THE LAIR OF BONES

THE LAIR OF BONES

↝ DAVID FARLAND ↜

A TOM DOHERTY ASSOCIATES BOOK
NEW YORK

THE LAIR OF BONES

Copyright © 2003 by David Farland

Edited by David G. Hartwell

Map by Mark Stein Studios

A Tor Book
Published by Tom Doherty Associates, LLC
175 Fifth Avenue
New York, NY 10010

Tor® is a registered trademark of Tom Doherty Associates, LLC.

ISBN: 0-765-30176-8

Printed in the United States of America

Kingdoms of Rosehaven

Internook

Ashoven

Eyremoth

Alnick

Eyremoth

Ice Sea

Heredon

North
Crowthen

Orwynne

South
Crowthen

Ghorat
Ocean

Erin's Pass

Lysle

Seward

Toom

Fleeds

Deyazz

Beldinook

Lonnock

Haversind

Kuhran

Mystarria

Caroll
Sea

Hawat

Dharmad

Muttaya

Carris

Brace Mountains

Kingdoms of Indhopal

Linah

Raj Ahten's
Ride

Indhopal

Alcair Mountains

Aven

Taif

Dead Sea

Kingdoms of Inkarra

Borenson's
Ride

Kartish

The Mouth
of
The World

Storm
King's
Demesne

Forests of Wold

N

For Mary

BOOK 11

DAY 4 IN THE MONTH OF LEAVES

A DAY OF DESCENT

ℬ PROLOGUE ℰ

STRUGGLES IN THE STREETS

Pride blinds men to the need for change. Therefore, for a man to walk the path to true wisdom, he must enter by the gate of humility.

—*proverb among the Ah'kellah*

When Raj Ahten's caravan approached the Palace of the Elephant at Maygassa, all the stars in heaven seemed to be falling, raining down in shades of red and gold.

In the still night air, the scent of spices from nearby markets hung near the ground: whole black pepper from Deyazz, cinnamon bark from the isles off Aven, and fresh cardamom. It was a welcome relief from the scent of death that hung like a pall over Raj Ahten's troops. His men, princes and lords of Indhopal dressed in their finest thick silken armor, wore rubies in their turbans and kept their heads high, swords held out in salute. Drummers and trumpeters acted as heralds.

The army rode as victors from the south, through the blasted lands that had been decimated by reaver's spells. The reavers, who spoke in odors, left their curses clinging to the soldiers and their mounts: "Rot, O children of men. Become as dry as dust. Breathe no more."

Even now, the smells brought Raj Ahten a vision of the giant reavers charging over the landscape. With their four legs and two arms, they looked something like enormous mantises. In their fore-claws, some wielded staves carved of stone, or enormous blades, or long iron poles with reaping hooks. The earth rumbled beneath the horde as it charged, while clouds of gree flapped and whirled above the reavers, squeaking like bats.

At the very head of Raj Ahten's army, his men brought a trophy: four bull elephants dragged a wagon laden with the head of a massive reaver, a fell mage. It was an awesome sight. At four tons, the head spanned wider than the wagon. The leathery skin grew as dark as the back of a crocodile, and the fell mage's gaping mouth revealed row upon row of teeth, each a pale green crystal, with some of the larger canines being as long as a child's arm. She had no eyes or ears. Along the lower ridges of her jaws, and again atop the bony plates that constituted the bulk of her spade-shaped head, her philia— her only visible sensory organs—swung like gravid dead eels with each jolt of the wagon.

Behind the elephants, near the head of the army, came Raj Ahten himself, the Sun Lord. He lay back on pillows, dressed in a gleaming white silk jacket, the traditional armor of old Indhopal, as slaves carried his palanquin. A screen of lavender silk hung like gossamer, hiding his face from his adoring subjects.

To each side of the palanquin, in a place of honor, rode four flameweavers. For now, they held their fires in check so that only thin vapors of smoke issued from their nostrils. Fire had burned away any trace of hair from their bodies, so that all four men were completely bald. The graceful smoothness of their scalps hinted at their power, and a strange light glimmered in their eyes even at night, like the twinkle of a distant star. They wore scintillating robes in shades of flame—the bright scarlet of the forge and the mellow gold of the campfire.

Raj Ahten felt connected to them now. They served a common master. He could almost hear their thoughts, drifting about like smoke.

His troops passed between a pair of huge golden censers where fires had burned continuously for a hundred years. This marked the beginning of the Avenue of Kings. As soon as his palanquin reached them, a thunderous cheer rose from the city.

Ahead, crowds had massed along the avenue to do obeisance. His people had strewn the streets with rose petals and white lotus blossoms, so that as the elephants walked, crushing the petals, a sweet fragrance wafted up. Sweeter to him still was the smell of scented oils burning in a hundred thousand lamps.

The crowd wildly cheered their savior. A throng had gathered to greet him, citizens of Maygassa and refugees from the south, more than three million strong.

Those closest to the palanquin fell down upon their hands and knees, bowing in respect. Their humped bodies, draped in robes of white linen and rising up above the lanterns set on the ground, looked like rounded stones thrusting up from a river of light.

Farther back in the crowd, some fought for a closer view. Women screamed and pounded their breasts, offering themselves to Raj Ahten. Men shouted words of undying gratitude. Babes cried in fear and wonder.

The applause thundered. The cheers rose up like fumes above the city and echoed from low hills a mile away and from the high stone walls of the Palace of the Elephant itself.

Raj Ahten grinned. The deed pained him. He had taken many wounds in the Battle of Kartish, wounds that would have killed any lesser man, and some of those were to his face. He lay back on his silken pillows, reveled in the gentle sway of his palanquin as the bearers marched in step, and watched the frightened doves circle above the city, floating like ashes above the light.

It seemed the start of a perfect day.

Gradually, something caught his attention. Ahead, people bowed to do obeisance, but among the humped shapes one man remained standing.

He wore the gray robes of the Ah'kellah, the judges of the desert. Upon his right hip, his robe had been thrown back, revealing the handle of his saber. He held his head high, so that the black ringlets attached to his simple iron war helm cascaded over his shoulders and down his back. Wuqaz? Raj Ahten wondered. Wuqaz Faharaqin come to fight at last? Offering a duel?

The humble peasants nearby looked up at the judge fearfully from the corners of their eyes, and some begged him to fall down and do obeisance, while others chided him for his deportment.

Raj Ahten's palanquin came up beside the Ah'kellah, and Raj Ahten raised his hand, calling for his procession to stop.

Immediately, the pounding of the drums ceased, and every man in the army halted. The crowd fell silent, except for the bawling of a few babes.

The air nearly crackled with intensity, and the thoughts of the flameweavers burned into the back of Raj Ahten's consciousness. *Kill him,* they whispered. *Kill him. You could burn him to cinders, make an example of him. Let the people see your glory.*

Not yet, Raj Ahten whispered in return, for since his near death in the battle at Kartish, Raj Ahten's own eyes burned with hidden fires now. *I will not unveil myself yet.*

Fire had claimed his life, had filled him with a light divine yet unholy. His old self had burned away, and from the cinders had risen a new man—Scathain, Lord of Ash.

Raj Ahten knew most of the members of the Ah'kellah. It was not Wuqaz who stood before him. Instead, his own uncle on his father's side, Hasaad Ahten, barred the way.

Not Wuqaz, Raj Ahten realized with palpable regret. Instead, his uncle had come on Wuqaz's mission.

Raj Ahten had taken thousands of endowments of Voice from his people, endowments that came from fine singers, from great orators. He spoke, and let the power of his voice wash over the crowd. In a tone sweeter than peach blossoms, as cruel as a blade of flame, he commanded, "Bow to me."

Everywhere among the crowd, millions prostrated themselves. Those who were already bowing flattened themselves further, as if to become one with the dust.

Hasaad remained standing, anger brimming in his eyes. "I come to give you counsel, my nephew," Hasaad said, "so that your wisdom may increase. I speak for your benefit."

By phrasing his words thus, Hasaad made certain that all in the crowd knew that he spoke by right. Custom dictated that even Raj Ahten, the high king of all the nations of Indhopal, could not kill an elder relative who sought only to counsel him.

Hasaad continued, "It is reported that already you have sent word, ordering your troops on Rofehavan's border to march to war." Hasaad shouted his words, so that they rang out over the crowd, but with only two endowments of Voice, Hasaad's words could not convey the emotional appeal that Raj Ahten's did. "The reavers have laid waste our fields and orchards in all of the Jewel Kingdoms. Our people face starvation. Do you think it wise to send more men to war, when they could better spend their time gathering food?"

"There is food in Rofehavan," Raj Ahten said reasonably, "for those strong enough to take it."

"And in Kartish," Hasaad said, "you have sent a million commoners to work the mines, hauling blood metal from the earth so that you heap upon yourself more endowments."

"My people need a strong lord," Raj Ahten said, "to defeat the reavers."

Hasaad asked, "You have heaped the strengths of others upon yourself for many years, claiming that you only seek to save your people from the reavers. Now the reavers are vanquished. You have already claimed victory over the lords of the Underworld. But it is not victory over reavers that you want. When you have stolen Rofehavan's food, you will force their people to give endowments." His voice grew thick with accusation.

Burn him now, the voices of the flameweavers sputtered.

"Two battles we may have won against the reavers," Raj Ahten answered in a tone that suggested grief at being questioned in so callous a manner, "but a greater battle remains to be fought."

"How can you know that?" Hasaad demanded. "How can you know that the reavers will attack again?"

"My pyromancer has seen it in the flames," Raj Ahten said, waving his hand toward Rahjim, a flameweaver riding to his right. "A great battle will flare up, more fearsome than any that we have ever known. Reavers will boil from the Underworld like never before. I go now to Rofehavan—to win food for my people, and to fight reavers in my people's behalf. Let every man who has access to a force horse ride at my side. I will lead you to victory!"

Cheers arose from the multitude, but Hasaad stood defiantly.

How dare he! Raj Ahten thought.

"You are a fool," Hasaad said, "to persecute the Earth King's people. Your rapacity is endless, as is your cruelty. You are no longer human, and as such, should be put to death like an animal."

Raj Ahten ripped back the veil that hid him from the crowd, and a collective gasp arose. The wizard fires in Kartish had seared every hair from his head, leaving him bald and without eyebrows. The flames had also burned away his right ear and scalded the retina of his right eye, so that now it shone as pale as milk. White bone protruded in a cruel line along his lower jaw.

The crowd gasped in horror, for Raj Ahten's visage seemed the very face of ruin. But he had taken thousands of endowments of glamour from his subjects, giving him a beauty ethereal, as overwhelming as it was impossible to define. In a moment, the gasps of horror turned into "aaaahs" of admiration.

"How dare you," Raj Ahten roared, "after all that I have suffered for you. Bow before my greatness!"

"No man can be great who is not also humble," Hasaad intoned in the calm, dignified manner common to the Ah'kellah.

Raj Ahten could not let his uncle continue to stand against him. He would seek to sway the crowds after Raj Ahten left, when the power of Raj Ahten's voice became only a memory.

He smiled cruelly. He could not kill Hasaad, but he could silence him. He begged his followers, "Bring me his tongue."

Hasaad grabbed the hilt of his sword. His blade nearly cleared its scabbard, but one of Raj Ahten's bowing servants yanked Hasaad by the ankles so that he went sprawling forward, and then faithful peasants leapt on the man, ending a brief struggle. Someone wrenched Hasaad's head around, while another man pried his teeth open with a dagger. There was a flow of blood, a clumsy cut.

In moments, a sweet young girl came skipping up to Raj Ahten, bearing the bloody flesh in both hands, as if it were a gift given with great respect.

Raj Ahten pinched the warm tongue between two fingers, showing his own disrespect for the gobbet of flesh, then tossed it to the floor of the palanquin and covered it with his slippered foot.

The peasants remained piled upon Hasaad, so that he could not breathe. Raj Ahten tapped the side of the palanquin twice, ordering the procession forward. "To the stables," he said. "I ride to war."

As his procession made its way toward the Elephant Palace, a knot of men dressed in black watched from the shadows of a darkened bedroom, in the uppermost chambers of an inn. Their leader, Wuqaz Faharaqin, said softly to the others. "Raj Ahten will not abandon the ways of war, and his people are so blinded by his glamour that they cannot see him for what he is."

Wuqaz felt within himself. For long years, he too had been blinded by

Raj Ahten's glamour. Even now, he fought the urge to bow before the monster, along with the rest of the crowd. But Raj Ahten had tipped his hand. He'd slain his own men in an effort to murder the Earth King, including one of Wuqaz's nephews. For that murder, Raj Ahten would have to pay. Wuqaz hailed from the noble tribe of Ah'Kellah, the judges of the desert, and his own language had no word for *mercy*.

A young man whispered, "How can we stop him?"

"We must rip the veil of glamour from him," Wuqaz said.

"But we have tried to kill his Dedicates," one of the men said. "We can't get into his castles."

Wuqaz nodded thoughtfully. A plan took form. In Kartish, the reavers had cursed the land. For hundreds of miles around, the plants had died, promising famine in the southern provinces.

This had forced Raj Ahten to move most of his Dedicates north to the Ghusa, a mighty fortress in Deyazz. According to conventional wisdom, no one could hope to break down its huge doors or climb its towering walls.

"Let us go to Ghusa," Wuqaz told his men. "Raj Ahten's greatest weakness is his greed. I will show you how to make him choke on it."

THE MOUTH OF THE UNDERWORLD

Rofehavan has always been bounded by the sea to the north and to the east, by the Hest Mountains to the west, and by the Alcair Mountains to the south. In an effort to assure that no war was ever waged over a desirable piece of land, Erden Geboren reached a concord with kings of Old Indhopal and the elders of Inkarra. He set the southeast border of his realm, where the three great realms met, in the most undesirable place on earth: at the opening to a vast and ancient reaver warren called the Mouth of the World.

—from A History of Rofehavan *by Hearthmaster Redelph*

"Milord, there you are," someone called. "I was growing worried. We've been waiting for hours." Averan woke. She recognized the voice of The Wizard Binnesman. She found herself in a wagon bed filled with sweet-smelling hay, new from the summer fields. For a pillow she used Gaborn's rucksack filled with chain mail and leather padding. All of Averan's muscles felt heavy and overworn, and her eyes were gritty. She lay with her eyes closed. Yet almost by instinct she reached out for her staff, her precious staff of black poisonwood. She touched it, felt the power in it surge beneath her hand.

Gaborn answered, "I hurried the best I could. But the horse was on its last legs, so I turned it loose and left the driver to care for it."

"So, the Earth King pulls a wagon to save a horse?" Binnesman scolded gently, as if worried that Gaborn might be pushing himself too hard. "Even those with great endowments have their limits—both horse and man." Binnesman laughed. "You look like an old farmer, hauling a load of rutabagas to market."

"It was only thirty more miles," Gaborn said. "And my cargo is far more valuable than rutabagas."

Averan found herself startled to greater wakefulness. She had been sleeping so soundly that she hadn't been aware that she slept in a wagon, much less that the Earth King himself pulled that wagon by hand.

Binnesman offered, "Here, let's hitch up my mount."

The wagon came to a complete halt as the wizard got off his horse and unsaddled it.

Averan sneaked a peek upward. Overhead, stars arced through the heavens as if intent upon washing the earth in light. The sun would not crest the horizon for perhaps an hour, yet light spilled like molten gold over the snowy peaks of the Alcair Mountains. To Averan it seemed that the light was sourceless, as if it suffused from another, finer world.

The heavenly display fooled even the animals. Morning birdsong swelled over the land: the throaty coo of the wood dove, the song of the lark, the jealous squawk of a magpie.

Close by, knobby hills crowded the road and the dry wheat growing along their sides reflected the starlight. Leafless oaks on the slopes stood black and stark, like thorny crowns. A burrow owl screeched in the distance. Faintly, Averan could smell water from a small stream, though she could not hear it burble.

She watched the steady rain of stars. The bits of light came arcing down in different directions, creating fiery paths against the sky.

"So, Averan is well?" Binnesman asked softly.

"It was hard for her," Gaborn answered. "She stood before the Waymaker all day, holding her staff overhead, peering into the monster's mind. Sweat poured from her as if she were toiling at a forge. I was afraid for her."

"And has she learned the way to, to this . . . Lair of Bones?"

"Aye," Gaborn said. "But I fear that the lair is far in the Underworld, and Averan cannot describe the path. She will have to lead us—that is, if you will come with me."

"If?" Binnesman asked. "Of course I'll come."

"Good," Gaborn said. "I'll need your counsel. I don't want to put too much burden on a girl so young."

Averan closed her eyes, feigning sleep, and took guilty pleasure in listening to them talk about her. She was but a child, yet in all the world she was the only person who had ever learned to converse with reavers, mankind's most feared enemy.

Gaborn had recognized that she went through an ordeal to see into the mind of the Waymaker, but even he could not guess how painful it had been. Her head ached as if a steel band bound it, and she felt as if her skull might split on its own accord. Hundreds of thousands, perhaps millions, of scents crammed her mind—scents that gave her the names of places and passages in the Underworld, scents that in some cases had been handed down from reaver to reaver over generations. In her mind's eye, Averan could envision the reaver tunnels in the Underworld, like vast arteries connecting the war-rens. There were tens of thousands of tunnels, leading to mines and quarries, to ranches and hunting grounds, to egg chambers and graveyards, to deadly perils and ancient wonders. Given a lifetime, Averan could not have mapped the Underworld for Gaborn.

Even now, she feared that she could not retain so much lore. The brain of a human is a tenth the size of that of a reaver. Her mind couldn't hold so much knowledge. She only hoped that she could recall the way to the Lair of Bones.

I *have* to remember, Averan told herself. I have to help Gaborn fight the One True Master.

She heard footsteps crunching on the road and tried to breathe easily. She wanted to rest, and hoped that by feigning sleep she could continue to do so.

Binnesman set his saddle in the back of the wagon. "Poor girl," he said. "Look at her, innocent as a babe."

"Let her sleep," Gaborn whispered. He spoke softly, not with the com-manding voice one would expect from a king, but with the gentleness of a worried friend.

Binnesman moved away, and wordlessly began hitching the horse to the single-tree on the wagon.

"Have you any other news of the reavers?" Gaborn whispered.

"Aye," Binnesman said, "Most of it good. We harried them all day. Many of the monsters died from weariness while fleeing our lancers, and our knights attacked any that slowed. At last report there were only a few thousand left. But when they reached the vale of the Drakesflood, they dug into the sand. That was about midafternoon. Our men have them sur-rounded, in case they try to flee, but for now there is little more that they can do."

Averan pictured the monsters at the Drakesflood. The reavers were enor-mous, each more than sixteen feet tall, and twenty in length. With four legs and two huge forearms, in form they looked like vast, tailless scorpions. But their heads were shaped like spades, and the reavers could force their way under the soil just by pushing down and then crawling forward. That is how they would have dug in at the Drakesflood. The move would afford them good protection from the lances of the knights.

"So that's the good news," Gaborn said heavily, "now what of the bad?"

Binnesman answered, "At the Mouth of the World we found reaver tracks heading in. It looks as if three reavers circled through the hills after the battle at Carris. Somehow they got past our scouts."

"By the Seven Stones!" Gaborn swore. "How soon before they reach their lair, do you think?"

"It's impossible to guess," Binnesman said heavily. "They may have already told their master how you defeated their army at Carris, and even now she will be considering how to respond."

Binnesman let that thought sink in.

"But how did they elude my scouts?" Gaborn wondered.

"I suspect that it would have been easy," Binnesman answered. "After the battle at Carris, the horde fled in the night while rain plummeted like lead. We had only brief flashes of lightning to see by. With our soldiers busy at the front, they left before we ever thought to try to cut them off."

Binnesman and Gaborn hooked the horse to the wagon, and both men climbed onto the buckboard. Gaborn gave a whistle, and the force horse took off at a brisk trot.

"This has me worried," Gaborn said.

Binnesman seemed to think for a long moment. At last he sighed. "Beware the Lair of Bones. Beware the One True Master. My heart is full of foreboding about this creature. No beast of this world could be so well versed in rune lore."

"You suspect something?" Gaborn asked.

"Seventeen hundred years ago, when Erden Geboren prosecuted his war in the Underworld, do you know *what* he fought?"

"Reavers," Gaborn said.

"That is the conventional wisdom, but I think not," Binnesman answered. "In King Sylvarresta's library are some ancient scrolls, levies for men and supplies written in Erden Geboren's own hand. In them, he asked for men not to fight reavers but to fight something he called a locus. I think he was hunting for a particular reaver. It may even be the one that Averan calls the One True Master, though I cannot imagine that any reaver would live so long."

"And you think that this creature is not of our world?"

"Perhaps not," Binnesman said. "I begin to wonder. Maybe there are reavers in the netherworld, more cunning and powerful than our own. And perhaps reavers here are but mere shadows of them, in the same way that we are mere shadows of the Bright Ones of that realm."

"That is a sobering thought indeed," Gaborn said.

The wizard and the Earth King rode in silence. Averan lay back again, eyes closed. Her mind felt overwhelmed.

The road had been leading down, and abruptly Gaborn jolted the wagon to a halt. Averan stealthily rose up on one elbow, and saw that they had reached a town, a small knot of gray stone cottages with thatched roofs.

Averan recognized it as Chesterton. Here the road forked. One highway headed almost due east toward the Courts of Tide. The other road went southwest toward Keep Haberd—and beyond that, to the Mouth of the World.

Overhead, a fireball lanced through the sky, huge and red. Flames streaked from it with a sputtering sound. As it neared the Alcair Mountains, it suddenly exploded into two pieces. They struck the snow-covered mountains not thirty miles away. The ground trembled, and moments later came sounds like distant thunder, echoing over and over.

"The Earth is in pain," the wizard Binnesman whispered.

Averan heard a child squeal in delight. Up the road, beside one of the cottages, a woman squatted on her lawn. Three girls, none older than six, stood with her, looking up at the heavenly display in wonder.

"Pretty!" the youngest child said, as she traced the trail of the fireball with her finger.

An older sister clapped in delight.

"Oh, that was the best one yet," their mother said.

Other than these four, the town slumbered. The cottages clustered in dark, tired mounds. The farmers within would not dare rise until the cows began bawling to be milked.

Gaborn drove the buckboard through town. The mother and her daughters watched them pass.

Now the earth shivered beneath them like an old arthritic dog. Binnesman had spoken truly. Averan recognized the earth's pain by more than just the earthquakes or the fall of stars. There were less definable signs that perhaps only one who loved the land could discern. She'd been able to feel it for days now as she walked, a wrongness in the soil, an ache among the hills.

"You know, Gaborn," Binnesman said at last, "you say that you will lean upon my counsel. Therefore, let me say this: I think you take too much upon yourself. You plan to seek out the Lair of Bones, and hope there to kill the One True Master. But you have not been called to be the Earth's warrior, you are the Earth King, the Earth's protector. You also talk of warring with the reavers, killing . . . perhaps thousands. But more than just the fate of mankind hangs in the balance. There are owls in the trees, and mice in the fields, and fishes in the sea. Life, every kind of life, may fade with us. The Earth is in pain."

"I would rejoice if we could heal its pain," Gaborn said, "but I don't know how."

"The Earth has selected you well," Binnesman said. "Perhaps we will find the way together."

The wagon raced over the road, and Averan lay back with a heavy heart, feigning sleep.

And what of me? Averan wondered. As a skyrider, she'd often had to travel far from home, and she had found some special places that she loved. She recalled a clear pool high in the pines of the Alcair Mountains where she'd sometimes picnicked, and the white sand dunes forty miles east of Haberd where she had played, rolling down the hills. She'd perched with her graak on rugged mountain peaks that no man could ever climb, surveying vast fields and the forests that undulated away in a green haze. Yes, Averan loved the land, enough even to live every day in its service.

That's what makes me an Earth Warden's apprentice, she realized.

The wagon rolled through the night with Averan lost in thought. It wound up into the hills. All too soon it came to a halt just outside a vast cavern, where dozens of horses were tethered. A bonfire crackled within the cave, where scores of knights were engaged in rowdy song.

"Averan, wake up," Gaborn called softly. "We're at the Mouth of the World."

He reached into the back of the wagon and as Averan raised her head, he retrieved the sack that held his armor, along with his long-handled war hammer. Binnesman got up and hobbled stiffly toward the cave, using his staff as a crutch.

"I had a dream last night," Erin Connal whispered to Celinor as they stooped to drink at a stream in South Crowthen, nearly a thousand miles to the northeast of Averan. The sun would not be up for half an hour, yet the sky glowed silver on the horizon. The early morning air felt chill, and dew lay heavy on the ground. "It was a strange dream."

She glanced suspiciously at South Crowthen's knights nearby, who were busy breaking camp. Captain Gantrell, a lean, dark man with a fanatical gleam in his eyes, stood ordering his men about as if they'd never broken a camp before. "Sweep the mud off that tent before you put it in the wagon," he shouted to one soldier. To another he called, "Don't just pour water on the campfire, stir it in."

By the surly looks he got, Erin could tell that his troops did not love him.

As the men bustled about, occupied with their work, for the first time since last night, Erin felt that she could talk to her husband with a measure of safety.

"You dreamed a dream?" Celinor inquired, one eyebrow raised. "Is this unusual?" He drowned his canteen in the shallow creek almost carelessly, as if unconcerned that Gantrell's men surrounded them, treating the crown prince and his new wife as if they were prisoners.

"I think it was more than a dream," Erin admitted. "I think it was a sending." Erin held her breath to see his reaction. In her experience, most people who claimed to receive sendings showed other signs of madness too.

Celinor blinked, looking down at his canteen. "A sending from whom?" he asked heavily. He did not want to hear about his wife's mad dreams.

"Remember yesterday, when I dropped my dagger into the circle of fire at Twynhaven? The dagger touched the flames and disappeared. It went through the gate, into the netherworld."

Celinor nodded but said nothing. He watched her suspiciously, daring her to speak on.

"I dreamt last night that I saw a creature of the netherworld, like a great owl that lived in a burrow under a vast tree. It held my dagger in its beak, and it spoke to me. It gave me a warning."

Celinor finished filling his canteen, then licked his lips. He trembled slightly, as if from a chill. Like most folk, he felt uncomfortable when talking of the netherworld. Wondrous beings, like Bright Ones, peopled it, but there were tales of frightening creatures too—like the salamanders that Raj Ahten's flameweavers had summoned at Longmot, or the Darkling Glory they gated at Twynhaven. "What did this . . . creature warn you about?"

"It warned me that the Darkling Glory could not be slain. A foul spirit possessed its body, a creature so dangerous that it strikes fear even into the hearts of the Bright Ones. The creature is called a locus, and of all the loci, it is one of the most powerful. Its name is Asgaroth."

"If you are convinced that this Asgaroth is a danger," Celinor asked, "then why are you whispering? Why not shout it to the world?"

"Because Asgaroth may be nearby," Erin whispered. A squirrel bolted up the side of a tree, and Erin glanced back at it furtively, then continued. "We can slay the body that hosts the spirit, just as Myrrima slew the Darkling Glory, but we can't kill Asgaroth himself. Once a locus is torn from one body, it will seek a new host, an evil person or beast that it can control." She paused to let him consider this. "When Myrrima slew the Darkling Glory, a whirlwind rose from it—and blew east, toward South Crowthen."

Celinor looked at her narrowly, anger flashing in his eyes. "What of it?"

"You say that your father has been suffering delusions. . . ."

"My father may be mad," Celinor said curtly, "but he has never been evil."

"You were the one who was after telling me how his far-seer turned up dead." Erin reminded him. "If he killed him, it may have been an act of madness. Or it may have been evil."

"I only suspect him," Celinor said. "There is no proof. Besides, his odd behavior began before Raj Ahten's sorcerers summoned the Darkling Glory. Even if you received a true sending, even if your 'locus' is real, there's nothing that should lead you to suspect my father."

Celinor didn't want to consider the possibility that his father might be possessed. She didn't blame him. Nor could she argue that his father's odd behavior had begun weeks ago.

Yet something that the owl of the netherworld had told Erin caused her concern. It had shown her the locus, a shadow of evil that inhabited one man, even as it sent out tendrils of darkness around it, tendrils that touched others—seducing them, snaring them—filling them with a measure of its own corruption.

Thus the locus's influence spread, rotting the hearts of men, burning away their consciences, preparing them to act as hosts for others like it.

Erin had never met Gantrell before, but the fanatical gleam in the captain's eyes, the way he had his men guard Celinor, the crown prince, as if he were a captured spy, made her suspect that he had been touched by a locus.

And then there was Celinor's father: claiming to be the Earth King, plotting against Gaborn, spreading lies about him to far-off lords who ought to have been Gaborn's allies.

Perhaps Celinor's father did not host Asgaroth, Erin thought, but he was dangerous by any standard.

"What are you two doing over here, all alone?" Captain Gantrell called out. He came sauntering up, the grin splitting his face only a thin veneer to hide his suspicion.

"Plotting my escape back to Fleeds," Erin said in a jesting tone.

"That wouldn't be wise," Gantrell said, attempting to mimic her light-heartedness and failing miserably. Erin could tell that he had no sense of humor. He looked approvingly to his knights, who had mounted their horses, and were now nearly ready to leave. "Well, let's see if we can make good time while it's still cool."

Erin forced a smile, but she grew more and more uneasy about Gantrell. Instinct warned her that rather than grin politely as if he were some unwelcome courtier, she'd be better off to slit his belly open and strangle him with his own guts.

Erin mounted her horse, exhausted from lack of sleep, and rode through the pre-dawn. Every few miles they passed small contingents of knights, all riding south. Camp followers in the form of smiths, washwomen, and squires rode in wains or trudged down the dusty roads. Drivers rode war wagons filled with lances, arrows, food, and tents, everything one needed for an extended campaign.

After passing a train of twenty ballistas mounted on wheels and drawn by force horses, Erin blithely asked Gantrell, "All this movement before the sun's even up. What country do you plan to invade?"

"Invade, Your Highness?" Gantrell asked. "It is but a normal repositioning of our defenses." He rode close enough so that she had to urge her horse aside, lest they bump legs.

"If you were afraid of invasion," Erin argued, "you would strengthen your fortifications, not mass troops on your southern border. So, who will you invade?"

"I couldn't say, milady," Gantrell answered with a maddening little smirk.

So they rode through the morning. The horses nearly pranced as they raced through the chill. The knights' ring mail chinged like cymbals to the drumming of the horses' hooves, as if making music to accompany some vast empyreal hymn.

Erin's fatigue lent the ride a surreal, dreamlike quality. Some thought South Crowthen to be a beautiful country, and it was true: the trees on the hills danced in particolored raiment of autumn colors, and in the more settled areas Erin would ride round a bend and discover a picturesque stone cottage dozing beneath a sprawling oak or elm. Nearby, a milk cow would crop the grass in some green field misted by morning dew, while stone fences that had stood for longer than men could remember neatly parceled out the quiet farmland. But when she rounded the next corner, she'd see another quaint stone house beneath a sprawling elm, with the milk cow's sister cropping the grass by the barn, and another endless stone fence parceling out the squares of dirt, and on and on and on it went until Erin thought that she would never again admire another cottage or cow or meadow or tree.

So she closed her burning eyes. "I'll only let my eyes rest," she told herself. "I won't sleep."

Erin feared that she would lose her mind. The dreams that came every time she succumbed to sleep were so vivid that she felt that now her horse was galloping through a dream, and when she slept, she would awaken to some truer world.

She dreamt. Only a vague flash of vision, an image of the great owl in its dark burrow. It had moved from its previous roost, and now huddled farther in the shadows. The gray-and-white pattern of its feathers looked like dead leaves plastered above bones.

Erin peered into its unblinking golden eyes, and said, "Leave me alone. I don't want to speak to you."

"You fear me," the owl said, its thoughts piercing her mind with more shades of emotion and insight than mere words could convey. "You need not fear me. I am not your enemy."

"You are madness," Erin said, willing herself to wake. The image faded.

The horses rounded a bend just at sunrise, and Captain Gantrell called, "Troo-oops, haw-aalt!"

Erin opened her eyes, imagining that they were stopping to let another wagon train pass.

Instead, near the road ahead lay a serene little pond covered in morning mist, and above it loomed a purple pavilion with gold trim: royal colors.

King Anders himself knelt beside the pool, his shirt off, washing himself in the cool morning air. He stood tall, lean, almost haggard in appearance, with a skeletal head and only a wisp of beard.

His Days, a historian who chronicled his life, brushed down a horse nearby, preparing to ride.

Near the king a plump old woman dressed in grayish rags squatted on a large rock, while squirrels darted around her in play. She would crack a hazelnut between her tough fingers and then toss it in the air. The squirrels made a game of racing over her shoulders or leaping into her lap to catch the nut before it touched ground.

Celinor nudged Erin, nodded toward the woman. "The Nut Woman, an Earth Warden from Elyan Wood."

In her dreamlike fog, Erin thought it to be one of the strangest scenes in her life.

So, this is mad King Anders, she thought, looking back at the pasty old lord with his sagging breasts—the man I may have to kill.

He didn't look frightening at all.

The king half turned, peering up from his morning ablutions with a frown, as if worried to hear the approach of troops. Yet he spotted Celinor and the frown disintegrated, blossoming into a heartfelt smile.

"My son," King Anders called, his tone conveying only solemn joy. "You've come home!" He grabbed a towel that lay draped over a nearby bush and dried himself as he rushed forward. Celinor leapt from his saddle, and hugged the old man as they met.

The hug was short-lived. Celinor pushed his father away. "What's the meaning of all these troops on the border, Father? Are you going to start a war?"

King Anders managed to look hurt as he answered, "*Start* a war? My dear lad, I may finish a war, but I've never been known to start one." Anders held his son's hands, but peered over Celinor's shoulder at Erin.

"And who have we here?" he asked. "Erin Connal? Your picture doesn't do you justice, fair lady."

"Thank you," Erin answered, surprised that he would recognize her face from a tiny picture painted on a promise locket nearly a decade past.

King Anders smiled a genuine smile, a smile of welcome and warmth and gratitude. His gray eyes seemed to stare into Erin, through her. He left Celinor, came to gaze upon Erin more fully.

Her horse shied away, but when he reached out and touched it, the animal immediately calmed.

King Anders raised his left hand in the air. "I Choose you, Erin Connal," he said. "I Choose you for the Earth. If ever you are in danger and hear my voice whisper within you, obey it, and I will lead you to safety."

Erin leaned back in her saddle, a grunt of surprise rising from her throat. Of all the words that he could have said, she expected these the least, for he used the very phrase that Gaborn had spoken when, as Earth King, he had Chosen her to be one of his warriors. Could it be that Anders, too, now had the ability to Choose, to select her as one of his soldiers and use the Earth Sight to recognize when she was in danger, then send her warnings?

No, it was blasphemy.

"By what right?" Erin asked. "By what right do you do this?"

"By every right," King Anders said. "I am the Earth King. The Earth has called me to save a seed of mankind through the dark times to come."

Erin stared at King Anders, dumbfounded. His manner seemed perfectly sincere. His gray eyes looked kind, thoughtful, and benevolent. He held himself with certitude. He smiled in a manner disarmingly warm. In physical appearance, he looked nothing like Gaborn. Yet in his bearing, it was as if Gaborn had been reborn in him.

"What do you mean, you're the Earth King?" Celinor asked.

"It happened but yesterday, in the morning. I must confess that I had been feeling strangely for days. I'd sensed that dark times were coming, that great things were afoot, and so I retired to the woods to ponder them. The woods seemed quiet, tense. All of the squirrels were gone. I went searching for the Nut Woman—"

At this, the Nut Woman got off her rock, and ambled over to the party, squirrels prancing madly around her feet.

King Anders continued, "I found her in her cave, packing some dried herbs and whatnot. She told me that she had taken the squirrels to safety, and only returned to get a few things. Then, she led me deep into the woods, to a certain grotto."

The Nut Woman put a hand on the king's shoulder, as if begging him to let her continue the tale. "There," she said, with a voice filled with awe, "the Earth Spirit appeared to us, and warned us that dark times are coming, darker than any this world has ever known. The Earth warned your father: 'Be faithful! Cling to me, and my powers will attend you. Abandon me, and I shall abandon you: *as I have abandoned the Earth King before you!*'"

Anders turned away as if the thought of a man losing his Earth Powers wounded him to the core. "Poor Gaborn, to be so cursed," Anders lamented. "Dear boy. I fear that all the good he tried to do will turn to evil. I doubted him. But he *was* called of the Earth, if only for a while. Now I must carry on in his stead, and see if I can undo the great harm I've done him."

Erin stared at them both darkly, unsure what to do, unsure what to think. She'd been prepared to meet a madman, and dispatch him quickly. Yet a niggling worry crept into her mind: What if he really is the Earth King?

The Mouth of the World, Averan thought, as she looked at the gaping cavern. I've flown over it a dozen times and seen the sheep cropping the grass on every hilltop near here. I'm not fifty miles from home.

The memory of home brought an ache to her heart. The reavers had destroyed Keep Haberd a week past. Just about everyone she'd ever known had been killed.

She leapt out of the wagon on legs that were still rubbery from sleep, and landed on the stony ground. To both sides of her lay a rut, as if this were an ancient road. But Averan knew better. She'd landed in the massive footprint of a reaver, the four-toed track of a huge female. It measured a yard in length and four feet in width. Countless other tracks surrounded it.

The "road" was really a reaver trail. A week past, tens of thousands of the monsters had boiled out of the Underworld here and spilled over the countryside. They had worn a rut in the ground sixty to seventy feet wide and several feet deep. Their trail, which wound over hundreds of miles, led through dozens of devastated cities.

Averan planted her staff in the ground, and found herself leaning on it wearily.

"Are you ready to take your endowments?" Gaborn asked as he shouldered his armor.

"You mean I'm going to do it here," Averan inquired, "not in a Dedicates' tower?"

"We're a long way from any towers," Gaborn said. "Iome brought a facilitator and some folk to act as Dedicates. Go find something to eat, and then we'll see to your needs."

Averan pulled her robes tight against her face. The air up so high had an autumn chill to it, and the wind came a bit boisterous, circling this way and that, like a nervous hound. She followed Gaborn to the mouth of the cave.

With each step they took, the singing grew louder. It reverberated from the cavern walls. "Why is everyone singing?"

"They're celebrating," Gaborn said. "The reaver horde has been brought to ground."

No wonder they sing, Averan thought. Seventy thousand reavers vanquished. There hasn't been a battle like that in ages. Still, so much wanton killing—even of reavers—left a sour taste in Averan's mouth.

At the cave's throat at least two hundred men crowded round the bonfire. Most were minor lords out of Mystarria and Heredon, though many were also Knights Equitable who called no man their king, and some were dark-skinned warriors who still wore the yellow colors of far-off Indhopal.

Still, dozens of peasants looked as if they had followed Gaborn's troops in from nearby villages. Most of them wore lambskin jackets and knit woolen hats. Some were just curious farmers and woodsmen out to see the Earth King, but most carried heavy axes and yew longbows, as if eager to swell the ranks of Gaborn's army.

Now that Gaborn had arrived, someone cried, "All hail the Earth King!" and wild cheers erupted.

Averan hung back at the mouth of the cave and glanced up. The flickering light of the bonfire illuminated the smoke-gauzed ceiling where gray-green cave kelp dangled in curtains. An enormous blind-crab crept along the ceiling precariously, clinging to rocks as it fed on kelp.

Even here at the cave's mouth, the flora and fauna of the Underworld looked strange and unearthly. Averan hesitated, for once she stepped into the cave, she feared that she would be leaving the world behind forever, and her journey down would begin.

She glanced back at the star-filled heavens. She breathed deep of the pure mountain air, and listened to the peaceful coo of a wood dove, then stepped over the threshold of the cave. Her journey had begun.

Nearby, a young knight sat on a stone, trying to knock a dent out of his helm. He glanced up at Averan with shining eyes. Local boys were breaking camp—pulling cooking pots from the fire, checking and rechecking their packs. A grizzled knight of Indhopal knelt on the ground with an oilstone, honing the steel bodkins on his arrows.

Everyone bustled about. She felt a sense of urgency, as if these folks had been waiting for Gaborn for more than just a few hours, as if they had been waiting for him for all of their lives.

Binnesman's wylde stood conspicuously among the crowd. He had designed the creature to be a warrior for the Earth. She was one of few women in the group, and she stood holding a war staff of stout oak. She wore buckskin pants and a woolen tunic. To all appearances, she looked like a pretty young woman, but she had a disturbing complexion. Her huge pupils were so dark green they looked almost black, and her hair fell down her shoulders in avocado waves. Her skin, too, seemed to have been dyed a vigorous green, the color of young leaves.

Averan walked over to the wylde. "Hello, Spring," Averan said, calling her by the name she had used ever since she'd first seen the green woman fall from the sky.

"Hello," the wylde replied. Her language skills still were limited. On the other hand, Binnesman had only created the thing a little more than a week ago, and no babe could talk at a week of age.

"How are you feeling today?" Averan asked, hoping to start a conversation.

The green woman gazed at her blankly. After a moment of thought, she said, "I feel like killing something, Averan."

"I feel that way some days, too," Averan said, trying to make light of the answer. But it underscored a difference between the two. Averan had first thought of the green woman as a person, someone who needed her help. But no woman had mothered Spring, and no man had fathered her; Binnesman had fashioned her from roots and stones and the blood of the Earth. Averan could never really be her friend, because the green woman only wanted one thing in life: to hunt down and kill the enemies of the Earth.

Averan had thought that there might be two hundred warriors when she walked into the cave, but now she saw that she had underestimated the size of the band by at least half, for many men could be seen hovering about farther back into the tunnel, deeper in the shadows. The sight gave her some confidence. She would want all of the Runelords that she could find marching at her back as she led them into the Underworld.

She felt worn to the bone. For the past week, ever since she'd fled the reaver attack on Keep Haberd, she'd been pushing herself hard.

Averan went to the fire, where some farm boy shoved a plate in her hand. A knight carved a slab of meat from a roasting mutton and slapped it on her plate, then scooped buttered parsnips and bread pudding from a pair of iron kettles.

It was fine food for such a rough camp, a veritable feast. The knights here were serving their best, for this might well be the last decent meal they ever had. Averan took the fare and began looking for a bare rock to sit on.

She went to a shadowed corner of the cave, where dozens of others were eating, squatted in the sand. She hunched over her plate. Here, at her back, a few feather ferns grew. She cut a bite of mutton, then happened to glance up.

Every man within twenty feet seemed to be watching her. Their faces showed undisguised wonder mingled with curiosity. Embarrassment warmed her cheeks.

So, she realized. They've all been talking about me. They knew that she had tasted reaver's brain and had learned their secrets in doing so.

She skewered the mutton with her knife, took a bite. The succulent lamb had been delicately seasoned with rosemary and basted in a honey-mint sauce.

"Not as good as broiled reavers' brains," Averan mused aloud, "but it will have to do."

Several farmers laughed overloud at the jest, even though it wasn't very funny. At least she'd managed to break the tension. Suddenly conversations started up again. Averan began chewing in earnest when a beefy palm slapped her on the back.

"Need some ale to wash it down?" Someone thrust a tin mug into her hands. She recognized the voice and choked out a cry of surprise. "Brand?"

Beastmaster Brand, her old friend, stood above her, grinning hugely. He stretched his one arm wide, inviting her in to hug, and Averan leapt up and grabbed him around the neck.

"I thought you were dead!" she cried.

"You weren't the only one," he laughed. "I thought I was as good as dead a few times myself."

The laugh sounded genuine enough, but not as carefree as it would have a week ago. Averan heard pain in it.

She gazed at him. Brand had been her tutor. He'd taken Averan in as a child and taught her to ride graaks at the aerie in Keep Haberd. He'd taught her to read and write, so that she could deliver the duke's messages. He'd trained her in the care and feeding of graaks. For such kindness alone, she would have been eternally grateful. But he'd been more than a master. He'd been a mother and father, lord and family, and dearest friend. The relief she felt at seeing him again, the sheer joy, brought a flood of tears to her eyes.

"Oh, Brand, how did you escape? When last I saw you . . . the reavers—"

"Were charging toward the keep," Brand said. In her mind's eye, Averan relived the moment. They'd been high above Keep Haberd, where she could look down over the castle walls and see the reavers charging. The reaver horde had charged in such vast numbers, and at such a fast pace, that he could not possibly have escaped.

"I set you aback old Leatherneck, and sent you into the sky," Brand said. "Then freed the last of the graaks from their tethers.

"Afterward, I just stood on the landing, looking down over the city. The reavers came in a stampede, and the world shook beneath them. They were like a black flood, rushing down the canyon. Most of the graaks fled. But young Brightwing, she kept circling the aerie, crying out, all mournful.

"The reavers hit the castle wall, and never even slowed. Our ballistas, our knights . . ." He shook his head sadly. "The reavers just shoved the walls down and rushed through the streets. Some folks tried to run, others to hide. The reavers were taking them all.

"With naught but one arm, I couldn't fight. So I stood there, waiting for the reavers to eat me, when all of a sudden something hits me hard from behind. The next thing I know, Brightwing is lifting me above the fray. She has my leather vest in her claws, you see.

"Now, I'm a fat old man, and I think that she's going to carry me to my death. But Brightwing flaps viciously and lugs me over the valley as if I were some young pig that she had a notion to eat. She wings along, and it seems to me that she's dropping faster than she's flying."

Averan stared in wonder. "How far? How far did she take you?"

"A mile and a half," Brand answered. "Maybe two."

Averan knew that the graaks could carry more than just the weight of a child. She'd seen old Leatherneck lift a bull calf out of a field, and the calf couldn't have weighed much less than Brand. And she'd heard that mother graaks would sometimes carry their enormous chicks from one nest to another, if the nest seemed to be in danger. But graaks could never bear such weight for any great distance.

"She must have taken you downwind from the castle." Averan knew full well that if they'd gone upwind, even at a distance of two miles, the reavers would have smelled him.

"Aye," Brand said. "That she did. And I had the good sense to stay put until the horde had passed."

"What of the rest of the town?" Averan asked.

Brand shook his head sadly. "Gone. A few got out on fast horses—Duke Haberd and some of his cronies—" He bit off the words he wanted to say, his voice choked with outrage at such an act of cowardice.

"But what of your adventures?" Brand asked more brightly, changing the subject. "You've grown much since last I saw you."

"Grown?" she asked. "In only a week?"

"Aye, you may not be a hair taller, but you've grown much indeed." He reached out and touched her robes. The old blue skyrider's robes were covered with tiny roots, as if seeds had sprouted in the wet fabric. Indeed, one could hardly see a trace of the blue wool anymore. The roots were twining together, forming a solid new fabric. It would be her wizard's robe, the garment that, as an Earth Warden, would hide her and protect her from dangers.

"Yes," Averan said. "I guess I have grown." She felt sad when she said it. She hadn't grown taller, but she felt a thousand years old. She'd seen too many innocent people die in the battles at Carris and Feldonshire. She'd seen more wonders and horrors in a week than she should have seen in a lifetime. And all of it had transformed her, awakened the green earth blood that flowed through her veins. She was no longer human. She was a wizardess with powers that mystified her as much as they did those around her.

Brand smiled broadly and said in a husky voice, "I'm so happy. . . ." He clasped her around the neck and just held her for a moment.

Then he pulled back, and his face became all business again. "So, you're going into the Underworld, are you?" Averan nodded. Brand seemed to be studying her. He continued, "I'd come with you, if I could. But I'm afraid that with naught but one arm, I'd be of no use. Sure, I can carry a pack full of food as well as the next man, but . . ."

"It's all right," Averan said.

"The thing is," Brand said, "there are other ways that I can help. I'm a strong man, Averan, always have been. I want you to have my strength."

Averan swallowed hard and blinked back a tear. "You want to be my Dedicate?"

"Not just me," Brand said. He nodded toward some of the local woodsmen sitting in the cave. "Lots of us would give anything to help—*anything*. We might not be worthy to march beside folks like you and Gaborn as Runelords, but we *will* do what we can. The king's facilitators has brought hundreds of forcibles!"

"I don't want to hurt you," Averan said. "What if you died, trying to give me your strength?"

"I think that I would die of a broken heart if you didn't take it, and that would be worse. . . ."

"I couldn't bear it," Averan said. "I couldn't bear the thought of finding you now just to lose you again."

"If you won't take an endowment from me," Brand warned, "I'll give it to someone else."

Averan wanted to argue, but at that moment a facilitator hurried from the back of the cave. "Averan," he called. He wore black pants and a black half cloak, with the silver chains of his office upon his neck. As she got up, Averan looked down sadly at Brand, and stumbled through the crowd. She followed the facilitator's billowing black robes into the recesses of the cave. He said, "His Highness has sought a great many endowments for you, child. Twenty endowments of scent from dogs we found, and twenty of stamina, eight each of grace and brawn, twelve of metabolism, ten each of sight and hearing, five of touch."

Averan's head spun at the news, at the sacrifices others would have to make. She'd leave dozens of people blind, mute, or otherwise deprived of vital powers.

Perhaps as horrific would be the changes that the endowments wrought upon her. With twelve endowments of metabolism, she'd be able to move faster than others, to run fifty miles in an hour, though to her it would only seem that time had slowed. Each day she would age nearly two weeks. Each year, her body would be more than a dozen years older. In a decade, she would be an old, old woman, if she lived at all.

He led Averan to a corner back in the cave where a dozen potential Dedicates squatted. The facilitator had seven forcibles—small branding irons made of blood metal—laid out on a satin pillow. His apprentices already had a girl on her back and were coaxing the sight from her. She seemed a small thing, not much older than Averan. She had kinky blond hair, a thin face. Beads of sweat were breaking on her brow. One apprentice sang in a piping voice and held the forcible to her arm while the other whispered words of encouragement. "Here she comes now," the facilitator's apprentice whispered in an urgent voice, "the hope of mankind, she who must guide our lord through the Underworld, through the dark places. It is your sight that will let her see, your sacrifice that will give us hope of success."

Hope of success? Averan wondered. The task ahead seemed daunting. The paths through the Underworld were as tangled as a massive ball of yarn. And what could she do when she reached her destination? Kill the lord of the Underworld?

I'm not ready for this, Averan thought desperately.

But the facilitator's apprentice kept it up, this litany, and the girl stared at Averan with pleading eyes. "Save me," she mouthed to Averan. "Save us all."

I'm the last thing she will ever see, Averan realized. And with her gift, my eyes will pierce the deep shadows. I shall be able to count the veins in the wings of a moth at a dozen paces.

Averan went forward timidly, and took the girl's hand. "Thank you," Averan said. "I'll do . . . everything that I can."

At that, the forcible blazed white hot, and the girl screamed in pain. Her pupils seemed to shrivel like prunes and go white before her eyes rolled back in her head. The girl fell backward, dazed with pain, and the facilitator's apprentice pulled the forcible away. A white puckering scar showed the rune for sight branded on her arm.

The facilitator's apprentice waved the glowing tip of the forcible in the air experimentally. It left a white trail, like living fire, snaking in its wake. Yet the trail remained hanging in the air long after the forcible had passed. He studied the glow, the width and breadth of it, and then looked to the master facilitator for approval.

"Well done," the facilitator said. "Continue."

The apprentice reached down to Averan and slid the sleeve of her robe up, revealing the scars from endowments taken in the past. With all of her former Dedicates dead, the scars had all gone gray.

The facilitator's apprentice once again began his birdlike singing and pressed the forcible to Averan's flesh. The glowing white trail broke off at the Dedicate's arm, and flowed into Averan. As it did, the blood metal flared white, and then dissolved into dust.

Averan felt the indescribable ecstasy that comes from taking an endowment, and as the endowments of sight flowed into her, it seemed as if the dingy cave exploded into brightness.

After that nothing would ever look the same again.

∽ 2 ∞

A LIGHT IN A DARK PLACE

By the love that binds us both together—
I vow to be for you a light in dark places,
and give you hope when hope runs dry,
to be your fortress in the mountains,
when your enemies draw nigh. . . .

—from Iome's wedding vow

A whooshing sound swept through the Mouth of the World, like the sound of wings, and the huge bonfire snuffed out. Iome glanced up. The Wizard Binnesman stood where the bonfire had been. He had just made a fold of ground rise up and surge like a wave to smother the flames.

Now he held his staff up, and a swarm of fireflies circled it, so that he stood in a haze of green light. Earth blood flowed in his veins, so that he had a green cast to his skin, and even the autumn colors of his robes held some of that hue, so that in this light he looked strange and unearthly. Iome imagined that he glowed like a Bright One, straight from old stories of the netherworld.

"Gentlemen, ladies, may I have your ears?" Binnesman asked loudly. "The time is at hand that we must prepare for battle. Let nothing that you hear this morning be spoken by daylight or before an open fire, for some pyromancers can overhear your words in the sizzle and pop of the flames."

With that, he glanced at Gaborn for a moment. "Your Highness . . ." Binnesman said.

Iome felt a thrill of anticipation. She had been waiting all night to hear Gaborn's plans. Yesterday she had begged to accompany Gaborn to the Underworld, and he had made no promises, only said, "I will think upon it."

A hush fell over the crowd. Everyone drew close. Someone called out, "We're with you, milord!" Shouts and war cries rose from all about.

Gaborn raised his hands and begged the men for silence.

"Over the past day," he began, "many of you have asked to come with me to the Underworld: High Marshal Chondler," he nodded with deference to Chondler, "Sir Langley of Orwynne, Sir Ryan McKim of Fleeds." He hesitated as he gave appreciative looks to each of these warriors. "And your great hearts are borne out by greater deeds. Each of you is more than worthy to follow me. But my mind has been much occupied on thoughts of how I can save my people, and I have had to make some hard choices. . . ."

At that, the strong lords around Gaborn all stood tall and proud, eager to hear whom he would choose as companions.

Gaborn gazed out over them, and in the darkness his pupils had widened enormously, so that almost the whole whites of his eyes seemed to have faded. By this, Iome knew that he had already taken several endowments of sight, so that he might better see in the Underworld.

"Those who will follow me," Gaborn said with finality, "will be three: the wizard Binnesman, his wylde, and the child Averan."

A gasp of dismay swept through the crowd, and Iome choked out a sob. She felt sick. She had hoped to accompany Gaborn, and had dared to imagine an army at her back with a few hundred warriors at the very least.

Several lords grumbled openly and looked as if they would march into the Underworld against Gaborn's orders.

Sir Ryan McKim of Fleeds shouted at the lords, "Shut yer yaps, all of you, or it's a few loose teeth I'll be giving you! If this man were but a common king, you'd show him better respect. How much more should we honor the counsel of Earth King?"

Gaborn smiled in gratitude at Sir McKim, and said, "It is not by force of arms that we will win our way to the throne of the fell queen. Binnesman, Averan, and I are all under the protection of the Earth. I suspect that that alone can help us win our way into the Underworld. And though I would gladly take an army at my back, I believe all would die."

Iome saw his look falter then. Gaborn's face seemed pale, as if he stared death in the face, and she suspected that the struggle to come might be grim indeed.

"Your Highness," High Marshal Chondler reminded Gaborn, "yesterday you mentioned that the fate of the world hangs in the balance with this upcoming battle. If we do not kill the reavers—"

"We're *not* out to kill reavers—" the Wizard Binnesman objected. "That was never my intent. The Earth is wounded with a sore wound, and deep. We must heal its wounds if we can. I suspect that in order to do so, we will have to destroy the three runes and their author. We may only need to kill *one* reaver. . . ."

"Aye," Chondler argued, "you've got to kill one reaver, but doubtless you'll have to face thousands more to win your way into her lair. No one has ever gone so deep into the Underworld. If my guess is right, this is an old nest, in the farthest depths of the earth. I myself have risked a journey into the Underworld on two occasions, but only on a dare, and never have I gone so far." He swallowed, looked around the tunnel, and the warriors all fell silent as he spoke. With the fire gone from the cave, the night grew dark and deep. The starlight outside could hardly lend more than shadows to a man's face. "Our forefathers used to hunt reavers down there, far below. Mostly they didn't dare the deep lairs—where the ground gets hot to the touch and the air is so thick you could cut it with a knife. The old books call it the Unbounded Warren, for the tunnels go on forever, and every reaver lair is like a hive, with hundreds or thousands of warriors to guard its nests."

Averan shouted, "Yes, but the great seals aren't near the nest! They're near the Lair of Bones."

"So," High Marshal Chondler said, "you'll be going as assassins, not as an army. Still, Your Highness, I respectfully submit that I or Langley might be of great help on such a quest. . . ."

Gaborn gazed evenly at Chondler for a moment, then his eyes flickered around the cavern. "There are great deeds to be done," Gaborn said, "more deeds than men to do them. Indeed, in the battles to come, each of you must play a hero's part. I sense danger closing from every side."

He gazed down at the floor and peered as if into the depths of the earth. Beads of sweat stood up on his brow. "The first enemy to strike will be in Heredon, a thousand miles north of here, in two nights' time. Even if I could send an army to Heredon's aid, it would not help. The Earth bids me to warn the people there to hide—to seek shelter underground."

Murmurs of wonder rose from the crowd, for Gaborn gave curious counsel indeed. "Hide beneath the ground, like a mole?" someone blurted. Strange though it sounded, the counsel of an Earth King could not be ignored.

"At dusk the evening after that," Gaborn continued, "war will begin to break out close to home. If it's battle your stomach wants," Gaborn said, "you shall have your fill . . . and more. For war is coming, war with a foe who will not spare women or children."

At this Gaborn leapt up on a huge rock, so that he could see above the crowd, and shouted, "Send messengers throughout all Mystarria: tell all those who can to gather at Carris. I need every man who can stand upright, every woman who can hold a bow, every child over the age of ten who is willing to stare death in the face. I need them all to gather on the castle walls.

"At sunset, three nights hence, steel your hearts and sound the horns of war. You are to strike, and strike relentlessly. Our enemies will show no mercy and give no quarter, and if we fail, the end of mankind may well be upon us!"

Lowicker shouted, "You mean to send women and children into battle? Will you be there to lead us?"

"By the Seven Stones, I hope so," Gaborn answered, but Iome saw the worry in his eyes deepen, and knew that he doubted his own strength.

Gaborn gazed out on the assembled lords. Men from a dozen nations gathered around him. "Sir Langley, take the fastest horse that you can find, and fly for your homeland at Orwynne. Bring every lord who will follow you back to Carris. You must reach it by sunset in three days' time."

"Aye," Langley said. With half a dozen endowments of metabolism, he could easily run fifty miles per hour. Langley had hardly agreed when he spun on his heel and fled.

"High Marshal Chondler, you want a great task, and I will give it to you: I ask that you begin fortifying Carris. Do not worry about gathering supplies, for you will not need more than the castle has to offer. If you do not win this battle, all is lost."

"By the Powers!" Chondler swore. It would have been a daunting task in any case, since the reavers had destroyed the castle walls. But Gaborn put the weight of the world upon the man's shoulders.

"And what of me?" Iome asked.

Gaborn looked at her sadly, as if he feared to break her heart. "If Carris falls, I will need someone to lead our people to safety."

"I'm a Runelord," Iome said, "and by right should fight at Carris. Indeed, should I not be in command?"

"I considered having you hold Carris," Gaborn said. "You were the last to leave Castle Sylvarresta, and no one cares for her people more than you. But Chondler is the better leader for Carris."

She knew that he sought an excuse to send her somewhere far away, out of danger.

"I swore on our wedding day to be a light for you in dark places,'" Iome said. "And there is nowhere darker than where you are going. Let me come. I will do all that I can to ease your journey."

Gaborn shook his head sadly. "You don't understand. It's not *safe*."

The way that he said it, Iome suspected that Gaborn feared not only for her but for his own life. Her heart pounded. She dared not argue with him further in front of his own men.

Chondler called to several Knights Equitable, and the men began to hurry away, grabbing arms and packs. The place suddenly became a madhouse.

With the members of the band selected, Gaborn quickly began choosing weapons. Averan, Binnesman, and the green woman each had their wizard's staves, and would not want to be encumbered with other arms. Gaborn had his customary horseman's warhammer, the long-handled weapon favored in Mystarria. He also bore a saber as a matter of habit. But neither weapon was well suited for fighting reavers in their lair. The warhammer posed a danger to anyone who might be standing too close when he swung it in combat. And Gaborn's saber would probably snap the first time it struck reaver hide.

So Gaborn studied some weapons that Marshal Chondler's men had retrieved from Castle Arrowshire for just this purpose, and now laid on the ground before him: reaver darts. These were heavy spears made of solid iron, much like a javelin in shape, but longer. Each dart, some eight feet in length, was pointed at each end and tipped with diamond so that it might better pierce reaver hide. Around the iron shaft a grip had been wrapped, made of rough cowhide.

It was an ancient weapon, rarely used over the past thousand years. It looked overly heavy, but with endowments of brawn the dart would be as light as a willow wand in his hand. Still, its very bulk made it clumsy, inelegant.

So what am I to do while Gaborn is out saving the world? Iome wondered. He had already rejected her plea to go with him, and she doubted that he would be easily persuaded. She carried his child, after all, and he would not subject the child to danger.

And Gaborn was afraid not just for her but for himself.

There are things I can do to help, Iome thought, even if he doesn't let me come, things that Gaborn would never do in his own behalf.

Iome had always been more pragmatic than Gaborn. She admired his virtue, his refined sensibilities. She loved him for his gentleness.

But there comes a time when we must no longer be gentle, she told herself.

Iome went back into the tunnel, past the smoldering campfire into the deep shadows where a pair of facilitators were transferring endowments to Averan. Half a dozen Dedicates lay about the girl, like spent sacrifices.

Iome waited until the head facilitator was free for a moment, and then approached.

"Gaborn will be leaving soon," she told him. "When he does, send word to our facilitators at Castle Sylvarresta in Heredon. I have many forcibles hidden in the uppermost tomb on the hill. I want the facilitators there to use them to vector endowments to Gaborn. He has Dedicates at Castle Longmot. It shouldn't be hard."

"How many endowments should we give him?" the facilitator asked.

"All that they can."

"Gaborn would never agree to that!" the facilitator said too loudly. "Even as a child, he has never loved the forcible."

"Of course not," Iome said, trying to shush him with a gesture. "He must not know what we do for him. I ask only one boon. Gaborn is an oath-bound lord. He will not take endowment by force, nor barter for them with the poor who have no other choice. Those who give the endowments must be adults who understand the danger and who give their strengths voluntarily, out of their own pure desire to serve others."

The facilitator studied her. He knew how hopeless Gaborn's quest would be. He also knew that the world could not allow him to fail. "You will lose him, you know," the facilitator said. "Even if he succeeds on his quest, with so many endowments of metabolism, he will age and die while you are yet young. And you risk something even more profane. He might well become the Sum of All Men, immortal, alone, incapable of dying."

The thought wrung tears from Iome's eyes. "Don't you think I'm aware of the dangers? This is not something that I do lightly."

"Very well," the facilitator said. "I will send word to Heredon at once."

As Averan finished taking her endowments, Iome strode deeper into the cave. Binnesman and his wylde followed in Iome's wake.

Farther back in the tunnel, Gaborn stood alone with a torch in hand, peering into the void while his knights broke camp.

The opening to the Mouth of the World was more than a hundred feet wide, but quickly it tapered down to a bit over twenty-five feet wide.

The reavers had recently reinforced the walls with mucilage, which hardened into a substance tougher than concrete. The mucilage had been shaped into riblike pillars that arced up gently to reach a point some thirty feet overhead. Every dozen yards a new set of pillars rose. At the apex, where pillars from each side of the tunnel met, ran a bony ridge the length of the crawlway.

The appearance of these pillars was disconcerting. When Iome peered down the tunnel, the supports looked like bony white ribs, as if the trail led through the skeletal remains of some vast worm, long dead.

From the roof above, cave kelp hung in long tendrils, and other hairy plants dangled.

"What are you doing?" Iome asked.

"Wondering how many torches we should take," Gaborn said. "Carrying too many would be a cumbersome burden, and taking too few will be a disaster."

"Waxroot burns well," Binnesman suggested. "We should find some growing along the way."

"I may have something better than torches," Iome said, glad to prove her worth. "I took the liberty of bringing a present from the treasury at the Courts of Tide." She went to her pack, which sat waiting nearby beneath some coils of stout rope, and pulled out a bag filled with jewelry, all set with opals. These were but a small part of the treasures of the Mystarrian court, and represented the vast hoard of jewels collected by Gaborn's ancestors over a period of more than two thousand years. There were no less than eighty cape pins with opals of every color, to match whatever a lord might have in his courtly wardrobe: black opals from the hills above Westmoore. Fire opals from Indhopal, pearl opals from beyond the Carroll Sea, a blue opal so old that Chancellor Westhaven had told her that no one at court knew where it had come from. There were golden opals flecked with red set in a tarnished golden crown, and necklaces, bracelets, and rings by the score.

She dumped the contents onto the ground near Gaborn's feet. The jewels gleamed dully in the glow of his torch. "Can you draw the light from them," she asked Binnesman, "as you did at Castle Sylvarresta?"

"Yes," Binnesman exulted. "These will be marvelous!" The wizard scattered the jewels into a circle, and then drew runes outside. He waved his staff above them and spoke an incantation, then whispered softly, "Awaken."

The stones began to glow dimly, each with its own luster. It was like watching the stars come out on a summer's evening. First, the blue opal caught a spark, and then others joined it.

Yet unlike stars, there seemed to be no end to their glory. Even without a dozen endowments of sight, the resplendent light that shot up from the opals would have bedazzled and pained the eyes.

Streams of lustrous white, like sunlight bouncing off a snowy field, radiated from many opals. But startling colors played among them: streams of blue water running from a sapphire lake, a ruddy gold like an autumn day, greens and reds so fierce that if Iome had had to describe them, words would have failed her.

The stones blazed, and their brightness was such that Iome felt the heat from them, as if from a fire. She was forced to look away, and thus she looked up and saw the colors dancing across the roof of the cave.

Averan gasped, and even the green woman made a cooing sound in wonder.

Binnesman quickly reached down and pawed through the opals, gathering up the brightest. Iome had hastily searched among the treasure chests before she came, and many of the stones that had seemed fairest to her then were cast aside.

"Softer now," the wizard said as he finished. The opals dimmed, so that no heat burned from them, and yet even their muted light was brighter than any lantern.

"Let us see here," the wizard muttered. "Who shall need what?"

The wizard first picked up a silver ring that held a fine white stone that blazed hot. "Take care with this one, child," he said, handing it to Averan. "You can cook your meals with it."

Averan put the ring on and rejoiced, "It fits like it was made for me!"

"Perhaps it was," the wizard jested.

The ring glowed fiercely, and Averan stroked it and whispered, "Softer now." The light from it dimmed, as if she wore a star upon her finger.

For his wylde, the wizard chose a necklace with dozens of golden opals in it. He draped it over her head, and the green woman merely stared into the stones, bedazzled.

Last of all, he picked cape pins for himself and Gaborn.

Gaborn's was the pin with the green opal, which blazed the brightest of all the colored stones. "A singular stone for a singular man," Binnesman said as he pinned Gaborn's cape.

He stretched out his hand above the rest of the jewels, preparing to snuff out their light, when Iome grabbed his wrist and said, "Wait. I'm going with you."

She reached into the pile of jewels and picked up the ancient golden crown. Not many of its opals were bright, but with the hundreds of opals therein, Iome suspected that she could see nearly a quarter of a mile back into the cave.

Gaborn stared at her evenly. "No, you won't be coming. I have another task for you." He glanced up, as if afraid that others might hear. "If Chondler fails us, if he is overwhelmed at Carris, then I suspect that all of my Chosen may die. But there may still be one slim hope."

"Name it," Iome said.

"Some folks might flee to safety on the sea," Gaborn said. "Reavers hate water, and cannot see far enough to safely reconnoiter the oceans. They never surface on islands. So why not take some people to safety? You could sail north, into the frozen seas where no reavers would dare follow!"

"So," Iome said, letting only the slightest tone of bitterness creep into her voice, "you still hope to send me to safety?"

"I'm hoping that you will lead our people to safety."

"Fine," Iome said. "Send word to Chancellor Westhaven for Mystarria, and to Chancellor Rodderman in Heredon, and let them make the preparations. They don't need my help."

"But—" Gaborn began to say.

"Don't play upon my sense of duty," Iome warned him. "I'm not some servant. I'm sworn to your service more closely than any man could be. I know what you're thinking. You want to send me to safety, but you are the Earth King, and the only place that I can be safe is at your side. You swore, you swore in your wedding vows, that you would be my protector."

"I don't know what we'll find down there," Gaborn argued. "I can't promise that you'll be safe."

"Then what good is your Earth sight?" Iome asked. "You're as blind to our fate as any common man. But I can promise you this. When others falter, I'll be your shield. And while you're thinking about how to save the world, I'll be thinking about how to save you."

Gaborn peered hard into her face, searching for an argument. He said as if the words were wrenched from him in agony, "All right. We will face the pit together."

❧ 3 ❧

WED TO A WOMAN OF WATER

*Of all the Powers, Water is the most seductive. Perhaps that is because it is
easily unleashed. But all too soon, the streams become a raging torrent that
cannot be stopped, and he who sought to master Water becomes but another
bit of debris, borne away to the sea.*

—*excerpt from* The Child's Book of Wizardry, *by Hearthmaster Col*

Sir Borenson and his wife Myrrima fled the village of Fenraven before dawn,
when the mist was lifting from the mire while the stars drifted from the heavens like sparkling cinders.

Borenson first raided the kitchen, grabbing a few sausages and some
loaves of bread, which he stuffed in his pack. Then he crept to the door of
the inn, warhammer in hand, and peered out into the street. Cottages hunkered dazedly in the darkness, casting long shadows, and the bare limbs of
trees rose up all around behind them like black fingers, silently straining to
catch the falling stars. Nothing in the village seemed to be awake. No smoke
from a morning fire yet drifted from a chimney. No dogs barked, no pigs
grunted curiously.

Yet Borenson's mind was uneasy, for he still remembered the hooded
man who had followed them two nights before. The fellow had ridden a force
horse in the darkness, braving the wight-infested bogs of the Westlands.
That showed that he was a bold man. But he had also ridden hooded, with
sheepskin boots pulled over the hooves of his mount to soften its footfalls, in
the manner of assassins out of Inkarra. He might have just been a lone highwayman, hoping to waylay unsuspecting merchants. But Borenson had long
ago learned to nurture his suspicions.

So he watched the street for several long minutes, peering into the shadows. When he felt reasonably certain that no one was watching, he whispered, "Let's go," and crept like a shadow out the door, around the side of the inn, and into the stables.

Inside the stables a lantern burned dimly, and the stalls were dark. The hay up in the loft smelled moldy, which one might have expected in late winter or early spring, but which seemed odd here in autumn. Borenson watched Myrrima as she lit a lantern. She did not wince when she lifted the light from its hook, and as she carried it to the stalls, she moved gracefully, seeming to flow smoothly over the ground like water. A night past, she had managed to banish a wight with cold iron, but its touch had nearly stopped her heart. Now, to all appearances, her healing was complete.

Myrrima held the lantern high as they neared the stalls, searching for their horses, and Borenson grunted in surprise, giving a little laugh.

"What?" Myrrima whispered.

"My piebald mare! Look, she's here! Someone must have found her." She was stabled next to Borenson's own warhorse. He'd found the little mare outside Carris, and in the past few days had become quite fond of her. But he'd lost her while fleeing the wight. She'd struck her hoof on a root while running in the darkness. "Do you think she'll be lame?"

"I hope not," Myrrima said. "I'm the one who found her outside town yesterday afternoon. Her hoof was split, and the poor thing looked ready for slaughter, so I used the last of Binnesman's salve on her."

"Binnesman's wondrous salve?" Borenson asked, peering through the slats in the stable at the horse's hoof. "I thought I'd used it all on you."

"You dropped the tin," Myrrima said, "but there was a tad left."

There was a white blaze on the mare's hoof, as if the poor beast had injured it a year ago, but otherwise it looked fine. The mare held her weight evenly, and did not limp as she ambled close to Borenson, to nuzzle him.

Borenson stroked the horse with a sense of loss. "The old wizard outdid himself with that batch. We'll not see the likes of that ever again, I fear." The salve had saved Myrrima's life, and Borenson's, performing wonder upon wonder. But now it was gone.

"Blessed be the brooks that flow from the slopes of Cerinpyre, and glad be the fish that swim therein," Myrrima said, almost singing. Borenson wondered at her words, for it sounded as if she quoted a song that he had never heard. But Cerinpyre was the name of a tall mountain west of Balington, where Binnesman had made the salve.

"How far is it to Inkarra?" Myrrima asked, changing the subject.

"It's seventy miles from here to Batenne," Borenson said. "If we make good time, we can be there before noon, and I can take my endowments at the home of the marquis. We'll reach the southern border forty miles beyond.

The passage over the mountains into the Hidden Kingdoms may be slow, but afterward, the roads should be good all the way to Iselferion."

"That's where the Storm King lives?" Myrrima asked.

Borenson nodded. "We should be there by nightfall. We can deliver Gaborn's message to the Storm King—and perhaps even learn the whereabouts of Daylan Hammer."

"Is it that simple?" Myrrima asked.

Borenson laughed at her naïveté, wondering just how much she knew about Inkarra. He peered hard at her in the darkness. "I meant it as a joke."

They saddled their horses. Borenson took the mare from her stall gingerly, to see if indeed she was healed. To his delight, she was more than just well. She seemed positively sassy.

So Myrrima and Borenson rode into the night, toward the hills south of town. For a bit, the land dropped, and they rode through a thick fog. Myrrima's horse drew close to Borenson's then, as if fearing more wights. Borenson looked to his wife, to see if she too was afraid, but Myrrima rode her horse with her head back, her chin raised, as if savoring the moment. The fog misted her skin, so that dew formed on her brow and droplets sparkled in her hair, and she gulped the foggy air greedily.

Borenson grunted in surprise. His wife seemed to be a changed woman after last night. He could smell the water in her breath, like the wind off a lake, and her hair smelled like a still pool. But it wasn't just her scent that had changed. It was her movements, too—the easy way she seemed to flow when she walked, the calmness and sense of peace that pervaded her.

Wizardborn. She had learned that she was wizardborn, a servant to water. The water's touch had healed her, transformed her. But she had rejected the opportunity to serve it, and elected to stay with him.

Yes . . . something was different about her.

The land rose steadily for several miles, so that they soon could see the foggy moors behind. Bands of forest and field alternated along the road, but the woods were quiet and dry, and the land seemed healthier than the bogs to the north had been.

Still, he warily watched the margins of the road for sign of the hooded man. He and Myrrima seldom spoke, and then only in whispers. Whenever they reached a patch of woods, they'd hurry the horses through at a gallop, and each time they topped a hill, he would stop and search the starlit stretches of the road behind for long moments.

Thus they made their way into the highlands of Cragenwold, a region of dense, rocky forests. The road was so seldom used that it seemed only a ruin. Partial walls stood among the bracken where stone had been stacked upon gray stone a thousand years past. Broken statues of ancient lords lined the road, the wind and water having worn away the hollows of their eyes. Their gaping mouths bore mute testimony that Old Ferecia had once been the proudest of realms.

But that had been long ago. Now black pines crowded about the ruins of graveyards. Owls hooted in the lonesome groves, letting their voices echo among the hollows.

The road wound up and down for an hour, yet each time the path went down, it seemed to rise higher again. The morning sun rose, ponderously large on the horizon.

Borenson could feel the dead in these woods, pressing against the shadows, as if restrained somewhere off in the mossy trees. Yet the spirits here did not feel evil. They had once been men much like him, and he did not fear such wights. Besides, the sun beat on his back each time he exited the trees, and so long as it did, the dead were powerless to manifest themselves.

With the coming of the sun, Borenson began to watch the road for sign of tracks, but saw nothing for miles until they passed over soggy ground by a brook: and there it was, a scuff mark where there should have been a clean track.

Borenson's glance flickered over the scuff. "Our assassin. Do you think it's fresh?" he asked. He reached behind his back and drew his warhammer from its sheath.

Myrrima hopped down from her horse. She had taken endowments of scent from a dog, and now she sniffed near the track, then tested the air. "Not fresh," she said. "A day old maybe. A man, by the smell of him, an odd one."

"Odd?" Borenson whispered.

"His smell reminds me of open lands and lonely hills. Maybe he's only been out in the weather for a few days, but I think its much longer. It's like . . . he'd rather sleep in the rain than in a cozy inn."

"Hunh," Borenson said. He glanced about. "More likely, Raj Ahten has had him watching this road for a month. We'll water the horses, take our breakfast here."

He got off his mount, and led it uphill, away from the brook. Here, hazelnut trees crowded at the edge of a glen, huddled together like gossiping old women. Down below, the road wound like a ribbon over hills toward Fenraven, and Borenson could glimpse bits of it through the trees farther up the highway.

He lit a small fire and watched the road ahead while the twigs burned away, letting the flame consume the bark from some larger sticks, until he had enough coals so that he could roast the sausages he'd brought from the inn. There was little movement on the road ahead. He saw a huge red stag warily walking along, antlers arching so that they rested on its back, legs stiff, nose high in the air. It was scenting for a doe. But there was no sign of the mysterious rider ahead, nor of anyone else.

Still, Borenson felt uneasy. He couldn't quite name the cause of his fear. It might just have been the trip to Inkarra. That in itself was dangerous enough.

But there was something more. His main worry was for Myrrima. Over the past weeks, he had been loath to let himself fall in love with her. As a guard to the crown prince, his first duty had always been to Gaborn. He'd never felt that there would be room for a wife in his life—or at least not a woman that he would love. He'd always imagined that if he took a wife, it would be some poor woman, a starveling who would make his meals and satisfy his other physical urges in return for a warm roof. He had not imagined that he would marry a beautiful woman, a strong woman who loved him fiercely, a woman with wit and charm.

Now he was more than smitten by Myrrima. Now he felt struck dumb, like a boy whose heart was churning for the first time with unimagined passions.

Last night with Myrrima, as they had consummated their love, had been perfect.

Yet he felt that something was wrong. He feared that she would leave him—or, more exactly, that something was trying to pull her away from him.

His thoughts kept returning to the hooded man. There was something sinister about him.

Myrrima remained down by the brook, hidden in the thick of the trees. Borenson imagined that she was bathing herself, or merely resting, or perhaps gathering more firewood. But when he'd put the thick sausages on some forked sticks and begun to simmer them over the coals, he realized that he had not seen Myrrima for far too long.

Not wanting to call out with the threat of highwaymen about, he hurried back down to the brook. Myrrima wasn't by the road, but he could see her modest footprints in the soft earth beside the stream.

She'd headed downhill, following the brook. Trailing her was easy. Moss and fallen leaves covered the muddy ground, making it firm enough for a man to walk on. The low music of water burbling over rounded stones covered his footfalls, and the scent of the stream filled the air.

Borenson lightly crept along, watching her trail. No other footprints followed her, and only in one spot did he notice anything suspicious—the tracks of an enormous wolf crossed her path. The sight reminded him that they were in the wilds.

A steep slope dropped away just ahead, and the brook suddenly pitched over it, spilling into a narrow pool. Just beyond it, a wider pool opened where the water was as still and as clear as glass.

Myrrima knelt on the green grass beside the pool among a field of posies. Cattails thrust up among some stones by the water, and beneath its surface one could see down into the depths. Silver minnows flashed among the black roots of a large pine.

Myrrima was not bathing. She merely sat gazing into the water, eyes unfocused, her bare feet dangling into the pond. As she sat, Borenson saw a little thrill at the water's surface, as if a single minnow, or perhaps even a larger fish, swam just below the surface, its dorsal cutting the water. It raced along in a near circle, then wheeled toward the heart of the circle, suddenly breaking into three parts that zigged out in different directions and disappeared.

The movement thus drew a rune on the surface of the pond, one that Borenson did not recognize. His heart thrilled at the sight. No sooner had the surface of the pond gone still when a new rune began to take shape. Borenson peered close, to see if indeed there were minnows or water beetles swimming there, but he could see nothing. The water moved of its own accord.

Suddenly, Borenson understood his fear. It wasn't an assassin that would take his wife, it was another suitor that sought to lure her away, one of the Powers.

I should have known, Borenson told himself. I should have seen it in the way that she flows over the ground, or inhales the morning mist, or in the way that dew sparkles in her hair. She's an undine!

Borenson picked up a small twig and angrily hurled it into the pond, disrupting the water.

Myrrima looked up, and a broad smile broke across her face.

"You said that you rejected Water," Borenson accused, struggling to control his voice.

"No," Myrrima replied. "I said that I love you more, and that I refused to go to the sea."

"But the Powers don't let us make that choice. You can't love both me and Water."

"Are you so sure?" Myrrima asked. "Can a man love his wife and his children, his horse and his dog, his home and his country? Can he not love each of them deeply, in their own way?"

"He can," Borenson said, "but life ever makes us choose between the things we love, and if you try to serve Water, it will lay its claim on you, the way that the Earth has laid its claim upon Gaborn."

"Gaborn serves a hard master," Myrrima said, "as firm and unyielding as stone." She cupped her hand and dipped it into the pool, then ladled water onto a rock next to her. "But Water yields. It fills the empty spaces around us and the voids within us, and then lifts us up. I can be borne away upon deep currents of Water and still love you. I told you last night that I love you, and that I won't leave you. It's true. I will never leave you."

Borenson knew that few who loved Water could resist its call for long, yet Myrrima's soft and reassuring tone almost allayed his fears.

"Come here," she said, patting the ground beside her. Borenson made his way down the slope and squatted on the grass at Myrrima's side.

She reached out and touched his hand. It is said that powerful wizards evoke odd emotions when they enter the presence of common men. Flameweavers arouse men's appetites—their greed for wealth, their lust for women, their hunger for blood, and their avarice—while Earth Wardens arouse a desire to procreate, or to till the soil, or to seek solace in dark places. Borenson had never really noticed such feelings before, until now. As Myrrima took his hand, he felt a sense of peace wash over him, a clean feeling that swept away his doubts and anxiety. He'd felt that same sense of ease last night, as the two of them lay tangled together in bed. He'd thought that it came from within, that he felt only the comfort that came with consummating their love. Now he saw that it was something more.

Myrrima took his right hand in hers, and looked deep into his eyes. Her own eyes were so dark that they were almost black, and the whites of her eyes were a pale blue. Even now, when there was no morning mist, droplets of water sparkled in her dark hair, and her breath smelled like some mountain freshet. But there was no trace of the undine about her. Her eyes were not turning as green as the sea. She was not growing gill slits in the hollow of her throat. There was no hint of silvery scales in her skin.

"Don't be afraid," she said, and the very words banished his fear. "Water requires a task of me, one that I am willing to give. A dark time is upon us, a dry time. Water needs warriors, to help bring stability and healing to the land. And I have been thinking: you and I are one. I would have you join me in my quest."

She's to be Water's warrior? Borenson wondered. That explained why he could see no sign of the undine about her. Perhaps it also explained her uncommon prowess in battle. It was *her* hand that slew the Darkling Glory when all others succumbed to it. And by her hand she had banished a wight, something no mere mortal should have been able to do. And she had slain dozens of reavers in battle yesterday. Yes, he could see that she was a fit warrior. More than that, he could see that the Water chose wisely, for it tailored its request to fit Myrrima's own penchant.

There was a hunger in Myrrima's eyes. "Please, join me," she said. "It is a battle that will leave no scars on the heart. Water will wash them all away."

What had possessed her to say such a thing? She knew that his guilt over killing the Dedicates at Castle Sylvarresta had nearly destroyed him. But did she also know that he had sought Water afterward, that he had made an offering beside a sacred pool?

He felt sure that even if she didn't know, her master did. And now it made an offer to him in return.

Myrrima reached down with her left hand, cupped it, and ladled a handful of water over their clasped right hands. Borenson resisted the impulse to pull away at the last instant, and the cool liquid spilled over his hand, a hand that a week ago had been so drenched in blood that he had never thought it could be clean again. She poured the water over him slowly, and it spilled down over his thumb and fingers, and around his palms, and streamed down his elbow. There was more water, he thought, than any cupped hand should be able to hold.

The water was warmer than he'd imagined it would be, as if it still held the kiss of summer. And when Myrrima washed him thus, all the pain and weariness in his right arm seemed to depart. He didn't just feel clean. He felt new.

Myrrima smiled at him, as if delighted by his surprise. She reached into the pool, and water striders darted away as she ladled out a second handful. "May Water refresh you," she whispered, as she poured it over his head. His mind seemed to go clear. All the fears he felt about her future, all the doubts he had about his own destiny, seemed borne away. She scooped up a third handful and let it wash down the front of his shirt. "May Water sustain you," she whispered, then leaned forward to kiss him, and added, "May Water make you its own."

She kissed him then, and took hold of his tunic passionately. With a mighty heave she shoved him into the pool. But she held him even as she did, still locked in an embrace, and her weight bore him beneath the water. The warm water was over him and under him and all around, and she clung to him, still kissing him, and he found no need to breathe, and had no desire to push her away. Instead, she merely held him, her lips against his, and he knew that indeed she loved him, almost as much as she loved Water.

Ꮽ 4 Ꮸ

THE BLIND-CRAB

Perhaps the most common inhabitant of the Underworld is the blind-crab. These creatures, whose philia and skeletal structure mark them as members of the same family as reavers, range broadly in size from the miniature lantern crabs of Waddles Cave in Alnick, whose glowing bodies can comfortably rest on a babe's thumbnail, to the behemoth crab of Delving's Deep, whose empty carapace could house a large family.

—from Denizens of the Deep, by Hearthmaster Quicks

Gaborn Val Orden descended into the Underworld. The few small signs of life right at the cave's opening soon gave way to desolation. Just inside the tunnel, the air began to turn cool, and after a quarter of a mile it had a biting chill.

The frigid air steamed the breath of the horses, and within half a mile, ice glistened on the tunnel walls and crusted the floor. On the ceiling some ice crystals looked as if they had not been disturbed in a thousand years. Ice fans splayed out as wide as a man's hand, and in such places, the lights from the opals reflected from the roof and the icy walls in a dazzling display.

Here on the floor in their path lay a dead reaver. Whether it had merely died of natural causes, or been killed by one of its own, or trampled by the horde as it raced through the cave, was hard to tell. The grim monster had been shoved up against the wall, as if the reavers had sought to get around it, and parts of it had been trampled. Its eyeless head was intact, shoved against the wall, its jaws gaping wide. A few small blind-crabs had been lured to it by its smell, but they too had succumbed to the cold, and lay around it in piles.

The tunnel was broad enough for five people to ride abreast, so ride they did, though the horses seemed jittery and ill liked the trail.

Reaver tracks were everywhere. The tramping of over seventy thousand of the monsters had worn a rut in the tunnel and cleared the floor of vegetation. Nothing grew upright, except an occasional column of fungi or a stray plant that lay splayed against the wall. And few vines or rootlike creepers swung from overhead to brush against them, for these too had snapped away as the reaver army marched beneath. The path led gently down, a trail that could easily be negotiated by horse or mule.

Averan rode in the lead. The girl had received endowments of scent from dogs, and by taking the lead, she hoped to detect the subtle odors of reaver speech, a tongue that only she could understand. The girl sniffled and wept softly as she rode. She had said a long and sad good-bye to one of her Dedicates, a big man named Brand, who had but one arm.

Iome rode close beside Gaborn. She was no warrior, though she had taken full as many endowments as any captain had in Gaborn's guard. At the rear came Binnesman and the green woman. The tunnel led down into the heart of the mountains at a gradual slope, and rarely veered. When it did, Gaborn felt certain that it did so only to avoid enormous boulders or exceptionally hard stone.

Despite the ease of the early trail, the reaver's tunnel was not free of damage. In places, bits of ceiling had caved in, leaving rocks and rubble on the tunnel floor. In another spot, the earth had cracked wide open. The fissure was but four feet wide but seemed to drop away endlessly below Iome as her mount jumped over.

Still, such was the skill of the reaver's workmanship that the tunnel held, for the most part.

Reavers are used to earthquakes, Gaborn realized. They must know how to cope with them as well as we do with the wind and rain.

But other acts of nature could not be so easily avoided. In places water had seeped through the rocks above, and over the ages had formed stalagmites and stalactites. The reavers had cleared these away just four days past as they marched through the tunnel. But in some places water would spill down the walls, forming shallow streams and icy pools, and ultimately these would find some crevasse to seep into. Such crevasses widened over time, and cut away the floor.

After a dozen miles, the caves began to warm. The ice fans disappeared, and quite suddenly the cave was filled with a dense, cool fog.

The horses slowed to a walk, and despite the fact that Gaborn could not sense any immediate danger, his heart beat faster. Until now, the view had been clear before them, and Gaborn hadn't feared that they would meet a reaver. At least, if they had met one, he'd have been able to see it. But now, the light thrown by his opal pin failed him, and he could hardly see his hand in front of his face.

The whole party was forced to dismount, and Gaborn walked for a bit in the fog, his skittish horse pulling at the reins with nearly each step.

He thought back to a conversation that he had had while Averan finished taking her endowments.

Gaborn's Days had asked, "Your Highness, I beg you to take me with you. At least let me ride part of the way."

Gaborn felt annoyed by the request from the historian. "You ask much of me, and never once have you given anything in return. You say that the Days are forbidden to become involved in political intrigues, that you are merely observers of the affairs of men, servants beholden to no one but the Time Lords. Yet I ask you one last time to become involved. Help me. Bid your Days around the world to warn the people: tell them to set sail north or south for the isles of the sea. If we do not defeat the reavers at Carris, there may be no other refuge."

To Gaborn it seemed a small request, one that could easily be fulfilled. Each Days had given an endowment of wit to another, who then granted his own endowment in return, so that the two Days shared one joint memory.

The Days that stood before Gaborn acted as the "witness" for the "twins," scrutinizing Gaborn's every word and deed. His twin acted as a scribe, and lived a retired life on an island in the cold seas north of Orwynne, where she wrote the chronicles of Gaborn's life.

Thus, with all of the scribes living together, they formed a vast network. In theory, the Days could do as Gaborn asked. They could warn every lord in every realm of the impending doom.

"This would violate our political neutrality," the Days answered Gaborn.

"Not if you warn all men equally," Gaborn said. "I don't ask you to favor any one nation above another. Warn all men. Help me save any man who will save himself."

For the first time in his life, Gaborn saw a Days flinch and seriously consider a request for help. By the Days's own law, if a prince, though he be but a child, should fall into a pool and begin to drown, the Days was not allowed to offer a hand.

"You understand," his Days answered after a moment, "that whether you want it or not, there would be political repercussions. Kings and queens would flee their own lands, or send their children into exile. Nations would tumble, populaces shift. Wars would erupt as men struggled for control of the islands in the north."

"At least some would live," Gaborn said. "At least in the northern wastes, they'd stand a chance against the reavers."

Iome's Days, a young girl who was new to the task, looked to Gaborn's Days and said, "We should take the request to the council."

"You would risk a schism!" Gaborn's Days objected.

"And you would risk the fate of mankind!" Iome's Days shouted back.

The two glared at each other, and Gaborn's heart pounded. Never had he seen two Days argue.

Gaborn's Days abruptly went to his horse and rode off in a fit of rage. Iome's Days said to Gaborn, "Your Highness, I will do what I can to honor your request."

"Thank you," Gaborn said. He reached out and squeezed her hand.

The girl looked at Gaborn's Days's fleeing back and shook her head sadly. "Old ones like him, they forget what it is like to love, to have family and friends. Their only love is watching, and their only friends are their twins."

"In this council of yours," Gaborn asked, "will you stand much chance against others like him?"

The girl shook her head. "I don't know. We serve the Time Lords. We keep the chronicles. But what will we chronicle if all men die? The advance of the reavers, the slow cooling of the sun, the end of all things? I think we have reached a time when we must take action, but if we do, we must all take it together."

So Gaborn walked in the fog, and sought with his Earth Sight to pierce the gloom.

"The fog won't last long," Averan assured everyone. "There's a larger passage ahead, a shaft going up, where hot air from the Underworld meets the cold air of the mountains."

"Gaborn," Iome asked, "is there danger ahead? Do you sense reavers?"

"Yes," Gaborn said trying not to sound too ominous, "I sense danger, but not for many miles."

He wondered at that. If the reavers were planning to set an ambush, what better place could they have to spring an attack than here in this dank fog?

Gaborn asked Averan, "You warned me yesterday about the dangers here. What are we likely to find ahead?"

Averan shook her head, as if clearing her thoughts. "Mainly there are reavers," Averan said. "Lots of them. But there are other dangers—deep canyons that reavers could climb, but maybe men could not. And there are other animals down here. . . ."

"With our endowments," Gaborn said, "I don't think we need to worry about animals."

Averan seemed to think for a moment, and then let out an exasperated sigh. "This . . . isn't what I remember. A week ago, the roof of this tunnel was choked with vines, and the floors were thick with vermin. That's what the

Waymaker remembered. But now the reavers have cleared the trail and smoothed the way. So I don't know exactly what we'll find on the road. And I'm not sure what roads we might have to follow. There are lots of tunnels near the Unbounded Warren, and there are paths that even the reavers fear to tread. If we're to get past the reavers, we'll need to take some of the less-used tunnels, the dangerous ones. I think we'll have to sneak in."

"You say we'll meet reavers," Gaborn asked. "Will there be guards?"

Averan thought for a moment. "I told you: the reavers you fought, they weren't warriors. They were farmers and tunnelers, butchers and . . . just common reavers. Few of them knew how to fight. Sure, they carried knight gigs and blades, but they didn't know how to use them. If there are guards ahead," Averan continued, "I can tell you what to watch for. Reavers like to burrow underground when they hunt. They'll be on the road, with dirt covering them, hidden so well that you won't even notice a bump. Nothing may show except for one or two philia, lying above the surface."

"I've always wondered," Binnesman said, "can they see us when they're underground?"

"No," Averan said. "Like I told you, they don't see like we do. They only sense shapes from their life-glow, from the lightning in their bodies."

"The force electric," Binnesman said.

"Whatever you call it," Averan said. "So they can't see through dirt any better than you could. But so long as a philium or two is lying above the ground, they can smell you coming, and they can feel vibrations from your movement. When you're on top of them, that's when they like to rise up, throwing you to the ground to disorient you. They want to kill you before you have time to move."

"So I've heard," Gaborn said bitterly. Averan didn't know it, but Gaborn had gone into the Dunnwood to hunt reavers only a day after he'd wed Iome. He'd hunted in an ancient cave where some reavers had holed up. Even though Gaborn was an Earth King, and even though he'd had his senses to warn his men of danger, few of his companions had survived that expedition. Nearly four dozen knights had died in an ambush like the one Averan described.

"There is danger ahead," Gaborn said. "Reavers, most likely. But it's not for—oh, ninety or a hundred miles."

"I just remembered something," Averan said, "something I learned from the Waymaker. There is an old warren ahead. I don't know how to convert distances in reaver to human terms . . . but I think maybe a hundred miles. The reavers stayed there for days before they came to the surface."

"It was a staging area?" Gaborn asked.

"There could be more reavers there, I think," Averan said. "An army—a big one. I remember seeing it in the mind of the fell mage. She needed to get her warriors out, to make room for the others that were coming."

Gaborn's heart went out of him. Seventy thousand reavers had attacked Carris. If there was a horde that size ahead, how could they hope to sneak past it?

"Is there a way around the staging area?" Gaborn asked, "a side tunnel that we can take?"

Averan gazed up at Gaborn's face. "Maybe we should go find another way into the Underworld."

"There isn't time," Gaborn said.

"We might be able to sneak past them," Binnesman said. "Or, if their guard is light, we may be able to fight past them, and hope to avoid pursuit."

The fog felt to Gaborn as if it were closing in. He was beginning to worry about Averan. She had learned much from the reavers, but she didn't know nearly enough to guide them. Or perhaps, more precisely, her head was so full of minutiae that she hadn't had time to put it all together.

"What about this fog?" Iome asked. "Can reavers see through fog?"

"Yes," Averan said. "They hardly notice it."

Almost as soon as Iome had spoken, Gaborn found the fog beginning to clear. Indeed, in a matter of a few paces, it was gone altogether. The tunnel branched, and warmer air seemed to be coming from the left fork, like a summer breeze, except that it smelled of minerals and dank places. The right fork led up at a steeper angle.

"Turn left," Averan said. "The trail almost always leads down, toward warmer air."

Now the tunnel began to show signs of life. The ice here had all melted, and with the confluence of heat and moisture, patches of wormgrass began to grow all along the floor and walls. Wormgrass was so named because the urchinlike shrub had soft spicules the width and length of earthworms. Cave kelp hung from the ceiling, and blotches of colorful fungi adorned the rock.

Most of the vegetation along the floor and walls had been devastated, so that now only ragged patches of flora could be seen.

Here and there blind-crabs roamed about, searching for food. These were nothing like the crabs that inhabited the coast or some rivers. They were more closely akin to reavers, and to Gaborn's mind looked more like giant ticks than crabs. They had six legs, each of which was long and thin.

The group mounted up, and began to ride their horses hard now. The road was clear before them.

Most of the young blind-crabs were absolutely colorless. Their shells were like flawed crystal, giving a clear view of their guts and muscles. Gaborn could see their hearts palpitating wildly in fear as the horses approached, and could make out the color of their latest meals. Most of the crabs were small, only a few inches across the back.

A few lost gree shot through the cave with the speed of an arrow, searching for reavers that served as hosts for the insects and parasitic worms upon which the gree fed. As they flew, their black wings wriggled and squeaked as if in pain. One landed on Iome's shoulder, mindless with hunger. Its head was spade shaped, like a reaver's, with tiny philia that ran along the ridge of its brow and down its jawline. It immediately hooked its clawed feet into Iome's cloak and began scrabbling about, searching for insects. Iome shrieked and grabbed it, then flung it against the wall.

Soon after that, the party came upon their first great-worm of the journey—gray like a slug, nearly nine feet long and as broad as a man's hand, leaving a slime trail as it fed on a colony of mold.

Gaborn was fascinated. He'd heard few tales of the Underworld, and many animals and plants, like this giant worm, had no names that he'd ever learned.

Now that they had passed through the fog, for hours they rode down into the very belly of the world. Often they reached branches in the tunnel, and more and more, the cross trails showed signs of heavy use by reavers.

At each juncture Averan would sniff the trail for the Waymaker's scent. Yet in spite of all the memories that the Waymaker had shared, even Averan found a few surprises.

They had ridden for several hours at a fast pace, when Gaborn noticed something: off the side of the trail was a small cave, crudely chiseled. Above it, clearly visible in the light of the gleaming opals, scratch marks looked to have been gouged by human hands.

"What's this?" Gaborn asked. "An animal's lair?"

"Not animal," Binnesman said. "Human. Erden Geboren's men often used to build such retreats in the Underworld, when they hunted reavers in times of old. The mark here is written in Inkarran. I'm not too handy with their tongue, but I believe that the sign calls this 'Mouth of the World Outpost Number Three.'"

"The Waymaker knew of hundreds of such fortresses," Averan said.

"I suppose that we had better check this out," Gaborn said. "We may want to take refuge in one of these before our journey is over."

Averan leapt off her mount, and peered into the narrow opening. She held her gleaming opal up before her, so that its reddish light showed the way. "The tunnel is chiseled into solid rock," she said. "The crawlway goes up a dozen yards, then turns to the left."

She climbed in first, and Gaborn got down from his own mount and followed the girl in.

Spongy black fungi, like wrinkled leaves, matted the floor. Gaborn
crawled over them and felt as if he were crawling on a wet blanket.

At the top of the tunnel he found a room large enough for ten or fifteen
people. A pair of blind-crabs, sensing the intruders' presence, scrabbled to
hide behind a tall stone jar that sat in one corner. An ancient reaver dart, its
haft nearly rusted through, leaned against a wall.

Moldering in another corner were the bones of a child. The flesh had
first dried on the skeleton, and then rotted away in patches so that the bones
clung together.

Gaborn counted the ribs, and found that it had been a girl, a small child
of perhaps four or five. The girl had been curled in a fetal position with her
thumb in her mouth when she died. A blanket was wrapped around her, an
Inkarran blanket woven from long strands of white goat hair.

Gaborn heard someone grunt. Iome had followed him up the tunnel. She
caught him staring at the pile of bones.

"Who would bring a child down here?" Iome wondered aloud.

Averan spoke up. "A few days ago, when I tasted the brains of a reaver, I
saw something. I saw . . . pens full of people down here in the Underworld,
kept so that the reavers could test their magic spells." Iome looked up at her,
stricken. "All the spells that they learned: to wring the water from a man, to
blind him with pain, to make his wounds rot, they had to practice on real
people. So, they caught people—never too many from one place: here a person, there two or three, and they brought them down here. Maybe this girl
was one of them."

"How horrible it must have been," Iome said, as if this were something
that had happened long ago.

Averan shook her head. "No, how horrible it must *be*. They're still down
here."

It was heartbreaking news. Gaborn had imagined that Averan's mind
was a vast cave, full of treasures waiting to be brought to light. But now he
found it full of bones and horror. "Do you know where they are?" Gaborn
asked. "Can you show me the way?" On top of all his other impossible
tasks, he'd have to find these people, bring them up from their prison, if he
could.

"At the bottom," Averan said. "Near the Lair of Bones."

Gaborn inhaled deeply. He was finding it hard to breathe in this tight
space. At first he'd thought that an outpost like this might be a good place to
camp, but now he knew that he could never rest in this one, not with the hollow eyes of the child watching him. He felt guilty for being alive, when so

many others were dead. He felt guilty for wanting life, when his earth senses warned that so many were about to die.

"Let's go," Gaborn said. His group had not ventured more than ten miles past the old outpost when Gaborn halted his horse, peered up the road, and said, "There is danger is here—not far ahead."

∞ 5 ∞

THE SHIVERING WORLD

A well-bred lady must be prepared in all things. It is not enough to simply excel at needlepoint. She must also be equipped to lead a nation. She should know how to gossip effectively, barter for mercenaries, plan a feast, skewer an assassin, comfort a sick child, and lead a cavalry charge.

—*from* A Young Woman's Primer, *by Andreca Orden-Cooves, Duchess of Galant*

Iome's nerves felt jittery and her stomach tightened. She'd known that she would find reavers in the Underworld, but she hadn't wanted to find them soon.

For the past seventy miles the reaver tunnel had been almost featureless, a dull thoroughfare through the Underworld made interesting only by an occasional blind-crab or great-worm. The drab stones offered little variation in color. But suddenly the path ahead opened up into a natural cave whose ceiling rose hundreds of feet in the air. The sound of rushing water thundered in the distance, and nearby Iome could hear it trickling along the walls, dripping from stalactites. The tunnels ahead were covered with white calcite that gleamed like quartz, and the reavers had pummeled it under their feet, so that their trail looked as if it were strewn with bright glass, or bits of stars. The keen scent of sulfur water filled the air.

"The reavers like the pools here," Averan said. "It's the last drinking water before they leave the Underworld."

"They're here," Gaborn said, nodding with certainty. "Up the road a ways. I feel the danger rising."

Iome had watched men battle reavers from afar, but had never fought one herself. The green woman, Binnesman's wylde, rose up in her stirrups, sniffing the air like a hound, peering ahead.

"Do you smell reavers?" Averan asked her.

The green woman shook her head. "No."

Gaborn looked to Averan for counsel.

"There could be guards posted ahead," Averan said. "They might have buried themselves."

You would never have any warning before they got you, Iome thought.

"I'll take the lead," Gaborn said. With his Earth Sight, Gaborn was the only one who could travel this path with any degree of safety.

They rode on.

Iome's senses were alert. As she rode, she held her opals up and lit the cavern perhaps more brightly than it had ever been lit before. The walls glittered like frosting in shades of honey and ivory. Warm sulfur water trickled and dripped over every surface, and over the ages it had built up deposits of stone in grotesque shapes. Stalagmites squatted like gargoyles on the cave floor while tubular stalactites hung overhead, twisting in serpentine fashion. Along both sides of the path, shallow green pools lay with steam curling up from their surfaces. Myriad reaver tracks deeply imprinted the mud of every pool.

Plant life was sparse, but feather ferns hung from crevasses near the roof. Something large, the size of an eagle, flitted overhead and circled a stalactite.

"Gree hawk!" Binnesman shouted.

Gaborn reined his horse and pulled out his sword, eyeing the creature as it circled twice more. In some ways, it resembled an enormous bat. But it had a head like a reaver's—blind, broad, heavily toothed, with frills of philia sweeping off its jaw and in a ridge along the back.

To Iome, with her six endowments of metabolism, the gree hawk did not seem to present much of a threat, but to a commoner it would have seemed to be flitting about at lightning speed.

Iome asked, "Will it attack?"

"They mostly eat gree," Binnesman said. "But if they are hungry, and if they are presented with an easy meal in the way of a lone traveler, they may attack."

Gaborn eyed the gree hawk. It wheeled near the roof of the cave for a moment, then landed back in a dark corner, near some red feather ferns. The ferns all snaked back from the creature, withdrawing into recesses in the wall so that in moments there was no sign of the ferns at all, merely the small holes into which they had fled.

Gaborn led the way. For three miles the trail followed the line of pools, and Iome saw a host of intersecting tunnels running here and there to unknown destinations.

Averan kept to the straight path, and soon there was a huge rumbling sound, an incessant thunder—water tumbling over rocks. Gaborn halted the group again, seemed leery of the path ahead. He sniffed the air.

Iome rose in her stirrups. She had no endowments of scent from dogs to aid her, and the only smell she could detect in the air was the sulfur water. Ahead, just around a bend, a waterfall seemed to be cascading over the stones. The water breaking on the rocks caused the whole cave to tremble.

Yet as Iome listened, she realized that something strange was happening. The rumbling was growing stronger.

"Flee!" Gaborn shouted. He began wheeling his mount around, and for a moment everyone struggled to keep up.

"Earthquake!" Iome warned, for she had felt that same rumbling two days past, when a quake humbled the Courts of Tide.

"No," Gaborn shouted. "Reavers are coming!"

How many reavers would it take to make the earth grumble like this? Iome wondered. Yet she knew the answer. She had heard a similar thundering across the plains at Carris.

Iome and the green woman were at the back of the group. Iome wheeled her mount as best she could, raced back the way she had come, but Binnesman's mount surged ahead of hers.

What are we to do? she wondered. Our horses can outrun them, but to what end? The reavers will only chase us back up the tunnel.

Iome raced past one path that branched to the right, but when she reached a second that climbed a steep hill and then disappeared into another passageway, Gaborn shouted, "That way! To the left!"

Iome spurred her charger uphill. It would have been too steep for a normal mount, and even with endowments of brawn and metabolism her horse struggled up the incline, floundering once so that she thought that they would go tumbling back downhill. But the beast got its feet under it and surged up into the opening. A path opened ahead of Iome—stalagmites rose up all around like ogres. It was a forbidding landscape.

"Not this way!" Averan shouted when she reached the summit. "The Waymaker knew this path. It comes to a dead end a few miles up the trail!"

"Yes, this way!" Gaborn argued. His own mount had just lunged to the top of the hill. "Hide!"

Iome trusted Gaborn's Earth Sight more than she did Averan's memories.

"Where?" Averan asked.

"This way," Gaborn shouted. "Follow me!"

He raced his mount a hundred yards, and then stopped, searching this way and that for a place to hide. "Up there!" he shouted. He pointed toward a narrow cleft between two stalactites near the roof.

"The horses will never fit through there!" Binnesman objected.

"Then we leave them," Gaborn answered. He leapt off his mount and pulled out his dagger, then cut the girth straps to his saddle. In an instant the saddle and all of the packs were off.

Iome's mount had its ears back, and its eyes were wild. It snorted in terror at the sound of the reavers' trampling feet. Iome leapt off and removed her saddle, ropes, and pack. Her mount reared up, frantically pawing the air.

She could see no escape for the beast. There was no light here in the Underworld, and the horses would not be able to run in the dark.

As Iome wondered what to do, Binnesman dismounted, but left his saddle on the horse, cutting off only his packs and his coil of rope. Then he took his opal cape pin off and pinned it onto the saddle.

He laid a hand on the muzzle of the gray imperial warhorse, and said softly, "You have carried me as far as we can go, my friend. Now, seek greener fields."

The stallion stared at him for a moment in curiosity, ears forward. Iome wondered if the animal understood the wizard, but this force horse had once been Raj Ahten's personal mount. The runes on it showed that it had four endowments of wit. Seldom were so many forcibles used on a mere horse. This mount learned almost as fast as a man would. Hopefully, it understood.

"Go, my friend," Binnesman urged. "I have provided light for the journey."

Around Iome, the ground rumbled continuously. It was as if giant stones were rolling through the cavern. The sound seemed sourceless. She almost expected reavers to come charging up the cave at that instant, but somehow knew that they were far away. The noise wasn't loud because they were close, it was loud because they were many.

The wizard turned away from his horse. Gaborn was already scrambling up the rocks, with the green woman in tow. Iome followed last.

The horses took off, went thundering down the tunnel, racing back the way that they had come.

"Here, now," Binnesman said to Iome. "You first." He hesitated as Iome stepped around him, between a pair of stalagmites that stood like grotesque guardians. There was no trail to their retreat. Iome had to look for handholds on her way up. The flowstone along the walls, though slick, offered many such opportunities.

She turned back to see what was keeping the wizard. He took some sprigs of parsley from his pocket and blessed them. He tossed them on the trail, then drew wards of protection on the ground with his staff.

Iome reached the sanctuary, squeezed in. Gaborn and the others were already inside. It was a small grotto, about forty feet long. Stalactites had dripped down over the ages, until at last they had joined with the stalagmites beneath, forming crude pillars. Several of these stood next to one another, becoming solid walls. The floor beneath showed that at times water had pooled in the small cavern, but now all was dry.

"The reavers will smell the horses," Averan said. "They'll come to investigate."

"But they won't smell us," Binnesman assured her.

Iome had to wonder. Binnesman was the most powerful herbalist she had ever known. His spells could amplify the natural properties of plants, magnifying their effect. But could even the incomparable Binnesman hide the odor of half a dozen men and horses from the reavers?

Her heart pounded. She studied the narrow grotto. There was no exit. Sweat stood out on Gaborn's brow; his tongue flicked out and whetted his lips.

What does it mean, she wondered, when even the Earth King is afraid?

The ground began shaking so hard that bits of stone flaked off the roof. Mingled with the distant rumble now came a hissing, the sound that reavers make as they draw breath. It sounded almost as if the tunnel were a windpipe, and the Earth itself were gasping.

Gaborn threw down his saddle and stripped his pack, ropes, and saddlebags off. He tossed them over his own shoulder, leaving the saddle. He stood up, and his eyes darted about nervously.

Iome and the others grabbed their own belongings.

"Get back," Gaborn warned them. "Get to the back of the chamber."

Averan was the first to go. Binnesman and the others followed. Gaborn held his reaver dart and stood at the mouth of the grotto, on guard.

Averan hung at the back of the cavern, listening. The rumbling grew. Tremors shook the floor, and dust rose all about. "They're coming fast," she said. "They're coming too fast."

"'Too fast?'" Alarm coursed through Iome.

"This is it," Averan said. "This is their entire horde, their army. This is the end of the world."

"What do you mean, this is the horde?" Iome demanded.

"Now the *real* warriors are coming," Averan said, "and all of them will come. They'll bring their most powerful battle mages, and . . . and—" She threw up her arms, unable to explain.

Iome suspected that even Averan couldn't guess what the reavers were capable of.

Three days. Gaborn had warned that there would be a great battle at Carris in three days. Iome calculated how fast the common reavers had run before, and realized that three days was about right. In three days the army that was marching from the Underworld would reach Carris.

Gaborn paced at the mouth of the grotto.

"What's wrong?" Iome demanded.

"The Earth . . ." Gaborn said. "The Earth warns me to flee, but I see no escape."

"Maybe we should go after the horses," Averan suggested.

"No," Gaborn said. "This is the right path. I just—I just don't see the way out."

Iome searched frantically. Everywhere, the white walls hung like dripping curtains of stone. Craters pocked the floor where pools had formed and then dried out ages ago. White ridges along each ledge showed where the waterline had been. Perfect blue-white cave pearls rested on the floor.

The water had to come from somewhere, Iome thought. She peered up. The roof above rose some twenty feet. Small stalactites hung overhead like spears. The ground rattled under her feet now, and Iome licked her lips, afraid that a stalactite would break loose and fall, along with the flakes of stone that had begun tumbling from the roof.

Then she spotted it—a tiny shaft so small that a badger could not have crawled through. It was near the roof, at the back of the cave.

"Up here!" she said.

Iome dropped her pack and ropes and climbed up the wall. Her fingers and toes found purchase in tiny crevices and indentations that no commoner could ever have used. The flowstone offered ample opportunity for support. With her endowments of brawn and grace, she felt almost as if she were a fly, climbing along the wall.

She reached the top. Her opal crown gleamed, and by its light she searched the hole. She couldn't see far back. She reached in. The hole narrowed, and became no wider than her arm. She grasped a knob of calcite, a cave pearl that had fused to the floor of the small spring, and tried to wrench it free. With so many endowments of brawn she was able to break it off, but even as she did, her hand snapped up and hit the roof of the cave, banging it. Her knuckles bled profusely. It was no use. The calcite deposits were as hard as quartz. She'd never be able to dig fast enough to widen the opening.

"Here they come!" Gaborn shouted. "Everyone to the back!"

He herded the others to the rear of the grotto. Iome clung to the wall like a fly, afraid to move. The wall shook beneath her grasp.

Silently, she prayed to the Earth Powers, "Hide us. Let them not find us."

Loud hissing rose outside the grotto.

"They've smelled us," Averan said. "There's no other reason why they'd be coming up this branch of the cave."

The acrid stench of horse sweat was everywhere. Even without endowments from a dozen dogs, Iome could smell it. She only hoped that Binnesman's spells could hide them.

The hope was short-lived.

In seconds a reaver reached the mouth of the grotto. The huge monster rushed up the cliff and wedged its head into the crevasse at the opening. The philia along its jaw line quivered as if in anticipation. Slime dripped from its fearsome jaws.

"He's found us!" Averan screamed. "He's shouting to the others, warning them."

There was no sound from the reaver other than his hissing breath. His shouts were smells, odors so subtle that Iome could not distinguish them.

The opening was only six feet wide, too narrow for a full-grown reaver to enter—at least that is what Iome thought.

But the monster shoved its head into the crack, and twisted its body sideways. It heaved once, and there was a snapping noise.

On the reaver's head were three bony plates joined by cartilage. Now the reaver shoved its head into the crevice, and the plates snapped back, so that it could shove its muzzle into the hole. It twisted onto its side, and its torso followed.

Iome could smell the stink of its hot breath. A gree flew up from the beast, dislodged by its acrobatics, and flapped around the small grotto with a squeaking sound.

Gaborn leapt forward, stabbed the monster in the muzzle with his dart. Even with all his endowments of brawn, the blow hardly pierced the monster's thick flesh.

Iome looked for a place to run. She could not see an exit up here.

The reaver hissed in outrage at Gaborn's thrust, and pulled its muzzle back, inching from the grotto. It backed out completely, and Iome's heart pounded in terror: behind it were more reavers, a tide of them sweeping into the small tunnel. Their bodies formed a black wall.

Yet even as they came to a halt outside, the trembling continued, growing louder. She realized that the main part of the reaver horde was still marching, passing them by, uninterested in a few intrepid humans that dared venture into their domain, or perhaps more concerned with advancing to war.

A larger reaver appeared at the mouth of the grotto and thrust a knight gig—a metal hook on a long iron pole—through the hole. Gaborn leapt just as the knight gig approached.

"Binnesman!" Gaborn shouted.

The reaver flipped its knight gig around expertly, and would have impaled Binnesman, then dragged him from safety. But Gaborn leapt down on the pole and ran up its length two paces, until he reached the reaver's massive paw. He struck with his dart, plunging it into the soft flesh between the monster's fingers. The reaver wheezed in pain.

There was a hissing at the reaver's back, a sound of rushing wind that sounded like *"Gasht!"*

Iome had heard that sound before, when reaver mages cast their spells.

A dark cloud roiled into the grotto, filling it with noxious fumes. Iome found her eyes burning, as if hot coals had been flung into them. She dared not take a breath, for even in the open air on the battlefield, a reaver mage's spells were devastating. Here in the confines of a grotto, their effect would be twenty-fold.

Think, Iome told herself. Gaborn said that there has to be a way out. But where?

The reaver drew his knight gig from the grotto, banging it against the walls. The pole must have been thirty feet long and six inches around. As it struck the left wall, a huge chunk of stone broke away.

Encouraged by this, the reaver swung the knight gig, hitting a far wall.

"He's widening the opening!" Binnesman warned. The wizard let out a breath, and was forced to draw air. He fell back against the wall, eyes tearing. He struggled to reach into his pocket for some healing herb.

The green woman rushed forward and would have done battle with the reavers, but Binnesman put a restraining hand on her shoulder. "No," he said, the word wrung from his throat in torture.

The floor! Iome realized. There were pools here, but no sign of a stream flowing away. That meant that the water had to have emptied through the floor below at one time. There might be an exit hidden down there.

She leapt from the roof of the grotto, twenty feet, jarring her ankles as she hit ground. She peered around the edge of the deepest pool. Her eyes burned, and she swiped tears away. At the back of the grotto she saw it—a tiny crevasse under the craterlike rim of a pool, not more than a foot long and an inch wide.

Gaborn raced to the mouth of the grotto and stabbed at the reaver's paw. As he did, a second knight gig thrust through the opening. Even with all her endowments of metabolism, it seemed to Iome that the gig wrenched through with incredible speed. Gaborn tried to dodge, and took a glancing blow.

The stroke flung him against the far wall.

"Kill a reaver!" Binnesman shouted to his wylde. The wizard stood with his back against a stone wall, gasping, and tried to pull Gaborn to safety.

The green woman, unleashed at her master's command, leapt forward. As she did, she waved her iron-bound staff in the air, making it do a little dance, forming a rune of power.

She jabbed the reaver's paw, and there was a sound like stone hitting meat. The reaver's massive hand exploded, sending shards of broken bone through flesh. The monster wheezed in pain and dropped its weapon as it struggled to back from the cave. For the moment, no other reavers could get near to attack.

Iome grabbed her own reaver dart, and plunged it into the tiny crevasse.

Stone broke beneath her, a clod as large as her hand. The spear pushed through. She lowered her head and peered down. She saw another cave beyond the grotto!

Iome's air was almost gone. Her lungs burned, but she dared not draw breath. Instead, she pounded the stone alongside the crevasse as fast as she could, widening the hole.

Averan let out her breath, and cried in agony. "Help! I can't see!"

Iome could do nothing for her. She dared not. She plunged the spear into the stone, breaking away a handful of calcite here, another there. Even with endowments of brawn, it was harrowing work. Her spear point felt blunted and all but useless in a matter of moments.

She toiled on.

Another large reaver entered the mouth of the cave, picked up the pole, and thrust it in. It hit the wylde on the ankle, throwing her to the ground.

Iome slammed her spear into the stone. A large chunk of calcite fell away, went sliding downward.

She could see the cave beyond! There was a path of flowstone, and it dripped down the hill until it joined what must have been the bed of a submerged river, for there the path widened.

She could hold her breath no longer.

She exhaled, and gasped.

The reaver mage's stench burned her throat. As air filled her lungs, she could almost hear the reaver's command, "See no more."

The wylde roared in anger and swung her staff. The blow struck a wall, sending shards of dust and rock everywhere. The reaver that had attacked her backed away.

Iome's eyes throbbed. The cords that held her eyeball convulsed and spasmed so that she could not focus. She felt as if a dagger had been thrust into each socket, and now her attacker was methodically twisting the blade. Even with a dozen endowments of stamina, she could barely see.

She grabbed Averan first, shoved her through the hole. Averan went tumbling a few yards, then slid on her belly the last dozen feet. As she reached bottom, she began to flounder and make a mewling noise, trying to crawl to safety. Iome found the girl's pack and shoved it after.

"This way!" Iome shouted.

She could barely make out her friends. Her eyes wouldn't focus. Gaborn, Binnesman, and the wylde were but partly glimpsed shadows, shifting about in a world of pain.

"Duck!" Gaborn shouted.

Iome ducked.

A swinging pole whipped past her head. She felt more than saw it. Half blinded, only Gaborn's warning had kept her from being brained.

She grabbed Gaborn. He hunched in pain, holding his ribs. She propelled him toward the exit. "Go!"

Last of all, she grabbed Binnesman.

The green woman still held the front of the grotto. Another reaver slammed its head into the crevasse, trying to wedge its way in, and she lunged forward, slugging it in the jaw. Bloody gobbets of reaver flesh rained through the grotto.

Iome felt about blindly on the floor. Binnesman had dropped his staff and his pack. Iome hurled both through the small opening, then tossed her own pack through, and slid down the exit.

She gasped air, fresh air! She lay for a moment on her belly, chest heaving, trying to clear her lungs of the reavers' curses.

"Foul Deliverer, Fair Destroyer—to me!" Binnesman called out weakly. In answer, the green woman came hurtling through the opening from above. She rolled downhill and landed against a stone wall with such a shock that if she had been human, she would have broken every bone in her body.

"Let's get away from here," Gaborn said. The ground still shook from the passage of reavers, and all around was a distant hiss.

Iome looked back. With all her endowments of sight and stamina, her vision began to clear quickly. It might take the reavers some time to dig through the grotto and find their escape route. But she had no doubt that they would follow.

Ahead, an ancient riverbed wound through the Underworld. There was still water in it here and there, small pools. Grotesque Underworld vegetation, like cabbage leaves, covered the walls. Tubers and hairy rootlike plants hung from the roof in twisted splendor, while giant fungi rose up like little islands from the tickle ferns that covered the floor. Still, there was something of a trail cut by the watercourse. It would be a hard path, a wild path. Where it led, Iome could not guess.

Their horses were gone. Gaborn was hurt. And the reavers were after them. A stalactite fell from the roof, shattered on the floor not a dozen feet away.

"Looks like we're through the easy part," Iome said.

ജ 6 ഇ

THE SHAFT

Dare to be a leader. When faced with great peril, men will follow anyone who hazards to make the first move.

—from the writings of Suleman Owat, Emir of Tuulistan

"Come!" Gaborn urged the group. "We have no time to waste."

Come where? Averan wondered.

In the reavers' tunnels, Averan knew the way. But here in this natural cave, without any reaver scents written on the wall to guide her, she was lost. The ground thundered beneath the feet of hundreds of thousands of reavers.

They had barely escaped the grotto. Averan gasped, struggling to clear her lungs of the reavers' curses. "I'm blind!" She squinted. Her eyes would not focus. Instead, the cords in them convulsed and twitched, and Averan peered through a red haze.

"It will pass," Binnesman promised. Averan peered at him, a vague shape in the darkness recognizable only by the color of light shining from his cape pin. For an instant his face came into focus. Such was the power of the reavers' curse that the whites of the wizard's eyes had gone blood red.

Averan's eyes burned like poison. She had never imagined such exquisite pain.

The whites of my eyes are probably as red as his, she realized.

Binnesman felt in the pockets of the robe, pulled out a tiny sprig. "Here," he said. "Eyebright!"

He broke the stem of the plant and wetted it with his tongue, then quickly painted a bit over each of Averan's eyes. The pain drained away quickly as Binnesman ministered to the others.

Averan grabbed her pack and ropes, peered along the cave both ways, upstream and down. Along the sides of the cavern, stalactites dripped from the ceiling and stalagmites rose up from the floor like a forest of spears. Only the center of the cavern was clear of them. There, water had flowed swiftly once, polishing away the debris. Now the rivercourse was overgrown. Binnesman had called the plants tickle fern. Their fronds fanned slowly, as if swaying in an invisible breeze.

In her mind, Averan tried to construct an image of what the reaver tunnels looked like. But in her mind, the image was a tangled ball of yarn. Perhaps the Waymaker could have envisioned it, but she doubted it. The reavers didn't negotiate the tunnels by sight. They didn't use maps. They followed their sense of smell.

Averan sniffed. The reavers had a name for this kind of stone. The name was a smell—the chalky scent of blue-white cave pearls. If this deposit joined with any other reaver tunnels, she might be able to figure it out by the scent.

"Downstream!" she said. "I think this cave meets an abandoned reaver tunnel downstream." A feeling of doubt assailed her. It would be miles from here, dozens and dozens of miles, and in a cave such as this, the trail might easily be blocked a hundred times.

Gaborn got up, squinting and gasping. He rested his weight heavily on his reaver dart, used it as a crutch. The blow he had taken to his ribs obviously pained him. So he merely stood for a moment, as if to let his endowments of stamina and metabolism heal his broken bones.

As he did, the high hissing sound of frustration came from the grotto above. Averan could hear the reavers clanking the stone with their knight gigs, trying to gouge their way through. With every blow, the floor of the cave shook.

Gaborn peered at Binnesman. "Can you seal the cave behind us?"

"Collapse the roof? That would be foolhardy," Binnesman said. "I don't have that kind of control." He thought for a moment, and added, "But perhaps a small spell is in order."

He climbed back up the tunnel to the mouth of the grotto, and returned a moment later, obviously pleased with himself.

The reavers still hissed, but the ground shook somewhat less.

"Let's get away from here," he said.

"What did you do?" Averan asked.

"There is a simple spell for softening stone," Binnesman explained. "That is how you make a roof collapse, or destroy a bridge. But it is similarly easy for an Earth Warden to harden the earth, to make dirt as flinty as stone, and stone as impenetrable as steel. I hope to keep those reavers busy digging for hours."

"So, you locked the door behind us?" Gaborn asked.

"One can only hope," Binnesman said.

Gaborn led the way, climbing over stalagmites and boxlike fungi, wading through tickle fern. He carried his reaver dart in one hand, and his pack and ropes slung over his back.

So they ran. Each of them had taken endowments of metabolism, which served them well. But of them all, Averan was still the slowest. Her nine-year-old legs were shorter than any others, and she had to take three steps for Gaborn's every two.

She struggled to keep up at first. But soon, it was Gaborn who slowed his party. Though his endowments would heal the blow he had taken to the ribs, he still wheezed in pain, even as they slowed.

The channel went down, always down. Often there were places worn away where there had once been wide pools. Most pools were dry, but in some basins a bit of water had collected. Averan could see scrabbers—a kind of blind lizard with winglike arms—that seemed to fly beneath the water. She raced through such pools, splashing water everywhere, lest she get bitten.

In other places, the walls of the old river channel narrowed where water had rushed down, and thus the path was much clearer. There was little sign of animal life. Large green-gray cave slugs oozed about, feeding on the tickle fern, and these in turn provided sustenance for some small blind-crabs. But Averan saw nothing big in here, nothing dangerous.

We're still far from the deep places, she thought. Still far from the perilous realms.

This was a desert. Most Underworld plants drew sustenance from heat, and it was too cold for much to grow here. Thus, there were no large animals about.

Even after they had run for miles, the ground still trembled and thundered from the passage of reavers. It was growing distant now.

They reached a narrows where stalactites hung from the ceiling in columns, and water dripped. Each person had to walk through the narrows in single file, and once they passed, Binnesman turned.

"Averan," he said. "Let's see if you can draw that rune I was telling you about."

He traced the rune on the stone with his finger, leaving a tiny scratch mark.

"Now," he said, "draw the rune with the point of your staff. And as you do, imagine your own strength, your own power, and the power of your staff fusing with the stone."

Averan recognized the rune. She'd seen it many times, carved into stone blocks on houses and on castle walls. For a commoner, to carve such a rune was meaningless, a charm that he hoped might protect him from danger. But for an Earth Warden to draw such a rune, it could be a powerful spell.

Yet Averan also knew that not all Earth Wardens had the same powers.

Binnesman could peer into stones and see things at great distances. But Averan had no skill with the seer stones. Similarly, she was discovering that she had powers Binnesman had never heard of.

Obviously, the old wizard was pushing her, hoping to discover Averan's merits.

She closed her eyes. She drew the rune, almost by instinct, and sought to funnel all of her strength, all of her power into it, until she trembled from the effort.

Close for me, she whispered. Close for me.

She drew the rune, and then as if of its own volition, her staff drew three more squiggling lines within it.

And then Averan felt something strange. In an instant, it was as if all of her energy were inhaled.

Averan collapsed; everything went black.

When she woke, not much time seemed to have passed. Her head was spinning, and it felt as if someone had wrapped an iron band about it, and was pulling it tight. A deep pain ached, far back between her eyes. Gaborn stood over her, calling. "Averan! Averan, wake up!"

She looked around. Everyone was staring at her, or staring at the narrow wall. Binnesman stood before the pillars, studying them intensely.

"Are you all right?" Gaborn asked.

Averan tried to sit up, and felt weak as a mouse. Her arms seemed to be made of butter, and her legs would not move at all. If she had run all day without stopping, she would not have felt more overworn.

"I'm all right," she said, struggling to sit up. She reached a seated position and the pain between her eyes deepened. Dizziness assailed her. She sat for a moment, unable to think, unable to focus.

Slowly, the strength returned to her muscles.

"Very good," Binnesman said. "Very good, though I am afraid that it was a bit much for you. Would you like to see your handiwork?"

He stepped aside and Averan gasped.

The crack between the pillars was gone. Instead, the rock looked as if it had turned to mud and smeared together, only to harden afterward. The surface of the gray stone itself glistened, as if it had been fired in a kiln.

"What did I do?" Averan asked.

Binnesman shook his head in wonder, then laughed. "Certain sorcerers among the duskins could shape stone to their will. By that power, the great rift in Heredon was formed, and the continents divided. It is the rarest of all of the powers of the deep Earth. I have not heard of a human who ever possessed such skills, but it seems that you have it in some small degree."

Averan gaped at the stone wall in shock.

Binnesman tapped it with his staff, listening as if for an echo. "This should hold them for a good while. Indeed, I suspect that the reavers may abandon any hope of breaking through, and instead be forced to dig around it. Let's go."

Averan made it to her feet. Everyone else ran ahead, but Binnesman stayed behind with Averan, keeping a watchful eye on her, as if afraid that she might fall again. She very nearly did, and if she had not had her staff to help her, she would have.

"When next we stop," Binnesman said, "if you have the energy, we should practice this newfound skill of yours. But this time, we'll try shaping something smaller."

"All right," Averan said, though in truth she didn't feel as if she ever wanted to try it again.

After they had run only half a mile, the cave floor suddenly dropped away into oblivion.

The tunnel narrowed and the old watercourse dropped almost straight down, varying only slightly as it twisted this way and that.

Gaborn peered down the hole. Its sides were covered with tickle fern and wormgrass. Averan could see perhaps a quarter mile down the tunnel. At that point, it seemed to twist away, but she could not be certain. The light was too dim to let her see farther. Averan looked into Gaborn's eyes, wondering if they should dare the shaft.

"The Earth warns us to flee," Gaborn said. "And this is the only way out."

Averan reached down and touched a tickle fern. Its fronds brushed her hands gently. She pulled at it, and the roots came away easily.

"Trying to climb the rocks with this stuff is dangerous," she said. "It's as slippery as moss."

"We can make it," Gaborn said.

The packs lay all around, and Gaborn began pulling off the coils of rope and tying them together, while Iome tied one end of the rope to a nearby stalagmite.

"Let me have a look at those ribs," Binnesman said to Gaborn.

"I'll be fine," Gaborn objected. "They're almost healed."

But Binnesman strode forward, unlaced Gaborn's armor, and pulled it off. Beneath his padding and tunic, Gaborn's ribs were a mess of blue and black bruises.

"They look worse than they feel," Gaborn said.

"Good," Binnesman said, "because if they felt as bad as they look, you'd be dead!" He placed his fingertips above the wound, never touching it. He frowned and muttered, "As I thought, four broken ribs. Even with all of your endowments, they won't heal fully for a day or so. But I don't understand how you got hit in the first place."

"I trusted my eyes more than my heart," Gaborn said. "I felt the warning to duck, but couldn't see the danger. Then the knight gig came through so fast."

"Let that be a warning," Binnesman said. "Do as the Earth commands. Forget about what your eyes can see, or what you think you know."

Binnesman reached into his robes, pulled out some melilot, and blew it onto the wound. When he finished tending Gaborn's ribs, he picked up Gaborn's mail and leather padding. He considered for half a second, then hurled it into the pit, where the mail clanked and thudded as it bounced down into the darkness.

"What?" Gaborn asked.

"It will only be a hindrance on the climb down," Binnesman said. "And we should find it on the bottom easily enough."

Iome and Averan had just finished tying the ropes together. They all looked at one another, and at the pit.

"Who should go first?" Iome asked tensely.

Gaborn walked to the edge of the pit, tossed his reaver dart down the hole. It clanged once, and then he threw the packs over. Last of all, he threw over the end of the rope, and jumped. Averan drew a startled breath.

But Gaborn merely twisted catlike in the air, then grabbed the rope. With so many endowments of brawn and grace, he began to scamper down as quickly as a spider.

Binnesman raised an eyebrow in surprise. Apparently Gaborn's ribs were better than they appeared.

Averan went to the lip of the shaft and peered down. She gripped her poisonwood staff tightly. She wanted to carry it, but didn't dare try. The staff was precious, though as yet it was unadorned. She planned to carve runes of protection into it as soon as she could. The poisonwood had chosen her, and in some way she felt that the staff was a part of her. She was wondering what to do with it when Binnesmen threw his own staff down the shaft, so that it cleared Gaborn by a yard. Then he had his wylde do the same.

"Go ahead," Binnesman told Averan. "The wood knows you. It will be waiting for you at the bottom."

Averan let her staff fall gingerly, fearing that it might shatter against a stone wall.

In moments they began to make the perilous descent. Gaborn led the way, followed by the wylde, Binnesman, and Iome, with Averan coming last.

The climb proved difficult. For the first hundred yards, Averan merely clung to the rope and lowered herself hand by hand. But all too soon, the rope came to an end.

At this point, she had to abandon it forever, and a sense of dread engulfed her. Each of them had brought some stout rope, and none of them would ever be able to use it again.

"Come on," Iome urged. She was just below Averan, grunting and struggling for purchase as she made her way down. "If you start to fall, I'll catch you."

Averan's heart raced. She felt powerful with her endowments of brawn, but still found it hard to find her first hand- and footholds. Rushing water had polished the rock over the years, leaving little purchase. The tickle ferns growing everywhere only added to the danger. She couldn't really look down very well to see where to place her hands and feet, and ended up having to climb down more by a sense of feel than by sight.

Worse than that, the ferns were not trustworthy. If she found a small handhold and was tempted to rely on the ferns, she discovered that the roots sometimes seemed to have dug in enough to give her purchase. But too often the ferns would rip under her weight without notice, and she would be left grasping blindly for something to cling to.

With her short legs and arms, she had a harder time reaching some handholds than the others did.

Binnesman noticed her predicament, and he let Iome climb down past him. He moved up so that he was below Averan. At times when things got scary, he would put a hand up to hold her foot, or offer her reassurance. "Don't worry," he'd say. "There's a good handhold just below you."

So Averan swallowed her terror and lowered herself, carefully placing each foot, each hand.

A quarter of a mile they descended below the rope, and a quarter more. The tunnel sometimes snaked this way and that, yet every time Averan dared to glance down, the tunnel plunged deeper into the abyss.

It was slow work.

She reached one spot and was about to lower herself another step when Gaborn called out, "Averan, stop. Move to your right, and try to find a way down."

He was far below her and could not possibly have seen her danger. But he was the Earth King, and he felt it. She did as he said, and dozens of times during the course of the journey he warned others to take similar measures.

More than a mile they climbed, and still Averan could see no end. Her nerves were frayed, and she found herself trembling all over.

Still the ground rumbled distantly, like faraway thunder, at the passage of reavers.

She felt astonished that no one had fallen yet. Even with Gaborn's help and all of their endowments, it seemed an impossible feat.

Gaborn reached a rocky ledge, the first perch they had found, and called a rest. Averan inched down, met the others. Iome leaned with her back against the rock wall, grimacing with fear. Gaborn squatted next to her, heaving to catch his breath. Binnesman leaned away from the ledge, respectfully, but his wylde walked to the very end of it and peered down.

Their perch jutted out only three or four feet, then the shaft jogged back down. Under normal circumstances, Averan would have been terrified to stand so close to the ledge. But right now it felt like a little bit of paradise. She looked up the shaft, into the infinite blackness.

Once the reavers break through my rock wall, she thought, they will be on our trail in an instant.

Reavers were great climbers. With their huge grasping fore-claws and their four legs, they could scurry up and down stone slopes much faster than a human could. And the shaft from the old river channel was just wide enough to make this an easy climb for one of the monsters.

She imagined reavers up above, and that made her want to hurry all the faster.

"Once the reavers reach the top," Averan dared say, "all they have to do is throw a rock down this hole, and we'll all be knocked off the wall and swept to our deaths."

Binnesman teased, "Once the rock hits you, you won't have to fear being swept to your death." He tried to offer a comforting smile, but Averan noticed that no one stayed long on the rocky perch.

Gaborn soon began climbing down, and everyone else followed. Averan's arms ached from the stress by now, and the skin had been rubbed raw from her fingers. Others were in as bad shape, for they left little smears of blood all along the rock wall. She let her mind go blank, ignored the pain.

The chute dropped another half mile, when suddenly Gaborn called, "Wait where you are. There's no bottom."

"What do you mean there's no bottom?" Iome called.

"I can't see a bottom," Gaborn said. "It just—it drops into nothing."

Averan huddled where she was, clutching some precarious handholds. The tickle ferns waved slowly, brushing like feathers against her wrist.

She tried to peer down, but Binnesman and the green woman blocked her view. There was light all through the shaft, where the opals released their inner fire, but the light ended perhaps a dozen yards below, and Averan could see what Gaborn meant—the shaft suddenly stopped, and below them was what seemed to be an endless drop.

Averan clung to the wall, heart pounding. Sweat streamed down her forehead. The nail of her left pinky felt as if it were about to pull off. She'd abused it tremendously.

She moved her pinky finger minutely, and the nail detached.

She dug her toes tighter into her footholds, and just leaned her head against the stone wall, wanting to cry. Her legs and arms were trembling now, despite her best efforts to keep still.

Do spiders ever get this tired of climbing walls? she wondered. Yes, she realized, they must.

She could hear Gaborn wheezing as he scrambled down farther, closer to the lip of the chasm.

"I think I see water below us," Gaborn called. "I'm pretty sure of it."

Averan's heart pounded in her ears. She sniffed. Yes, she could smell water. She realized now that the scent had been getting stronger for what seemed like hours. The whole cave was moist, and condensation had been dripping from some of the rocks. But she could smell water, a large body of it, rich in sulfur.

Our packs, she thought dully. We threw our packs and our weapons down there. They'll all be underwater. Gone. Our food.

The realization left her weak, and Averan clung to only one hope: that her staff would float. If she swam around enough, she would find it.

It was a focus point for her magic, and somehow, though she lost everything else, she felt that she could survive so long as she found her staff.

"There's only one way down," Gaborn said. "We have to jump. There's a lake down there. I can see the shore."

"Wait!" Averan said. "You don't know what might be living in there!"

But Gaborn didn't wait. He threw himself from the ledge. Averan listened, counting slowly, until the splash reached her ears.

She reached a count of eighty-nine.

Eighty-nine seconds? she wondered. No, she realized. I have twelve endowments of metabolism. I have to divide that by thirteen. It's more like seven seconds. How far can a person fall in seven seconds?

She didn't have any idea. She only knew that it was a long way.

What's the worst that can live in the lake? she asked herself. She had eaten the brains of several reavers, and from them had learned much about the Underworld. There had been scrabbers in pools up above. They would probably be in the lake—unless there were blindfish down there to eat them.

The Idumean Sea was full of blindfish—great eels thirty feet long that could swallow a child whole, whisker fish as big as a boat. And then there were creatures that weren't fish, that were just as dangerous, like the floating stomachs—blobs of jellylike substance that would latch onto your flesh and just begin digesting you.

What's the worst that could happen? Averan asked herself, and she realized that all of her fears were groundless. Gaborn was the Earth King. He wouldn't let her jump to her death. The worst that might happen is that a few scrabbers would nip her.

She climbed down. By now, Iome had jumped. They were taking their time, giving each person a few seconds to swim away. Binnesman told his wylde to jump, and she leapt off into nothingness.

"I'm not a very good swimmer," Averan whispered to Binnesman.

The wizard laughed weakly. "Don't worry, child, I float like cork wood. Let me jump, and then wait for five seconds. I'll be there to help you."

Averan set her feet, then peered down, over her shoulder. She saw Binnesman climb down the shaft, to the very lip. Below, she could see the cave now. Gaborn and the others had their opals on, and the lights from them shone like stars in the night. They were swimming in a great pool, shaped almost as round as a cistern, and waves radiated away from them. Gaborn made toward a pile of rocks near the far wall.

It looked almost peaceful, like night swimmers enjoying a dip in a lake.

Binnesman pushed back from the wall and kicked away. She saw his face briefly by the light of her opal necklace, his expression looking perfectly peaceful. He went over backward, with his arms splayed out to the sides, and then the darkness swallowed him. Averan began counting.

Distantly, she heard a sound that set her heart pounding more fiercely—the rasping breath of a reaver.

Where? she wondered. Hiding in the rocks below? She tilted her head, strained to hear. With her endowments of hearing, all noises seemed unnaturally loud, amplified.

No, she realized. The sound is coming from above.

"The reavers are after us!" she shouted.

She didn't give Binnesman his full five seconds. She merely leapt.

The drop through the darkness seemed endless. Averan had never dived so far. The closest thing that she had ever done was to jump into the pond from the old tree at Wytheebrook.

She went down in a ball, arms wrapped around her knees. She counted almost to a hundred as she fell, then hit the water.

She plunged down and down. The water felt surprisingly warm. She held her breath, struggled to swim upward. By the light of her opal necklace, she peered through the water. Blindfish, as bony as pike, lanced through the black waters, at once both frightened of something as large as she and attracted by her splashing. She could not see the bottom far below.

Averan swam for the surface. Her robe weighed her down, and she considered casting it off. But it was a wizard's robe, a garment that would protect her and hide her, and she dared not lose it.

So she swam to the surface and splashed about, trying to get her bearings. Almost immediately, her hand hit something hard, and she grabbed on.

A sense of power surged through her as she touched her staff.

For a moment she floundered about, wondering at her luck. But she felt that it was more than luck.

I wanted my staff, and it came to me, Averan told herself.

Binnesman swam to her. "Here, child, grab my arm."

"Reavers," Averan told him as she took hold of his robe. "I heard reavers in the shaft above."

He didn't answer. He merely shoved his own staff into her hand. "Here. Hold on to this for me." He began to swim. Averan clung to the staves, and Binnesman pulled them along. Both staves seemed to float unnaturally high in the water.

Averan knew that reavers couldn't swim. They sink like a stone. But they could walk on the bottom of a lake like a crayfish for short distances.

This lake was small, small enough so that a reaver could probably crawl out of it. But would the reavers know that? Would they know how to get out? They could see a hundred yards with decent clarity, but the world was all a blur at anything more than two hundred.

They wouldn't be able to see the shape of the lake below. They would only smell it and the scent of the rock walls. Would the smell of the rock be powerful enough to let them guess the size of the lake? Would they dare jump in?

Averan didn't know. Reavers could be very brave. Their skin was so hard that it almost acted like armor, and reavers were terribly strong. This gave them a sense of invulnerability.

Some of them will come after us, Averan felt sure. She didn't know why she felt that way, until she searched through her thoughts.

Cunning Eater. She'd gorged on his brain a couple of days ago. He had been a reaver warrior, and she remembered the way he felt about humans. It was a sinister mix of fear and loathing over the past victories men had made against reavers combined with an appetite so insatiable that she knew it would drive him to hunt.

From across the water, Gaborn called, "Don't worry about the packs! I already got them. Hurry!"

So the packs floated, Averan thought.

But the reaver darts are gone.

Averan paddled, helping Binnesman reach shore. In moments they emerged from the black water. Light from the opals reflected from the waves, sending beams to dance against walls that dripped of white crystal.

No sooner had they reached the bank than a huge reaver hurtled down from the shaft, sending waves to lap against the shore.

"Hurry! This way!" Gaborn shouted, nodding toward a dark arch where the ancient river channel had worn through stone.

"Wait!" Averan argued. "We have to kill the reaver that came into the water. If the ones up in the shaft don't smell its death, they'll follow."

"No! Run!" Gaborn urged. "Now!"

"Come, child," Binnesman said. He pulled her from the water, set her on shore. "Grab your pack." Their packs lay in a pile where Gaborn had set them.

Averan slung her pack over her back. Binnesman tossed a pack to the wylde, reached for his own. He looked worn. He had as many endowments of metabolism as Averan did, but even with them, he moved with the deliberateness that comes with age.

A cavern opened like a black maw. Gaborn stood in the mouth of it. "Binnesman," he shouted, just as Binnesman shrugged on his pack, "flee!"

Binnesman dropped his bag and whirled just as something monstrous surged from the water.

Nothing can move that fast, Averan thought.

Even with all her endowments, the reaver burst from the lake in a blur. Water streamed from its spade-shaped head, and splattered on the rocks before it.

Binnesman whirled to meet it, his face a mask of panic, raising his staff protectively with both hands.

Before she even realized that the reaver was armed, Averan saw the dark blur of its blade—a huge hunk of steel some twenty feet long—slice through the air.

One instant, Averan saw the blow coming, and the next there was a whack of metal shattering wood, the snap of bones. Binnesman hurtled forty feet through the air.

"Help!" Averan screamed.

She raised her staff protectively. The reaver loomed above her, its massive jaws wide enough to swallow a wagon. Runes glowed with a faint blue light along its forearms. Never had she seen a blade-bearer so glorious and deadly. She smelled him, and with her endowments of scent, his name suddenly seemed to seep into the corners of her mind like a shadow. This one had been known to every reaver she had eaten. His name was spoken in fear: Consort of Shadows.

Among all of the servants of the One True Master, he was the most cunning and subtle. Averan's mind blanked in terror.

For a tenth of a heartbeat, he seemed to halt, watching her. Then his blade whirled to sweep through Averan.

She was conscious of little. Binnesman was gone. She felt numb.

"Dodge!" Gaborn shouted.

Averan threw herself aside as the reaver's blade hit. Metal cleaved through the rock where she had been. Something streaked overhead to meet the reaver, a shrieking blur that howled like a wolf in pain.

"Blood!" the wylde screamed.

She lunged with her staff, as if to bash the Consort of Shadows.

But as suddenly as he had attacked, the reaver bounded aside, landed on a wall, and scuttled up its side like a spider. He began sending a stream of information in the form of scents. Averan smelled the scent of the wylde, followed by a scent that meant *I am confused,* followed by a scent of *Warning, this one brings death.*

The Consort of Shadows backed up the wall, its philia waving. The green woman raced up to the cavern wall, screamed in frustration. She threw down her staff, leapt up to a little ridge, began climbing after the monster, seeking toeholds in the stone. The walls of the cave were covered in calcite, and tickle fern grew on it like moss. Some of the stone was as white and frothy as cream, while other parts were as mellow gold as honeycomb. Over the ages, deposits had built up on the wall, little knobs, like half-formed stalagmites. The green woman climbed swiftly, and the Consort of Shadows moved back up the cave, until he was clinging to the roof like a vast, obese spider.

The wylde mewled pitifully, "Blood, blood!" She reached the roof and floundered about, seeking to follow her prey.

The Consort of Shadows lunged. He leapt sixty feet in a blinding flash and clung to the ceiling with his feet. He grabbed the wylde in one paw, reared back, and smashed her against the rock. Averan thought that she heard bones snap, and the wylde screamed in rage.

Then the reaver flung her back into the pool. For a moment, there was no sound at all but that of water lapping against rock.

Warily, the Consort of Shadows studied them, clinging to the cavern roof, his philia waving in a frenzy.

Suddenly the wylde surfaced, splashing about, screaming in rage.

The Consort of Shadows backed away and retreated up the shaft.

He's gone, Averan thought in relief. But she knew that it was only for the moment. He was studying them.

"Averan, Binnesman," Gaborn called.

Binnesman can't be dead, Averan thought. He's supposed to be my teacher.

But Averan knew what a reaver's blade could do. The huge hunk of steel weighed hundreds of pounds. It wasn't honed as sharp as a sword, but if a blow didn't slice a man in two, it would still shatter every bone in his body.

She'd seen men killed by reavers—corpses hacked into gruesome pieces—a head here, and a hand there, blood spattered about as if by the bucketful, innards draped over tree limbs like sausages hanging from the rafters of an inn.

The wylde was going mad. The green woman keened like an animal in pain, splashed to shore. Averan wondered that it had survived at all.

Averan shakily struggled to her feet. She didn't want to look at Binnesman, for she knew what she'd find. She imagined his blank eyes staring into space, the guts knocked out of him.

"Binnesman?" Gaborn called as he rushed toward them.

Averan had to look. There was still a possibility that he might be alive.

Binnesman lay on the cave floor, sprawled on his back. His face was pale, drained of blood, and his hands quivered as if in death throes. Flecks of blood issued from his nose and mouth. Miraculously, he was all in one piece, though the reaver's blow had struck him in the chest.

"You're alive?" Averan asked.

"Glad to hear it," Binnesman said, but the labor he had to put into speaking the jest belied the tone, and his eyes were full of fear.

He's not alive, Averan decided. But not dead yet either. He's dying. She knelt, took his hand, and squeezed hard. Binnesman gasped, struggling for breath. He didn't squeeze in return. He had no comfort to give her.

Gaborn rushed up to Averan's back.

She glanced up to see his face, pale with shock. Iome came slower.

"Why didn't you run?" Gaborn asked.

"For a hundred years," Binnesman said, struggling for breath, "I've been the wisest person I know." A coughing fit took him, and flecks of blood flew from his mouth. "It's hard to take advice."

Iome was at Gaborn's back now, and she just stared at Binnesman with pain-filled eyes.

Binnesman's hands fluttered and Averan looked back to his face. He was gazing at her now, imploringly. "Not much time," he said. "Get my staff."

"It's broken," Averan said. But suddenly she had a wild hope that even broken, the staff would be able to heal him. She rushed to it. The wood had not merely cracked; it had splintered in pieces, sending shards in half a dozen directions. Averan wanted every piece. Earth Power was stored in every splinter, and runes of healing and protection had been carved all around the base of the staff. She wanted all of it. When she had all the pieces, she rushed back to Binnesman.

"I'm sorry," he was telling Gaborn. "I failed you all." His breath was weak, and more blood came gushing from his mouth with every word he choked out.

"Don't try to speak," Iome said. She knelt by his side and held his hand.

"Things must be said," Binnesman told Iome. "Foul Deliverer, Fair Destroyer," he whispered. "I unbind you."

The green woman howled with glee like an animal. Averan glanced up. The wylde was peering up toward the ceiling at the shaft, as if seeking a path to the reavers.

"Averan?" Binnesman called. He gazed about, but his eyes were no longer focusing.

"I'm here," she said. "I have your staff."

As proof she began laying the broken shards on his chest, as if they were bits of kindling. He fumbled about, grasped a piece.

"Averan, I must leave you. You must guide them. Listen to the Earth. It will be your only teacher now."

He gasped for breath, and then could not speak at all.

Averan felt as if the world were reeling out of control beneath her. She couldn't believe that Binnesman was dying. Old wizards like him were supposed to be indestructible. Averan found herself trembling.

"Bury him!" Gaborn shouted. "Quickly."

"What?" Iome asked.

"Beneath the soil!" Gaborn raised his left hand and whispered desperately, "Binnesman: may the Earth heal you; may the Earth hide you; may the Earth make you its own."

Of course! Averan had slept beneath the earth three nights past, relieved of the need to breathe, to think. She'd never slept so soundly in her life. Nor had she ever felt as invigorated afterward.

None of them could save Binnesman, but while there was still life in him, perhaps the Earth could do it.

The cave floor was almost solid rock, with only a few pebbles here and there.

Averan grabbed her staff, struck the ground, and whispered, "Cover him."

From all around, detritus converged in a rush, pebbles and dust rolling across the cave floor, covering Binnesman, so that he lay beneath a quilt of gray sand, flecks of stone, and cave pearls.

What a pretty grave, Averan thought.

Grief welled up in her. She feared that Binnesman was gone forever, that nothing that they did could help. After all was said and done, he'd be lying here in a pretty grave.

Gaborn glanced up at the dark shaft above. He placed a hand on Averan's shoulder, as if to offer comfort. "We'd best be on our way," he said warily.

Iome knelt beside the grave for a moment and pressed her hand into the fresh soil, leaving her imprint, as was sometimes done at peasants' funerals. She brushed back a tear and picked up Binnesman's pack.

The green woman kept pacing the shore of the lake, seeking a route to the reavers. There was a scrape on her face, where the Consort of Shadows had bashed her into the stone wall. Other than that, Averan could see no sign of damage.

It was frightening to see the wylde's inhumanity laid bare. It was more than the green woman's indestructible nature that bothered Averan. Her total lack of concern for her fallen master was chilling. Averan kept hoping to find some sign of human sentiment in the wylde, but the green woman could offer no affection, no compassion, no grief, no love.

She paced the shore, howled in frustration at not being able to reach the reavers.

"Spring," Averan called to the wylde, using her private name. "We're leaving."

The green woman ignored her.

Gaborn eyed the creature, worry etched into the lines of his face. "Foul Deliverer, Fair Destroyer," Gaborn called. "Hear me: we go to hunt the great enemies of Earth. You would best serve your master by coming with us."

If the wylde heard at all, Averan could not tell.

Averan smelled reavers up in the shaft, whispering, wondering what to do. Dozens hid there. She suspected that the wylde could smell them, too.

"Let's go," Gaborn said, grabbing Averan's hand. Iome was already forging ahead, down the old river channel. Gaborn pulled Averan, their footsteps echoing behind them.

For a long time as they raced down the cavern, Averan could hear the keening cries of the wylde.

ಐ 7 ೞ

TIES THAT BIND

The transfer of endowments is more of an art than a science. Every facilitator has heard of those sublime cases where the transfer of endowments seems miraculous—where, for example, the strength of a lord is greatly enhanced after the application of a forcible, yet his Dedicate's strength seems hardly diminished—or rarer yet, those cases where effects seem to linger even after the Dedicate passes away. By learning the art of making a perfect match, it is our hope that such wondrous cases will, in the future, become the norm.

—from The Art of the Perfect Match, *by Ansa Per and Dylan Fendemere, master facilitators*

A few hours past dawn, Myrrima and Borenson reached Batenne, an ancient city whose tall houses were built in the old Ferecian style, with well-cut stones that fit seamlessly together. The roofs were made of copper plates from nearby mines, green with age, overlapping like fish scales. Old manors in the hills soared above expansive gardens where marble statues of nubile maidens, all swinging exotic long swords, could be glimpsed among the golden-leafed willows.

They bypassed the city and rode to the Castle of Abelaire Montes-fromme, the Marquis de Ferecia. The castle, with its stately towers, sat on the highest hill above the city. The outer walls had been limed over the summer, and they gleamed so brightly that when the morning sun struck them it pained the eyes. It almost seemed as if the castle were a bit of bright cloud fashioned into walls. The guards at the gate wore polished silver armor, enameled with the red graak of Ferecia upon their chests. Their helms sported visors with slits so small that the warriors within seemed eyeless. They bore long spears of blackened iron, with decorative silver tips.

Myrrima tried not to look at her own clothes, still wet from her dip in the pool and muddied and stained from the road. She gazed about in wonder.

"Close your mouth," Borenson warned softly, "you'll not be catching any flies around here."

"It's so beautiful," Myrrima said. "I've never imagined such a place." Indeed, as they rode into the courtyard, the cobbled stones were so perfectly level that they might have been laid that very morning. A mosaic showed the red graak upon a white background. Along the margins of the road, the lawn was perfectly clipped. Gardens of jasmine trailing down from window boxes in the castle's archery slots joined with mallow and rose on the lawns to lend the air a natural perfume. Hummingbirds swooped and darted among the bruised shadows of the towers, sparkling like gems when they caught the sunlight.

Myrrima saw anger on her husband's face. "What's wrong?" she asked under her breath, lest the guards hear her.

"This—" Borenson said, nodding toward the castle. "The people of Carris bleed and die on the castle walls less than three hundred miles from here, while the marquis and his dandy knights cower in splendor. I have half a mind to toss the fine flower boxes from the tower windows, and hurl the marquis out after them."

Myrrima didn't know what to say. The marquis was a powerful man from one of the oldest and wealthiest families in all of Rofehavan, while Borenson was only a Knight Equitable. For days now she had been afraid that she would lose him. She could feel him slipping away. His growing resentment toward Gaborn, the marquis, and indeed all lords was certainly part of the problem.

By the time that they reached the marquis's Keep, Borenson was in a black mood. His jaw was set, and the blood flowed hot in his face. A servant showed them into a stately antechamber where fine paintings of the marquis and his ancestors hung in gilt frames. Enormous candelabras graced the mantel above the fireplace.

"Wait here," the servant begged.

Borenson paced like an angry dog, and looked as if he would go follow the servant at any minute, tracking down the marquis. Yet they had not waited two minutes when a young man raced in, face flushed and eyes shining with eagerness.

"Sir Borenson, is it true?" the lad begged. "Is the Earth King battling reavers at Carris?"

Borenson looked that lad over. "Do I know you?"

"I'm Bernaud—"

"The marquis's son?" Borenson asked in disbelief.

"At your service," Bernaud said with a half bow.

A wicked twinkle sparked in Borenson's eye. "Aye, your king is battling reavers," Borenson said, "as you will be—soon."

At that moment, a servant entered through the same open door. "The marquis begs you to join him for breakfast in the Great Room."

Borenson and Myrrima followed the servant, with Bernaud trailing, into the marquis's Great Hall. An enormous table, some fifty feet long, occupied the length of the room. The table was set with enough pastries, fruit, and boar's ham to feed a dozen men, but the marquis sat there all alone, as if brooding over which dainty to taste.

Above the table, the shields of the marquis's ancestors adorned the walls. Each shield, plated with gold foil, was a monument to the great families from which the marquis had descended. Myrrima knew little of such lore, yet even she recognized some of the devices: here was the crouching lion of Merigast the Defiant, who stood fast against the sorcerers of the toth at Woglen's Tower when all hope of rescue had failed. And there were the double eagles of King Hoevenor of Delf, who drove the arr from the Alcair Mountains. Each shield was elegant, and many had been forged by the finest craftsmen of their era. Yet most impressive of all was a small round shield above the head of the table, a crude thing that almost looked as if a child might have fashioned it on his own. On it was painted a red graak, wings spread as it soared above two worlds. Myrrima did not doubt that it was the shield of Ferrece Geboren himself, son of the Earth King Erden Geboren. In his own day he had been called The Ferocious, for he was fearless in battle. According to legend, at the age of thirteen he had instigated the journey to the netherworld with the Wizard Sendavian and Daylan of the Black Hammer. There Ferrece implored the Bright Ones to fight in mankind's behalf. In all the lore of knights, no man was more universally admired than Ferrece Geboren.

It was a sad reminder that Ferecia had once been a proud land. An even sadder reminder of its ruin was the marquis himself, who sat just beneath the shield in a silk housecoat, looking down his nose at Myrrima and Borenson. He held a white perfumed kerchief up to his face, and by his sour expression seemed appalled that two people as squalid as Myrrima and her husband should appear in his appointments.

"Oh dear," the marquis said, "Sir Borenson, it is so good to see you! You look . . . well."

"And you," Borenson said with a strain, the veins bulging in his neck. "Although, last time we met, you had four or five endowments of glamour to your credit. You look to be . . . a much more withered specimen of humanity without them." The marquis's face paled at the insult. Borenson affected a cough into his hand, and then clapped the marquis on the shoulder in a manner that was common with men in arms. The marquis looked down at the offensive hand, eyes popping.

Borenson seemed as if he were ready for murder, and the marquis looked as if he might faint.

"I, I, I trust that all is well with . . . our king," the marquis stammered.

"Oh, the kingdom is in a shambles, as I'm sure you know," Borenson said. "So, Gaborn sent me to give you an urgent message. As you also know, he is battling reavers south of Carris."

"Is he?" the marquis affected ignorance.

"He is," Borenson affirmed, "And he wonders where his old friend, the Marquis de Ferecia is hiding."

"He does?" the marquis asked.

"You did receive the call to battle?"

"Indeed," the marquis pleaded, "and I prepared to ride at once, but then Raj Ahten destroyed the Blue Tower and my men were left with less than two dozen endowments between them. Surely, one cannot be expected to fight without endowments!"

"One can," Borenson said dangerously, "and one must. At Carris men, women, and children charged into the reavers' ranks without regard for their own lives. They fought with the strength of desperation because they had no choice."

"A nasty business, that," the marquis said, appalled.

"And now," Borenson said, "it's your turn." Beads of sweat began to break on the marquis's brow. He held the perfumed kerchief closer to his face. "You are to equip your soldiers and ride toward Carris at once, giving battle to any foe that presents itself, be it man or reaver."

"Oh dear," the marquis moaned.

"Father, may I go?" Bernaud cut in.

"I think no—" the marquis began.

"A fine idea," Borenson urged. "You'll want to present your son to the Earth King, both as a show of family solidarity and to receive his blessing. Any other choice would leave you . . . exposed." He studied the marquis's neck as if pondering where the headsman might make a cut.

The marquis was in torment, but his son said, "Father, now is our chance! We can show the world that Ferrece is still one of the great houses. I'll apprise the guard!"

The lad ran from the room, leaving Borenson to hover above the marquis.

Myrrima found her heart pounding. Borenson and the marquis had no love for one another, but Borenson was playing a dangerous game. Gaborn had not ordered the marquis to battle, had not made any threats veiled or otherwise. Yet Borenson threatened the man with the king's vengeance.

Borenson smiled dangerously. "A fine lad, your son." Now he got down to the real business at hand. "Have you a facilitator handy? I'm riding for Inkarra and need three endowments of stamina."

"I—I've a facilitator," the marquis stammered, "and suitable Dedicates may be found, but I'm afraid that I haven't any forcibles."

"I brought my own," Borenson said. "Indeed, I have a dozen extra which I should like to present to your son."

Outside the castle, Bernaud shouted to the captain of the guard, warning him to prepare some mounts.

The marquis gave Borenson a calculating look, and suddenly the terror in his eyes seemed to diminish. His face went hard.

"You see it, too, don't you?" the marquis asked. "My son is more a man now than I could ever hope to be. He looks much as his grandfather did, when he was young. In him the House of Ferrece might hope to return to grandeur."

Borenson merely nodded. He would not feign any affection for the marquis.

The old man smiled sourly. "So, the king orders us into battle. Let the fire take the old trees, and make way for the new." He sighed, then peered up at Borenson. "You're gloating. You'll be pleased to see me dead."

"I—" Borenson began to say.

"Don't deny it, Sir Borenson. I have known you for what, a dozen years? You've always been so secure in your own prowess in battle. No matter that I had wealth that you could never match, or a title above your own, every time you've entered my presence, you've given me those insufferable looks. I know what you think of me. My ancestors were kings of renown. But over the centuries bits of our kingdom have been bartered away by one lord, or frivoled away by the next, or stolen from a third who was too weak to keep what he rightfully owned, until the last of us . . . is me. When you were but thirteen years old you looked at me with disdain, knowing what I was: a minnow freakishly spawned from a line of leviathan."

"You beg me to speak freely," Borenson nearly growled, "and through your own self-deprecation, you almost relieve me of the necessity." He leaned on the table, so that his face was inches from the marquis's, and he stared him in the eyes, unblinking. "Yes, I'll be glad to see you dead. I have no stomach for men who live in luxury and whine about their fates. When I was a lad of thirteen, you looked down your nose at me because I was poor and you were rich, because my father was a murderer and yours was a lord. But I knew even then that I was a better man than you could ever hope to be. The truth is that you, sir, are a milksop, so weak in the legs that you could never father a child of your own. You say that Bernaud favors his grandsire, but I suspect that if we look among your guardsmen, we'll find one that favors him more. Fie on you! If you were any kind of a man, you'd do your best to kill me right now for speaking thus, whether you had endowments or no."

The marquis's jaw hardened, and for a moment Myrrima thought that he would grab the carving knife from the boar's ham and bury it in her husband's neck. Instead, he leaned back in his chair and smiled wickedly. "You've always felt so constrained to prove yourself. The lowborn always do. Even now, as captain of the King's Guard, you feel the need to challenge me." The marquis had obviously not heard that Borenson had abandoned his station, and Myrrima wondered what the marquis would have done had he known. "But," the marquis added, "there is no need for *me* to fight you. *You* and your shabby wife are the ones going to Inkarra, and we both know that the Night Children will send your heads home in a sack by dawn. As for me, I go to battle the reavers—a foe I judge to be far more worthy and implacable than you."

For a moment, Myrrima thought her husband would kill the man for his insults, but Borenson laughed, a genuine laugh filled with mirth, and the marquis began to laugh in his turn. Borenson slapped him on the back, as if they were old friends, and indeed for a moment the two were united, if only in their hatred for each other, their scorn for each other, and their desire to unleash their anger upon other foes.

Borenson and Myrrima made their way to the Dedicates' Keep behind the castle. Like everything else in the marquis's domain, the Dedicates' Keep was overnice. The walls of the keep, along with its towers, had been limed, so that the building fairly glowed. The courtyard gave rise to stately almond trees. Their leaves had gone brown, and the grass was littered with golden almonds. Squirrels hopped about madly, burying their treasures. A pair of Dedicates played chess in the open courtyard next to a fountain, while a blind Dedicate sat off in the shade with a lute, singing,

> "Upon the mead of Endemoor
> a woman danced in white.
> Her step was so lissome and sure
> She stunned the stars that night.
>
> But far more stunned was Fallion,
> whose love grew stanch and pure.
> Thus doom's dark hand led to Woe Glen
> the maid of Endemoor."

"You hate the marquis?" Myrrima asked as they walked.

"No," Borenson said. " 'Hate' is too strong a word. I merely feel such contempt for him that I would rejoice at his death. That's not the same as hatred."

"It's not?"

"No," Borenson said. "If I hated him, I'd kill him myself."

"What did he mean," Myrrima asked, "when he said that the 'children' would send our heads home in a sack?"

"Night Children," Borenson said. "That is what the word *Inkarran* means. It comes from *Inz*, 'Darkness,' and *karrath*, 'offspring.' " He spoke the words with such an accent that Myrrima imagined that he knew the language well. "The Inkarrans will send our heads home in a sack."

"Why?" Myrrima asked.

Borenson sighed. "How much do you know of the Inkarrans?"

"I knew one back home, Drakenian Tho," Myrrima said. "Drakenian was a fine singer. But he was quiet, and, I guess, no one knew him well."

"But you know that our borders are closed?" Borenson asked. "Gaborn's grandfather barred Inkarrans from his realm sixty years ago, and the Storm King retaliated. Few who have entered his realm have ever returned."

"I've heard as much," Myrrima said. "But I thought that since we were couriers, we would be granted safe passage. Even countries at war sometimes exchange messages."

"If you think we're safe, you don't know enough about Inkarrans," Borenson said. "They *hate* us."

She understood from his tone that he meant that they didn't just actively dislike her people, the Inkarrans hoped to destroy them. Yet Myrrima had to wonder at such an assessment. She knew that Inkarrans were outlawed in Mystarria, but it wasn't so in every realm among the kingdoms of Rofehavan. King Sylvarresta had tolerated their presence in Heredon, and even did some minor trading with those Inkarrans who followed the spice routes up through Indhopal. So she wondered if Borenson's judgment wasn't clouded in this matter by the local disputes. "And why would you think that they hate us?"

"I don't know the full story," Borenson said. "Perhaps no one does. But you know how Inkarrans feel about us 'Dayborn' breeding with their people?"

"They don't approve?"

"That's putting it mildly," Borenson said. "They won't talk about it to your face, but many Inkarrans are sickened by the mere thought of it—and for good reason. Any child from such a union takes on the skin, the hair, and the *eye* color of the Dayborn parent."

"Which means?" Myrrima began.

"A full-blooded Inkarran, one with ice white eyes, can see in total dark-ness, even when traveling through the Underworld. But many half-breeds can see no better at night than we do, and the dark eyes follow down from generation to generation. The Inkarrans call such part-breeds kutasarri, spoiled fruit of the penis. They're shunned in their own land by some, pitied by others, forever separate from the Night Children."

Myrrima remembered the half-breed assassin that had tried to kill Gaborn.

"But," she argued, "even some in the royal families are kutasarri. Even the Storm King's own nephew—"

"Shall never sit on a throne," Borenson finished.

"Here's a mystery," Myrrima said. "Why would a kutasarri from Inkarra agree to act as an assassin? Why would he try to kill Gaborn? Certainly it wouldn't be for love of country."

"Perhaps he merely wants to prove his worth to his own people," Boren-son said. "But there may be more to it. The Inkarrans do not just hate us for the color of our eyes. They call us barbarians. They hate our customs, our way of life, our civilization. They think themselves superior."

"That can't be the whole argument," Myrrima said. "I've seen Inkarrans in Heredon. They didn't seem to hold us in contempt at all. There has to be something more."

"All right," Borenson said, "A history lesson, then. Some sixty years ago, Gaborn's grandfather, Timor Rajim Orden, discovered that many Inkarrans who were entering our lands were criminals fleeing justice, so he closed the borders. He turned back many of their traders, and told the minor nobles to put on trial any man that they believed posed a threat. Three minor Inkarran nobles in Duke Bellinghurst's realm thus went to trial, and proudly admitted that they were more than criminals—they were assassins bent on killing the king's Dedicates. They were from a southern tribe of Inkarra, one that despises us more than most, and had sworn to destroy us barbarians in Mys-tarria. Bellinghurst executed the men summarily, without first seeking King Orden's approval. King Orden was a moderate man, and some say that he would have merely outlawed the offenders. But I think that unlikely, and in any case, it was too late. So he sent their bodies home as a warning to all Inkarrans.

"When the dead men reached their own land, their families cried out for vengeance to their high king. So King Zandaros fired off a choleric missive protesting the executions and cursing all northerners. Gaborn's grandfather sent a skyrider over the mountains, telling Zandaros that if he refused to patrol his own borders, then he had no business protesting our attempts to protect ourselves. A day later, a skyrider from Inkarra dropped a bag on the uppermost ramparts at the Courts of Tide, at the very feet of King Orden. In it was the head of the child that had borne the message to the Storm King, and with the head came an edict warning that the citizens of Mystarria—and all of the other kingdoms in Rofehavan—would no longer be tolerated in Inkarra. Soon after, the Inkarrans began building their runewall across the northern borders, a shield that none dare now pass."

"But that was a long time ago," Myrrima argued. "Perhaps the new high king will be more tolerant?"

"Zandaros is still the High King of Indhopal. It's true that he's old, but he's more than a king, it is said. He is a powerful sorcerer who can summon storms, and he uses his powers to extend his life."

"But," Myrrima protested, "in sixty years, surely his anger has cooled. His argument was with Gaborn's grandfather, not with us."

"Aye," Borenson said. "That's my hope. It is the only thing that might save us. We come as the envoys not of the old king but of a new, and we bear entreaties of peace. Even that black-hearted old badger should respect that."

There was a pregnant silence. Borenson loved his wife, and was offering her one last opportunity to abandon their quest. But Myrrima said with finality, "I won't be left behind."

"Very well," Borenson said.

Borenson gave over three forcibles of stamina to the marquis's facilitator, an elderly man who studied the forcibles with glee, as if he had not seen so many together in a long, long time. The facilitator went to a logbook and came back shaking his head. "Only two folks have offered to give stamina in the past year. Would you like to wait until our criers find a third?"

"That could take weeks." Borenson sighed. "Give me what you can now, and send out the criers. Perhaps you can vector the third endowment to me?"

"Done," the facilitator said, disappearing from the room to make the arrangements. For a moment they stood in the silence, and Myrrima gazed about at the work chamber filled with implements of the facilitators' craft. There were scales for weighing blood metal, tongs and hammers and files, a small forge, thick iron molds for making forcibles. A chart on the wall showed the various runes that allowed the transfer of each type of endowment, like sight and wit, along with possible minor variations in the shape of the runes. Cryptic notes written in the secret language of facilitators were scrawled upon the charts.

Myrrima gazed curiously at Borenson. She noticed that he was pacing, and his face seemed a bit pale. "How do you feel?"

"Fine," he replied. "Why?"

"The facilitator back in Carris said that he'd vector endowments to you: metabolism, brawn, wit. But you're not moving any faster now than you did two days ago. Do you think he forgot?"

"No," Borenson said. "The facilitators keep copious notes. I'm sure he's just too busy. The city was—" He searched for the right word for the destruction of Carris. The walls of the city had buckled under the onslaught of the reavers, and many of its finest towers had fallen. The lands for thirty miles around lay black and blasted, every plant dead. The corpses of reavers, black monoliths with mouths gaping wide, littered the fields along with dead men. The reavers' curses hung over the city—a reek that demanded that the men inside dry up, be blind, and rot and putrefy. Recalling the nightmare of Carris, Myrrima could think of no word to describe it. *Destroyed* was too weak. Demolished? Devastated? Borenson offered "Expunged."

"Still," Myrrima said, "plenty of people survived. He should be able to get Dedicates."

"But those people want nothing more than to get away from Carris," Borenson said. "The facilitators had their hands full just trying to move the Dedicates, boat them downstream. I'm sure that he'll get the endowments vectored as soon as he can."

Though he reassured Myrrima, Borenson didn't seem so confident himself. He began to pace about the room. In all likelihood, his Dedicates were floating downriver now, perhaps on their way to the Courts of Tide. If the facilitator was with them, he'd be looking for a place to settle them, and Myrrima knew by report that most of the towns along the river would be too full of injured and homeless refugees to take on a large number of Dedicates. Under such conditions, it might be days or weeks before the facilitator returned to his normal duties.

Borenson's lack of endowments put an uneven burden on Myrrima. As a soldier she didn't have Borenson's years of training, but she had more endowments and was definitely stronger, faster, smarter. In every way, she was more prepared for a journey to Inkarra than he.

Perhaps that was why Borenson paced. He went to a window, looked out, sighed, and then sat down with his back against the wall. He was pale, trembling all over. Sweat stood out on his forehead.

"What's wrong?" Myrrima asked.

"I don't know if I can do this anymore," he said. "I've seen too many Dedicates die."

Myrrima knew what he was thinking. He had been forced to butcher Raj Ahten's Dedicates at Castle Sylvarresta—thousands of men, women, and children in a single night. And he was thinking of his own Dedicates that Raj Ahten had murdered at the Blue Tower.

"You know," he said softly, "the marquis was right about me. As a young man, I always wanted to be a Runelord. I wanted to prove myself, and I thought that taking endowments would make me powerful. But it doesn't just give you power. It gives you new responsibilities, and leaves you open to . . . whole new worlds of suffering."

Within the hour the facilitator brought the Dedicates, two robust young girls, aged eleven and twelve. They stood just behind a curtain in the receiving room, a comfortable room, gaily painted, with warm couches to put the potential Dedicates at ease. Myrrima could hear the girls talking to the facilitator, begging for assurances that their widowed mother and younger brothers would receive food from the king's stores.

"Fine young sacrifices, both of them," Borenson whispered angrily as he peered through the curtain.

He trembled as the facilitator drew the stamina from the girls, along with their screams of pain. And when the forcibles kissed his own flesh, even the rush of ecstasy that came with taking an endowment did not stop him from shaking. As the facilitator's aids carried the girls away afterward, both of them pale and weak with shock, Borenson vomited on the facilitator's floor.

ಐ 8 ೞ

HOLLOW WOLVES

The hollow wolf may have taken its name from its unusual profile. It is long of leg, with a stomach that hugs the beast's backbone and looks perpetually empty. But I favor the theory that the creature takes its name from its icy, soulless eyes.

In the days of mad King Harrill, the creature was hunted nearly to extinction. However, on an outing the king heard a chorus of their haunting voices, deeper and more resonant than those of their smaller cousins.

"Ah, what beauteous music these wolves do make. Let their voices fill these mountains forever!" said he, banning the hunting of the creatures for nearly forty years, until the mountains became overrun.

After his death, the hunt resumed. Indeed, entire armies were deployed in what became known as the "War of the Wolves."

—*from* Mammals of Rofehavan, *by The Wizard Binnesman*

South of Batenne, the road up into the Alcair Mountains became a desolate track. In places, the forests covered it completely, and often Myrrima and Borenson found themselves riding through trees, squinting vainly for sight of the road. But as they began to climb above the forests toward the jagged icy peaks, the ruts and stone walls along the road could be easily discerned.

The voices of hollow wolves could be heard in the distant mountains, eerily howling, like the moan of wind among rocks.

They had just stopped to put on heavy cloaks, and were in the last of the thinning trees where mounds of snow still huddled in the shadows of boulders, when Myrrima became aware of another rider.

"Our friend is near," Myrrima said. "I can smell him up the road."

"The assassin?" Borenson asked.

She got off her horse and warily strung her bow. She drew an arrow from her quiver, and spat on the sharp steel bodkin, anointing it with water from her own body. "Strike true," she whispered. She looked to Borenson.

Borenson drew his warhammer. He seemed self-conscious. He was not a Water wizard, but Myrrima had washed him and offered the Water's blessings upon him. He spat on the spike, and whispered, "May Water guide you."

She peered up the road. The land rose steadily. Dwarf pines, nearly black against the fields of blinding snow up above, grew in ragged patches on the slopes of the mountain. There wasn't much cover, not many places for a man to hide. But Myrrima felt sure that the assassin was far enough ahead that he could not have spotted them.

"How far?" Borenson asked.

"A mile or two," Myrrima said.

"You take the right side of the road, I'll take the left," Borenson said. They tied their horses to a tree, then split up. Each of them crept through the woods on opposite sides of the road.

The snow was rife with wolf tracks. Myrrima strained her senses, letting her gaze pierce the shadows, listening for any sound—a cough, the snap of a twig. She sniffed the air. The wind was blowing in odd directions among the trees. She'd lose his scent one moment, smell it twice as strong the next.

There was little cover here, and after half a mile of sneaking, the trees gave out almost completely.

Myrimma leapt over the ground and raced ahead, her feet softly shushing in the snow. With five endowments of metabolism added to her brawn and stamina, she could run effortlessly for hours. More important, she could run faster than most horses. She hoped that this speed would give her the advantage in any fight.

She raced along at fifty or sixty miles an hour, head low, scenting for the smell of the assassin. She had never run like this since taking her endowments. It was queer.

Time did not seem to pass any differently. She ran at a good pace, but not overly quick. Yet when she rounded a bend, she could feel an odd force tugging her, so that she quickly learned to lean into her turns. And when she topped a rise, her stomach would do a little twist as she went airborne.

She felt sleek and powerful, like a wolf as it races after a stag.

The air grew thin and chill. Frost stood up in the dirt where the day's sun had not yet penetrated the shadows. Higher up the mountain, the sun glinted on snow. She was nearly past the treeline when the odor of the assassin's horse came suddenly strong.

She drew to a stop, and watched the road ahead. She could smell the brittle scent of a fire, its ashes gone cold. The assassin had made camp uphill, to her right among a knot of trees. She hoped that he might be asleep.

Myrrima peered at the spot for a long moment, but saw no movement, and could not make out any form that seemed vaguely human.

She crept off the road two hundred yards, and circled up through a gully into the trees. She saw no sign of anyone, yet the smell of horseflesh grew stronger. She let her nose guide her into the thick copse of pine, up a ridge, past a fallen log.

She did not spot the assassin's camp until she was less than forty feet from it. He hid in the midst of thick trees, their branches forming a natural roof. At some time in ages past a depression had been dug there, and a small rock wall built up to chest height in a semicircle, forming a crude defense. She saw a horse's ears poking above the rocks, and Myrrima froze for a moment.

She could hear the assassin, drawing deep, wheezing breaths. She scented the air. She could smell blood and rot. The man was injured.

Myrrima looked behind her. Borenson had seen her run, and he was leaping up the hill toward her, trying to catch her. He slipped in a deep snow-drift, and for a moment snow churned in the air all around him as he fought back to his feet. She raised a warning hand, dropped to cover behind a tree, and waited for him.

When he drew near, he was huffing for breath. He tried to still it. He peered into the dense foliage, saw the little camp there, and nodded. He motioned for her to circle the camp, come at it from behind.

Myrrima crept along the edge of the wood, walking in slushy snow. A twig crunched beneath her foot, under the snow. She could barely see the top of the horse's head there in the camp. The horse's ear went erect.

Wolf tracks littered the ground here at the edge of the camp. Myrrima looked up and saw a white form against some dark trees uphill. A huge wolf was there, as motionless as the snow. Suddenly it spun in its tracks and bounded away over the ice field, emitting a soft woof.

At that instant, she heard another twig snap behind her. She turned and saw Borenson, warhammer held high behind his head, charging toward the hidden camp.

A rush of wind came screaming through the trees toward them. It didn't come from uphill. Instead, it was like a tornado leaning on its side, aiming toward Myrrima and her husband. The forest shook like thunder, while bits of pine needles, cones, and icy shards of snow suddenly whirled in a vortex, obscuring Myrrima's view.

Her heart nearly froze in her chest. For a moment she thought that the Darkling Glory must be near, for she had experienced nothing like this outside the monster's presence.

"Sorcery!" she cried, stunned motionless.

A blinding blast of wind and ice came whipping over her, knocking the arrow from her hands.

Pinecones and twigs pelted her; shards of ice slammed into her eyes and teeth. Myrrima squinted and raised her hand protectively, trying to see through the tempest.

With a roar, Borenson charged. The storm turned on him. He leapt into the pit.

His warhammer fell and with a sickening thud slammed into flesh. A wailing cry arose. *"Ooooooooh!"*

Wind rushed about the trees then, circling like a storm.

The man's cry kept ripping from his throat. Pine needles and ice lashed through the air in a maelstrom, then went rushing south up the slopes toward Inkarra.

Myrrima heard the scream *"Noooooo!"* in the wind, as it drew farther and farther away, echoing among the canyons.

She ran up to Borenson, knowing what she would find.

He stood over a corpse, struggling to free the spike of his hammer from a wizard's head. The dead man wore the blue tunic of Mystarria's couriers, with the image of the green man on his chest. But his long silver hair proclaimed him to be of Inkarran birth. His eyes were flung open, and his mouth drawn in a little circle of surprise or pain.

His horse whinnied pitifully at the sight of strangers, and tried to rise. But its legs had been shackled.

"Pilwyn coly Zandaros," Myrrima mouthed the man's name.

"This is the wizard that tried to kill Gaborn?" Borenson confirmed.

She nodded. Pilwyn had been both an assassin and a wizard of the Air. Myrrima shook her head in confusion. "What do you think he was up to? Waiting in ambush?"

Borenson was already studying the ground, the shabby camp. The hobbled horse had lain in its own excrement for hours. It gazed at Borenson imploringly.

Myrrima saw no sign of food, no extra wood for the fire. There was nothing left of the campfire but lightly smoking ruins.

Borenson knelt over Pilwyn's corpse. Four days past, Sir Hoswell, who had been one of Iome's guards, had shot Pilwyn with an arrow. The wound would have killed any commoner in a matter of minutes. The arrow had punctured Pilwyn's lung. But wizards of the Air were notoriously hard to kill. Beyond that, Pilwyn was a Runelord with endowments of stamina. So he had merely plugged the cavity in his chest with a crude bandage. But now Myrrima could see that black blood crusted the wound, and it had swollen horribly. Maggots crawled around the lip of the bandage.

"He wasn't long for the world," Borenson said. "He'd have died in a few more hours, even if we hadn't come along. If the infection hadn't killed him, the hollow wolves would have."

"But why was he following us the other night?" Myrrima asked.

"My guess is that he wasn't," Borenson said. "We're all on the road to Inkarra, fellow travelers. He probably pulled off the road to rest and heard us pass, then just crept along behind us. He may have even hoped for our aid. But he was an Inkarran in Mystarria—an outlaw." He sighed.

Myrrima went to the body. She reached down to pull the bandage back, look at the old wound. She felt a cool wind whip around her hand as it neared the man's chest—suspected that she had just touched protective runes written with wind.

Up the hill, through a thin veil of trees, she heard the horrid ghostly wailing of his voice, and could see the plume of windblown ice still racing away, now nearly a mile uphill.

Borenson gazed in that direction. "His elemental will reach Inkarra long before we do," he said, and Myrrima wondered about her own elemental, the thing growing inside her. She imagined that when she died, the Water within her would merely leak from her mouth and eyelids, leaving a moist puddle.

Borenson went to Pilwyn's mount, removed its hobbles. The beast struggled to its feet.

Borenson then leapt up on the stone fence above the camp. He did not speak, but his posture, the tilt of his head, asked, "Ready to go?"

Myrrima asked, "What should we do with the body?"

"Leave it," Borenson said. "The wolves will have him."

"But he's the Storm King's nephew," Myrrima said. "We should show him some respect."

"We can't dig a hole, and I won't take him over the mountains to Inkarra," Borenson argued. "King Zandaros would be none too pleased to learn that we killed his nephew on our way to beg his favor."

"You're right," Myrrima said. "Of course you're right. But I don't feel easy about it. Wizards don't just die. After I slew the Darkling Glory, its elemental hurled boulders around as if they were apples. Binnesman warned that the elemental was still capable of great evil. Pilwyn's elemental is small, but that *thing* is headed for Inkarra."

Again she felt the foreboding that had been growing all day. Something, or someone, would seek to take her husband from her. Could it be the wizard's elemental?

"Look at the bright side," Borenson said. "At least we got a good horse."

With three force horses, the trip through the snow went fast. Or at least it would have seemed so to an outsider. Had you seen them, you would have tracked the force horses galloping up the mountainsides, churning snow and ice with each hoofbeat. When the road leveled, they seemed to almost float above it, such was the length and grace of their stride.

But Myrrima had endowments of metabolism now, more even than her mount, and to her senses the horse did not seem to be moving fast at all. Instead, she felt as if the stuff of time had stretched. The sun lumbered interminably into the sky, and gradually slanted toward darkness. Thus one day seemed to be expanding to fill five. Myrrima felt every second of her life waning past.

Their journey had begun before dawn. In that time, they traveled hundreds of miles.

The journey up the slopes was tedious. Myrrima never even got to see one of the much-vaunted hollow wolves up close. In the distance she saw a pack of them sweeping over the snow—white on white—wafting ghostlike over the slopes of a nearby mountain. Even from a distance they looked huge.

The hollow wolves saw her party and redoubled their speed, hoping to catch up, but they were no match for force horses. Borenson let the mounts race for an hour.

When next they stopped, they were near the mountain peaks. The snow was now six inches deep and crusted from last night's freeze. Myrrima followed its course up the mountains with her eyes. The snow-covered trail looked broad and easy as it wound through the hills. It had been cut wide enough to accommodate wagons, and was none too steep.

Somehow, in Myrrima's imagination, the Alcair Mountains had always seemed impassable. Perhaps for one without endowments the journey would have been more challenging. But she suspected that there wasn't so much a physical challenge in crossing the mountains as there was a political one.

At the mountaintops, stone wheels stood against the sky. The wheels looked to be more than thirty or forty feet tall. The line that they formed zigzagged crazily, marching up one ridge, then diving into a ravine, like rocky pearls to decorate the hills. On each stone wheel a rune had been carved. Myrrima eyed them, not quite able to make out the design.

"Don't look at the runewall!" Borenson warned. "Not unless you have to. Keep your eyes on the road!"

Myrrima averted her gaze, but now felt curious. What was the runewall? The runes looked as if they had been carved on individual tablets of stone and then rolled into place. The making of this massive bulwark had been a monumental task. The border between Rofehavan and Inkarra spanned a thousand miles. Building a barrier like this would have taken tens of thousands of masons a period of decades.

The fact that gazing upon it was forbidden made it that much more enticing. Myrrima wanted to feel the awe of it.

"I had no idea it would be so vast," Myrrima said. She studied the ground.

The snow here was dirty, streaked with ash. She looked for the source of the ash, but could see no sign of a fire. There were no trees so high, only low shrubs here and there that thrust their dead branches up between the rocks.

She dutifully kept her eyes on the road as the horses plodded step after weary step, and felt a most peculiar sensation. The stone bucklers loomed enormous in her mind. It was as if the very shadow of them weighed upon her consciousness. As she drew nearer, she could feel them, demanding her regard.

She had to will herself not to look. She had to force herself to focus on a rough stone road ahead, or the twisted roots of a dead bush, or plain rock casting an uneven shadow in the snow. Even when she did, her eyes sought to flit away, to land like sparrows upon those monoliths that formed the runewall.

The desire to look and be done with it burned her mind, left an acid taste in her mouth. She could close her eyes and feel the stone tablets looming above her. She could track them thus.

An awful certainty grew in her: to keep her eyes closed was better than to look.

Suddenly at her back she heard a loud thump, and the mount that she trailed pulled at its reins. Carefully keeping her eyes averted, she turned to glance back at the horse. Its eyes had gone wide, as if in shock, and it stared in frozen horror toward the monoliths.

Myrrima worried that the animal had picked a lamentable time to look up, but knew in her heart that it was no accident. Even this dull beast felt the forbidding presence of the wall.

If a horse can look upon it, I can too, Myrrima thought. And instantly her eyes darted toward the road ahead. She was just beneath the skyline now, not more than fifty yards away.

A vast archway spanned the road. Overhead, the skies were blue, but clouds on the far horizon lay opalescent beneath that dark arch, making it look for all the world like a blind eye.

An inscription above the arch was written in both Rofehavanish and Inkarran: Beyond This Point, Your Tribe is Barren.

She struggled now to avoid looking at the monolithic stones raised up like shields on either side of the arch. But she had let her gaze stray too far, and now it was taken hostage.

She saw vast round stones, like wheels or shields, on either side of the road. Her eyes went to the northernmost stone. Inscribed upon it was a trail, a groove in the rock, leading downward and inward, like a map. She recognized that it was a rune, a mesmerizing rune, and powerful. She tried to look away, but could not. Her eyes were forced to follow that groove along its tortured path, winding down, down. And as it wound, she felt the weight of ages slowly passing by, wheeling beneath her. Civilizations could rise within each turning of the wheel, and worlds could rot. Great cities formed, and in her mind's eye, Myrrima saw them crumble. Their foundations sank and moldered among forgotten forests. Monuments to proud kings wore away. Their squalid children fought and sought shelter among the ruins. In time they began the process of building again. Still the wheel turned, and Myrrima was swept away among the dreams of proud lovers, the boasts of warriors, the wild utterances of poets and prophets, and still the wheel turned toward its devastating conclusion.

Her heart surged in panic, and her mouth went dry.

Looking at this will kill me, Myrrima thought feebly. She fought it, tried to close her eyes and twist away. A groan escaped her, but she stared on, her eyes following that twisted groove along its fearsome course—as towers rose and dreamers dreamed and proud lords made war under a hazy sun—until it all stopped.

Immediately an emotion surged through her, struck her with awful force.

You are nothing, a voice seemed to roar through her mind. *All your deeds and dreams are futile. You strive for beauty and permanence, yet you are less than a worm on the road, waiting to be crushed beneath the wheels of time.*

The conviction of this, the power of it, overwhelmed her. The visions elicited by the rune proved the argument. How dare one like her seek to enter Inkarra? She was loathsome. Better to turn the horse back now and run it madly over some cliff than to proceed.

Myrrima never thought about what she was doing. She merely groaned and reined in her mount, tried to turn it, and spurred its flanks with her heel. She sought escape.

Nothing that had ever happened to her was as cruel as the thought of facing that rune. Until now she had lived in relative peace, not knowing of its existence.

But now that she had seen it, she could never be free. Better to be nothing. Blind with panic, she did not see the cliffs below.

All the heavens had gone black, and she fled through a dark tunnel toward oblivion.

"No!" Borenson shouted. "No!"

Her husband came off his horse and grabbed her own mount by the reins. He was fighting the beast, trying to subdue it and the Inkarran's horse at the same time. Myrrima could not see him, but felt his hands grab her wrists, pull the reins. She gouged her mount's flanks. She was riding his big strong warhorse, and as the beast pawed the air, she felt certain that it would deliver a crushing blow to Borenson's skull, as it had been trained to do. But Borenson had been its handler for years, and perhaps that alone saved his life.

He wrestled the horse down, shouting at Myrrima, "Don't look! Don't look at it!"

Myrrima was blind with panic, but suddenly she began to see as if through a haze.

Borenson peered up at her. His own eyes went to the runewall, and he gazed at the horror there. Fierce tears welled up, and he stared in defiance. "It's a lie!" he raged at her. "I love you! I love you, Myrrima. Damn those bastards."

He turned and led the horses onward. Each step seemed to fall painfully, as if his legs were slogging through molten iron.

Myrrima clenched her eyes shut and faced the wall. Her heart hammered. I faced a Darkling Glory, she told herself. I bested a wight. I can fight this, too. Yet somehow, the vile runes terrified her more than other monsters ever could. She could do little to help Borenson but urge the horse forward with a kick of her heel.

Thus Borenson forged on against the repressive wards, dragging Myrrima someplace she could never have gone herself.

She felt the weight of the wards grow above her. Even with eyes clenched shut, she could see their loathsome shape now, stamped on the back of her brain as she bowed in submission. *Your birth was a misfortune, a chance collision of wantonness with abandonment. You are no better than the secretions from which you were formed.*

And farther away, as if from some hollow in the hills, Borenson roared in defiance, "Don't believe it."

And then she was beneath the arch. She could almost feel the weight of it as if it leaned upon her back, crushing her.

And then she was past it, and still she felt it behind her. Sobs wracked Myrrima now.

"I love you," Borenson said calmly as he strode forward.

Myrrima would have lashed her horse and sped away into Inkarra but for the fact that Borenson kept it firmly in control.

With each step, the power of the wards faded. In a sense, she felt like a dreamer who has awakened from a nightmare. The dream was fading from her memory with each step of the horse, for the mind was not meant to feel such torment, and ultimately could not hold it for long.

Myrrima was half a mile beyond the wall, maybe more, by the time she was able to open her eyes and raise her head a bit. Borenson had taken the reins of all three mounts and led them over the pass and down toward Inkarra. His own mount bumped her leg to her right, the wizard's mount to her left.

She gazed down the slopes. Ahead, a sea of mist rose above Inkarra. It was warmer on this side of the mountains, much warmer she realized, as if the wall did more than keep out unwanted northerners but also kept out the cold. The thin layer of snow vanished just down the hill, and shrubs here still rose up among the rocks, showing green leaves.

But beyond that, beyond those few signs of life among the stones, she could only discern a rolling sea of fog. "Beyond this point, your tribe is barren." Barren of what? She wondered. Barren of hope? Barren of pride? Barren of comfort?

Borenson rounded a sharp corner in the road, and Myrrima suddenly saw to her a left a small cave, the mouth of a fortress carved into the stone.

At the mouth of the cave stood three men with ivory skin and long silver hair wrapped in corn braids, which were all coiled together and hung over their right shoulders. They wore blood-red tunics that did not quite reach their knees, and beyond that, Iome could see no other article of clothing except their sandals, tied with cords that wrapped around the ankles and knees. For armor they wore steel breastplates, perfect circles, upon their backs and chests. They wore similar disks on bands upon their foreheads, and another upon their upper arms. Two of the men bore longbows, and the third carried an Inkarran battle-axe—two slats of wood bound together with a row of spikes between, so that it looked like the jawbone of some sharp-toothed beast.

"Halt!" an Inkarran warrior called in a thick accent as he strode forward. "You are our captives!"

ᛒᚩ 9 ᚸᚳ

ABYSS GATE

Few have dared explore the depths of the Underworld, and fewer still have dared assault reavers in their lair. The exploits of Erden Geboren, whose Dark Knights hunted in the Underworld for years, are the stuff of legend now.

—from Campaigns in the Underworld, *by Hearthmaster Coxton, from the Room of Arms*

Long and long the riverbed wound through the Underworld. Gaborn ran in a daze of grief. His side ached from the blow he'd taken from the reavers, but the physical pain was nothing compared to the concern he felt at the loss of Binnesman.

The wizard had been the one to introduce Gaborn to the Earth Spirit. He had been a wise counselor and friend.

More than that, he had been Gaborn's strongest supporter. As an Earth Warden, he had been set apart for one duty only: to protect mankind through the dark times to come. Gaborn was the Earth King, with powers of his own, regardless of how diminished. But Binnesman's powers and wisdom had been incomparable.

With him gone, what will become of us? Gaborn wondered.

He felt ashamed to even worry about such a thing. But he knew the answer. Binnesman had said it himself. If he failed, mankind would be lost.

Averan raced beside Gaborn on her short legs, weeping bitterly. Iome stayed back and tried to urge the child on, her face a blank mask.

They had been running through the bed of the ancient river, where water had dribbled over rocks, leaving crater-shaped pools. They reached a wide cavern, where a tiny stream dripped down from a high wall, filling some pools.

Iome asked Gaborn at last, "Can we stop here for a rest?" The sound of reavers running overhead was a dim rumble. Gaborn stretched out his senses, felt for danger. Yes, he could feel it everywhere. Battles coming to Heredon, death to Carris, the creeping darkness that could swallow the world. With every hour that they ran, the darkness was one hour closer.

But for the moment, the danger to the three of them was not great. "We can stop." His mouth was parched from lack of drink, and his belly clenched like a fist. With all his endowments of stamina he could endure much, but even a Runelord needed some refreshment.

He hadn't eaten a decent meal since when? Yesterday at dawn? With his endowments of metabolism, his body registered that as something closer to ten days.

"We can't stay long," Averan said, her voice thick with fear.

"Why?" Gaborn asked.

"That reaver," Averan said, "the one that . . . hit Binnesman. I smelled him. I know him. All of the reavers know him. He's called the Consort of Shadows. He won't leave us alone. He'll hunt us until we're dead."

"What do you mean?" Gaborn asked.

"Among the reavers, he's a legend," Averan said. "He's the One True Masters' favorite, her mate. He's a hunter, sent to track down sick and dangerous reavers."

"Dangerous?" Iome asked.

"Among reavers," Averan explained, "the most feared illness is something they call worm dreaming. Tiny worms eat into the reaver's brain, causing phantom smells and visions—worm dreams. In time the worms cause terrible pain, forgetfulness, and death.

"So, when a reaver gets worm dreaming, to keep it from spreading, the sick reaver is killed and its carcass is burned.

"Such a death is a disgrace. For if a reaver dies and another eats its brain, then its memories, its experiences, are partly learned by the one who ate it. But reavers that aren't eaten don't get to share their memories."

"In other words," Gaborn reasoned, "a reaver can hope to gain a sort of immortality." Gaborn had known that reavers ate their dead. He'd even known that they obtained the memories of the dead. But he'd never imagined that living reavers would hope to be eaten.

"Yes," Averan said. "Every reaver hopes to be so well thought of that its death will spark a duel among others for the right to feed on its brain. And at feasts where the most powerful sorceresses gather, the brains of wise reavers are considered to be a treat.

"So, the most powerful reavers, like the Waymaker that I communicated with yesterday, have memories that stretch back a hundred generations in an unbroken chain."

"I see where you are going," Gaborn said. "To be thrown away, burned, is such a disgrace that some of them fight it. That's where the Consort of Shadows comes in?"

"Yes," Averan said. "Reavers who get burned die the 'greater death.' It's a permanent death, and they're disgraced by it. So when they begin to see signs of worm madness, the reavers often hide those signs even from themselves. They try to live out normal lives, be consumed, and die with honor.

"But as their minds begin to waste, their dreams become more frightening, and their fear of discovery grows. So they flee the warrens.

"They come out here, far away from the hives, into the barrens where they live as rogues."

"That would explain something," Gaborn cut in. "Years ago, a reaver attacked the village of Campton. My father sent some men after it, but all they found was a sickly reaver, dragging its legs."

"Yes," Averan said. "Some go all the way to the surface—unless the Consort of Shadows catches them. He's relentless, and deadly. He's curious about us. He'll come for us. I'm sure of it."

"Perhaps," Gaborn said. "But the danger is small right now. We should take nourishment while we can." He continued to sense for danger. With the loss of Binnesman their chances of defeating the One True Master had diminished.

Averan went to the nearest pool, peered into the water. "There's no scrabbers in here," she said dully. "Only blindfish." She knelt close, sniffed. "This water is fresh."

All of the water they'd passed in the last few hours had been contaminated with sulfur. Gaborn hurried over, peered into the shallows. The crater-like pool was perhaps thirty feet across, and two feet deep. Dozens of blindfish, a dull gray in color and the length of a man's hand, swam about ponderously. These were not the leathery, spiny, sulfur-tasting fish of the Underworld, but looked more as if they had descended from some breed of bass.

For miles now the ground had been covered with tickle fern and clumps of colorful wormgrass, but with the advent of fresh water, rubbery gray man's ear surrounded the pool.

Averan dipped in her hand, took a long drink. Soon, everyone was doing the same.

"We'll camp here for an hour," Gaborn said at last. "Get some rest. We'll have fish for dinner. It will help stretch our supplies."

Iome looked up at him. "Before we do, shouldn't we . . . make plans. What will we do without Binnesman?"

Gaborn shook his head. "I . . . he's not dead."

"He might as well be," Iome said.

Gaborn shook his head in exasperation. "Of all the people in the world, Binnesman should have known best how important it was to heed my warning."

"But sometimes even the wisdom of the wisest men fails," Iome said. "From now on," she begged Averan, "when Gaborn tells us to do something, do it."

Gaborn didn't think that they would forget the lesson. But it grieved him that it had to be learned at such a dear price. He studied the fish swimming lazily in the pool. Catching them would almost be like picking berries. He waded into the water.

"Gaborn," Iome said, "lie down and rest. I can catch the fish." Her fierce look told him that she would not take no for an answer.

What had she said to him earlier this morning? "While you're out saving the world, who will be saving you?" She was taking those words to heart. Gaborn felt in no mood to argue.

He found a patch of gray man's ear, then lay down on it while Iome and Averan caught the fish. The plants made a spongy mattress.

Gaborn lay still, listening.

On the wall of the cave above him hung a curtain of cave straws, a kind of stalactite that formed over eons as droplets of water dripped down through hollow tubes. The cave straws looked like agates or jade of varying colors, ranging from a soft rose hue to bright peach. They were beautiful to look at, sparkling gems, and the sound of water plunking from the straws onto the calcite floor created a resonance that echoed loudly. Gaborn wasn't sure if it was the acoustics of the cavern or if it was his endowments of hearing, but the dribbling water reminding him of the soft tinkling of bells. And distantly, the pounding feet of reavers were like the roll of drums.

Gaborn played a game in his mind. Binnesman had suggested that up until now Gaborn had been asking the wrong questions. He'd concentrated on tactics, various weapons he might use to fight the One True Master, and nothing that he imagined could save his people for long.

Darkness is coming, Gaborn thought, a full night like we've never witnessed before. How can I save my people?

He imagined raising armies, attacking various nations—Indhopal, Inkarra, South Crowthen. It mattered not at all.

Darkness was coming, and attacking others offered no hope.

As he lay pondering, Averan pulled up some old dead tickle ferns and started a small campfire. Then she emptied the packs, setting things next to the fire to dry. She pulled out apples and nuts and whetstones and bits of flint and set them in one pile, then threw away the wet loaves of bread that had been destroyed by the water. When she finished, she repacked everything, leaving only some spare clothes and other oddments to dry.

The burning ferns had an odd peppery scent that only made Gaborn that much more hungry. Unfortunately, it would take nearly fifteen minutes for the fish to cook, and with his endowments of metabolism, it would feel more like two or three hours.

He glanced across to the far side of the cavern. The walls there looked almost flat, as if they had been carved by hand, and he spotted a couple of odd-shaped holes that looked like windows here and there, up near the ceiling of the cave. Stalactites hung from the roof, ugly things of dirty brown stone.

Gaborn dropped his mouth in surprise. He had only thought it *looked* like a fortress, but now he could see details: yes, down there was a gate, but part of the roof had caved in, landing at its door. Over the ages, the stone walls had buckled a bit, so that they wavered on their foundations. Stalactites hung like spears, hiding some of the windows.

"Human?" Gaborn wondered. "Or duskin?"

His heart hammered in excitement. Wondrous things could be found in duskin ruins—metalwork so fine that human hands could not match it, moonstones that shone with their own eternal light.

Gaborn got up and crossed the riverbed until he reached some fallen stones from an old wall. They were coated with mud, like that on the outer walls, making them all but invisible. There had once been a portcullis here, and the wooden gate had been bound together with iron bars. Now the iron had all gone to rust, and the wood had rotted through ages ago.

Gaborn grabbed an iron rod and pulled on it. The gate all but collapsed. He kicked in some old timbers, and made his way inside.

The floor looked as if it were coated with plaster. At some time in the past, the fortress had flooded, leaving a thick coat of mud on both floor and walls. A few Underworld plants struggled up like black bristles from the floor, but it seemed that, for some reason, little could thrive here.

A yellowish creature with a broad back, like some strange eyeless beetle, came scampering toward Gaborn, waving its small claws in the air. Gaborn stomped on the bug with an astonishing effect.

There was a pop and a flash of light, and then the dead bug began to burn steadily with a sulfur smell.

A blazer, Gaborn realized. He'd heard of the bug once, long ago, in the House of Understanding. "They are the only animals known," old Hearthmaster Yarrow had said, "that do you the courtesy of cooking themselves when you're ready to eat. Unfortunately, they taste worse than fried cockroaches."

Gaborn peered about. He'd found what might have been a Great Room. On one wall the tattered remains of a tapestry still hung like a banner, but the colors had so faded that Gaborn could not even begin to guess at what it might have pictured. Ancient oil lamps rested in nooks in the walls; here and there was an odd piece of refuse—part of a rotted chair, the skeletal remains of a chest of drawers.

Mystarrians built this, Gaborn realized. I've seen clay lamps like these in the House of Understanding, in the Room of Time.

This place was old, very old. But Gaborn could not guess how old. He thought he knew, but dared not admit it to himself. Only three times in recorded history had Mystarria dared attempt to conquer the Underworld. Erden Geboren himself might have slept in these rooms, led warriors through these corridors during the first of those attempts.

The hair rose on Gaborn's arms. He could almost feel the presence of spirits here, of men who had died in battle.

A narrow staircase was chiseled into the stone at the back of one room. He climbed the stairs to the second floor. An ancient wooden door blocked the way.

Words were carved into the door. They were all in old script, a corrupt version of Rofehavanish that Gaborn could barely make out. The door had rotted away, leaving blank spots for some words.

"I, Beron Windhoven . . . this fortress . . . year of Duke Val the Wise! . . . Below . . . much foretoken of reaver."

"Duke Val the Wise?" Gaborn tried to guess at the age of the writing from memory. His mother's line came through Val. Val the Wise was the son of Val the Foresworn, who had conquered the Westlands seven hundred years ago.

So, this place was old even then, Gaborn realized. Which meant that King Harrill could not have built it.

Gaborn pulled the door latch; it came off in his hand. He gave the door his shoulder, and it cascaded inward.

There was little to see. Four dozen small rooms had been cut into the rock. It had the look of a barracks. There were privies chipped into the stone, but no ancient weapons, no rare antiquities plundered from duskin ruins.

Anything of value had been hauled off centuries ago.

Another staircase led upward. These would be the officers' quarters. Gaborn climbed the steps with a growing sense of reverence, came to a T. The left hallway led to a large room whose door had been kicked in. Gaborn suspected that Beron Windhoven must have claimed the room as his own. Part of the ceiling had collapsed into the room, and Gaborn dared not enter.

But to the right stood an ancient door of blackened metal, and upon it was a crest that Gaborn knew all too well: the face of the green man stared out at Gaborn through leaves of oak, all wrought into the metal of the black door.

Erden Geboren once slept in this room, Gaborn realized. He planned his wars and guided his men from here. I know the name of this place now: Abyss Gate, the Dark Fortress.

Knowledge of the whereabouts of this place had been lost in time, but its name was still remembered in the lore of Mystarria. Gaborn would have imagined it bigger, would have thought that it had housed a thousand men, for it loomed large in legend.

There comes a time in a man's life—if he is lucky—when he feels as if he has met his destiny. There comes a time when he recognizes that every path he has chosen, every plan he has so painstakingly laid, delivers him to a doorstep where he will confront his fate. And what may happen next is only a dimly hoped dream.

Gaborn had that premonition now.

Every step I have ever taken has led me in the footsteps of Erden Geboren, Gaborn thought. Why not here? Why not now?

In the distance, the sound of the reaver horde rushing through caverns above was like a distant thunder.

Gaborn reached out and scraped the door with his dagger, cutting a silver groove. The door was all of silver beneath the black. The door had tarnished that much over the centuries.

Everything else of value here had been carried away, but such was the regard that others held for the Earth King that no one had dared plunder this door.

Gaborn pulled the handle. The door was locked, but the keyhole was a mere indentation in the shape of the green man. Gaborn put his signet ring to the notch and turned. His signet ring had been cast in this very shape for more than a thousand years. The lock resisted at first, then broke free.

He pushed the door open.

The room was austere in the extreme. Gaborn had seen prison cells that were larger. Up here, sealed behind its door, the room had remained dry. The furnishings did not look so much well preserved as petrified. A cot with a wooden frame occupied most of the room. Upon it lay a reed mat and a brown woolen blanket. The bed had been left unmade.

A small table stood by the bed with a chair beside it. Upon the table lay a wooden plate and knife. A weathered book wrapped in leather lay next to the knife, along with an inkpot shaped like a lily, and the remains of a quill. A simple riding robe hung upon a peg on the wall, and a pair of tall boots peeked out from under the bed.

It looked as if Erden Geboren had simply eaten breakfast here ages ago and left, locking the door—never to return.

A realization struck Gaborn: that is exactly what happened. Erden Geboren had been at Abyss Gate, guiding his Dark Knights as they fought the reavers belowground, when he learned of the treachery at Caer Fael.

After an endless war fighting reavers and toth and nomen, he'd heard that the people of his own city had turned against him, the Earth King.

Little was known about why they rebelled. Some historians suspected that the cost of his war had been too great—he had led his knights through the Underworld for more than a dozen years, after all. Others argued against that, imagining that rogues and bandits had rallied against him in one last bid for domination. But one thing was certain: he died at Caer Fael, and no wound marred his body.

Now nearly eighteen hundred years later, Gaborn found himself in Erden Geboren's room, a chamber undisturbed since the very hour that he had ridden to his death.

Gaborn half expected to see the Earth King's shade patiently hovering in a corner, waiting to speak to him.

He gingerly touched the book, untied the cords that bound it, and opened it to the first page. The leaves were mere loose sheets, and some were flaking into dust. A drawing occupied the title page—a great oak tree, and beneath it two creatures that looked like men with wings, but with faces like foxes. Each creature bore a long sword with a wavy blade. The picture had been painstakingly drawn in ink, though the artist showed no talent. Gaborn recognized that this was a work of love, most likely a rough draft by Erden Geboren meant to be refined by better hands into an illuminated manuscript. He could not read the title, for the characters and language were in a tongue older than any that he knew.

Still, Gaborn found himself trembling with excitement. He flipped through the pages. The writing was in an ancient language, Alnycian, a tongue that had been spoken at court for a thousand years but was all but forgotten now. Gaborn could not read it, yet here was a book scribed in Erden Geboren's own hand. He flipped to the next page. The script was strong and graceful. The ink was dark upon the yellowed pages. But the manuscript was far from finished. Words had been crossed out and passages inserted in their place. Questions were transcribed in the margins. This was obviously a work in progress.

Old Hearthmaster Biddles will love this, Gaborn thought. The tome would be cause for celebration among the keepers of the Room of Time. He tucked it into his shirt.

There was little else in the room: an old tin bell, gray with age, four copper coins upon a shelf. Behind the door Gaborn found an ancient reaver dart somewhat longer than the norm, unlike any that he had ever seen. It was a kingly piece, fashioned not of steel but carved from one length of reaver bone, most likely from the shoulder of a large blade-bearer. There had been a leather grip wrapped around the shaft, but it was old and useless. The diamonds that tipped the dart were unusually large, long, and thin.

Gaborn smiled. The very weapon of Erden Geboren. The reaver bone would have hardened over the ages, becoming stronger than ever, and the grips could be replaced easily enough.

He would have wanted me to have this, Gaborn thought.

He took the reaver dart, then stood in the doorway for a moment, just observing.

Erden Geboren had been a humble man, Gaborn decided. The room showed no penchant for adornment, no love of display.

He closed the door once again, and locked it.

Iome had a dozen fish cooking on rocks around a small campfire. She glanced up at him, saw the gleaming amber javelin.

"What have you found?" she asked, a smile broadening across her face.

"The fortress of Abyss Gate," Gaborn said. "Erden Geboren's old bed-chamber was there, untouched through the ages. I found his own reaver dart!"

"What else?" Iome pressed him.

Gaborn said, "An old book, a manuscript I think."

"In Erden Geboren's own hand?" Iome asked. She looked as if she would get up and dance.

Gaborn nodded at her evident delight, but looked around in rising concern.

"Where's Averan?" Gaborn asked.

"She walked up the trail a way," Iome said. "She said that she wanted to pee in private, but I think she's very upset about Binnesman. She just wants to be alone."

Gaborn reached out with his Earth Sight. Yes, Averan had gone down the trail a way. He could sense no danger around her.

Gaborn pulled out the volume, and Iome unwrapped the leather that bound it. She opened to the title page, and read slowly, " 'The Tales' . . . no, I think that is 'Lore of the Netherworld, as Told by One Who Walked Among the Bright Ones.' "

"You can read this old tongue?" Gaborn asked in astonishment. "I've never heard it spoken outside the House of Understanding, in the Room of Tongues. Where ever did you hear it?"

"I learned it from Chancellor Rodham," Iome said. "He was quite the scholar and thought it infinitely more worthwhile for me to learn Alnycian than needlepoint."

Gaborn studied her in frank amazement. "History has been silent as to what Erden Geboren learned from the Bright Ones and glories," Gaborn mused. "Now we know why: he never finished his book. This is fabulous. Only the most powerful wizards have ever walked the path between our world and the netherworld, the One True World."

Iome flipped to the second page. "This is old," she said. "It's hard to deci-pher." She struggled to read.

"'Mine voice is coarse . . . a crude tool, I fear. Mine tongue is of brass, untrustworthy. How may I recount the words of Bright Ones and glories who thunder, who . . . '—I don't know that word—'men with words of light, who whisper to . . . ' or is it 'in? . . . the ears of our spirits? Listen to the words of glories, if thou canst. Unless my poor voice fails, as I fear. Yet still I hope that thou shalt hear.'"

Gaborn was immediately riveted. Iome glanced up to see his expression. She flipped open a page at random, halfway through the book, and began to read. "'Then the Fael saith unto me—'"

"What's a Fael?" Gaborn asked.

Iome said flippantly. "Something that saideth things unto Erden Geboren." She began to read again. "'Learn to love all men . . . ' He can't decide whether to use the word 'equally' or 'perfectly.'"

"If you loved all men perfectly," Gaborn suggested, "wouldn't you love them equally?"

Iome nodded and continued. "'Do not esteem one man above another. Do not love the rich more than the humble, the strong more than the faint, the kind man more than the cruel. But learn to love all men equally.'"

"Hmmm," Iome said with a thoughtful look on her face, as if the words disturbed her. She began to close the book.

Gaborn had never heard words like that, had never heard anyone other than a king who dared utter a commandment about how men were to treat each other.

A Fael must be a king among the Bright Ones or glories, he decided. "Keep reading."

Iome forged ahead with great deliberation. "'Then asketh I: "How can I love all men with equal perfection?" And the Fael answereth . . . '" Iome grunted in consternation. "Erden Geboren has got a lot of this blacked out. In part, he seems to say that we learn to love those that we serve, and he writes that 'Thou must learn to serve each man perfectly.' But he's scribbled a note in the margin, asking, 'How mayest I fixeth' . . . I think he means 'fix in people's minds,' 'that serving a man perfectly meaneth to serve his best . . . ' —I don't know that word—'in defiance of his own wants? For truly some men wanteth that which is evil, and still we are bound to provide them with only that which is good. Those men under sway of the . . . lo . . . loci fighteth goodness by rote, never guessing that the minions of the One True Master command them.'"

Gaborn's head spun as if he had been slapped. "Are you sure it says that?" he asked. "The One True Master?"

"It does!" Iome said.

"Is he talking about the reaver queen?" Gaborn asked. Binnesman had suggested that Erden Geboren had been hunting for a particular reaver, one that he called the locus, but neither the wizard nor Gaborn could guess what it might be that he sought.

"It sounds to me," Iome said, "as if he is talking about something more powerful than a mere reaver."

Gaborn grunted, wondering. The Days taught that there was only one evil: selfishness, a trait that all men have in common. That seemed a sufficient explanation for evil. After all, who among men does not desire endless wealth, or unfailing health, boundless wisdom, or unending life? Who does not crave the love and admiration of others?

Certainly, such longings are only too human, Gaborn thought, and in themselves, they are not evil. For, as Gaborn's father had once pointed out, a man who craves wealth and is thus driven to greater labors blesses both himself and those around him. The woman who wants wisdom and studies long into the night enriches all that she meets. And often Gaborn wished that he could become the kind of lord who could win the undying affection of his people, because to him it seemed an accurate measure of how well he governed.

It is only when we crave such things so much that we are willing to destroy others to get them, Gaborn told himself, that we engage in evil.

"The One True Master . . . is what Erden Geboren was hunting when he died," Gaborn mused. "He prosecuted his war with the reavers for more than a decade. Could it possibly be the same creature we are hunting for now, after so long, or is the name merely a title used by the reavers' lord?"

Gaborn suddenly had some questions for Averan. Could this One True Master have lived for seventeen hundred years? What more could she tell him about it? He looked up the tunnel. She hadn't returned.

"Averan?" Gaborn called. His words echoed through the cave.

There was no answer.

"Averan?" Iome called.

But it was pointless. Gaborn used his Earth Sight, feeling for danger. He sensed her presence, a mile up the tunnel.

"Where is she going?" Gaborn wondered, and panic swept through him, for he sensed where she was going: into danger.

ᛒ 10 ᛇ

THE CONSORT OF SHADOWS

A child must lean on faith to guide him because he lacks both the wisdom that comes from experience and the foresight that comes from a mature mind. While some promote faith as a virtue, I prefer wisdom and foresight.

—Mendellas Draken Orden

Averan had left the camp with her mind in a muddle. She felt a keen sense of worry, and it grew with every minute. The Consort of Shadows was on their trail, and she knew that he would never leave them alone.

Right now, Averan suspected that he would be waiting for them to return back up the cave. Most likely he would dig a hole somewhere along the tunnel, bury himself and hide with nothing but one or two philia above the ground.

Given its reputation as a hunter, Averan doubted that even Gaborn could evade the Consort of Shadows forever.

Their only hope was to find another reaver tunnel, one that led deep into the warrens. And the prospect seemed slim. The Waymaker had never been in this shaft, and Averan felt lost.

For a while she walked alone with her worries. They were getting deeper into the Underworld. The air felt warm and heavy. With the warmth, king's crown began to adorn the walls; it was a bright yellow fungus that slowly grew from a central infestation, then died out in the middle, leaving a golden halo that slowly spread. In the distance Averan heard a strange sound.

She stopped. It sounded almost like the throaty purr of a large cat.

There can't possibly be cats down here, can there? she wondered. But there were blindfish and crabs and other animals that lived aboveground. It seemed remotely possible that a cat might live down here, too.

There are lots of strange things in the Underworld. But none of the reavers she'd eaten had ever seen a cat.

Averan proceeded cautiously to a bend, peeked around. Several cave lizards, like bloated newts, squatted beside a small pool, and were sputtering at one another loudly, as if by doing so they could claim a prize. They sounded almost as if they were purring.

Keeper had known of these lizards. They would dig holes and live in soft mud. Their flavor was mushy and tasteless. Yet despite Keeper's vast lore, the reaver had never heard their songs.

Averan walked near them. The lizards spun their blind heads toward her, listening, and then leapt into the pool.

Just past them, the old riverbed ended. Hundreds of smaller tunnels, each as narrow as a wolf den, riddled the stone walls where crevasse crawlers, like giant millipedes, had burrowed into the soft stone. The constant tunneling of crawlers had weakened the cave, collapsing the roof.

The only way past is through the holes, Averan realized. But going into one of those narrow holes was risky. Crevasse crawlers could grow to be fifty feet long, and they were carnivores.

The crawler's tunnels could extend for miles. I'll need to find a way through, Averan thought. She imagined how proud Gaborn would be when he learned that she had scouted a path for them.

Shaking, Averan went to the nearest hole, sniffed at it. Nothing. It smelled only of the local stone and feather fern. No crevasse crawlers had been in it for ages.

At the third hole, she detected the musk odor of crawler eggs, and immediately backed away. At the twelfth hole, she finally found what she was looking for, the vague scent of *different* air blowing up through a passage. Either the hole led to a reaver tunnel or it would give her access to another cave.

Averan hesitated. She studied the burrow. She could crawl through it, but could Gaborn and the others?

Yes, she decided, with some work.

She climbed on her tiptoes and peered in. The burrow was just broad enough so that she could crawl upright without difficulty.

Which means that the crevasse crawler that dug this tunnel is big enough to swallow me whole, Averan realized. I shouldn't do this. Gaborn would be mad.

But Gaborn was waiting for his fish to cook. What if the reavers came after him? He'd be looking for an escape route fast. He was counting on her to lead the way.

Yes, I should do this, Averan told herself. By scouting the path, I could save the party valuable time.

"Averan?" Gaborn called from back up the tunnel. "Wait!" She stopped, heart pounding.

She turned and watched back up the tunnel. Soon, lights reflected from the walls, announcing Gaborn's arrival.

He came running round the bend, and saw her.

"What are you doing?" he demanded.

"Just exploring," Averan said. "There's a cave-in here. I was looking for a way past."

"It's dangerous," he said, the concern clearly etched in the lines of his face.

"It's our only way out," Averan argued.

Gaborn peered back along the trail they had come. The distant sound of reavers charging through the Underworld came as a low rumble. He licked his lips, and shook his head.

"I agree," Gaborn said. "But I sense danger ahead. Not . . . death. But I fear that if we take this course . . ."

"What?" Averan asked.

"I don't know." Gaborn said. "Perhaps I should lead the way." He studied the hole, then stepped back. "No. The Earth warns that I can't go down there, and neither can Iome."

"Then I have to go," Averan offered. "It can't be that bad. I smell fresh air. This hole should take me to the other side of the tunnel."

Gaborn peered at the burrow, as if seeking some hidden danger there, and nodded slightly. "Yes," he whispered. "That's the one."

"Let me go first, then," Averan said.

"Wait," Gaborn said, stopping her with a touch. "The fish should nearly be cooked. We'll eat, and come back later."

Averan could tell that he was stalling. Gaborn had a cornered look in his eye.

After a quick dinner, during which Gaborn kept peering into the distance, lost in thought, Averan felt ready to face the burrow. With Gaborn and Iome behind her, Averan scooted into the narrow tunnel. Dried black goo littered the floor, drippings from the crevasse crawler. It was an oil that the monster secreted to lubricate its cave. Reavers liked the taste of it.

"There's nothing in here to be worried about," Averan told Gaborn.

"Perhaps," Gaborn said, "but take nothing for granted. I sense danger here. It may be something small. Just remember that you're not a reaver. A bug that is insignificant to a reaver may be devastating to you."

"I'll be careful," Averan promised. She forged ahead. Gaborn needed her help.

She scooted through the tunnel quickly, listening for the rattling that accompanied crawlers as they slithered through the rocks.

She reached the exit after only a few hundred yards, and poked her head out.

The exit opened into a large cavern. She was back to the riverbed, but things had changed. The stone here was red, and must have been soft, for the river had fanned out. Over the ages the roof had collapsed again and again, carving a vast chamber. The ceiling soared two hundred feet above her, and stalagmites rose up from the floor like some petrified forest, while stalactites hung down like giant teeth.

On either side of the path, tanglers grew—plants with roots that criss-crossed the cavern floor. Giant bulbs lay lazily in the center of this network, like huge seed pods. But Averan knew that as soon as her foot touched one of the roots, the pods would wriggle around on their necks of creeper and try to swallow her.

She carefully lowered herself to the ground and sniffed the air. She walked forward a pace or two.

A whisper of reaver scent hung in the air. She smelled the word, "Wait." It might have been a shouted command given a hundred years ago, or it might have been something whispered much more recently. There was no way to tell.

"Gaborn," Averan called. "I'm past the cave-in. Come ahead."

She dared go no farther without Gaborn at her back.

But if reavers have been here, Averan reasoned, then this cave must lead to a major tunnel. And if I can find the tunnel, find some scent markers, I can figure out how to reach the Lair of Bones.

Cautiously, Averan peered down at the tangler, watching to make sure that her feet weren't near any thin gray roots, lest they snake around her ankle.

Ahead, stalagmite columns pierced the air on either side of her, and a natural stone bridge arched over a deep chasm. Far below, by the sound of it, water churned through a gorge.

Suddenly a single pebble dropped from above, plunking at Averan's side. She peered upward and yelped as something huge dropped like a vast spider. She tried to leap away as an enormous paw swatted down on her, cupping over her.

"Reaver!" she cried.

She wriggled between its talons, lunged toward the safety of the crawler's tunnel. A tangler vine, wakened by the presence of the reaver, whipped out and snagged her feet. She sprawled to the ground. The tangler's podlike head swiveled toward her; the pod opened, splitting into four pieces, revealing a strange, toothless mouth full of fibrous hairs. It lunged at her, but never reached her.

The reaver pulled hard at the roots, ripping the vine that held Averan's ankle, and the tangler vine went limp. She tried to lunge to her feet, but too late. The reaver's paw swept her up, crushing her in its grip.

Averan wriggled, tried to draw a breath. Even with all her endowments, her strength could not match that of a reaver. It held her in a fist of iron, and spun about. It leapt over the tanglers and bounded across the stone bridge.

"Gaborn," Averan cried. "Help!"

She craned her neck to peer backward.

Averan beat on the monster's fist, and it responded by shaking her so hard that she feared her head would snap off.

Averan caught the monster's scent. She knew this reaver. How did he find me? she wondered. How did he get here so fast?

In a daze Averan gasped for a breath as the Consort of Shadows whisked her off into darkness.

‫ఌ 11 ౿

FEYKAALD'S GIFT

Where there is hope, the loci sow fear. Where there is light, the loci spread darkness.

—excerpt on the nature of loci, from The Lore of the Netherworld, *by Erden Geboren*

Raj Ahten's army was heading north of Maygassa through the Great Salt Sea, the sun splashing down upon the shallows for as far as the eye could see. In his retinue were three flameweavers, a dozen force elephants, and another three thousand Runelords of various strength. Most of these were nobles who wore armor of thick silk in shades of white or gold, and turbans of blood red adorned with rubies the size of pigeon eggs. Though they were few in number, they were a powerful force, for these were no hireling soldiers; these were princes and kings and sheiks of the old Kingdoms of Indhopal, as rich in endowments as they were in gold. Furthermore, they were men bred to cunning and ruthlessness, for they had been born to wealth and war, and had long ago learned to keep that which they laid claim to.

The bridles and saddles of their horses and camels flashed with gems, and their swords and lances were tipped with the finest steel.

So they rode, their animals' hooves splashing. Riding across the salt sea was easier than riding around it at this time of the year. In the winter, it would deepen and become impassable by horse, but for now the water was less than a foot deep and barely covered the white salt pan of the lake. Still, it stretched for as far as the eye could see. The noonday sun beating upon distant wavelets sparkled, so that every horizon seemed to beckon with empty promises of silver. Beyond the sea, to the north, a line of mountains could be descried.

Raj Ahten rode in the lead all dressed in white silk, upon the back of a gray imperial warhorse. With each step, the horse's hooves splashed. The water quickly dried on its belly and legs, leaving a crust of white salt. Raj Ahten wore a white kaffiyeh to keep off the midday sun and to hide the scars on his ruined face.

As he rode, in the distance he spotted a single rider making his way across the sea toward them. The rider, swathed all in black, leaned forward like an old man, and rode a black force horse that nearly stumbled beneath the weight of its saddlebags.

Raj Ahten had over a thousand endowments of sight. His eyes were keener than an eagle's, for no eagle can spot the heat that radiates from a human body at night. Nor could it count the hair on a fly's legs at twenty paces. Though the rider was but a distant blur to a common man, Raj Ahten knew his name: Feykaald, his faithful servant.

"O Light of the World!" Feykaald shouted, when at last he rode near. "I bring a gift, a treasure stolen from the very camp of the Earth King!"

He reached back into his saddlebags and pulled out a handful of forcibles, like miniature branding irons, each as small as a metal spike with runes engraved into its head.

"My forcibles?" Raj Ahten brought his army to a halt with a raised hand. Feykaald nodded. Gaborn's father had taken nearly forty thousand of them from Raj Ahten's trove at Longmot. "How did you get them?"

"They were on a wagon full of treasure, in the king's retinue," Feykaald said. "He had nearly twenty thousand left! The Earth King was hunting reavers yesterday at noon, south of Mangan's Rock, doing battle with the horde that destroyed Carris, when I managed to get these."

"What did he plan to do with them?" Raj Ahten asked.

"He is taking them to the Courts of Tide, I think," Feykaald said. "There, he will use them to strengthen his army."

"And what of his troops?" Raj Ahten asked. "Who does he have in the way of champions?"

"Langley of Orwynne is his only champion, a lord who has taken hundreds of endowments. Other than that, Gaborn's army is in ruins. Your strike at the Blue Tower devastated them. His warriors are weak, broken. And to the north, Lowicker's daughter prepares to strike against him in revenge for her father, whom Gaborn slew."

Foolish young King Orden, Raj Ahten thought.

The forcibles were invaluable. If Gaborn had dared use them properly, had invested a dozen of his finest men with endowments, he could have created some champions capable of stopping Raj Ahten. As it was, only this Langley stood between Raj Ahten and Gaborn.

"You have done well, my old friend," Raj Ahten said. "The news you bear gladdens me as much as the treasure. For your reward, you shall have a hundred forcibles. Go now, take them to the facilitators at the Palace of Ghusa, in Deyazz. Tell them that in two nights, my army will ride down into Mystarria, like reapers in a field of wheat. Have them transfer endowments to me through my vectors. I must have them by nightfall."

"All four thousand?" Feykaald asked.

"Indeed," Raj Ahten said. It would take twenty facilitators working around the clock for nearly two days to transfer so many endowments.

"O Radiant One," Feykaald objected, "Ghusa is a lonely outpost. Where will your facilitators find the Dedicates?"

"Have them raid the villages nearby," Raj Ahten said. "There should be plenty of orphans about who would sell their wit or brawn for a bellyful of rice."

"As you please," Feykaald said with a bow. He looked to the east. "The forcibles will be in Deyazz by dawn." He turned his horse to the west, kicked its flanks, and was gone.

ᛒᚩ 12 ᚳᛒ

A MURDER OF CROWS

When Erden Geboren was selected by the Earth to be its king, he renamed his land Rofe-ha avan, which means "Freedom from Strife" in Alnycian, and ceded lands to a dozen of his most faithful servants. The first to be granted lands was the Wizard Sendavian, who adopted for his device the black crow, a symbol of cunning and magic, and named his realm Crowthen. The kingdom was split in two when he died, so that his twin sons might each rule over his own realm.

—from A History of Rofehavan, by Hearthmaster Friederich

Erin Connal rode throughout the day in the retinue of King Anders. The king kept the Nut Woman on her mount to his left, where squirrels darted about on her saddle and made a game of hunting for hazelnuts in the pocket of her gray robes. Celinor rode to the king's right, tall and regal, so that the three of them took up the whole of the road. Thus, Erin Connal was forced to ride behind them, with Captain Gantrell on one side, and the king's Days on the other. Fifty knights in silver surcoats with the black crow of South Crowthen rode at her back. Erin was surrounded.

The party snaked south through the mountains, with their green hills and sprawling oaks and scenic cottages. King Anders did not press his force horses for speed, for at every cottage and every village he would stop and peer at the inhabitants. After a moment, he might raise his left hand and utter solemnly, "I Choose you. I Choose you for the Earth. If ever you hear my voice giving you warning, heed me, and I will lead you to safety."

Sometimes he would look at a man or a woman, and after a long moment he would merely drop his head sadly, and pass them by.

Thus, because Anders Chose his people, the ride south went by at a creeping pace, making less than ten miles every hour.

The day was cool, and the clouds began creeping toward the south, high and sere, a gauzy veil that hid a sun that seemed to be as cold and lifeless as the blind eye of a dead man.

Erin felt that the day was somehow strange, surreal. To her it almost seemed as if the line of clouds was following them. Ahead, on the horizon, a thin line of blue sky still held a promise of fair weather. But above them and at their back, the billowing vapors followed, like a dog wearily treading at the heels of its master. It did not matter if the party rode fast or slow. The clouds matched their pace.

Heedless of the strange signs in the heavens, Celinor talked to his father. Over a period of several hours he calmly related all that had befallen him since he'd gone to Heredon. He began with his first meeting with Gaborn, then told of his and Erin's battle with the Darkling Glory, and rendered his account of their race to Carris where Gaborn found Raj Ahten's troops occupying the city while a dark sea of reavers surrounded it. He related how Gaborn had used his Earth Powers to Choose Raj Ahten and his men along with all of the citizens of Carris so that they might defend themselves from the reavers. But even after Gaborn summoned a world worm to kill the fell mage that led the reaver horde, Raj Ahten would not bend the knee to Gaborn. Instead, like a dog he sought to ambush Gaborn after the battle. Gaborn used his powers to try to kill Raj Ahten, and for that act of sacrilege, the Earth withdrew them. He told how Gaborn could now sense danger to his Chosen, but could no longer warn them how to avoid it. Instead, he had to suffer as his people were slaughtered and torn from him.

As Celinor talked, Erin held silent. She did not trust King Anders. Her thoughts were muzzy from lack of sleep, and she was so tired that the very ride today had an unreal quality. All of the trees and hills seemed to be too defined and have sharp edges, and the light that flowed from heaven was overwhelming and tinged with yellow. She could detect some cold, but she was too weary to feel pain or pressure, or even to think much.

Throughout Celinor's recitation of his journey, King Anders rode with his head bowed and eyes nearly closed, deep in thought. It was as if he wanted to see the battle, and so was conjuring the image in his mind, living it as Celinor had done. From time to time he would break in on the narrative to ask questions. Usually, the questions were benign. For example, he asked, "The spells that the fell mage cast, you mentioned that one of them wrung the water from you. How so?"

"When it hit," Celinor answered, "it made the sweat instantly rise from every pore, and made you feel as if your bladder would burst, you had to pee so bad. Once the sweat started, it didn't stop. My clothes were drenched by the count of five."

"And what about the need to pee?" King Anders asked.

"I did it where I stood, as did every other man," Celinor said. "We were in the thick of battle, and had no time for niceties. Besides, there was no stopping it."

King Anders nodded appreciatively at that, and let his son continue.

The account lasted for hours. Every question that King Anders asked, Celinor would answer easily—too easily for Erin's taste.

She was reminded again that King Anders had sent his son to see Gaborn as a spy. And though Celinor said that he mistrusted his father and was worried that the old king had gone mad, killing his own far-seer, Celinor still acted the part of a spy. He spared nothing. Erin wasn't sure if it was King Anders's own skill at eliciting responses—for during the entire conversation, his demeanor was simply that of a kindly man who wanted to understand the whole situation more clearly—or if Celinor just had a loose tongue.

Celinor told everything, down to the time that Erin chose him for her husband, in the way that horse-sisters did.

"Really?" King Anders responded to the news, looking back at Erin. "You married her? Your mother will be mortified!"

"How so?" Celinor asked.

"She would have wanted a big wedding in the South Garden—months of planning, a thousand lords in attendance."

"I'm sorry to disappoint her," Celinor said.

King Anders turned back and smiled warmly at Erin. "Oh, she won't be disappointed. Of that, I'm certain."

When Celinor had finished his tale, King Anders asked, "You say that Gaborn traveled with a great trove of forcibles. How many of them were there?"

"Five big boxes," Celinor said. "I suspect that Gaborn's father captured them from Raj Ahten when he took Longmot. Each box had to be lifted by two force soldiers, so they could not have weighed less than three or four hundred pounds. I made it to be four thousand forcibles in each box."

"Humph," King Anders snorted in surprise. "A great trove indeed." The soldiers at King Anders's back made appreciative noises at the mention of the treasure.

"Aye," Celinor said, "it was a great treasure, and there were more besides. You could hear Gaborn's facilitators chanting night and day at Castle Sylvarresta, giving endowments, though Gaborn was loath to take any for himself."

"Loath?" King Anders asked.

"He does not like the kiss of the forcible," Celinor answered. "They say he is an oath-bound lord."

"How many endowments does he have?" Anders asked. This was a deeply personal question, the kind of thing that one never discussed in public, in part out of social nicety, in part because it was so dangerous. It was the kind of thing that only an assassin would worry about.

"I haven't seen his scars," Celinor said, "but I know that he lost his endowments when Raj Ahten killed his Dedicates at the Blue Tower. Afterward, he took a few endowments at Longmot, but it could not have been many—I'd guess perhaps fifteen—three each of brawn, grace, and metabolism, four or five of stamina, maybe a bit of sight and hearing. He has not taken any glamour or Voice, that I could tell."

King Anders nodded appreciatively. "It sounds as if he is a good man. I only wish that he were a better king. Remember, Celinor, none of us who are in power can afford the luxury of such scruples."

"Some folks think that scruples are a necessity, not a luxury," Erin said. She regretted the words before they even left her mouth.

"That they are," King Anders said turning around as best he could to face her with a warm smile. "I meant no insult to Gaborn. He is doing his best to manage a dire situation. Still, I feel that if he cares for his people, he owes it to them to take more endowments. True, a few Dedicates will die here and there—a loss that we all regret. But if Gaborn's people were to lose their king . . ."

He sighed.

Erin studied his face. Anders showed no outward sign that he planned to try to kill Gaborn and take his forcibles, but Erin could not help but suspect that such schemes were spinning in his head.

King Anders gazed at Erin sidelong. "You don't trust me, do you?" Erin didn't answer. The only sound was the clopping of the horse's hooves as they pounded the dry dirt road. "Why not?"

Erin dared not tell him the truth, that she did not trust him because his own son feared that Anders was mad. He might have killed his own far-seer, and he had done all that was within his power to dispose of Gaborn.

Even now, Erin wasn't sure why King Anders was heading south to Mystarria. He said that he was going to try to stop a war that he had set in motion. But he wasn't going in haste.

Celinor filled the uncomfortable silence by blurting, "She had a dream about you. She dreamt that you were a locus."

King Anders looked as if he would deny the accusation outright, but after a moment of thought gave her a queer look. "A what?"

"She dreamt of an owl in the netherworld," Celinor went on, "that told her to beware of a creature called a locus, a, a sort of a focus for evil. It can get inside a man and wear him like a suit of armor."

King Anders raised his hand and stopped his men. He turned his horse around and studied Erin narrowly, as if trying to think of a proper response.

"You dreamt of an owl?" King Anders asked. "Tell me, was it barn owl, or more of a hoot owl?" At her back, several knights guffawed in suppressed laughter. One made hoot owl noises.

Erin felt blood rise to her face. She was outraged by the fact that Celinor had told his father her secret. She never would have spoken openly of her dream. "It was an owl of the netherworld," Erin said, "in a burrow beneath a vast, vast tree."

"And it said I was a . . . locus?"

"No," Erin said. "It didn't name you. It only warned me that a locus had come to our world, hidden in the Darkling Glory that Myrrima slew. As for whether or not it's inside you, I only know that it will be looking for a host, and you've been acting queer."

For a moment, Erin thought that the men around her might take her seriously, but King Anders said, "Dear girl, in this dream of yours, didn't any toads or mice speak up in my defense?"

At that, the troops broke into a chorus of howls, and Erin's face went hot in anger. King Anders let them laugh for a moment, then held up his hand for silence. "I'm sorry," he said. "That wasn't any way to speak to my daughter-in-law. I didn't mean to embarrass you. I'm sure that you had a most distressing dream—"

"It wasn't a dream," Erin said hotly. "It was a sending, a true sending." For an instant Anders got a pained expression. Behind him, Captain Gantrell rolled his eyes. "Raj Ahten's sorcerers summoned the Darkling Glory in Mystarria," Erin explained, "at a town called Twynhaven. They burned the whole of it, using the folks there as human sacrifices to bring about their dark magic. They opened a door to the netherworld, and let the creature through. On our way back from Carris, Celinor and I stopped at the town. We found fiery runes among the ash, still glowing as they snaked across the ground in a large circle. The door to the netherworld still looked as if it was open. So I tossed my dirk down into the runes. It fell through the fire, and disappeared. It never touched the ground. We knew then that the door was still open."

At this the men around Erin fell silent. They might laugh at her dream if it was only a dream, but each of them had heard of sendings, and as she explained the circumstances that led to her strange visitations, they began to look more apprehensive than amused.

"Later that night," Erin said, "I dreamt of an owl in the netherworld that held my dagger in its beak. He was the one who sent me the warning."

The Nut Woman spoke up. "It was a true sending, or I'm no wizard! I feel it in my bones. But take my word, it was no owl that spoke to you. It was a

Bright One, or even a Glory. Much that is seen even in a true sending takes on the nature of a dream."

Erin drew a breath in surprise. Could it be that a Bright One or a Glory spoke to her? These were creatures of legend. They had helped great folk like Erden Geboren. But she couldn't imagine that one would help her.

"Why would he appear to her as an owl?" Celinor asked.

"Because something about him is like Ael, the wise lord of the nether world," the Nut Woman said. "Perhaps it's his name, or maybe the owl is a favored pet. But mark my words, we should heed this warning!"

There was a long moment of silence. Erin looked about. She was surrounded by men wearing the crow of South Crowthen, and a thought struck her. King Anders wore the symbol of a crow, and owls hate crows. They'll kill them if they can, and a murder of crows will surround an owl in its tree at dawn and spend the day tormenting it, until they bring it down.

Is this why the messenger appears to me as an owl? Erin wondered.

King Anders said, "All right, let us imagine that it is a true sending. Why would you think that this . . . locus you called it? . . . why would you fear that it might come to me?"

"When Myrrima slew the Darkling Glory at Castle Sylvarresta," Erin said, "an elemental rose from it, a great howling tornado. It went east. Binnesman said that it was capable of great evil still."

"It could have come as far as Crowthen," King Anders said with worry in his brow, "though many leagues lie between Castle Sylvarresta and my realm. And there are several cities between us—Castles Donyeis, and Emmit, and even the fortress at Red Rock. If what you say is true, this creature could be anywhere, inside anyone. It could inhabit a knight, a merchant, a washwoman. There are tens of thousands of people in those cities."

But Erin suspected that it would not be content to merely occupy a washwoman. It had been a Darkling Glory, a lord of the netherworld. And a creature like that, bent on evil, would seek power. It wasn't just the direction that the elemental traveled. There was the matter of the far-seer that fell from Anders's watchtower, and the fact that he roused allies to fight Gaborn.

King Anders sat for a long moment, as if in deep thought. Finally, he sighed and addressed one of his men. "Sir Banners, take three men into Heredon, to the eastern provinces, and search the cities. See if you can find any sign of this locus—any murders that have been committed, any robberies." Anders fell silent for a moment and bit his lip as he thought. "Perhaps I should go myself. I could use my gift to look into the hearts of men, and rout this creature out. It wouldn't be able to hide from me, or Gaborn."

"That is, if it's in Heredon still," Celinor said. "It could be in Crowthen. Or maybe it passed us all by completely, and went off to the east somewhere."

King Anders nodded thoughtfully. "You're right. I could waste months looking for it. Besides, I have more pressing business to attend. I feel it in my bones. Our quest lies to the south, in Mystarria."

So Banners took his men north, and King Anders rode south. Erin dared speak no more of her concerns, and time after time she considered how King Anders had responded to her news of the sendings. He had been quiet and gentle in his expression, but she had seen how he huffed when he spoke, as if he struggled to control his response.

She watched him throughout the day, and noted that most of the time he wore a beneficent smile. Often he would chuckle for little reason—when the sun came out from behind a cloud, or when a squirrel leapt from the Nut Woman's horse onto his own. But he did not giggle maniacally as the wind-driven wizard from Inkarra had.

What had the owl told her—that the Asgaroth was the subtlest of all the loci?

Certainly a subtle creature would not declare itself. It would stay hidden, wreak its damage from a concealed position.

Yet something that King Anders had said bothered Erin. A locus could be anywhere, inside anyone. It could be hiding in Gantrell, or even in Celinor for all that Erin knew.

Erin wanted to know more. She wanted to question the owl of the netherworld.

She'd been fighting sleep for two days, and so in the afternoon, as the sun dropped toward nightfall, during one of the group's many stops to let the horses rest, Erin went alone to an old hickory tree by the road and leaned with her back against it.

Despite the noise and commotion around her, she soon fell asleep. She woke in the netherworld.

It was night, and Erin found herself inside the hollow of the vast tree. Lightning was flashing outside, thunder snarled through the heavens and a storm howled through the branches of the tree, shaking the limbs so that they creaked beneath the blow, and the leaves hissed and rattled.

She could hear cries in the wind, too. Wolflike howls and the blood-curdling screams of Darkling Glories. This was no natural storm blowing outside, she felt sure.

Erin peered about in the darkness, seeking for sign of the owl. By flashes of lightning, she made out the now familiar knots and roots that could be seen in the hollow of the tree. The bones of deer and small animals lay in a pile beneath the owl's roost, and in a far corner were steps leading down between some forked roots into a deeper chamber. Above the entry, a woman's face had been carved into the roots, and her hair seemed to cascade down around the tunnel's opening.

She climbed up some steps and peered outside. The limbs of the vast tree swayed, and their shadow blotted out the sky overhead. But lit by flashes of lightning, Erin could see the batlike shapes of Darkling Glories sweeping across the sky in a vast flock.

Her heart began pounding. She slipped back from the opening. She stumbled down the stairs and raced deeper into the burrow, past the face of the carved woman that was sometimes lit by lightning, deeper into the hole where no light could find her at all. The journey took her down stairs that wound deep underground. At last she reached a landing where the echo of her breathing told her that she had entered a vast stone chamber. She could see nothing.

In total darkness, she halted.

Where is the owl? she wondered.

Owl, are you here? Erin shouted wordlessly. *I need your help!*

She called thus for long minutes, but there was no answer.

She thought back to the last time that she'd seen him. She'd told him then that she didn't want to talk to him anymore. Perhaps he'd left.

Maybe he's outside, Erin thought, fighting the Darkling Glories, or fleeing from them.

Or maybe he's here, and he doesn't risk answering for fear that his enemies will hear.

Very softly, like a whisper of thought, she heard his voice. "Yes," the owl said. "Your enemies flock all around you. Can you not smell the evil? Even now, they bend near to hear your thoughts."

Erin's eyes came open. She found herself awake, heart pounding, beneath the great hickory tree. Its leaves had begun to hiss in a rising wind.

Down the hill, the knights of Crowthen watered their horses beside a small stream where clumps of lush green grass still hung above the waters.

King Anders and Celinor huddled together in conversation, and as she looked down at them, Anders gazed up at her. There was something suspicious in his stance, the way he watched her. Was he talking about her?

Celinor glanced up at her, too. Erin kept her eyes closed to slits, feigning sleep. Both men looked away.

They were talking about her, she felt certain.

Erin got up swiftly, hurried downhill. The knights had let their mounts forage, and the horses milled about, seeking lush grass. One of them passed between Erin and Celinor, and stood munching for a bit.

Erin came up behind it, heard King Anders ask, "Are you sure that she didn't take a blow to the head in the battle at Carris? All of this talk of hers—it speaks of madness."

"It was quite a row," Celinor said. "The reavers were everywhere. But I'd have noticed if she got hit in the head. More likely, this madness was with her all along."

King Anders sighed deeply. Erin hunched low and grabbed the horse by the bit, so that it would shelter her from their view. Then she stood, listening.

"You're not upset that I married her?" Celinor asked.

"Upset?" Anders asked. "Dear me, no! You could not have chosen a better match. If she is Duke Paldane's daughter, it puts you well in line for the throne of Mystarria, and perhaps even Heredon."

Celinor had not spoken of Erin's lineage earlier this morning. As a horse-sister of Fleeds, Erin's mother had chosen the best man she could to act as stud, but she'd never bandied Paldane's name about, and Erin had only told her husband that name in strictest confidence, realizing the potential that the revelation had for causing political turmoil in Mystarria.

Now Celinor had spilled his guts to his father.

What kind of man did I marry? Erin wondered. He'd gone to Heredon to spy on the Earth King and learn all that he could about Erin Connal and her suspicious lineage. He'd seemingly taken her into his confidence, telling her that he suspected that his own father was mad.

Now it seemed that nothing she told him remained secret. Could he be playing her and his father against each other?

After a long pause, King Anders spoke. "I worry about your new wife. If she keeps imagining that she has sendings, you know what we will have to do."

"Cage her?" Celinor asked.

"For her own good," Anders said, "and for the good of your daughter."

Erin's stomach did a little flip.

"My daughter?" Celinor asked.

"Yes," Anders said. "When I Chose Erin this morning, I sensed not one life but two within her. The child that she carries has a noble spirit. It will be one of the great ones. We must do everything that we can to protect them both, to make certain that the child comes to full term."

There was a long moment of silence, and suddenly Erin saw a shadow beneath the horse as her husband approached.

"Erin," he said. "You're awake?"

Celinor took the horse's reins. He stood looking at her over the beast's broad back. His eyes were cool and hard. He knew that she had been listening. She knew that if she weren't careful, they'd put her in chains right now.

"Aye, that I am," she said. "Did I just hear your father say that I've a child in me? A daughter?"

"Yes," King Anders said, approaching with a broad smile. "By midsummer you'll be a mother."

Erin thought for a moment, wondering what she should do, how she could escape. To run, to fight, would be folly. The crows surrounded her. So she chose to be discreet. She reached over the horse and stroked Celinor's chin, then kissed his cold lips.

"Looks as if I found me a grand stud," she said. "It only took one night in the barn for us." She smiled broadly, and Celinor studied her for a moment, before he smiled in return.

King Anders laughed, as if in relief. "Let's saddle up. With this rising wind, I think a storm is coming. We should try to make the castle at Raven's Gate before it gets too dark."

Raven's Gate was a vast and ancient fortress that marked South Crowthen's border. Right now, it was bristling with tens of thousands of Anders's soldiers, nearly the whole of his armies. And Erin recalled something her mother had once said about the fortress. "Deep have they delved the dungeons at Raven's Gate, and none who enter ever escape."

BOOK 12

DAY 5 IN THE MONTH OF LEAVES

THE DARKNESS DEEPENS

ಬ 13 ೞ

THE MASTER

No man can hope to lead others until he first masters himself.

—Mendellas Draken Orden

Gaborn studied the tangler as whipcords of vine lashed out and giant pods snapped vainly at the air. Even with all of his endowments, he dared not try to pass it yet. He saw where the tangler had caught Averan's foot, the vines clutching her leather boot. Closer to hand, Averan had dropped her staff. Her cries still seemed to ring in the air, yet he saw no other sign of her.

"Up there," Iome said at his back, "is where the reaver must have hidden, waiting for her. Are you sure that she's still alive?"

"She's alive," Gaborn said, sensing deep inside himself. "But the reaver is getting away fast."

"Even with all her endowments," Iome said, as if in resignation, "she couldn't get escape. She has endowments of scent from more than a dozen dogs. She's learned the ways of reavers, learned their tongue. And one still got her. What hope do we have?"

"Reavers hide their scent," Gaborn said in Averan's defense. "I can't smell that a reaver has been here at all. There's nothing we could have done to avoid it."

"Where do you think its taking her?" Iome asked.

Gaborn shook his head. "I . . . couldn't guess." He didn't sense imminent death in store for her. So her captor didn't intend to eat her now. The tangler was going quiet.

Using his reaver dart, Gaborn ran forward a couple of paces and vaulted over the beast. He stalked forward a few paces, stood on the land bridge, gazing down into the chasm. His opal pin would not let him see the bottom, though he could hear a river swirling beneath him. Farther above, he could still hear the sounds of reavers rushing through their tunnel, a constant thunder.

Averan was alive for the moment, but he sensed death advancing toward her. *The reaver is taking her home for some reason,* Gaborn decided.

He felt lost. He'd brought Binnesman and Averan down into this damned hole to guide him, and now he was stripped of both their counsels.

"Is it possible," Iome asked hopefully, "that the reaver isn't taking her anywhere? Averan is a wizardess. She summoned the Waymaker yesterday, and held it for hours. Maybe she's controlling it."

"No, I don't think she's in control," Gaborn said. "The Waymaker was almost dead from fatigue, and she had her staff to help her. If she were controlling this monster, I think she'd bring it back to us. I only know that she's alive for now, and she is the only one who can lead us. We have to find her."

Gaborn held up his light, revealing the path ahead. The land bridge spanned perhaps forty yards, and there he could see the beginnings of a reaver tunnel. The walls were sealed with mucilage, and bonelike pillars supported the roof. Gaborn ventured, "I can track Averan. Her scent is everywhere."

He stood for a moment, uncertain.

"What's wrong?" Iome asked.

"I think we are in for a long chase, with a fight at the end of it," Gaborn said. He turned back to Iome. She stood on the far side of the tangler vine. "Use Averan's staff to vault over," he said.

Iome took half a minute to build up her courage, then ran a step, using a rock as a stair, and leapt. With all of her endowments, her jump carried her fifteen feet in the air, and eighty feet in distance.

And then they were off. They did not walk or even jog. Gaborn sprinted, and Iome hurried after him.

He found that his recent meal refreshed him like a feast, invigorating both mind and spirit. Worry over Averan weighed on him, but with the nourishment, it seemed as if the fog had lifted a bit.

So they ran. Scrambling through the reaver tunnel wasn't easy. Gaborn found that as he sped, odd things happened to his body. His own sense of movement told him that he was going no faster than normal, but he could not round a sharp corner with ease, since his forward motion tended to throw him off course. Thus, he had to lean into his turns at what seemed an unnatural angle. In some ways it was much like riding a force horse.

He also had to pay attention to his footing on the rocky, uneven trail. There was the constant hazard of tripping or twisting an ankle on stone, though plants grew over the path. Wormgrass and molds vied for control of the rocky walls. Rootlike bushes hung from the roof, yellow and white ten-

drils often cascading down like frozen waterfalls. Sometimes they formed curtains, barring the way, and only the fact that a huge reaver had passed
through, ripping the foliage down, had cleared the path at all. In many
places, seepage dampened the cave. Black hairlike moss grew beside the
water, with golden drops of sap in it, while rubbery plants sprouted tiny
brown pods the size of cherries. Gaborn found both to be particularly haz-
ardous. The moss was slippery, while the pods could roll beneath his feet.

Added to these difficulties was the lack of light. The coruscating glow
from their opals seemed bright when one stood still. But when he ran fifty
miles per hour, Gaborn needed time to choose where to put his feet, to decide
whether to speed up or slow down or to leap over a bit of tangle root or pick
his way through it. Most important, he had to remain alert for new dangers.

More than once he found himself running headlong into a lumbering
crevasse crawler or giant blind-crab, and would have to dodge around it.

Thus, even with endowments of sight, he squinted into the gloom,
watching at the limit of vision.

Once, he sensed that he was winning the race, that Averan was only a
mile or so ahead. But he and Iome rounded a corner and found their path
blocked by a huge stone.

The reavers had constructed a door. The door seemed to have been
carved from the rock itself, for it rested on a stone hinge that hung from the
ceiling. The panel appeared to be three feet through the center. By pushing
at the bottom, Gaborn discovered that the door wouldn't budge.

It had been locked.

He beat against it in frustration, and then he and Iome went to work.
Using shards of rock from nearby, they hammered and chiseled through the
bottom of the door, a process that took what seemed like hours.

Gaborn felt weary by the time they started on the trail again, and
Averan had been carried far, far away.

There was no sun or moon to track the turning of the earth. There was
only darkness fleeing from the light of their opals, returning to reclaim all
they left behind as they raced along.

The trail wound, tunneling through veins of soft rock, twisting through
boulders, sometimes taking odd turns for reasons that only reavers would
understand.

But always the trail sloped down.

Gaborn measured time by the pounding of his feet, by the gasping of his
breath, by the waves of sweat that trickled down his cheeks. The heat and
humidity began to soar as the miles receded.

Sometimes they reached side tunnels or shafts that rose like chimneys.
Each time they did, Gaborn would stop and sniff at every passage, checking
for Averan's scent.

They spoke little. Gaborn found himself alone with his thoughts, and he found himself wondering at the book that Iome carried in her pack: Erden Geboren's tome.

Had he really been searching for the One True Master? And if so, what was it?

Two days ago when Averan first mentioned the creature, Binnesman had seemed confused. He'd asked, "Are you sure that it is a reaver?"

Averan had been sure. But now Gaborn wondered. What exactly was a locus? He felt that his Earth Sight was failing him. Binnesman had said that it was because he was still asking the wrong questions. Perhaps once Gaborn understood his enemy better, he'd know how to fight it.

He felt sure that the book would tell more, but Iome couldn't read and run at the same time.

Indeed, they reached a tunnel that slanted steeply down, and found that the tickle fern was gone, trampled. The ground lay in waste. Reavers frequented this trail.

A second door confronted them.

Gaborn called a halt. "I'll hammer away at the door. You should get some food. If you can spare a moment, I'd like you to read to me."

He reached into his pack, pulled out some apples and a flask of water. He took a bite of apple, picked up the nearest stone, and began hammering at the door.

Iome munched her own apple as she sat down to read. Alnycian was not an easy language, Gaborn knew. It had been dead for hundreds of years, and most scholars spoke the most recent variety, but Erden Geboren had written back when the tongue was still vibrant. Thus, his spellings, word choice, and grammar would all lie outside the norm.

Iome opened the book, skimmed through.

"Tell me as soon as you find anything interesting," Gaborn said.

Still huffing from the long run, Iome said, "Erden Geboren begins by summing up his early life in a few sentences. He was a swineherd in the Hills of Tomb, until the Earth Spirit called him. Then he tells how he met the Wizard Sendavian, who guided him and Daylan Slaughter—that must have been Daylan's name before he won the Black Hammer—upon 'paths of air and green flame' to the netherworld."

This was all the stuff of legend. Iome didn't bother to go into detail. Then she said, "But once he gets to the netherworld, he suddenly changes the style of his book. He begins inserting subtitles, breaking it into chapters."

"See if you can find anything about the locus," Gaborn suggested.

Iome skimmed down the headings silently for a minute, flipping a dozen pages of text, until she said, "Here's something: 'Upon Meeting a Locus.' I'll try to translate it into a more modern style."

" 'The locus was an most hideous creature. The Bright Ones kept it locked within a cage, hidden in a green glade in a narrow box canyon. It was a difficult journey to reach it, and the monster beat its wings against its prison bars wildly as we approached. The wings had black feathers and a span of perhaps thirty feet. The creature itself had a form somewhat like a man's, with stubby legs and long arms that ended in cruel talons. But there was a blackness about the beast that defied the eye. Squint as I might, I could not pierce the depths of its cage. It was as if the monster absorbed the light around it, or perhaps bent it, wearing it like a black robe. Air circled the beast, swirling about, carrying with it the scent of rot. Rather than seeing the creature clearly, I got only a vague impression of sharp fangs, cruel talons, and glaring eyes.' "

Iome paused, shaken.

Gaborn said, "Erden Geboren is describing the Darkling Glory, isn't he?"

Even mentioning the monster made Iome shiver. "Perhaps," Iome said. "Or maybe we're mistaken. Maybe these aren't the same creatures." She read on.

" 'The bars to its cage were of blackened iron. Glowing violet runes encircled the base of it, and a roof covered the crown.

" 'As I drew near, I felt entranced by the creature. I peered hard to view it, drawing closer and closer. Yet the nearer I got, the more the darkness about it thickened, obscuring my view.

" 'It was not until I was nearly upon it that I became dimly aware that the Bright Ones were speaking to me: nay, shouting to me. But I could not hear them. Their voices were dull, as if they called from miles and miles away. Instead, all I could hear was the creature, urging me, "Come! Come to me."

" 'I saw a door on the cage. I could see no . . . ' " Iome paused. "I think the word must be 'lock.' " She began again. " 'It looked as if the door would sway open with a touch of the finger, yet the dark servant could not open it.

" 'As I drew near, the creature made no move. Its wings quit beating so wildly against the cage, and it regarded me almost as if it were made of stone.

" ' "Open the door," I could hear it whisper. "Open it." Distantly I could hear the Bright Ones shouting, but their words.' "—Iome struggled to make sense of the statement by context—" 'had no intelligence,' it says. But I think he means, 'conveyed no understanding.'

" 'I did not intend to open the door. I only thought to experiment, to touch the gate.

" 'I was about to do so when Daylan grabbed me from behind. He shouted in my ear, but I could make no sense of his words.

" 'He pulled me back from the cage and threw me on the ground, then stood over me gibbering.

" 'The locus raged at me with a sound of thunder, and it seemed that all of the heavens roared with it. "I see you, King of the Shadow World! I shall sift your world as wheat, and cast off the chaff thereof." I could feel the hatred of the servant, could smell it in the air, as palpable as the stink of dead men.

"'At some length, I was able to make out the words of Daylan. "Didn't you hear us?" Daylan cried. "Can't you hear me?" His face was red with worry, and tears of'—I think the word must be 'frustration'—'filled his eyes.

"'"I heard you not," said I, coming to my senses.

"'Then the voice of the Fael did pierce me, that I heard it clearly. "Beware Asgaroth. He is a most subtle child of the mother of all loci, the One True Master of Evil."'"

Gaborn yelped as he slammed a rock against his hand. The green light of his opal pin shone down as he turned toward Iome. But it was not the pain of the wound that had made him cry out.

"The One True Master—" he said, "I thought she was the One True Master of All Reavers, or something like that, not . . ."

"Of Evil," Iome offered.

Gaborn felt as if his head were spinning. The creature he was going to face was an enemy that even the Bright Ones and Glories feared. No wonder they had come to fight beside Erden Geboren. Iome continued to read.

"'Many words did the Fael speak unto me, words that were understood in the heart. I realized that if I had touched that door, tried to open it, strength would have failed me. The door was bound with runes so powerful that a common man like me could not have broken it. Yet if I had tried, I would have succeeded in opening another door: a door into my heart.

"'"Asgaroth could have filled you," the Fael told me. "Its evil desires could have become your desires. It could have filled you, as blackness fills the hollows of the earth."

"'An unnamable fear seized me. So shaken was I that I could not stand.

"'"The locus is not the creature that you see before you," the Fael said. "The Darkling Glory can age and die, but the shadow hiding within it is immortal. When the Darkling Glory dies, its essence will move on, seeking a new host. Thus we have sought to imprison Asgaroth, rather than destroy him. Many Glories were destroyed trying to bring him here. A thousand times a thousand shadow worlds Asgaroth has helped to seize."'" Iome faltered for a moment, and said, "Erden Geboren doesn't like the word 'seize.' He has crossed it out once, suggested 'destroy' or 'sway' or 'capture.'" She read on, "'"But so long as we hold him, he can do little harm."'"

Iome closed the book, and sat for a moment. Sweat poured down her face, and her clothes clung to her like rags. "Do you think that Raj Ahten's sorcerer is the one who set the Darkling Glory free?"

Gaborn wiped some sweat from his own brow with his sleeve. The running, the growing heat, had left him feeling oily and gritty. He wished for a bath. He had seen the sorcerer enter the fiery gate at Twynhaven, and seen him come back out only moments later. Had the sorcerer had time to break into the cage? Or had he only met the monster there, after some accomplice freed him on the other side?

Asgaroth was its name. Could the monster that Erden Geboren described two thousand years ago be the one that had stalked Iome at Castle Sylvarresta only a week past?

He felt sure that it was. It had come in a cloud of darkness and swirling wind, sucking all light from the sky, wrapping night around it as if it were a robe. Thunder had boomed at its approach, while lightning snarled. It had spoken "as if with a sound of thunder."

"Well," Gaborn said. "It seems as if you have found yourself a worthy adversary."

"I didn't pick a fight," Iome said. "It came hunting for me."

Gaborn grinned, hoping to allay her concerns.

"Wait," she whispered. "It didn't come hunting for me. It came for our son, the child that I carry in my womb."

"Why?" Gaborn asked. A fear struck him, and a certainty. The Darkling Glory had come for his son, and as Gaborn stretched out his senses, he felt danger stalking the child.

"It isn't just killing a child that the Darkling Glory enjoys," Iome said as if to herself. "The clubfooted boy was with me, and the Darkling Glory didn't seek *his* life. Wait—" Iome's face fell and she clutched her womb, then let out a gasp. "Wait!"

"What is it?" Gaborn asked.

"The Darkling Glory—" she said. "Or the locus within it, it didn't want to *kill* the child. It merely asked for him. It demanded him."

"What do you mean?" Gaborn asked.

"I think it wanted to possess the babe," Iome said, "as a hiding place!"

"Of course," Gaborn said. "The Darkling Glory has fled the netherworld. It might even be worried that its enemies will come looking for it. So it needs a place to hide. And what better place than in a mother's womb?"

By voicing Iome's concerns, perhaps Gaborn gave them weight and heft. Iome began to sob. She covered her womb protectively with Erden Geboren's manuscript.

"I, too, worry about where it has gone," Gaborn said. "But with my Earth Sight I can see the child's spirit. There is no darkness in you. The child in you is like any other, alive, but as yet unformed. I sense no malice, no evil intent."

Iome shook with fear as Gaborn held her. She peered into the darkness, her eyes unfocused.

Gaborn asked Iome, "How long will it take you to translate the rest of Erden Geboren's book?"

"I don't know," Iome said. "It's slow going. I could do it in a week, maybe."

"I don't need it all," Gaborn said. "Just . . . tell me everything he says about the loci and the One True Master."

Gaborn drained his flagon. It was water that they had taken from the pools at Abyss Gate, and it tasted strongly of minerals. He drank deeply, then sat for a moment. There was absolute silence, a silence so deep that it seemed to penetrate the bones. The distant pounding of reaver's feet was gone. He had heard it when they looked over the spot where Averan was captured. When had it gone silent?

Aboveground it never grew this quiet. There was always a jay squawking, or the rush of wind through trees, or the bawl of sheep in a distant meadow. Here, there was nothing.

It overwhelmed him. It was as if the earth loomed above him, a sky of stone and iron, waiting to fall. He could smell it all around, the mineral tang.

It feels like a thunderstorm, Gaborn thought. That was the closest thing to it, like on a summer evening when the air grew heavy and the clouds slogged over the horizon, as black as slate. All of the animals would fall perfectly silent and hide. Even the flies quit buzzing.

That's how quiet it was now, only deeper. It penetrated the skin and made the hair prickle nervously on the back of his arms. Ahead and behind there was only night so deep that he had never felt the like of it.

We're in a wilderness, Gaborn realized, far, far from any human habitation.

He reached out with his Earth senses, then sighed heavily, looked at Iome. "Averan keeps moving. I suspect that we've run a hundred miles and we could have gone no faster, but my Earth Senses warn that Averan is far ahead." He paused, as if considering what to say next. "There are reavers between us and her, I think. I sense danger." He did not tell her how great the danger was. He couldn't quite express it. It was as if there was a wall between them and Averan, a wall of death. Gaborn might make it, but could Iome?

Iome shook her head in near defeat.

Gaborn beat at the door for a bit, knocking off flakes now and then. When he grew fatigued, Gaborn let Iome work as he mended his shoe and put a new leather grip around Erden Geboren's ancient reaver dart.

After only a few turns at the wall, Iome broke through. She sighed and nodded down the tunnel. "They're up there waiting for us, aren't they—the reavers? I can see it in your face."

"Aye," Gaborn said.

"Well then," Iome said, climbing to her feet with the help of Averan's staff of black poisonwood. "Let's go make trouble."

࿇ 14 ࿐

THE LIGHT-BRINGER

After seventeen years of prosecuting this war underground, one might think that my men would most crave fresh air, clean water, good food, or the company of a woman. But no, we are beginning to learn how desperately a man can crave light.

—Fallion the Just, Reporting on the Toth War

The Consort of Shadows raced through the Underworld, its feet thundering over stone. Averan floated in and out of consciousness, struggling for breath.

She opened her eyes. The tunnels were a blur. The mucilage seals had begun to erode. Shadows of twisted stalagmites, like deformed giants, lumbered forward in the small light thrown by her opal, then were swallowed again by the darkness.

The reaver grasped her firmly to make sure that she didn't escape, much as Averan had held lizards and frogs as a child. The more she had fought, the harder the monster gripped her.

So she faded back to sleep until she jolted awake. The Consort of Shadows had just leapt a fifty-foot cliff and was racing through a maze of stalagmites. As he did, he cupped Averan close to his chest.

He doesn't want to kill me, she realized. He's trying to keep me alive. The best thing I can do is to go limp.

She wasn't sure that he was being tender enough to keep her alive. The skin of his massive paw was as thick as a bolster and as tough as scale mail. His three fingers were so wide that they enveloped Averan's body from shoulder to heel. With every step he took, the monster dealt out a jolt. Averan felt sure that she was covered with bruises.

Powerless before the beast, Averan dazedly watched the scenery go by. She had no idea how long the Consort of Shadows had been carrying her, but he ran at a tremendous speed.

A fold of reaver's skin was pushing against Averan's ribs. She wasn't sure if she dared try to move, lest the monster grasp her tighter.

She could think of only one thing to do. She cleared her mind, as Binnesman had taught her, and imagined the Consort of Shadows. She envisioned his great, spade-shaped head, as she'd seen it when he rose black from the waters, and she imagined how his philia quivered as he studied his prey. She imagined the feel of his feet as they struck the stone of the tunnel floor, and the sense of purpose he felt as he raced on and on. Soon her mind did a little flip, and she saw, the world through the "eyes" of the reaver.

He registered the force electric in the rocks around him as ghostly blue images, almost as if they were a fog. Plants and animals along the path were much brighter. Blind-crabs scurried from his path, blazing like stars in his field of view.

The path ahead was marked with old reaver scent. Even if it hadn't been, the Consort of Shadows knew it well. He had hunted in the barrens most of his life.

"Where are you taking me?" Averan asked.

The Consort of Shadows jolted to a halt. He held Averan up to study her, and his philia waved.

"Are you speaking?" the reaver asked. She could feel wariness in the monster, "Or am I worm dreaming?"

"Yes, I can speak," Averan said.

She felt a fleeting question. "Is this how humans talk to one another?"

"No," Averan said. "I am a wizardess, a protector of the Earth. I can speak to your mind. But most people don't talk like this."

A memory came to the Consort of Shadows. There had been an Earth Warden among the reavers. The Consort's ancestor had murdered the wizard in a grim battle, and the Consort had later eaten the ancestor's brain.

"Your grandfather killed an Earth Warden!" Averan said. "I see it in your mind."

"The One True Master ordered his death."

Averan saw snatches of the battle unfold in the memory of the Consort of Shadows. The Consort's grandfather had crept up behind the wizard, leapt on him and ripped off his forelegs. Once the Earth Warden was helpless, his attacker brutally pried apart the three bone-plates on the wizard's head while he still lived, to torture him until the very last moment, when he scooped out the wizard's brains. Now the Consort of Shadows held some of the wizard's memories.

"That's horrible," Averan said.

"Proud was my ancestor to have done this deed," the Consort of Shadows said.

He boasted, but Averan saw that the monster tried to hide more uncomfortable feelings. The memories of an Earth Warden lived inside him.

True, the Consort of Shadows hungered for human flesh. But he also sensed something that other reavers could not. Men were creatures of the Earth, too, beloved by their Creator. They were as valued by the Earth as reavers and blind-crabs, as world worms and tickle fern.

"Where are you taking me?" Averan asked once again.

"A place for humans," the Consort of Shadows replied. A scent came into his mind, the stench of unwashed people huddled in a dark cavern, the air redolent with the stink of urine and feces. Keeper had also known of the place. It was a cell where the One True Master experimented on people, testing her new spells. Dread knotted Averan's stomach.

"Your master will kill me there," Averan said.

"In time," the Consort of Shadows agreed.

"Please," Averan begged, "let me go. You know the power of the Earth Spirit. You know that I mean you no harm."

I must not speak of this human, the Consort of Shadows thought. Others will think I am worm dreaming.

Abruptly, Averan felt as if a gate slammed shut between her and the Consort of Shadows. Like the thief who had stolen her horse at Feldonshire, he pulled back from her scrutiny, broke their tenuous connection.

The huge reaver raced through the Underworld, the tunnel a grotesque blur. He clutched Averan so tightly, that she could hardly draw a breath. She tried to summon the attention of her captor, to beg him not to squeeze so tightly, but without her staff, she was almost powerless.

Averan dreamt of fire—slow-roasting coals that reddened the bottom of a campfire, and of tongues of flame as scarlet as those of the flame lizards of Djeban that snapped out and licked her skin till it was raw.

When she woke, as she often did while in the grasp of the Consort of Shadows, she would find herself racing along at a dizzying pace, plunging into the black depths of the Underworld through garish ribbed tunnels, past steaming pools that roared and thundered, past mud pots and the bones of strange Underworld creatures.

She woke once, after what seemed like days, gasping for breath, and found that the Consort of Shadows had stopped to speak with some other reavers. It was a war party of twenty-seven. They were led by a grizzled old veteran named Blood Stalker.

"Hide," Consort of Shadows warned in a spray of scent. "Set an ambush.

Assassins are coming from above, to hunt the One True Master. I have captured one of them, but more follow."

"I shall not hide," Blood Stalker said, in odors that hissed from his anus. "The One True Master has set runes of power upon us. I am strong now, stronger than you."

Averan did not slip into her captor's mind to learn what he was thinking. She already knew. Blood Stalker was a proud warrior, and even now he raised his tail higher than the Consort of Shadow's tail, as a sign that he hoped to win the right to breed. His philia were waving excitedly, and all of his muscles had tensed.

The Consort of Shadows had long held such a reputation for ferocity that none dared challenge him. Now Blood Stalker imagined that he was equal to the contest.

"You may be strong," Consort of Shadows said, "but so are the assassins that follow. Kill them and prove yourself worthy to challenge me."

His huge paws tightened involuntarily upon Averan, as he prepared for battle. And as they tightened, Averan's breathing was cut off. She struggled to keep from suffocating until she fainted.

When next she woke, it seemed to be hours later. The Consort of Shadows was feeding. He had torn the back off an enormous blind-crab, called a "mugger," and he used his tongue to scoop out the crab's entrails. Averan lay on her belly on the floor for a moment, seemingly forgotten.

Dazed, she wandered in a strange world, half in and half out of dream. She imagined that she roamed an empty plain, gray and without form. The ground was flat and featureless, with only cracked clay beneath her feet, as if from an interminable drought.

And in the dream she raised her staff, and the ground began to tremble. Rocks and clay rose up in a circle all around her, forming a ridge about a hundred yards across that became a strange and magnificent rune. And from those rocks and ridges, animals began to take shape. The gray clay at her feet shaped itself into a tiny stag only two feet long. The stag lay upon its side, mouth open, head tilted backward. At first the form was vague and general, a lumpy creature that a child might have wrought. But in moments the image became more and more refined, as if worked by the hands of an invisible sculptor. Suddenly, when the stag seemed perfect to Averan, it began to move, kicking about as if it were a babe, seeking to stand upon its own feet for the first time. It struggled to its knees, then climbed up, and suddenly the gray figure blossomed into color, a tawny red at the back, white at the throat, with living eyes that glinted in the sunlight. The creature bounded away, past Averan's feet.

And as suddenly as the stag had formed, she turned her gaze and saw that it was happening everywhere across the vast rune. Tiny boars were taking shape, squealing with delight. Elephants trumpeted in a far corner, and snakes wriggled past her foot. A flock of tiny doves, smaller than moths, fluttered before her view, as if rising into the mountains. Everywhere she began to discern hopping frogs and wriggling fishes, butterflies in bright clouds, reavers and whales.

Filled with wonder, Averan strolled along the gray earth, studying the rune, seeking ways to improve it.

Ah, if I could only make such a rune, she thought.

Then she became aware of her surroundings once again. She opened her eyes, fumbling for her staff. But it was gone, and the Consort of Shadows was feeding.

Averan considered making a run for it.

She squinted furtively. Fortunately, her white opal ring still glowed, and by its light she could see that the reaver had brought her far down into the Underworld. The tunnel that she was in now had changed. The stifling heat and high humidity made the air muggy, and because of the heat and moisture, hairlike plants as gray and thick as a wolf's pelt covered the tunnel floor. Wormgrass and feather fern battled for control of the walls, and rootlike plants dangled from the tunnel roof. The broken shells of blind-crabs and the round shapes of elephant snails littered the floor. More important, not far ahead, some crystalline rods grew near the wall and blocked the floor of an adjoining cavern. Each rod was as clear as quartz, and many reached as much as eight or nine feet in height. Each hollow rod came to a jagged point. Averan recognized them from reaver memories: the homes of flesh eaters.

Each tube was a cocoon, spun by a pregnant creature that looked like a crab stretched impossibly thin. Once the cocoon was complete, the crab crawled inside to die. As the eggs inside her hatched, the young devoured their way out of her womb, consuming her. These young, each not much larger than a flea, made the flesh-eater tube their lair.

They crawled to the lip of the tube and waited for something to brush against it—a reaver, a blind-crab, or mordant, it didn't matter. Any animal would do.

Then the flesh eaters would burrow into their victims. They would be carried through the bloodstream, where they wreaked damage on its organs.

Reavers feared the tubes of flesh eaters. If such tubes began to grow in one of their tunnels, they would sometimes seal off the crawlway and dig a new route.

Thus, the tunnel that Averan was in now was dangerous. The number of plants dangling from the ceiling and growing from the floor showed that common reavers had abandoned it. But the Consort of Shadows often trod dangerous paths.

I could run in among the flesh eater tubes and hide, Averan thought. As long as I don't get near the tip of the tubes, the bugs won't get me.

But she didn't dare. Not with the Consort of Shadows watching her. Instead, she used her summoning powers, concentrated upon the Consort of Shadows to learn what he was thinking, to feel what he was feeling.

"I should eat the human," Consort of Shadows thought. "No one would deny me the pleasure. She is small and worthless."

Yet another voice whispered inside him, as if it were the voice of an intruder. "No creature that the Earth has formed is worthless, especially not this one. She is not just its creation, she is its advocate."

"This is only worm dreaming," he told himself.

Consort of Shadows grabbed Averan violently, whisked her up against his chest, and began to run, scraping his hide against the far wall of the crawlway in order to avoid the flesh-eater tubes.

I've lost my chance to escape, Averan thought desperately.

She knew what was happening to the Consort of Shadows. Just as she had eaten the brains of reavers and thought at first that she would go mad, the Consort of Shadows had done the same. His grandfather had eaten the brain of an Earth Warden, and ever since, almost as if in punishment, the Earth Warden's thoughts had haunted those who partook of its brains.

Averan lay limp in the Consort's huge paw, rejoicing in the fact that he was holding her gingerly, and she feigned sleep. She tried to keep a loose contact with his mind, to learn what she could. But the Consort of Shadows seemed to run almost as if in a trance. He did not speak, did not think. His mind had become as eerie and as quiet as a tomb.

She hoped that he'd put her down again soon, give her a chance to escape.

The Consort of Shadows stopped for a moment and opened a stone door that led into a broader corridor. This tunnel was perhaps sixty feet wide, and the floor was rutted from use by reavers. He closed the door behind him, as he had all of the others. Her captor passed some scent markers, and Averan suddenly realized where she was: nearing the Lair of Bones. She was already inside the Unbounded Warren.

Time and again now she saw tunnels branch off, other reavers ambling about. She saw some howlers—blotchy yellow creatures like enormous spiders—coming out of one tunnel, dragging the squirming carcass of an eighty-foot worm behind them. She saw glue mums spitting out mucilage as they shored up a damaged wall. She saw young reavers, no more than ten feet tall, trundling behind a matron.

What she did not see were blade-bearers or sorceresses, the guardians of the lair.

They had all gone to war.

Suddenly the Consort of Shadows turned at a side tunnel. Averan spotted a pair of blade-bearers standing at guard. Both of them were enormous, with glowing runes branded into their heads and arms.

Inside the chamber beyond, Averan could smell the stench of human bodies, filthy and diseased.

"Take care with this one," the Consort of Shadows told the guards.

"It shall not escape," the guards said.

The Consort of Shadows trundled deeper into the tunnel, and Averan, with her endowments of scent from more than a dozen dogs, found the reek of filthy humans to be more unbearable with each passing step. She smelled the odor of sour sweat mingled with piles of feces and pools of urine, and the rot of infected flesh, fish guts, and unburied dead.

For the first time in hours, the Consort of Shadows seemed to come out of his reverie. The monster's stomach churned in disgust at the scent.

He hates it in here, Averan realized. All of the reavers hate being here. The stink is too much for them.

The Consort of Shadows reached the middle of the large chamber and tossed Averan to the floor. Averan heard a woman cry out from a far corner, half in fear, half in wonder, and then the Consort of Shadows turned and was gone.

Averan lay in a heap for a moment, peering around. The cavern was not huge. The mucilage on the walls was eroding away, so that bare rock showed in some places. Stalactites hung from the roof, and the floor was uneven. The scent of sulfur water came from a nearby pool.

In the far corners of the room, people huddled. They were mere humps on the floor, their clothes so grimy that they had taken on the hues of the dirt. Only their eyes could be seen through masks of grime, eyes wide with wonder. Gradually, Averan began to make out more features: here a face so pale it looked like an Inkarran boy, there the leathery brown of an Indhopalese woman.

The more Averan peered about, the more she realized that all of the humps around her were people. Sick people, starving people, wounded people, but alive.

"Light!" an old man cried. "Wondrous light!"

And someone echoed his sentiment in Indhopalese, "Azir! Azir famata!"

The humps began to move, and people rushed toward her on hands and knees. Averan realized that, deprived of light, most of them had probably been scurrying about like this for weeks or months.

"Who are you, Light-Bringer?" a woman called, pleading. "Where do you hail from?"

"Averan. My name is Averan. I was the king's skyrider at Keep Haberd."

"Keep Haberd?" a man asked, a mere skeleton. "I am from Keep Haberd. Can you tell me how it fares?"

Averan didn't dare tell him that the reavers had killed everyone. The fellow scuttled toward her, along with the others, until they pressed about her, their stinking flesh overwhelming, their eyes wide with wonder at sight of her glowing ring. The skeletal fellow reached up to paw it, stroke it gingerly. Soon twenty dirty folk surrounded her, fawning.

"See how it shines!" a woman cried, reaching to stroke Averan's ring, but not daring to, "like a star fallen from heaven."

"Nay, no star was ever so filled with luster," another insisted.

"What year is it?" a man demanded, as if he were some captain among the king's guard.

"Year one of the reign of Gaborn Val Orden in Mystarria," Averan answered, "who followed on the heels of his father, Mendellas Draken Orden, who died in the twenty-second year of his reign."

"Five years," an elderly man said in a thick Indhopalese accent. "Five years since last I saw light."

"Ten for me," a sickly fellow croaked.

For a moment, there was silence, and the prisoners in this dark place looked about at one another.

"Gavin, where are you?" a young woman asked.

"Here," a man said from a few feet away.

The two of them stopped and gazed at each other in wonder, with love shining in their eyes. Everyone fell silent. The woman began to weep.

These folks have never seen each other before, Averan realized. How would it be to live here in darkness for years, never having seen the face of a friend?

The lost souls wore rags, if they wore anything at all, and several of them seemed to have had more than one broken bone or game leg. The reavers that imprisoned them had not been kind.

Near a far wall lay a pile of bones, both fish and human. Beyond that, Averan could see no sign of food. She asked, "How—how do you live down here?"

"We don't live," the Indhopalese man answered. "We just die as slowly as we can."

ஐ 15 ☙

FORMS OF WAR

Every group of people develops many words for those things that concern them most. In Internook, men have seven words for ice. In Indhopalese, there are six different words for starvation. In Inkarra, there are eighty-two words for war.

—*Hearthmaster Highham, from the Room of Arms,*
On the Eighty-two Forms of War

The Inkarrans held Sir Borenson and Myrrima prisoner at the mountain fortress until it was nearly dark. The Inkarrans took their weapons and placed both of them in manacles. The fortress seemed to hold about twenty soldiers, none of whom wanted to go outside during daylight, where the glare on the white snow all but blinded them. So the westering sun was barely riding above the clouds as they marched into Inkarra.

They could not ride horses. Inkarrans rarely rode them at all, and certainly wouldn't be able to do so tonight. The trail plunged down the mountain slopes through thickets and rock, then dove into the mists and trees. The combination of darkness, shadow, and fog would make riding impossible. So Borenson's fine horses were left at the fortress.

Still, all of the party had endowments of metabolism. Shackled at the wrists, Borenson and Myrrima nearly raced downhill in the twilight, making good use of the last of the sun's rays.

The party made good time in spite of the suddenly rather unbearable mixture of heat and humidity. In the late afternoon, the mists rising up the forested slopes felt as warm as a gentle steam.

By nightfall they were heading down steep mountain roads. The warmer climate here gave rise to vastly different flora and fauna than what was found north of the mountains. There were pines, but they were taller than any trees that Borenson had ever seen, and their bark was a dark red instead of gray. There were birds here, too, but these dusky magpies had longer necks than their northern cousins, and their raucous cries sounded alien to his ears. Everywhere, he saw strange lizards scurrying about—racing beneath ferns, hopping off rocks, leaping from tree branches to sail into the shadows on leathery wings.

Nothing could have prepared him for the strangeness of Inkarra, the misted forest, the exotic perfumes of the peach-colored mountain orchids that grew across the road. Sir Borenson had been raised on Orwynne, an island in the Carroll Sea not more than two hundred miles north of here. Yet once he crossed the mountains, he felt as if he had entered a world of which he had never dreamed.

Night closed in on them soon, and the Inkarran captors traveled noise-lessly in near total darkness. They did not speak, did not give their names. The Inkarrans tried to guide Borenson and Myrrima as best they could, moving them this way and that to avoid roots that stretched across the rutted road, but the two daylighters kept tripping. The path couldn't have been any less negotiable if Borenson was blindfolded. Borenson's feet were getting bruised and bloody from the abuse.

After two hours of this, the party came to a halt. Borenson could hear laughter, the nasal voices of Inkarrans sounding odd to his ear.

"We wait," one of the guards said in a thick accent

"What for?" Myrrima asked.

"Lamps. We at village. We bring you lamps." One Inkarran headed off through the woods.

Borenson peered all about. There were no lights to show him where the village might be. Indeed, he could make out nothing at all, beyond a deeper darkness that showed him the bole of a nearby tree.

"I thought you used flame lizards to guard your houses," Myrrima said.

"Draktferion very expensive," the guard explained. "Eat much meat. This poor village. No draktferion here."

Borenson soon heard rustling in the trees, the sound of approaching feet, and he heard the shy laughter of children. Apparently, he had drawn a crowd.

At last he saw light, a pair of swinging lamps. The lanterns, which hung from chains, were like rounded cups made of glass. In each cup burned Inkar-ran candles, strange candles as yellow as agates, as hard as stone, and without wicks. Borenson knew of them only from legend. Once lit, each candle would burn without smoke for a week or more. Indeed, he could see no flame from the peculiar candles. Instead, they merely glowed like bluish white embers.

As the guard passed through a crowd of children, the lanterns lit them briefly. The youngest children ran naked, while the older ones wore shifts of white linen. Their pale faces were as white as their clothes. To Borenson, they all looked like ghosts, like a convocation of the dead.

The guard tied a lamp around Borenson's wrist, and one around Myrrima's. In its soft glow, he could hardly make out the ground at his feet.

Still, it was enough.

All through the night they walked, until they came down out of the mountains altogether, into flat lands where no trees shadowed their path. They passed village after village, but there was little to see.

The villagers lived belowground, in hollows under the hills. In some richer areas, draktferions did indeed stand guard at the mouth of each village. There, the flame lizards would spread wide their hoods and hiss at the first sign of a stranger, fluorescing. By the flickering bloody light that they threw, Borenson could see the peculiar stelae that marked the entrance to the Inkarran "villages." The stelae were carved of stone and stood some twenty feet tall. At the top was a circle, like a head, with two branches extending from the base, like arms. On the stelae, carved in stone, were the surnames of the families who lived in the town below.

As they approached a broad river, Borenson was aware that they passed farms. He could smell the rice paddies, and at last they reached a village, where the guards hurried them through a market where merchants hawked white peaches, fresh red grapes, a dozen kinds of melons, and dragon-eye fruits. Freshly killed crocodiles, snakes, and fish hung beside the road, where vendors would cook them while you waited.

The guards bought some winged lizards glazed with some sweet sauce, along with melon, and Borenson and Myrrima fed hungrily while one of the guards disappeared in a crowd.

"Come," the guard said when he returned. "Boat take us downriver!"

In minutes, the guards had Borenson and Myrrima hustled into an Inkarran longboat. The boat was some sixty feet long and fairly narrow, made of some strange white wood that buoyed high on the water. At the bow of the boat was carved the head of a bird with a long beak, like a graceful crane.

The boat was filled with Inkarran peasants, ghostly white faces. Some of them carried bamboo cages that housed chickens or piglets.

Borenson sat near the front of the boat, looking off into the water. The air was still. He could hear night noises—the peep of tree frogs, the croak of a crocodile, the calls of some strange bird. The laughter and voices of the Inkarrans in town rose like music.

The sky overhead was still hazy, but the moon wafted above the mist, and now he could see the river dimly. Its shores spread broader than any river in Mystarria, mightier. He could not see the other side.

"How far must we go to see the Storm King?" Myrrima asked one of the guards.

"This not for you to know," he answered. "Keep silence."

Soon the boat was full of passengers. The guard handed Borenson and Myrrima each an oar, and they rowed together out into the deep. A hundred yards from shore, the current grew swift, and the boat glided under the moon-light. The passengers quit rowing, and left the work to the steersman.

One of their guards, a nameless man with high cheekbones and eyes that reflected red by the light of the lanterns, finally broke the silence.

"We reach Storm King's fortress by dawn," he said in a thick accent. "You sleep. You go sleep."

"Will the king see us?" Borenson asked.

"Maybe," the guard answered. "Chances good to see king. Not good to get favorable response."

"Why not?" Myrrima asked.

"You savages. All northern men savage."

Borenson snorted in laughter, and the guard bristled. He uttered some curse in Inkarran. "No laugh! You no laugh at me! I tell you this for own ben-efit. Not laugh at Inkarran. Never laugh, unless he laughs first. That giving permission to laugh."

"Forgive me," Borenson said. "I wasn't laughing at you. I was laughing at the idea—"

"The idea not funny," the guard retorted. He waited a moment, as if doling out silence as punishment, and then continued, "We Inkarran most civilize people on Earth. You people barbarians. You kings rule by force of arms. When man not follow him, you king resort to brutal. He send army to butcher women and children. This is barbarian way."

Borenson did not bother to correct the man. The Inkarrans had little contact with his people, and they would believe what they wanted to believe. It was true that women and children sometimes died in war, but that wasn't the goal of war, only a perennial byproduct.

"In Inkarra, we not make war against innocents," the guard said. "We choose victims and methods, very careful."

"You mean that your lords fight one another?" Myrrima asked. "In hand-to-hand combat?"

"Among you people," the guard answered, "there is but one kind battle. But we see many way settle dispute. You seek take man's life when he anger you." Borenson didn't dare interrupt him, didn't dare mention that the kings of the North used diplomacy far more often than battle. An Inkarran would not believe the truth. "But Inkarran, we have dozen form war. Each has own rules, own strategies."

"Like what?" Myrrima asked.

"Gizareth ki," Borenson suggested.

"Yes," the guard said, "*gizareth* mean 'a man's honor,' *ki* mean 'unmake,' or 'undo.' So, in gizareth ki, goal to destroy . . . how say? 'word' of man?"

"Credibility," Borenson said. "You destroy his credibility.

"And how do you fight such a war?" Myrrima asked.

"Rules simple: you cannot lie to destroy man's credibility. That civilized way. You must . . . unmask deceit before witnesses. Once contest begin, it must end within one year."

"And you call this war?" Myrrima asked.

Borenson answered, "Don't be fooled. They take gizareth ki very seriously. A man is defined by his word, by his honesty. There are men here, truthsayers, who train for decades to learn how to tell when someone is lying or telling the truth. When you declare war on someone, you can hire one or more truthsayers to denounce the person. They'll dig up every noble thing that the person has ever done, and then shout about it in the public square. Everyone will gather around to listen, because they know that the truthsayers are just warming up. For once they've discussed your virtues, they'll denounce your vices in such excruciating detail that . . . well, many a prince has thrown himself down a well. And once they're done with you, they'll repeat it again, and again, and again."

"For one year," the guard said. "At end of year, must stop. And victim may retaliate; he hire own truthsayers. Once person suffer at truthsayer, he cannot be made to suffer again for ten years."

"And what do you accomplish by destroying a man's honor?" Myrrima asked.

"If lucky," the guard said, "victim will change, grow. There prince in legend, Assenian Shey, who was called to war by brother. Truthsayers, they denounce his vices—" The guard counted them off on his fingers. "He waste talent, cruel to animals, glutton, let father die after robbers waylay him. The list, it grow endless. Everyone agree that young prince shameless. Still, he manage hold place of power. When his mother died, he become king.

"Ten years pass. The king's brother hire truthsayers once again. After careful examination, truthsayers spoke only of king's virtues. This bring great shame to jealous brother.

"So, you see," the guard concluded, "here we civilized. Here, not all battles end with death. We can make war on man's estate, or on his sanity. This is way of civilized people."

"Hmmmph," Borenson grunted. "You talk about your warfare as if it were more virtuous, but not all of your stories end so well. I'm familiar with the eighty-two forms of war. In the milder forms, you seek to destroy only a man's wealth, or vanity, or reputation, but in the most heinous form, the mak-outhatek ki, you're not satisfied with killing just one person, you seek to erase both his future and his past. You plunder his holdings, humiliate him before his people, butcher his wife and children so that he does not leave seed in the earth, put him to death, and destroy all those who dare even mention his name. I agree with you that war is a shameful thing, but you Inkarrans haven't found a way to avoid the horrors of war, you've just perfected them."

"Be careful such talk," the guard warned Borenson in a voice edged with anger. "Some say forms of war should expand, that in addition to make war on city or family, we should entomb entire nations."

Borenson laughed dangerously. "I'd like to meet those folks."

"Then you in luck," the guard said. "You will."

"What do you mean?" Myrrima asked with worry in her voice. "Is the Storm King one of those people?"

"He no love Rofehavan, but he not one of those people. Still, you will visit during . . . kamen to, festival for pay tribute. Lords from all Inkarra must appearance. You surely meet some who wish destroy your kind."

Borenson fell asleep to the sound of water lapping against the hull of the boat, and near dawn he woke as the Inkarrans on the boat began to stir. Sometime in the night, the cloud cover had broken above them, and stars shone now. Heaven was giving them another fiery display. Dozens of shooting stars streaked through the sky in a perpetual blaze.

Borenson could smell a sea breeze, a smell that always reminded him of home, and he could hear the roaring of a great waterfall ahead. To the north, the heavens shone down on a great city. Patches of farm were laid out in neat squares, and he could see the ghostly Inkarrans working their fields by night.

They had reached the outskirts of the Storm King's capital. The boat soon pulled into some busy docks, where fisherman unloaded their catches of the night. The guards ushered Borenson and Myrrima off the boat, and into the dusty streets.

Here in the city, draktferions lit the hilltops. The guards steered him toward the tallest hill, where hundreds of the fierce lizards blazed. Borenson knew that he had reached Iselferion, the Palace of Fire. The road leading up was paved with cobblestones, unlike all other roads that he'd seen in Inkarra, and the sprawling trees and grounds were well maintained.

As he reached the bottom of the hill, he could see an enormous stele, with a three-pointed crown atop it, that announced the Storm King's residence.

The guard led them up a gentle slope, and then down a tunnel that stopped at an iron gate.

Borenson had never been inside an Inkarran burrow. The mouth of the tunnel was wide enough so that several people could walk abreast, but not so wide that one could drive carts into it. An iron gate guarded the mouth of the burrow. Spikes hammered into the gate were meant to keep out even a charging elephant. The gate was open, and they went down a long corridor. Kill holes and archery slots could be seen in the walls. No sconces lit the way. Borenson's tiny lantern gave the only light. The only sound was a distant boom as waves crashed against the rocks at the base of the cliff. The surrounding blackness became complete as the guards led Borenson and Myrrima into the palace of the Storm King.

They passed through several darkened antechambers, each descending several hundred feet, when at last a door opened into a vast room. It was enormous, oval in shape, with high ceilings. Its plastered walls had been painted white, and equidistant around this chamber hung a dozen Inkarran lanterns, similar to the one that Borenson carried. Within the chamber, Inkarrans milled about. Most of them seemed drunk, as if returning from a night of revelry, and many laughed. He saw men in their strange tunics, often being held by women in long dresses. They spoke among themselves in whispers, and shot curious glances at Borenson and Myrrima.

In the far corners, merchants had thrown carpets on the floor of the room, and sat hawking bolts of cloth, food, armor, just about anything one might find during a fair.

"As see," the guard whispered, "lords here from many land."

Borenson could hardly see the Inkarrans at all. The lamplight was too dim to suit his human eyes. Nor was he certain that he could tell the dress of a lord from that of a pauper.

The guards turned them over to an officious fellow who led them down some long corridors in near total darkness, until at last they reached what Borenson figured was an audience room. There, two women in white dresses came and cut off his long red hair, using sharp metal scrapers. Borenson sat transfixed. Both women were beautiful. He could not help but inhale their strange, exotic scent. Their bodies seemed to have been rubbed in oil perfumed with orchids. When they finished with Borenson's head, they shaved his eyebrows, but left his beard. They laughed at the effect, and then left, and the guard escorted them to another chamber.

This room was different from those before. It had a single lamp in the center, and several large stones lay about it. By the stones' size and the way that they lay strewn about, he wasn't sure if they were adornments or if they were meant to be used as chairs. One corner of the room had a little pool in it, and a stream tinkled down from some rocks, so that the whole room smelled of water. Fresh herbs had been strewn on the floor, and from some dark corner a cricket sang. Borenson could discern large crabs scuttling about in the pools.

"Here you wait," the guard said, "until king speak to you."

They rested on the stone. The cricket sang beside the quiet pool. Borenson lay on a rock, until at last the king arrived. With him came several men—counselors, it seemed, and courtiers, all in rich attire.

The Storm King himself entered the room first. He was a gnarled old man with a bent back, a bald head, and a silver moustache that hung almost to his waist. Like all Inkarran kings, he bore a reaver dart in lieu of a scepter. The dart was made of silver, with a head carved of white diamond, and his only garment was a white silk tunic. Nothing about him was adorned at all, and the question crossed Borenson's mind, "What does *he* love?"

The old Storm King glared at Borenson, but his gaze softened when he looked upon Myrrima.

Borenson studied the counselors and courtiers. From the anger in their eyes, he suspected that they hated his people more than the Storm King did. Indeed, he suddenly suspected that they were more than mere courtiers. The Storm King was the High King of Inkarra, who exacted tribute from all others. By their fine silk robes, Borenson suspected that many of these were kings from far realms.

Borenson dropped to both knees, and Myrrima knelt on one knee behind him.

"Sir Borenson," King Zandaros whispered in thinly accented Rofehavanish. "I understand that you bring me a message."

"Indeed, Your Highness."

"You do not need to kneel to me," the king said mildly. "Feel free to look me in the eye."

Borenson rose to his feet, and behind him he could hear Myrrima do the same.

"You realize," King Zandaros said, "that it is against our law for men of Mystarria to travel in Inkarra. You must have seen our wards in the mountains. Did they not warn you that your life is in peril?"

"Only great need drew me here," Borenson said. "I came in spite of the wards."

"You must be a man of great will," the king said, "to pass them. However, it is also against your law for men of Inkarra to travel in Mystarria, is it not? As I am sure that you know, our people have been killed for breaking your law. Should we not, therefore, kill you?"

"It was our king's hope," Borenson replied, "that an exception might be made, due to the fact that we travel only as his messengers."

"You are . . . close to the king?"

By custom only a relative or close friend should bear the king's message in Inkarra. "I have been his bodyguard for many years," Borenson said. "He has no father, no mother, brothers, or sisters. I am his closest friend."

"Yet you come under his command?" the Storm King asked. It would not do for some lackey to bear the message.

"No," Borenson said. "I was released from his service. I am a Knight Equitable, and come now as his friend, not as his servant."

Zandaros whispered, "And what if no exception is to be made to our law? Are you prepared to die?"

Borenson had been expecting this question. "If you intend to kill me," he said, "then I would ask for only one boon: that you let me deliver my message first."

The king thought for a moment. "Agreed," he whispered gently. "Your life is forfeit, along with that of your wife. I shall do with them as I deem fit. Give me your message."

Borenson had expected such a show of power.

"My lord," Borenson said, "an Earth King has risen in Mystarria, in the person of Gaborn Val Orden. And against him, other kings have raised their hands: Raj Ahten of Indhopal, Lowicker of Beldinook, and Anders of South Crowthen. Gaborn has driven back these enemies, but is concerned with a much greater threat. Even now he fights reavers that have been a scourge to Carris. You've seen how the stars fall at night, and how the sun grows large on the horizon. You cannot doubt that we are in great jeopardy. Deep in the earth, the reavers have created magic runes—the Seal of Heaven and the Seal of the Inferno. By uniting these runes with the Seal of Desolation, the reavers will wreak great havoc across the world. Gaborn wishes to put aside old enmities, and asks that you unite with him in his battle against the reavers."

King Zandaros thought for a long moment, then pointed at Borenson's chest. "How many reavers has your king killed?"

"Some seventy thousand attacked Carris. When last I saw Gaborn, his knights were charging them on the plains of Mystarria. I would say that he had killed at least thirty percent of them. Those that remained seemed . . . worn and humbled. I do not doubt that he will bring them all down."

"He has slain twenty thousand reavers?" Zandaros asked, his voice thick with suspicion.

Behind the king, Borenson heard someone whispering excitedly in Inkarran, followed by gasps of astonishment. Indeed the kings and counselors there began to argue loudly, and two of them made violent motions, pointing off to the north. The Storm King silenced them all with a harsh word and a wave of his hand.

"So," Zandaros whispered. "Your king sues for peace, and asks the help of Inkarra. He must be desperate indeed."

"It is not just desperation that drives him," Borenson said. "He is not like other kings. He didn't make the old laws. He does not want to count Inkarra among his foes. He feels the need to protect men of all nations through the dark times to come."

At that, King Zandaros laughed mirthlessly. "Inkarrans like dark times," he whispered. He went and sat down on a stone, near Myrrima. He motioned for Borenson to sit beside him. "Come, tell me more about this Earth King of yours. How many endowments does he have?"

Borenson sat beside him. "Gaborn has few endowments, Your Highness. He does not like to put men to the forcible. He has none of glamour or Voice anymore. And only a few each of brawn, grace, stamina, and metabolism."

"I hear that Raj Ahten has taken thousands of endowments. How then can Gaborn hope to stand against him?"

"He relies on his Earth Powers to protect him," Borenson said. "And on his wits."

"And you say that this king of yours would protect us, too?"

"He would," Borenson answered.

At the Storm King's back, there was a derisive bark, and one of the lords began raging insults. But the Storm King's demeanor remained pacific. He stared deep into Borenson's eyes, and then gazed over at Myrrima.

"And you agree?"

"I do, Your Highness," Myrrima whispered.

The old king peered hard at her, and sniffed the air. "You are not the lackey of any Earthly King," he said at last. "Of that much I am certain."

Myrrima nodded as if he had paid her a compliment.

"And what of the rest of your message?" the king asked. "I understand that you search for someone?"

"Gaborn seeks the help of Daylan Hammer, whom we believe to be here in Inkarra."

Zandaros nodded and turned his back, staring at the knot of men who stood there. "Perhaps you should look harder in your own lands. The kings of the south knew more of him than I did. There was a matter against him some time ago, a war of makeffela ki. Daylan of the Black Hammer fled the battle, and has not been seen in many long years. It is said that he may be living in Mystarria, where any Inkarran that might pursue him would be killed on sight, though he may have gone farther north."

Borenson took in this news. He had never heard of Daylan Hammer being anywhere in Rofehavan. But if he was afraid of Inkarrans sworn to vengeance, he could be hiding anywhere.

"How long ago was this?" Borenson asked.

King Zandaros turned to one of the kings behind him, an old fellow with an almost grandfatherly look about him. "Sixty-one years," the old fellow answered. "Please forgive bad Rofehavan talk I make. Wife can tell more."

King Zandaros patted Borenson on the shoulder, and stood as if to leave. "You and your wife are free to go, Sir Borenson. King Criomethes here will tell you all that you need to know. Feel free to enjoy our hospitality here at Iselferion for as long as you like."

At that, King Zandaros turned to leave the room. A lord behind him, a tall man with sweeping silver hair, all dressed in a black tunic, growled angrily and made some demand.

Zandaros turned to Sir Borenson. "My sister's son asks a question of you. It seems that he suffered many things yesterday in a dream. He believes that one of my nephews, Pilwyn Coly Zandaros, is dead, and that you might know something of this?"

Borenson didn't know how to answer. He could see rage in the tall fellow's eyes, and dared not admit that he had killed Zandaros himself.

Myrrima spoke up quickly, her voice as soft and liquid as water. "It was Pilwyn Coly Zandaros who caused us to initiate our visit, Your Highness," Myrrima said, "when he sought to assassinate the Earth King."

"Assassinate?" Zandaros asked.

"He bore a message case," Myrrima said, "and on it was inscribed a curse in runes of Air. He claimed that that message came from you."

The lord behind the Storm King suddenly grew fearful and backed away. Zandaros whirled on him with lightning in his eyes. He smiled cruelly, like a cat considering how to torment a mouse.

"I apologize for that," Zandaros said. "Our kingdom is ever rife with intrigues. Believe me, reparations will be made. And if Pilwyn is indeed dead, then it only relieves me of the chore."

"What of an answer?" Borenson asked. "What would you have me tell King Orden?"

Zandaros turned on him and nodded graciously. "I think that I should like to meet this king of yours that has killed twenty thousand reavers. Indeed, I have a sudden urge to hunt at his side. I leave within the hour. I hope to reach the mountains by dawn. Would that be advisable, milady?"

Zandaros gazed into Myrrima's eyes, as if asking if that was what she wanted. Something had passed between them, Borenson felt sure.

"Yes," Myrrima said. She seemed to be pondering, almost in a trance. "He will need your peculiar strengths."

The Storm King whirled and left, and many of the other lords followed at his heel, except for two men who stood by the door. One of them was the grandfatherly king that had spoken earlier. The other was a handsome young Inkarran, dressed in black silk, so much like him that he had to be his son.

"I King Criomethes," the old man introduced himself again, "and this son, Verazeth. Our kingdom far south. Please, follow."

Borenson glanced back uncertainly at Myrrima.

"Please," Criomethes said. "You guest. You hungry? We feed."

By now, Borenson's stomach was cramping from want of food. The lizard he'd eaten last night, and the bit of fruit, had not filled him.

"Yes, we're hungry," he said, thinking to himself, hungry enough even to eat Inkarran food. "Thank you."

Criomethes took his elbow and led him back the way that they had come. "This way," the king said. "Is time for feast here. Our room quite small. For this I sorry."

They walked through shadowed corridors until they reached the great hall. A throng filled that hall, young Inkarran lords dressed in dark, deep-hooded cloaks, with their armor gleaming beneath. They were already making preparations to ride with the Storm King. There was excitement in the air, a smell of war.

King Criomethes led them into a side corridor, along busy streets that seemed to stretch for miles. They passed doorway after rounded doorway, each covered with nothing more than a curtain, until at last the king steered them to a large room.

"Come in, come in," the king said. He stood aside from the door and urged Borenson inside, slapping him on the back.

Borenson stopped just outside the doorway, hesitant to enter a room before a king. A cooking fire burned dully in a hearth, and four girls were frying vegetables in its coals. Thick furs and pillows covered the floor, and a tall golden carafe sat on a low table, along with several half-empty glasses of wine.

"Please," Criomethes said, gesturing for Borenson to enter. Borenson stepped inside, and Criomethes came on his heel, still patting him on the shoulder like an old friend. "I glad Zandaros spared life. You be very useful."

At that, Borenson heard a gasp behind him, and turned to see Myrrima stumbling toward the floor. Prince Verazeth stood over her, and Borenson saw the glint of gold from a needle ring on his hand. At that very instant, he felt something prick his shoulder, where Criomethes had been touching him.

"Wha—?" he started to say.

His shoulder went numb instantly, and his arm went slack.

A poison, Borenson realized, a paralying drug.

His heart pounded furiously in terror, causing ice to lance through his arm. The Inkarrans were masters in the art of poisons, and their surgeons used a number of paralyzing drugs collected from the skins of flying lizards and various plants.

Borenson reached for Criomenes, thinking to deal him a death blow, but the room spun violently, his thoughts became clouded, and he grabbed the man for support.

His legs seemed to turn to rubber and he dropped to the carpets, no more able to remain upright than if he were a sack of onions.

᥉ 16 ೞ

THE BETRAYAL

A man who loves money above all else will feel most betrayed when his wealth is plundered. A man who loves praise will feel most violated when others speak ill of him. And the man who loves virtue will break when evil is done in his name.

—Hearthmaster Coldridge, from the Room of Dreams,
On Measuring a Man's Heart

Gaborn and Iome raced through the Underworld, measuring time by the pounding of their feet, by the wheezing of their breath. The ribs of the tunnel flashed by as white as the cartilage of a windpipe. Gaborn imagined that he was traveling down the throat of some fell beast. Going down, ever downward, until he reached its belly.

He chased the Consort of Shadows ceaselessly, going ever deeper into the earth, sweat storming from his brow, through a landscape of nightmare, past mud pots that splattered gray mud like pain, beneath tunnels where reavers had channeled steam that thundered through pipes of mucilage. The deeper they ran, the more grotesque and abundant the landscape became. Gaborn ran for what seemed days, stopping only long enough to drink greedily from a pool of tepid sulfur water or choke down something from the provisions. But no amount of drinking could assuage his thirst, and no amount of food seemed to give him the strength he needed to keep running.

The path slanted through the Underworld, sometimes leading down trails not meant for humans—through vertical chimneys where reavers had carved handholds and footholds.

He felt a great threat ahead, not more than a few miles now, a wall of death.

As he ran, Gaborn also reached out to sense the danger rising in Carris. He tried to imagine his Chosen people, living pleasant lives in safety. But all he felt in their future was death.

Once, after drinking, he leaned with his back to the wall, wrapped his arms around his knees, and bowed his head, letting the sweat drain from his chin. He squatted on the floor of the cave near a fetid stream, in a place where blind-crab shells were piled thick on the ground like discarded breast-plates in an armory.

"What's wrong?" Iome asked.

Gaborn tried to answer in measured tones. "I'm worried. I think it must be well after midnight now. The threat to Heredon is diminishing. I think our messengers are warning the people to hide there. But in Carris the threat keeps growing. All evening, I've sensed . . . people gathering. Almost everyone that I Chose in the city is returning. I can feel them stirring, coming together."

"But," Iome rightfully argued, "you told them to return."

"Not like this," Gaborn said. "There were women at Carris that I Chose, and children. So many of those little ones are going back. Hundreds of thousands. They must think that the castle is safer than the villages nearby, but it's not. They must think that they can help in the fight. . . ."

He shook his head in dismay. He imagined them hurriedly preparing the defenses in the castle. The women would be boiling rags for bandages and preparing food in advance of the battle. The children would be collecting rocks for the catapults and fletching arrows, while the men worked at shoring up the breaches in the castle walls. "The sense of danger is rising so high," Gaborn said. "It's . . . I fear I've sent them to fight a battle they cannot win. I think I've sent them to their slaughter."

Iome knelt beside him. "You're doing your best."

"But is it good enough?" Gaborn asked. "I'm sending people to war, and against what? If they fought reavers alone, that would be enough. But we are fighting an enemy we've never even guessed at—the One True Master of Evil."

Iome went quiet, and the silence around them deepened. Even with endowments of hearing, Gaborn could detect nothing. The silence around them, the immovable wilderness, was overwhelming. The only sound came from a few elephant snails nearby, their huge shells clacking together as they fed on moss. Even the sound of Gaborn's voice did not carry more than a few feet beyond his face.

Iome opened Erden Geboren's book and scanned through the headings. Gaborn sat for a moment, waiting for Iome to find something of interest. He noticed a twinge, as if a wave of fresh air washed over him. As it did, he felt suddenly lighter, more refreshed. He'd noticed it once or twice before, over what felt like the past hour or two.

No, he realized. I've noticed it a dozen times. Someone is vectoring endowments to me.

He'd last taken endowments in Heredon—brawn, stamina, grace, metabolism, wit. Now his messengers had gone to Heredon, telling the folk of the dangers to come. The endowments had to be vectored by the facilitators at Castle Groverman. But why would they do it?

Iome scanned through the headings of Erden Geboren's book. Gaborn peered at her. Was she moving more slowly than she had an hour ago?

No, she couldn't be, he thought. Perhaps someone is vectoring metabolism to me. Now that he thought about it, it had been less of a labor running for the last stretch. Iome had kept falling behind.

"Gaborn," Iome said. "You mentioned that the danger is growing less in Heredon. Can you tell me how my friend Chemoise will fare?" For years, Chemoise had been Iome's maid of honor, and they'd been inseparable.

Gaborn reached out with his Earth Senses. Felt the danger rising around the girl. "If she hears my warning and takes heed, there may be hope for her."

"May be?" Iome asked.

"Iome," he said, "you don't want to play this game. Don't ask me to name the names of those who will die. Nothing is certain."

"All right," she said, biting her lip. She pointed at something in the book. "Here's a chapter on fighting a locus. It says that 'Against a locus, no weapon forged of steel can prevail.'"

Iome flipped to the next page, and frowned. She began rapidly skimming through the next dozen pages. "If we cannot kill it with steel," she offered, "then we must find another way."

Her voice sounded unnaturally deep and slow.

"Something is wrong," Iome said. "Erden Geboren was going to talk about how to fight the locus, but the pages have been ripped out."

"Ripped out?" Gaborn asked. "Why would someone rip them out?"

Iome frowned, then gave Gaborn a hard look. "Think about it: Erden Geboren told people what he was fighting seventeen hundred years ago, but in all of the legends, in all of the myths, all we've ever heard is that he fought reavers. There can only be one answer: someone doesn't want us to fight the loci."

"Or perhaps," Gaborn countered, "someone took the pages precisely because *he* wanted to know how to fight the creature."

"I wish I could believe that," Iome said.

The heat was unbearable, worse than the hottest day Gaborn had ever witnessed. He took another drink from the pool, but no amount of water could quite refresh him.

Another twinge hit him, barely perceptible. His muscles tightened. He felt sure now. Someone was vectoring endowments to him.

When a Runelord took an endowment, if he took it directly from the Dedicate, he received more than just the attribute, he normally felt a rush of ecstasy. But coming as they were through vectors, Gaborn only sensed the virtue that grew inside him each time a facilitator transferred an endowment.

He got up and peered forward, down the long tunnel. He stretched his senses, reached out with with his Earth Sight. The sense of impending doom had lessened. With each endowment he received, the threat diminished. Ahead, the wall of death was cracking.

Iome must have noticed something amiss. "What's happening?"

"My facilitators," Gaborn said, "have begun vectoring more endowments to me."

Iome looked up at him with sadness in her eyes, resignation, but no surprise.

"Did you tell them to do this?" Gaborn demanded.

Iome nodded. "You wouldn't have taken more endowments yourself, so I sent a message to the facilitators in Heredon, asking them to vector the endowments to you."

Gaborn's heart fell. The facilitators were vectoring greater endowments to him—brawn, grace, stamina. Each time they did, they put the life of a Dedicate at risk. So many of Gaborn's Dedicates had died at Raj Ahten's hands already that he would not have dared seek more endowments.

"No promises were to be made to the Dedicates," Iome said by way of apology. "No offers of gold, no threats. Those who give themselves are doing it out of their love for their homeland, nothing more."

"How many endowments did you tell them to vector?" Gaborn asked heavily.

"All that they can," Iome said. "If all four of our facilitators work through the night, they should be able to give you a thousand or more."

Gaborn shook his head in horror at all of the suffering, all of the pain he would cause the Dedicates. Another burst of virtue passed through him, and he felt the desire to move faster. He stared at Iome, and could not begin to tell her how deeply she had betrayed his trust. The new Dedicates would be at risk, not just from men like Raj Ahten but from the stresses of giving endowments. Sometimes, men who gave brawn would die of weakness as their hearts failed; or those who gave grace would have their lungs cease up, and never draw breath again.

"Why?" he asked.

Iome shook her head, and tears began to pool in her eyes, as if to say *I'm sorry*. Instead, she said what she had to: "Our people need us to be strong now. If we don't kill the One True Master, nothing else matters. I'd have taken the endowments myself, if I could. But I don't have your gifts. I didn't dare waste any more forcibles on myself."

Gaborn looked down at her, dismayed. By granting so many endowments of metabolism, his people might well doom him to a solitary existence, moving so fast that he would be all but incapable of carrying on a normal conversation, a life where he could age in a matter of months or years, while his loved ones lived out their normal lives. They could make a sacrifice of him.

Gaborn wasn't just hurt. He felt as if something inside him had broken.

"Don't look at me like that," Iome said. "Don't hate me. Just . . . I just want you to live." Gaborn had never seen such grief in a woman's countenance. It was as if she were being torn in two.

"Life for me isn't just existing," Gaborn said. "It's how I choose to live that matters."

Iome took his face in her hands and held it, peering into his eyes. Even now, he could not meet her gaze, but stubbornly looked down at her lips. "I want you," Iome said. "I want you in my life, and I mean to save you by any means possible."

He closed his eyes, unable to confront what she had done. She was stronger than he, more willing to bear the guilt that came from taking endowments, more willing to bear shame, more willing to sacrifice the things that she loved for the common good.

For a long moment, she held him. Then she kissed him once on the forehead, once on the lips, and once on each hand.

"Go now," Iome said. "I can't keep up with you any longer. I'd only slow you down. I'll follow as best I can. Mark the trail for me."

Gaborn nodded heavily, then peered at her. "May I have Averan's staff? She'll need it when I find her."

Iome handed him the simple staff of black poisonwood. Gaborn felt in his heart, considering the path ahead. Yes, the wall of death awaited him just a few miles up the tunnel.

I'll either clear a path for Iome, Gaborn thought, or die in the attempt.

Gaborn held Iome for a long moment, and whispered into her ear. "I love you. I forgive you."

He turned and raced down the tunnel, redoubling his pace, becoming smaller and smaller. For a moment he looked the size of a young man, and then a boy, and then a toddler, until at last he turned round a bend and was gone altogether.

ೞ 17 ೮

THE BONE MAN

Even in the driest desert, a flower sometimes blooms.

—*a proverb of Indhopal*

Averan was in the fetid prison where lost souls huddled around her in the blackness, drawn to the light of her ring like moths. They were staring at the gem, at her.

Averan tried to sit up but fell back in a swoon. Her head spun and sweat streamed from every pore.

"Get her some water," one shaggy old man said. Soon, a half-naked girl brought water in her cupped hands, and gave Averan a drink.

"There's more blindfish in the stream," the girl reported.

"Fish?" Averan asked.

Barris said, "Fish. It's about all that we have to eat. There's a river that runs underground, and the fish swim up through it. We have no fire to cook them with, and they taste like rancid oil and sulfur. But if you pick through the spines and the bones, there's meat on them."

Averan's stomach churned at the thought. She still had her pack on. "There's supplies in my bags," she told the group. "Apples and onions, cheeses, nuts and dried berries. It isn't much, but split it among yourselves."

No one moved to touch her pack until Averan pulled it off her own back and handed out the food. There wasn't much, enough for each person to have an apple or a handful of nuts. Yet the folk seemed greatly touched by the gesture, and Averan heard one man weep in gratitude as he bit into an onion.

There was a long silence, and one old man, his face lined with wrinkles and gray in his hair, asked, "You was saying that you hail from Keep Haberd?"

"Aye," Averan admitted.

"I'm from there," he said. "But I don't remember much anymore. I try to imagine grass or sunlight, and I can't. There were people that I knew, but their faces . . ."

Averan didn't want to talk about it. She didn't want to admit that Keep Haberd had been destroyed, its walls knocked down by reavers, its people slaughtered and eaten. Everyone that this old fellow had known would be dead. "Do you have a last name?"

"Weeks, Averan Weeks."

"Oh," the fellow said. "Then you must know of Faldon Weeks?"

"That was my father's name," Averan said. "You knew him?"

"I knew him well," the old fellow said. "He was a prisoner here, captured in the same battle as me. I remember that he was married to a small woman whose smile could light the stars at night. But I don't remember a daughter."

"He was here?" Averan asked, disbelieving. She had been told that reavers had eaten him. She had never guessed that he might have been carried down here.

"He always dreamed of going home," the old fellow said. "But he could not hold on forever. Even with endowments, none of us can hold on forever. And now our endowments have been taken. He succumbed within the very hour that it happened."

Averan peered into the fellow's face. Here was someone who had known her father. The man was little more than bones with a bit of skin draped over him. He was so thin that his eyes seemed to bulge in their sockets. His only clothing was a scrap of dirty gray cloth tied around his loins. He looked as if he might expire at any moment.

With sudden certainty, Averan realized what had happened. Raj Ahten had killed the Dedicates at the Blue Tower. When he'd done it, Averan had lost her own endowments, and had grown so weak that she thought that she would die. How much worse would it have been if she'd been a prisoner down here, with nothing but an endowment or two of stamina to sustain her?

Tears welled up in her eyes, and she began to shudder, as if she would collapse. "My father is here?"

"Yes," the old fellow said. He pointed back to a far wall, where white bones glistened wetly, and blind-crabs still scuttled about the remains. "But there is nothing left of him."

Ten years, Averan thought. Ten years he'd been down here, and she had missed meeting him by only a week.

Bitterly, Averan cursed the reavers that had brought them here, and wished them all dead.

She found herself sobbing. The old man reached out timidly, as if begging permission to comfort her, and she grasped him around the neck, hugging him.

These could have been my father's bones, Averan thought. This could have been the smell of his unwashed neck.

A sullen rage grew in her, and she swore to take revenge.

෨ 18 ෬

AN UNEXPECTED PARTY

There is no surer refuge than a close friend.

—*a Saying in Heredon*

"Hide underground tonight!" Uncle Eber told Chemoise as he came in the door that morning, bringing home from the village a pail of fresh milk and a loaf of bread. "That's what the Earth King said to do. Hide underground. I just heard it in town from the king's messenger."

Chemoise looked up from the breakfast table. She was at her uncle's estate in the village of Ableton, far in the north of Heredon. Her aunt had just finished cooking some sausages and had asked her to sit until Eber got home. And grandmother sat in her rocker before the fireplace, deaf as a doorpost and half-blind as well.

"Why did he send messengers?" Chemoise asked. "He could have just told us that we are in danger."

"I . . . don't know," Eber said. "He's off way down in Mystarria. Maybe the Earth King's warnings won't carry so far. Or perhaps he wanted to be sure that everyone was forewarned, not just his Chosen."

Chemoise looked around the room with a rising sense of panic. It was early in her pregnancy, but for the past few days, the very mention of breakfast had made her too ill to eat. She was beginning to feel that sense of fragility that often accompanies gestation. So coming down for breakfast had given her a sense of accomplishment.

Now this. "Underground?" she asked. "Why?"

"I'll bet it's the stars," her aunt Constance offered. "They've been falling every night, each night worse than the night before!"

Chemoise's heart skipped a beat. She knew little of such things. She'd heard of men mining iron from fallen stars, and so she imagined that perhaps it would rain down like grapeshot from a catapult. But that couldn't be right. Falling stars were hot. The stars wouldn't be like grapeshot; they'd be more like fire raining from the skies, fire and molten iron. After last night's meteor showers, with the fireballs roaring through the heavens, it wasn't hard to imagine such a thing.

Uncle Eber shot Constance a furtive look, warning her to be quiet. He didn't want to trouble Chemoise with wild speculations about what might happen. That look worried her even more.

Chemoise often missed her life at Castle Sylvarresta. At least if I were there, she thought, I might have heard more about the threat. Even if the folks in the castle didn't know any more than Uncle Eber does, there would have been some juicy speculations.

But Chemoise knew of things more terrifying than meteor showers that Gaborn might warn them about.

"Perhaps another Darkling Glory is coming," Chemoise offered. The threat hung in the air like a cold fog.

Constance set the spatula beside the stove and began wiping her hands. She turned the subject, "So, where will we stay tonight?"

"I've been thinking we could use the winecellars," Eber responded. "They're old and dusty, but they go back quite far under the hill." A dozen years ago the estate had had some large vineyards. But blight had killed the grapes. With the loss of both his crop and the plants, Eber hadn't been able to afford to replant, so he'd leased his fields to sharecroppers.

"Those old tunnels?" his wife asked in surprise. "They're infested with ferrin!"

The thought of the little ratlike creatures gave Chemoise a shiver.

"The ferrin won't mind a bit of company for just one night," Eber said. He nibbled his lip. "I've invited the sharecroppers to stay with us."

"That's half the village!" Constance said.

"I invited the other half, too," Eber confessed. Constance opened her mouth in surprise as Eber set the bread and milk on the table and made a great show of sitting down, waiting for Constance to bring his breakfast. "There's nowhere else for them to go!" he apologized. "Only a few folk have root cellars, and the nearest caves are miles from here. We'll be safer together!"

"Well then," Constance said with a tone of false cheer, putting the sausages on the table. "We'll make a party of it."

Chemoise and Constance hiked up to the wine cellars half a mile behind the hill. The air had a strange quality today. The sky was hazy, and yet seemed to be heavy and looming. The path in front of the cellars was choked with tall grass, shrubs, clinging vines, and wild daisies. A few pear trees were growing before the door. This late in the season only a few dry leaves still clung to the trees.

It took some hard work even to wrench the door open. The odor of mold permeated the old winery. The floors were thick with dust, and little trails showed where ferrin had walked. A pile of their dung moldered next to the door.

"Yech," Aunt Constance said. "What a mess!"

The cellar had been dug far back into the hill so that the wine could age at an even temperature. Chemoise left the door open and waded through the dust, past some vines white from lack of sunlight, back into the dark storerooms. After twenty feet, the tunnel branched. To her right lay a little shop with hammers and benches where a cooper had made barrels. "Well," Constance said. "The heavier hammers are still here, but it looks as if the ferrin stole all the lighter chisels and files."

Straight ahead were rows and rows of old wine barrels. Winged termites crawled about on the nearest ones. Signs of ferrin were everywhere in the little trails on the floor. There were ferrin spears leaning against one barrel, and some ferrin had made a conkle—a fiendish image constructed of straw and twigs—and set it in a corner. Strange paintings, like scratch marks made with coal, surrounded the conkle. No one quite knew why the ferrin built them. Chemoise imagined that they hoped it would frighten away enemies.

She tapped the nearest wine barrel to see if it held anything. Inside, some sleeping ferrin awoke. They began snarling like badgers and whistling in alarm, then raced out the back of the barrel through a small hole.

Soon the whole wine cellar reverberated with such whistles, ferrin talk for "What? What?"

The calls seemed to echo from everywhere, and Chemoise spotted little holes dug into the walls behind the barrels. Fierce little ferrin warriors wearing scraps of stolen-cloth poked their heads out of the holes.

"What a mess!" Aunt Constance said, coming in behind. "We'll never get it all cleaned up in time."

"Would you like some help?" someone called. Chemoise turned. In the doorway stood a young man of perhaps eighteen years. He was tall and broad of shoulder, with blond hair that swept down his back and halfway covered his green eyes.

It had only been four days since Chemoise had come to Ableton. As of yet, she had met only half of the villagers. But she hadn't been able to help noticing this young man plowing a field across the valley.

"Chemoise," her aunt said. "This is Dearborn Hawks, our neighbor."

"How do you do?" Chemoise asked.

"Fine, thank you," Dearborn replied. He was staring at her, as if her aunt didn't exist, as if he wanted to speak to Chemoise but couldn't find the words. By now, he couldn't help knowing all about her, at least the rumors that her uncle had spread. "Uh," he offered lamely, "I, uh, I promised Eber that I'd come early, to help clean up."

"Well then," Aunt Constance said, "I'll let you two get to it, while I go do some baking."

There was a clumsy silence as her footsteps echoed out the door. Dearborn stood for a long minute. Chemoise knew what this was. She was going to have a babe in seven months, and her aunt and uncle were trying to find the lad a father.

"So," Dearborn finally managed. "You're new in the village?"

"You haven't seen me before, have you?" Chemoise asked.

"I think I'd remember if I had," Dearborn said, smiling appreciatively. "In fact I'm sure I'd remember. I, uh, I live across the valley, in the old manor."

Chemoise had seen it, a dilapidated building that had been old two hundred years ago. The Hawks family was large, ten children at least, from what Chemoise could see. Dearborn had two brothers who were close to his age. "I've seen you," she said. "You're the oldest?"

"Aye," Dearborn said. "And the best looking. And the hardest worker, and the cleverest, and funniest."

"Ahah. That must give you a lot of comfort. Say something clever."

The young man looked as if he wanted to bite his own tongue off for making a fool of himself. He looked up at the ceiling and said at last, "A true friend is one that will bear your burdens when you are down, and bear your secrets to the grave. And no lesser kind of friend is worthy of the name."

It wasn't exactly clever or funny. It was more sincere. "Are you implying that I have burdens that need to be borne, or secrets that need to be kept?"

"No," he answered. "It was just a thought."

Chemoise felt sorry for the cold welcome she'd given him. He knew that she carried a child, and had probably guessed the rest. Yet he'd come acting as if he'd elbowed his brothers aside to be the first to meet her. "Well then," she said, "let's see if you're as industrious as you are clever."

With that they pulled up their sleeves and went at it. Dearborn began rolling the old wine barrels from the back in order to make room for the party. Some barrels had ferrin families living in them, and as soon as he began to roll them out, the ferrin would whistle in terror and come bolting out of one hole or another, diving into the tunnels that they'd dug into the winery walls.

Others barrels were used by the ferrin for food storage—and thus held a bit of wheat stripped from the fields, or dried cherries, or rubbery turnips plundered from gardens. Two barrels had been used as graveyards, and were filled with old ferrin bones.

All of the barrels stank of musk.

They were halfway done pulling the barrels out when Aunt Constance brought some tea.

"I think we should burn these barrels," Chemoise said. "The ferrin have peed all over them."

But Aunt Constance would have none of it. "No, we'll put them back tomorrow. The ferrin would starve without their food stores, and there are mothers living there, with wee babes to feed." She looked pointedly at Chemoise's stomach. Uncle Eber and Aunt Constance had only managed to have one daughter of their own, and she had died in childhood, so she was perhaps a bit tenderhearted when it came to children. "Ferrin don't eat much, you know—a few cherries that fall from the trees, mice and rats and sparrow eggs, things like that. The rats down in the wine cellar were terrible until Eber brought some ferrin up from Castle Sylvarresta. Ferrin don't like wine, you know. Now we always put a load of hay in the winery come fall, to help keep their nests warm through the winter."

"You brought them here?" Erin asked. "I thought they were wild."

"Down south, in the Dunnwood, they live wild," Constance said. "But not up here, dear. It's too cold in these mountains come winter."

In southern Heredon, the wild ferrin were enough of a nuisance that the tax collector would pay two copper doves for every ferrin hide you brought in. Many a poor family avoided taxes altogether by collecting the bounties. But Uncle Eber and Aunt Constance didn't seem the kind to want to slaughter a whole village full of ferrin for a few coins.

"All right, then," Chemoise promised, "we'll work around them."

So Chemoise and Dearborn spent the morning clearing out the room and sweeping the dust from the floor. The dust cloud raised a stink, and the ferrin whistled in outrage and kept poking their heads from their burrows to let the big folk know about it.

Chemoise found that she and Dearborn worked well together. He was a farmer, used to guiding a plow, and chopping down trees for firewood, and shoeing his own horse. He was strong enough to move the heaviest barrel, and graceful enough to wrangle it around without stepping on Constance's feet while she swept and mopped.

Indeed, as they worked, she found that it almost became a dance. Dearborn would wrestle the barrels while she swept. She found herself continually drawing close to him, and sometimes she'd look up to find that he was gazing into her eyes, but they never touched. Instead, he'd merely smile shyly and look away.

Sometimes he tried to make small talk, joking and asking about her "husband." She told him how Sergeant Dreys had died at the hand of an assassin after only two months of marriage.

She watched Dearborn withdraw at the news. He hadn't really wanted to know about her "supposed" husband. Instead, he wanted to know how he fared against his memory, and he knew that it was not an equal contest. Dreys had been in the King's Guard, and had made sergeant by age nineteen. He'd have been a captain by forty, and would most likely have been retired as a baron of the realm. He would have had title and lands, and serfs working his fields.

Hawks could not compete against that. He was the oldest of ten, and had the birthright of his family. But it wouldn't fetch him much in the long run. His father was a farmer and a landowner, almost as wealthy as Chemoise's Uncle Eber, but once the farm was split among the six boys, they wouldn't all be able to make a living on it.

Hawks had little to offer a woman. So he worked. He tried to make light of it, but she soon saw the sweat staining the back of his tunic. Hawks took most of the barrels outside, and since Constance had said that she would want them replaced later, he piled them on each side of the path, and then, with the help of old shelving boards, stacked them overhead, making a sort of arch that the townsfolk could walk under. There were at least two hundred old barrels.

By noon, the tunnels were nearly cleared, and the smell of mold and dust and ferrin had receded, but there was still much to do. Both Chemoise and Dearborn just went outside and sat down, too tired to continue.

Downhill just a tad, her uncle's manor squatted. The foundation was stone. The mud and wattle on the sides had all been whitewashed, and a new load of thatch was on the roof. A pair of geese fed in the garden out back, and her uncle's old plow horse stared at her dolefully from the corral behind the barn.

It was a good life here in Ableton. Everything a person needed seemed to be close at hand. Her uncle had been living here, eating from his own garden from the time that he was born forty-six years ago. If Chemoise needed a new dress, Mrs. Wycutt would sell her a bolt of cloth, or sew it for her for a couple of copper doves. If her uncle needed a new plow, the smith could have it done in a week. Everyone knew everyone, and everyone watched out for everyone else.

Chemoise had thought that this would be a fine place to raise her son. She knew the child would be a boy, for she'd loved Sergeant Dreys so much that when he died, she'd lured his spirit back into her womb.

Now she felt apprehensive. The sky had gotten heavier since dawn. The haze was as thick as cream, and Chemoise could feel an electric thrill in the air. "There's going to be a storm tonight," Hawks said. "I'll bet that's what the Earth King was warning us about—grand storm, with lots of wind. I'll bet it knocks whole houses down."

"I hope not," Chemoise said. "I'd hate to see my uncle's house knocked down."

"Stay close to me," the Hawks boy offered, "whatever it is."

She almost laughed, but she could see sincerity in his eyes. He was offering to protect her, and no matter how melodramatic his appeal, she would not mock him for it.

Aunt Constance came out to check on the situation. She inspected the rooms, and said, "Give me an hour."

She came back half an hour later with twenty women from the village. They finished pulling out the last of the barrels, and in the back of the storeroom found three old kegs that still held wine. Uncle Eber was called upon to test it. The first barrel had gone to vinegar, but after a sip from the second, he declared, "Why, this is worth a king's ransom! Tonight we will have a party indeed!"

So the women swept and mopped the cobblestones, and strewed the floors with fresh rushes and pennyroyal to clear the air. The old door had rotted half away, so the miller, who was also the closest thing the village had to a carpenter, came and put up new posterns of fresh oak, and bolted together some planks to make a door so thick it would keep out a cavalry charge. The villagers brought in bedrolls and tables and chairs, and slowly the party room began to take form.

Then folks began to bring the food, as fine a feast as was ever served on Hostenfest. One table was loaded with plates of eels, just fished from the River Wye, and a pair of roast geese, and a suckling pig stuffed with baked apples and cinnamon. Another table was heaped with breads—hazelnut rolls, and butter muffins, and loaves of dark rye with wild honey. A third table was reserved for bowls full of salads made with fresh greens from the garden and the woods, sweetened with rose petals. It also held fruits—grapes just plucked from the vines, and ripe woodpears—along with carrots, beans, and buttered turnips. The last table was for desserts: chestnut pudding, nutmeg custards, and blackberry cobbler—all to be washed down with the finest wine that anyone in the village had tasted in years.

Aunt Constance was mindful of the ferrin, and she made sure that plates were set near the mouth of every burrow, with a few meaty bones on them, and plenty to drink. The growls of outrage that had come from the ferrin all day turned into whistles of delight, and often one of the little rat-folk would rush out of the warrens and snatch a bit of bread or some other delicacy, then race back into its warren.

Thus, the party began two hours before sunset. It was a strange affair. There were smiles and genuine laughs when a good joke was told. Some boys played lutes and drums, and Chemoise danced with Dearborn after the tables were cleared.

But behind the smiles there was worry. What would come tonight? Why had the Earth King warned everyone in all of Heredon to hide? Was a war coming? Would the ghosts of the Dunnwood be riding over the land?

It didn't take long to find out.

Just before sunset, a strange wind began to blow from the east. One of the boys who had been keeping watch at the door, atop the pile of barrels, yelled, "Come see this!"

Everyone rushed outside. The sky was covered with lowering greenish bruised clouds to the east, a strange and sickly haze that baffled the eye. Miles to the west, a wall of darkness approached. Blowing dust and chaff blotted out the sun. The wind began to rage, a boisterous gale circling this way and that, as if to announce a rising storm.

Veiled lightning crashed in the distance, grumbling again and again, as if the sky cursed in tongues of thunder.

Chemoise's heart froze. "I've only heard such a sound once before—at Castle Sylvarresta. It sounds like a Darkling Glory is coming!"

‮ℬ‬ 19 ‭ℭ‬

A WARM WELCOME

Inkarran politics are subtle and hard for an outsider to grasp. The royal families are at war on so many levels that only one thing is sure: for every friend you make in Inkarra, you will make a dozen enemies.

—*from* Travel in Inkarra, *by Aelfyn Wimmish, Hearthmaster in the Room of the Feet*

Cold water slapped Sir Borenson's face. He woke in near total darkness and tried to reach up to wipe himself dry, but the shackles on his hands were chained to his feet, and he could not move.

He could smell the musty scent of Inkarran blankets, and the peculiar odor of Inkarran flesh, a scent that somehow reminded him of cats. He could smell the mineral tang of an underground room, but he could see almost nothing. He knew that people surrounded him. He could hear them breathing, moving about.

He tried kicking with his feet, but they were chained to his wooden bed, as was his neck.

In the darkness, King Criomethes stirred, setting an empty flagon next to his head. "So, you wake now. Very good."

"Where am I?" Borenson demanded in almost a shout. He wrenched his head around. He could see just the slightest glow of coals in a hearth. By their light, he could pick out some shapes in the room—a few pillows on the floor, low tables. Nearby, in almost total darkness, lay another board made of heavy wooden planks. A woman was chained to it, hand and foot, lying on her back. "Myrrima?"

"She not hear you," Criomethes said. "The poison, she get more than you. Still sleep. We let her sleep."

"What are you doing?" Borenson asked. He sensed that hours had passed. He recognized this room. The fire had been burning merrily in the hearth when he and Myrrima first entered.

"Must talk to you," Criomethes said. The old king came and leaned over Borenson in the darkness. His pale skin was as white as cloud, and Borenson could make out some of the details of it. His eyes were cold, so cold. He peered at Borenson as if he were a bug. "You very willful man. I like."

"Willful?" Borenson asked.

"Take willful man to pass wards in mountains," Criomethes said. "Great will. Few can do this, no?"

It had taken every ounce of determination that Borenson had to cross that border. No words could describe the torment he'd felt as he forged ahead, plodding on with each step, even as the wards filled him with self-loathing.

"I don't think many would try."

"Ah," Criomethes breathed out, as if deeply satisfied. "In Inkarra, most men take endowment from family. You know this? Father, when old, give endowment to son. Uncle give to brother's son. This best way. Endowments transfer best from father to son. You know this?"

"No," Borenson said. "I've never heard that."

"Unh," Criomethes said. "That because Rofehavan facilitators very fool. Very backward."

"I'll take your word on it," Borenson said.

Criomethes smiled, a grandfatherly smile, yet somehow sinister. "Taking endowments only in family, not good," he said after a moment. "It weaken family. My thought, best take endowment from enemy. Yes?"

Borenson knew where this was going.

"You my enemy," Criomethes said in a tone so cold it hinted at murder. "Understand?"

"I understand," Borenson said. "You hate all of my people."

"I buy you endowment. From you. Want endowment. Best endowment is will? Understand?"

A flood of fear surged through Borenson. For ages, rumor said that the Inkarrans transferred endowments of will, but no northerner had ever seen the rune that controlled it.

Borenson knew what was being asked of him. What he didn't know was the cost. How could a man live without will?

"I don't understand," Borenson said, stalling for time. He considered calling for help, but this room had been at the end of a long hallway.

"Please," Criomethes said. "Must understand. Will. Will is good.

Will . . . it make all endowment strong. It add much effect. Give man strength, he pretty strong. Give man strength and will, he become very strong. Ferocious! See? Give man wit, he pretty smart. Give him wit and will, he become very smart. Sit up, think all night. Very cunning. See? Give man stamina, he not very tired. Give him stamina and will, he unstoppable. So, you sell me will?"

"No," Borenson said, trying to buy time.

"Oh, too bad," Criomethes said. "You think about it." He stepped aside.

There was movement over by the fire. A shadowy figure hunched above it, peering into the coals. Borenson recognized Prince Verazeth, all dressed in black. He advanced on Myrrima. He reached down and picked up something, a metal rod that looked like a long, thin knife.

"Wait!" Borenson said. "Let's talk about this."

But Verazeth didn't want to talk. He stepped over to Myrrima, grabbed her tunic, and ripped, exposing her bare back.

"Stop!" Borenson begged. He heard squeamish cries across the room. The Inkarran women were still here. "Help us!" he called.

Verazeth plunged the dagger into Myrrima's back at a shallow angle, burying its entire length just under the skin. There was the sound of sizzling flesh, and steam rose from the wound. Even in her drugged stupor, Myrrima cried out, her head arching back up off her wooden table as far as it would go.

"Zandaros!" Borenson screamed with his might. "Help us!"

"No one help you!" Criomethes said calmly. "Zandaros and other lords leave hours ago. He chasing after reavers you tell about. All day gone by. No one help you. No one help wife. Only you can help wife. Understand?"

"You won't get away with this," Borenson said. "Zandaros will be angry when he finds out."

"Zandaros not find out," Criomethes said. "We not want peace, not want open border. My friends, they tell Zandaros that you go home."

Prince Verazeth left the burning metal in Myrrima's back, and she whimpered as he returned to the fire and picked up another poker. He spat. The poker made a sizzling sound.

In the dim light, Borenson saw the profile of the prince's face. He was smiling. His silver eyes reflected the red coals of the fire.

He enjoys this, Borenson realized. There was a coldness to his smile that hinted at something worse than malice—complete indifference.

"Is shame," Criomethes said. "Wife very beautiful. Is shame to scar her. Is shame to torture, make die."

Verazeth approached Myrrima, and Borenson's heart beat wildly. He kicked at the chains that bound him, tried ripping free, all to no effect. The oversized chains and shackles were made to hold a man who had many endowments.

Verazeth plunged the second knife under Myrrima's skin, just above the kidneys, and smiled as he twisted it into her flesh.

Myrrima's head arced up, and every muscle in her went rigid, but the chains that held her were as strong as those that held Borenson. She let out a howl of pain that broke his heart, then fell back in a stupor.

"Please, stop!" he said. "Let her live!"

"You sell?" Criomethes asked.

"Yes!" Borenson said.

"Must want sell very bad," Criomethes said. "Must want sell more than want life itself. Must want give with all heart."

"I know," Borenson said. "I know. Just let her go. Promise you'll let her live!"

"Of course," Criomethes said. "You give me will, she live. I promise. I man of honor."

"You'll set her free?" Borenson demanded.

"Yes. We take her hills, set free."

"Let her go, then," Borenson said.

The old king nodded to Verazeth, and said, "Drug her again, then take her to hills and leave, as we have make promise."

Verazeth seemed angered by the demand, and Criomethes glanced toward two of the women in the group and barked some orders. He explained to Borenson, "I send women to make sure wife is set free."

Borenson wished that he had something better than the word of Inkarrans on this, but he could think of no way to guarantee his wife's safety. He suspected that the Inkarrans, with their twisted sense of honor, really would let her live. Yet he feared that they would try to cut Myrrima's throat to ensure her silence. He only hoped to buy her some time, give her a chance to escape. "All right," he said. "I agree to give my will. But I want to see you set Myrrima free."

Verazeth drew the knives back out of Myrrima's flesh, and set them in the fire.

"We keep knives hot, in case change mind after wife gone," Criomethes said. "Remember. Must want transfer will very bad."

"I know," Borenson said.

One girl threw a bucket of water on Myrrima, and she came out of her faint, lay shaking her head and weeping. In time, the poison wore off, and her eyes came open.

She looked to Borenson, "What's going on?" Myrrima asked, voice shaking.

"I'm buying your freedom," Borenson said.

"Buying?"

"With an endowment."

Comprehension dawned in her eyes, followed by outrage.

"Don't do anything stupid," Borenson said. "You can't fight them. Just leave. Live your life in peace."

Myrrima took his cue and only lay for a moment, weeping helplessly. Borenson felt grateful. Few women in Inkarra were ever granted endowments, and he hoped that the Inkarrans would not suspect Myrrima.

Criomethes nodded at Verazeth, and the young man unlocked the shackles on Myrrima's feet. She sat up, rubbing her the metal cuffs on her wrists, and winced at the wounds in her flesh.

"Go," Borenson told her. A woman helped Myrrima slide from table to floor, and she peered at Borenson for a long moment, as if to take a last look.

She limped to him and threw her arms over him, the heavy chains of her fetters clanking cruelly, and kissed him on the face.

Verazeth grabbed her shoulder, pulled her away, then escorted her down a dark hallway.

"Will remove wife's cuffs," Criomethes said, "when she away from here. Now, sit and look on me, your lord. Your master. No move. Keep perfect still."

Borenson felt someone pull up his right pants leg. He glanced down. In the shadows, an old facilitator with a ghostly white face leaned over him with an inkpot and needles.

∂ 20 ∞

A DISTANT FIRE

Of all mages, flameweavers are the most ephemeral. For the fire that fuels them also consumes them—first the heart, and then the mind.

—*from* Advanced Wizardry, *by Hearthmaster Shaw*

High in the Hest Mountains, Raj Ahten led his army beneath skies so clear that he almost felt he could touch the setting sun.

No snow had fallen in these mountains in almost a week. By day the sun crept up and burned away the layer of white. By night the ground grew bitter cold and every pebble on the trail froze into place. The firm footing made for a safe ride. The force horses ran swiftly, for though they had nothing to eat here on the escarpment where grass could not grow, they knew that refreshment lay in the warm valleys below, in Mystarria.

So it was that Raj Ahten rode down into the pines in the late afternoon when he came upon a vast army.

Dirty brown tents squatted haphazardly beneath trees. The horses in camp were starved, with ribs and hips showing beneath dull hides.

As Raj Ahten's army bore down upon the camp, its few guards grew frightened and blew their ram's horns.

"Peace," Raj Ahten said as he topped a rise and stared down the guards. "Your lord has returned."

These were ragged troops, commoners. Here were archers and pikemen, smiths and washwomen, camp followers and harlots. He had sent this army over the mountains nearly a month ago in preparation for his invasion of Mystarria. They had not arrived in time for his first battle at Carris, being bogged down in an early snow.

But they had made good time in the past week, and would be able to accompany him now. The captain in charge of the troops rushed from his tent, carrying a half-eaten bowl of rice.

"It is our lord, the Great Raj Ahten," a guard shouted, warning the captain to look sharp.

"O Light of the World," the captain called as he tossed his dinner to the ground and drew near, trepidation plain on his face. "To what do we owe this honor?" The captain, a grimy man named Moussaif, hailed from a great family. He had won this post by accident of birth rather than from any skill as a leader.

"The time has come," Raj Ahten said, "to claim Mystarria. Roust your men from their dreams. They must reach Carris by tomorrow at dusk."

"But, O Light of Understanding," Moussaif apologized, "my men are faint. We have had little food and no rest for days, and Carris is still thirty miles away. We just set camp an hour ago. The horses are tired."

"Your men can rest at Carris," Raj Ahten said. "They can eat Mystarrian food and drink Mystarrian blood for all I care. Tell every archer to bring a bow, a quiver of arrows, and nothing else. Tell every pikeman to bring his pike."

"But, O Fire of Heaven," Moussaif argued, "Carris is well defended. I was there at dawn myself, and rode close enough to see. Fifty thousand people are working like ants to rebuild the towers, and great columns of horses and men were entering the city. Its defenders number twice what you found a week ago!"

Raj Ahten stared down from his horse, seething.

"Of course," Raj Ahten told himself. "I should have known. Gaborn felt the danger rising at Carris. He knew I would bring it down. So he hopes to make one final stand."

"It is not you that worries him," Moussaif said. "My spies got close enough so that they could hear some workmen talk. They say that reavers are marching on Carris once again."

In a fit of rage Raj Ahten spurred his horse up a nearby ridge, to a lone peak where only a stunted pine grew. With his endowments of sight, he peered down upon the world, like an eagle from its perch.

To the south, more than three hundred miles off, he could see a veil of blowing smoke, and feel the heat of distant fires. The power in them called to him, whispered his name. Beyond the flames lay an endless black line of reavers that stretched over rolling hills. There had to be tens of thousands of reavers coming to battle, perhaps hundreds of thousands.

Ahead of their lines, he could see the distant glint of sunlight on mail, and the twinkle of flames. The knights of Rofehavan were trying to stall the reavers in their march, slow them with a wall of fire.

To the west, but thirty miles away, he could see the workers at Carris, struggling to repair the castle walls and prepare for battle.

Raj Ahten closed his eyes. He had nearly died at the hands of reavers when last he visited Carris. He had grown since then. In Deyazz, his facilitators vectored endowments to him. Raj Ahten could feel virtue filling him in waves, renewing his strength and vitality.

But he had gained more than just mere endowments. A hidden inferno burned inside him now, enlightening his mind. He consulted the flames.

Attack, Fire hissed in a voice like flickering flames. *Many will die. Make a sacrifice of them to me, and I will give you victory.*

"I hear and obey, my master," Raj Ahten whispered.

He smiled. A battle was rising, such a battle as had never been seen before. He had some surprises in store for his enemies—men and reavers alike.

ও 21 ৫

RAVEN'S GATE

Never fear a man based upon his outward form, but upon his inner spirit.

—Erden Geboren

By the time Erin reached Raven's Gate, the night skies had grown black with torment, and peals of lightning tore through the shredded clouds. A hard rain pelted down, pinging off helms and armor, dribbling beneath surcoats, drenching capes. The horses splashed through puddles, and mists rose so thick from the fields that Erin felt as if she breathed more water than air.

Raven's Gate cast an imposing shadow on the horizon. Three enormous black towers loomed above the castle walls above the fields. The middle spire rose much taller than the rest, like the highest tier of an obsidian crown.

A broad river ran to the base of the fortress. Upon its banks, rich planta-tions and cottages sprang among the rolling hills, presenting a tapestry of fields and gardens.

Erin watched the castle drawing closer, lit by flickering thunder. She had never seen Raven's Gate, with its legendary Tower of Wind. Here the Wizard Sendavian had paid homage to the Powers of the Air in ages past. Here the kings of South Crowthen had guarded their Dedicates for nearly two millennia.

Here at least twenty thousand knights filled the fields before the castle with pavilions. Squires and cooks had kindled fires within every pavilion, so that they glowed with their own inner light, like gems at the base of a black mountain.

As King Anders rode near the pavilions, lightning flashed above. Dark siege engines squatted among the fields, ballistas by the score. Captain

Gantrell blew his war horn, and knights sprinted from their tents with weapons drawn, preparing to barricade the highway.

As King Anders rode to a wall of human flesh, his knights and their squires shouted, "Anders! Anders of Crowthen! All hail the Earth King!" Heralds blew their silver coronets, squires banged shields as if they were drums.

The pavilions housed more than just the lords of South Crowthen. Erin saw merchant princes from Lysle all dressed in purple robes and shining armor; and dire Knights of Eyremoth looking pale as ghosts in white; while Duke Wythe of Beers out of Ashoven stood tall and haughty in his gray robes.

Not all among the camp were Runelords. Many archers, and camp followers, crowded close for a look at Anders, along with hopeful young men with naught but sheepskin for armor and cudgels for weapons.

Anders had emptied his realm, gathering all of his warriors here. His troops only awaited his command before marching across the border.

These lords and commoners alike stood with strange expressions, eyes gleaming with wonder and love for their lord.

Erin had never seen folk so ready to fight and die for their king. Indeed, it gave her pause. If indeed Anders did harbor a Darkling Glory's locus, and if she sought to strike him down, she saw now that she would never escape his realm alive.

King Anders's gray warhorse reared back and pawed the air. He raised his left hand and shouted to the horde of warriors, "I Choose you. I Choose you for the Earth."

The people cheered and pounded their weapons against their shields. To the north lightning flashed and thunder rumbled, as if the very heavens sought to surpass the people's applause.

They believe that he's an Earth King, Erin realized.

"Gentlemen, I apologize for the weather," King Anders said as the rain hammered on his helm. His men laughed. "We dare not ride in this storm at night, but be set for tomorrow. At dawn we ride to Beldinook to confront Lowicker's daughter, who even now marches forth to prosecute her unjust war against the people of Mystarria. But the Earth has called me to be its king, and I must protect mankind. Erden Geboren fought for twelve years before the nine kings bent their knees and bestowed upon him the iron crown. I will not repeat his folly. Tomorrow, Lowicker's daughter will bow her head to me, or we will take it off!"

The men cheered wildly, and a bolt of lightning sizzled across the heavens, arcing from cloud to cloud as it tore at the sky. Thunder roared, and the ground rattled.

Erin stared hard at Anders's back. She didn't like his words. He would have either dominion or bloodshed. That wasn't the kind of Earth King Gaborn had been.

But a mad thought entered her mind: Perhaps that's the kind of king he should have been. Perhaps Anders *is* an Earth King.

Erin had still seen no evidence that Anders had any prescient powers. She had not heard his voice in her mind warning her of danger.

Dare I test him to learn if he is a true Earth King? she wondered. If I try to stick my sword in his back, will he feel it coming? And even if I did test him, would it be a true test? What are the powers of a Darkling Glory's locus? Can it mimic those of an Earth King? A great weariness was on her. She had been fighting fatigue all the long day as she rode south. Her eyes felt heavy and full of grit, and her mind seemed to be turning like an ungreased wheel, slowly grinding toward ruin as the sands wore it down. She didn't trust her own judgment now.

And what if I kill him? she wondered. I have no proof that he harbors a locus. He might be nothing more than a madman. It would be a small deed, a dirty thing, to kill a man for his madness. And if he's not mad, if indeed he does have a locus in him, what then? I can't kill it. It will simply find a new host.

Either way that she looked at it, Erin could not raise her hand against the old king, for his death would avail nothing. It was his *unmasking* that she needed.

The men continued to cheer as King Anders rode into Raven's Gate. Erin followed in her sodden clothes, fighting sleep. The castle wall rose high, some eighty feet, and as Erin rode under the arch, she felt as if darkness swallowed her.

They continued up a short lane, to the base of the Tower of Wind. Footmen took charge of the horses. Erin got off her mount, stiff legged, and made her way into the keep.

Celinor took her hand, looked down at her smiling.

King Anders told them, "Freshen up before dinner. I'll meet you in the tower loft. We have much to discuss."

Celinor led Erin up six flights of stairs to a kingly bedchamber. A small fire flickered in the hearth. The room felt cozy, almost overwarm. At the door, Celinor ordered a maid to find suitable dry clothing for his wife, then he stripped off his wet clothes and armor. He stood naked for a moment, wiping down his armor in front of the fire. Outside, thunder raged.

Erin took off her own soggy riding cloak, leather armor, pants, and boots, but left on her long undertunic. As she hung her things by the fire, Celinor set down his oil rag and took her in his arms.

"Let's try out the bed. My father won't mind if we're a few minutes late for dinner."

"We'll not be needing a bed," Erin said. "You've already got your seed in me."

Celinor's face fell, as if he were hurt. "You're angry about something, aren't you?"

"You told your father about the sending. You told him that Paldane is my sire. You broke every confidence I've ever placed in you! And now you wonder that I'm angry?"

"I—" Celinor began, "I didn't mean to hurt you. Of course I told him everything. My father and I keep no secrets. I never have to worry what he's thinking, for when he is with me, as soon as a thought enters his mind it comes out on his tongue."

"That's no excuse," Erin said. "You can control your own tongue."

"I'm trying to win his confidence," Celinor argued. "How can I hope that he'll trust me with his innermost thoughts if I don't seem to reveal my own? If he is mad, I need to know it. I need proof of it."

"You went to Heredon as his spy," Erin said. "Tell me, are you still his spy?"

"Of course not," Celinor said. "But he must believe that I am."

"And what of me?" Erin demanded. "He sent you to learn my lineage. Did your father demand more of you? Did he tell you to be courting me?"

"Now you're the one who is talking madness!" Celinor said. He backed away a step and shook his head.

"You think I'm mad?" Erin said. "You told me that you thought your father was mad! Is everyone mad but you?"

"You've met my father now," Celinor said. "What do you think? Is he mad? Or is he the new Earth King? Is it possible that he is everything he says that he is?"

"I think," Erin said, "that your father is either a madman or is infected by a locus."

"And what of the Nut Woman?" Celinor asked. "She's an Earth Warden, and she backs up his tale."

"I don't know." Erin's head was whirling. She looked hard at Celinor. "I asked you a question a moment ago, and you never answered."

"What question?"

"I asked, 'Did your father send you to court me?'"

"What kind of question is that?"

"An honest one, from the heart. You say that you and your father keep no secrets. Will you keep secrets from me? Tell me, did your father ask you to court me?"

Celinor's smile faltered. She saw now that he had been trying to smile in the face of her accusations. He stood gazing at her for a long moment, sadness and worry warring in his countenance. "Yes," he admitted. "He thought it would be well if I courted you—that is, if indeed you were Gaborn's kin."

Erin turned away, her back going rigid with anger.

Celinor put his hand on her shoulder. "But that's not why I wanted you," he said. "I wanted you because you're strong, smart, and beautiful. From the moment I met you, I fell hopelessly in love with you."

He turned her around, and she thought that she could detect sincerity in his eyes. She stared hard at him and wondered, What kind of man are you? Dare I speak my mind to you ever again?

No, she decided, I can't.

It was all she could do to keep herself from killing him.

Only one thing held her back. She didn't know who was more dangerous, the father or the son.

That night, Erin Connal went to dinner in the uppermost chamber of the Tower of Wind, high above the plains. Six hundred steps the staircase climbed.

From time to time, as she ascended the winding stair, Erin would pass archers' slots. From these she could peer below.

To the south, ages ago, the Great Rift had sliced the land in two, so that Raven's Gate roosted on the lip of a cliff. From these lofty heights, one could peer down onto the green plains of Beldinook. An ancient road climbed the cliff, weaving this way and that, until it met the city gates.

By the time Erin reached Anders's chamber atop the tower, she could see for miles. The wind whistled around the tower, and lightning snaked across the heavens.

Anders was not in the room when Erin and Celinor entered. A fine feast lay spread about on a small table, but Anders had left it. He'd thrown open a door, and stood out on the parapet, the wind lashing his hair.

He grinned when he became aware of Erin and Celinor, and came in. "I was admiring the view of Beldinook," he said, "as Sendavian must have in his day. I cannot imagine that one of the wind-born like him would have been able to stay inside on a night like this. Come, let's to dinner."

The king sat at the small dinner table in the center of the room and carved from a venison roast. He held silent all through dinner, and did not look up at Erin, nor at Celinor, who often exchanged curious glances.

Erin found the silence to be disquieting.

"Father," Celinor asked after several minutes. "Did you want to talk to us?"

King Anders peered up at them as he had forgotten that they were in the room.

He is mad, Erin thought.

"They say that bad news should never be taken with dinner," the king answered, fumbling his fork, "for it is not easily digested."

"You have bad news?" Celinor asked.

Anders swallowed a piece of venison, nodded his head, and would say no more. Indeed, he merely peered at his dinner, as if a bite of turnip or mouthful of wine might supply an answer to the question. After a long moment, he continued eating.

Erin's stomach was tight with hunger, so she shoved a few bites in her mouth. When the king finished, they all pushed their plates back.

King Anders smiled, and gave his son a pained look. "As you know, I've played Gaborn falsely in the past. I asked you two here, I asked Erin here, so that I could apologize."

"Exactly how did you play him falsely?" Erin asked.

"I sent messages to King Lowicker of Beldinook and warned him to beware the pretend Earth King. I also plotted with Internook to invade Mystarria, and these two lands granted support. Others were more reticent to rush to judgment, though, as you can see, many a foreign lord has come to join my army. Only one man alone I did not seek to entice into my war—Raj Ahten, for I feared that he was beyond even my power to redeem.

"But since the Earth called me to be its king, my heart has grown uneasy. You see, every man, woman, and child is precious to me now. Every one of them. Yet I've sent the kings of the earth to battle Mystarria. Without endowments to protect them, the folk of Mystarria are doomed. My only hope is that we can reach them before Gaborn's enemies do, and thus bring enough aid to turn the tide of war."

Erin drew close and suggested, "If haste is needed, then let's ride now, as fast as we may."

"My heart forewarns that we would lose many men if we ride tonight," King Anders said. "Even if we could ride in such a storm as this, would our horses have the legs to fight when we reached Mystarria? Would our warriors be fit? I think not. Better to rest briefly. Still, haste is called for, and I am making haste. I've sent messengers to Lowicker's daughter, and to the warlords of Internook, begging them to withdraw. But I cannot guarantee that these two will stay their hands. Rialla Lowicker is filled with rage at her father's death, and the warlords of Internook are ruled by greed, not reason. So we must be prepared for battle. A ragged band of tired knights would avail little. A powerful army must ride from the north, like a mighty wind, blowing succor to the people of Mystarria. We must save Mystarria."

He peered at Erin for a long moment, and said, "So I have given you cause to mistrust me. I only ask one thing of you. As my new daughter, I ask your forgiveness, and your indulgence, as I struggle to make recompense for my wrongs."

Erin studied King Anders. His face was skeletal, and he sat leaning forward, like a child with his elbows on the table. His perpetual expression of worry so mirrored Gaborn's that Erin could almost imagine that the two were one. She seemed to feel the efficacy of his words. He really did want to save Mystarria.

Yet nothing that he had yet said or done indicated he was anything more than a befuddled old man who hoped to undo the wrongs he had set in motion. Nothing proved that he was an Earth King.

"All right," Erin said. "I'll give you a second chance."

After dinner, Erin left Celinor to talk with his father and went to her room. Her eyes felt full of grit, and all of her muscles were so worn that that she knew she could not last any longer. She would have to suffer through her nightly dreams.

She sharpened her long dagger, then lay on the big four-poster bed, placing her blade under her pillow. The bed felt softer than any cot she'd ever slept on, and she felt almost as if she were sinking into the mattress, sinking and sinking but never quite falling.

She woke in the owl's burrow. It was dawn in the netherworld, and the storm that she'd felt earlier in the day had passed. So much sunlight slanted under the canopy of the great tree and into the hollow that she got her first clear view of the owl's den.

It was much like a hollow in any earthly tree. Knobby roots thrust from the floor where they would, while others made shelves above the door. But this was no animal den. Erin could see signs of human habitation. A woman's face had been carved above the opening to the burrow, and a similar image had been carved above a passage farther back, round the bend of a root.

A pile of bones glinted under the roost where the owl usually sat. Erin went to it and gazed down. There were strange bones, the remains of monsters—something like a giant frog with antlers, and another creature that might have been a fawn, if not for its wide-set eyes and ungainly fangs. Feathers and dust lay in piles on the bones, along with the white excretions of the great owl.

Erin peered round the corner, to the woman's face carved above the passage. Her face was beautiful, surreal. Her long hair cascaded down, framing the doorway. Beyond it, a tunnel angled down into the ground, with flagstones paving the way, forming a stair down into the darkness.

Erin breathed deeply. The morning air smelled sweeter than a summer field, but a hint of musk and deep places added spice to the odor. She pinched herself, and felt pain. She felt awake. Indeed, she'd never felt so alive.

In tales of the netherworld, it was said that in the beginning, all men were Bright Ones who lived beneath the First Tree. Erin wondered if this vast tree was indeed that tree of legend, and if the hole that gaped before her led down to some forgotten home. Forgotten or abandoned.

Perhaps the Bright Ones are all dying off, she told herself. Surely, if the flocks of Darkling Glories I saw flying in my vision yesterday are real, then the end of the Bright Ones cannot be far off.

She squinted, searching the walls for a sign of an old sconce with a torch in it, or perhaps a fireplace carved into a nook where a faggot might lie. But she found nothing to light her way.

She turned back, and was about to risk going out into the daylight in order to explore this world that she was condemned to visit in every waking dream, when she heard the rush of wings. Darkness blotted out the light that streamed through the opening of the burrow.

Suddenly, the great owl swooped to its roost, the wind from its wings stirring up motes of dust that shimmered in the air. In its massive beak wriggled something that might have been a rat, if it had weighed less than fifty pounds.

The owl set its prey on the ledge, laid one claw over the creature, adjusted its wings, and sat with head lowered, peering at Erin for a long moment.

"Is it safe to talk?" Erin asked.

"For the moment," the owl said. It hesitated. "You fear me." Its thoughts smote her, carrying the owl's sadness. "You are a warrior, yet you fight sleep to avoid me. I mean you no harm."

"You're a stranger," Erin said. "I'd be leery even if you lived on my own world."

"You need not fear me," the owl said, "unless you are in league with the Raven."

In her mind's eye Erin saw the Raven, a great shadow that blotted out the sun. She it was who had sought to wrest control of the Runes of Creation from the Bright Council. She it was who had blasted the One True World into millions of parts, giving birth to the shadow worlds that she now sought to claim or destroy.

"It's not in league with the Raven you'll find me," Erin said. "Yet I don't trust you. Or maybe I worry that I'm going mad, for I've never dreamt of anything like you before, but now you haunt my every sleep."

The owl peered at her, unblinking. "In your world, do not people *send* dreams to one another?"

"No," Erin said.

The owl said nothing, but Erin felt sorrow wash over her, and knowledge enlightened her. In the netherworld, sendings were valued as the most intimate form of speech. It had greater power than mere words to enlighten both the mind and heart, and when men and women fell in love, they often found themselves wandering together at night in shared dreams, no matter what great distances might separate them.

"I see," Erin said. "You don't mean to worry me—only to offer comfort. Yet the things you show me bring no comfort at all."

"I know," the owl said.

"I've been hunting for your Asgaroth," Erin said. "I don't know where he is hiding."

"Long have I hunted Asgaroth, too," the owl whispered, and Erin felt the weight of that hunt. She saw in her mind the figure of a man, a lonely man who wore a sword upon his back, tracking endless wastes. The owl had hunted Asgaroth across countless ages and upon many worlds. A hundred times he had found the creature, and many times he had stripped the mask from Asgaroth's face.

"When I first dreamt of you," Erin said, "you held my dagger, and you summoned me."

"Yes," the owl said softly. "I seek Asgaroth, and I need an ally among your people. Beware," the owl whispered. "Asgaroth comes." It folded its wings over its chest and faded like a morning mist.

At the mouth of the burrow, the shadow descended. Black wings blotted out the sun, and the smell of a storm filled the small hole. The creature that strode down the steps squatted as it walked, its long knuckles scraping the ground. The thing had a man's shape, but its fangs and clawed fingers spoke nothing of humanity. Darkness flowed at its feet.

A Darkling Glory stalked toward her, cold and menacing.

Erin's eyes flew open just as her bedroom door began to crack. Her heart hammered. She'd left a single candle burning on the nightstand.

Celinor came into the room, looking solemn. She felt certain that Asgaroth's locus was near, so she clutched the dagger under her pillow, heart hammering, and prepared to sink it into Celinor's throat as soon as he lay on the bed.

But just behind Celinor came his father, King Anders.

One of them was a locus, Erin felt certain, but she didn't know which.

"Ah," King Anders said in a kindly tone, "I'm glad that you're awake."

"We just got a courier from Heredon," Celinor said. "A vast horde of reavers has issued from the Underworld, and is marching through Mystarria. Gaborn has sent out a call for help to every realm of the north. He begs that any who can come to his defense bring lances or bows and reach Carris by sunset tomorrow."

King Anders's skeletal face seemed pale. "We must answer his call before first light," Anders said. "I can bring precious few of my troops in so short a time, but I've already sent a messenger to tell Gaborn that a new Earth King rides to his defense. We will bring what comfort we may!"

BOOK 13

WHEN TRUE NIGHT FALLS

ஐ 22 ை

A WIND FROM THE EAST

The world is full of burrowing creatures—great stone worms whose diameters are larger than a house, crevasse crawlers with their sharp teeth and seg-mented bodies, blind-crabs and pouch spiders, and even tiny weevils called chervils, that can burrow into a man's armor. But reavers are hunters, not burrowers. They live in holes tunneled by other animals, and seem to dig only when trying to dislodge their prey from some small cavity.

—*from* Binnesman's Bestiary, Animals of the Underworld

Gaborn raced through the Underworld in a tunnel where mud pots spattered pale calcite against the white walls of the crawlway. Behind those walls, he could hear steam roaring upward through hidden chimneys, as if the reavers that fashioned this place had tried to wall out vast rivers of boiling water. It was a rolling thunder in his ears.

The light from his single opal pin was fading. He didn't know how much longer it would last. It seemed that he had been running for days now, per-haps weeks. He sensed danger ahead, stopped and peered down the trail.

The path intersected a crude cavern, a hole bored by some massive rock worm. Part of the roof had collapsed, leaving dirt, gravel, and boulders on the floor. It was perfect for an ambush. The main tunnel had been polished by the tread of countless reavers. But the side tunnel was wild. Red shagweed grew to the height of a man's knees.

Indeed, blister worms had crawled from the side cave and now infested the floor by the thousands, dining on dung left by the reaver horde. The worms, sluglike creatures the length of a finger, were gray, shot through with crimson veins. The worms' flesh secreted a poison that blistered the skin, but a large blind-crab, oblivious to the poison, was raking through the dung, feeding.

Gaborn could see no fresh sign of reavers at the crossroad, no philia peeking suspiciously from beneath a pile of dirt. Yet he sensed death lying in wait.

A reaver was there; perhaps more than one. He caught a faint odor, like flesh that quickly transformed to mold. Reavers were whispering in scents.

Gaborn peered up the trail and felt a sudden rush of energy. His facilitators in Heredon were granting him more endowments. He wasn't sure if he had just gained more brawn or stamina, but the effect was gratifying to one who had been running for so long.

Gaborn clutched his weapon tightly, his sweaty palms gripping the leather straps that bound the reaver dart, and prepared to step forward.

"Wait!" the Earth warned. Gaborn could see no reason to wait, but as he did, he felt a wash of power, and his muscles unclenched just the smallest bit. He had just received an endowment of grace.

He lifted his foot, leaned forward, and the Earth whispered wait again. Suddenly he understood the warning. The danger had just grown less, but it was still too great. The Earth Spirit forbade him to move forward until he had enough endowments.

And so Gaborn stopped and made a small fire. He made a paste of flour, water, salt and honey from his pack, and then cooked himself some fry bread.

As he ate, his powers continued to grow. Brawn, stamina, grace, and wit were all added to him. With each endowment, Gaborn felt more hale, more . . . permanent.

He continued to strain his senses for a long hour, whiffing faint scents that drifted across the cave floor.

At last, when he had eaten his fill and digested some food, he climbed back to his feet. He picked up a large flat rock and carried it up near the intersection, then threw it low to the floor, so it skipped as if on the surface of a pond, grinding the blister worms into gooey bits and startling the crab that fed among them.

The effect was instantaneous. A great reaver lurched up from the ground in front of him. The soil seemed almost to explode. Dust and pebbles flew up.

Confused, the monster grasped wildly at the stone, seeking its prey. A second reaver dropped from the roof of a side tunnel to the left. A third mage lurched from a cavity to the right, a deadly crystalline staff gleaming in its hand.

A bolt of green energy sizzled from the staff, smashing into the blind-crab. Gaborn smelled the stench of death, and as if a voice rang in his mind, heard the words, "Rot, thou child of men."

As their leader recognized that Gaborn had not run into its trap, it rushed forward with tremendous speed and power, and for a moment Gaborn watched in astonishment.

He somersaulted backward a dozen paces, hoping that in the narrows, they would have to attack in single file.

The huge leader lunged, hissing in frustration.

Gaborn leapt into its mouth—knees high so that his feet cleared the rows of scythelike teeth on its bottom jaw. He hit its raspy tongue, and found the beast's mouth wet with slime, so that he slipped as if on wet stones.

Gaborn shoved his reaver dart into the soft spot in the monster's upper palate, striking its brain. The monster responded by shaking its head roughly, trying to dislodge him.

Gaborn clung to his reaver dart, holding on for dear life, for the reaver's teeth were as sharp as daggers and would shred him like parchment.

Gaborn's weight caused the javelin to waggle. Hot blood showered over him as the monster provided the impetus to scramble its own brains.

Shortly, the reaver staggered and fell, its mouth gritted tightly. Gaborn drew his spear out.

The largest and fastest of the three reavers was dead, but Gaborn's Earth Senses were screaming, "Dodge."

Suddenly the dead reaver's mouth was pried open, and one of its companions slashed with its deadly claw.

Gaborn launched himself from the dead reaver's cavernous mouth.

The reaver mage stood just feet away, its paws occupied with holding its dead master's mouth open. Gaborn struck before it could react, hurling his javelin into the monster's sweet triangle.

The reaver let go of its master's jaws and lurched backward, stumbling into its companion. It reached up and tried to pry the reaver dart free, but must have done more damage than good. For as soon as it pulled the dart out, a gush of brains and blood came with it, and the mage stumbled and fell.

The battle with the third reaver lasted for several minutes, as Gaborn weaved and dodged to escape its attacks. Yet for all practical purposes, the battle was over before it had begun.

Soon, all three reavers lay dead.

Gaborn had received nothing more than a vicious cut.

But as he staggered over the battlefield, where dead blister worms lay in heaps, he was amazed. The little worms were all dead. They lay in piles of moldering flesh. Even the blind-crab that had been feeding on them was dead, bits of mold and putrescence oozing from its mouth.

Gaborn's cut began to fester. The reaver mage had been powerful. Indeed, Gaborn could feel the food turning bad in his stomach.

And yet he lingered for a moment, for the spell was so familiar. Gaborn sensed Earth Power here. The spell had been a healing spell, he decided, like those that Binnesman pronounced upon the wounded. Only it was reversed.

Gaborn began to choke, as if his lungs would rot in his chest, and he staggered away from the foul place. Patches of fungi, like liver spots, were forming on his hands.

He ran a few hundred yards, and on impulse, pulled off his backpack. His food was all covered with mold. He had nothing in there worth carrying, so he tossed the pack to the ground.

He ran on for hours, until his healing powers closed his wounds.

Who am I fighting? he wondered. What am I fighting?

Back in Heredon, two weeks ago, he had imagined that Raj Ahten was his nemesis. But the Wizard Binnesman had warned that Raj Ahten was only a phantom, a mask that a greater enemy hid behind.

He'd imagined then that Binnesman was speaking of Fire, was trying to tell him that one of the greater Powers fought him. And then Iome had warned that a wizard of the Air had attacked her, and he imagined that two of the greater Powers were allied in battle.

But something that Gaborn had just seen made him wonder even at that. The reavers' spells showed that they were twisting the Earth Powers. At Carris they had caused wounds to fester, and sent blindness upon men. They had hurled black mists that shredded a man's flesh.

They had wrung the water from men. Water?

It wasn't just Fire and Air that allied against him. Even the forces of healing and protection had been subverted. Even the Earth that he served seemed to have turned against him.

Earth, Air, Fire, Water.

A creature called the Raven had tried to wrest control of them once before, long ago, in a time of legend.

What was it that Binnesman had said in his garden, when the Earth Spirit first appeared to Gaborn? Other Powers would grow. But "the Earth would diminish."

Gaborn wondered. The Earth had withdrawn from him, left him bereft of his ability to warn his Chosen people of danger. But had the Earth withdrawn because of Gaborn's own moment of weakness or because of its own?

Gaborn ran on, and on, until his Earth Senses warned that death was approaching his people in Heredon.

Night was falling aboveground.

It had been a day and a half in common time since he'd entered the Mouth of the World. But there was no measuring time anymore. It had been less than two weeks in common time since Raj Ahten launched his attack on Heredon. It had been ten days since Gaborn had become the Earth King.

But with his endowments of metabolism, time stretched out of all proportion. Days seemed to draw out into weeks, weeks into months.

He ran through a tunnel where tiny crystalline cave spiders, so perfectly clear that they seemed to be cut from quartz, hung from thick silken strings. He had seen such spiders before in Heredon, but then they had climbed up their webs so quickly that they had seemed to be droplets of water, dribbling upward.

Now they were frozen motionless. The whole world seemed to be frozen, and all eternity was but a moment.

He reached a place where tunnel floors were flooded to a depth of several feet. He picked up his pace, raced over the water. Each time the sole of either foot touched the surface, it would begin to sink as if in soft mud. But he raced on, letting the surface tension buoy him.

He didn't know how many endowments of metabolism he had anymore. At least forty. He had heard that it took that many before a man could run on the water. But he could have had a hundred endowments.

He had no way to measure time except by the slap of his feet over stone, and the pounding of his heart.

There is a limit to the number of endowments of metabolism a man can take. Common wisdom said that one should never take more than a dozen, for when he reaches that point, certain subtle dangers arise. All of the runes by which facilitators transferred attributes were imperfect. The rune for metabolism made the muscles move swiftly, made the brain think clearly, but it often did not make all of the organs work with the same efficiency.

Thus, one who took vast endowments of metabolism and held them for long often became jaundiced and sickly, and within weeks would fall to his death. Adding two endowments of stamina for each endowment of metabolism could ease the problem. But rarely could a lord afford so many forcibles, and so a man who took great endowments of metabolism in a time of need was like a star that blazes brightly as it fades.

Gaborn wondered if the facilitators would kill him with their forcibles.

He did not stop to rest, did not sleep. With almost every step, he felt stronger.

There is a limit to what endowments can do. Once a man takes five endowments of wit, he forgets virtually nothing. At twenty endowments, every heartbeat, every blink of the eye, becomes etched in memory, and there is little benefit to taking more endowments beyond that point.

The same is true with brawn. A warrior who takes ten endowments of brawn might lift a horse, and Gaborn had seen more than one drunken knight attempt the feat. But adding more endowments does nothing to strengthen the bones, and so the warrior soon reaches practical limits. True, he might lift a horse, but in doing so he stood in grave danger of snapping the bones in his back or ankles.

A warrior who takes five endowments of stamina also reaches a limit: the point where he needs no sleep. It is true that he might grow fatigued, but a moment of rest is as refreshing as a night in bed.

Gaborn had never wanted to be like Raj Ahten, to horde endowments that benefited him little.

Yet as Gaborn ran, he could feel himself being added upon. He felt as if he had grown beyond all natural limits. He could not even guess how many endowments he had. A hundred of brawn? Even when straining to leap a sixty-foot chasm, he moved effortlessly. A thousand of stamina? He felt no weariness. It soon felt as if vigor and wholeness oozed from every pore.

And with each few steps, as the facilitators in Heredon vectored him more endowments, the vigor grew.

He felt as if he were a fruit ripening in the sun, ready to burst its skin from its own copiousness. He felt as if he were only dreaming of the race through the Underworld, as if he'd left his body far behind, and now glided on wings of thought.

Raj Ahten must feel this way, he thought. I could run across a cloud.

He raced through the cavern, crossed the water. Ahead, a squat brown creature, like a giant slug, oozed along the cavern floor—a mordant, digesting everything that it touched. The floors of the tunnel were riddled with holes now, the burrows of blind-crabs and other small animals.

Gaborn halted to drink from a warm pool. The water could not slake his thirst. And though he gathered some gray fungi to eat, it could do little more than ease the knot in his empty stomach.

He felt a death as one of his Chosen was torn from him. In Heredon the killing had begun. Gaborn stretched out with his Earth Sight. He felt his own death lurking in the dark corridors ahead, even as he felt death rushing toward his Chosen people in Heredon. Even with the warnings he'd sent, tens of thousands would die tonight.

He halted for a moment to gnaw on some gray man's ear and mourn his people. He felt that tonight was but a portent of worse things to come.

Aboveground and more than a thousand miles to the north, in Heredon a storm swept the land. Thick clouds, dark on the bottom but green at their peaks, rose like a wall. Lightning flashed at their crowns as a keening wind thrashed the fields.

"Inside!" Chemoise's uncle Eber shouted to the villagers of Ableton. "Everyone, hide, quickly! This is what the Earth King warned us against!"

Many a young lad would have argued and stayed gazing out the door, just to prove his bravery, but they had heard rumors of the goings-on at Castle Sylvarresta and knew that to ignore the Earth King's warning could have only one result: death.

"Get inside," Eber urged. "Whatever it is that's coming this way, it will kill you."

"Aye," a dozen other men all grumbled. "It's the king's will."

So Eber closed the door and brought down the bolt. Old Able Farmworthy surprised everyone by pulling out a leather bag full of soil from his fields and sprinkling it on the ground in front of the door, forming a rune of protection. Afterward, he poured a libation of wine over it. He warned, "Don't anyone disturb this dust."

The old man was no Wizard Binnesman, but he was a successful farmer whose heart was close to the land. Chemoise wanted to believe that he had some power, and perhaps everyone else did, too, for no one dared touch his rune.

The music had stopped. The feast was over.

Night had just begun, though no one was in the mood to celebrate now. Instead, the townsfolk all sat on the floor, fearing what the evening would bring.

Chemoise strained to hear outside. The wind moaned as the storm grew.

Soon the stout new door began to rattle on its hinges. "Someone's out there, wanting to get in!" a woman said. "Who could it be?"

Chemoise thought it only sounded like the wind banging, for no one called out for help on the other side. Or if they did, the rising wind was carrying their voice away.

She peered about the room. There were only sixteen families in the village. She did not know them well enough yet to tell if everyone was present. Could someone have left a child outside?

Eber began calling out names, "Caln Hawks, are you and yours all here?"

Caln looked about. "Aye!"

"Dunagal Free, you and yours?"

"Here!"

And so it went.

Eber and Aunt Constance were both here with Chemoise, and grandmother sat at the dinner table, the poor old thing painfully unaware that anything was amiss.

"We're all here," Eber said when he finished.

"But someone is out there!" the woman argued.

"I know—" Gadamon Drinkwater suggested, "it's that old shepherd what lives in the hills."

"No," Eber said. "I warned him this afternoon. He takes his sheep to a cave in times of storm. He planned to stay up there with his flock."

"It's not someone at the door," Able Farmworthy said. "It's some*thing.*"

The wind moaned as if in pain and pounded on the door, thrashing it. Sticks and leaves were flung against the stout wood, and it shuddered under the impact. Chemoise's hair stood on end.

She had heard how the Darkling Glory raged even after it was slain, turned into a whirlwind and raced to the east. Now it appeared that it had returned.

Distantly, a squeaking arose, as if bats circled outside. Chemoise could barely discern it under the howling of the wind, the sudden crash of thunder. With the sound came a stench, the smell of filth and hair.

"Rats!" an old woman said. "I smell rats!"

Slowly the sound swelled in volume, and the stink grew with it. Rats were coming—not just dozens or hundreds, not even thousands, but tens of thousands.

In her mind's eye, Chemoise could envision them rushing across the valley, through the dry stalks of the wheat fields, leaping into the creek and swimming over it with grim determination. Climbing atop the rock walls of the sheepfolds and racing along them as if on a road.

Until, presently, the rats were at the door. They squeaked and chittered outside, and there was a grinding noise as they began to gnaw the wooden doorposts away.

Uncle Eber shouted, "To the back of the room!"

Chemoise's stomach churned with fear. Most of the women and children raced to the back of the cellars, seeking to hide. But Chemoise looked around for a weapon, grabbed a broom, and went to the door. Some lads from town had brought swords and warhammers, just in case. But against rats they would prove to be clumsy weapons.

Dearborn Hawks took her broom. "Here," he said, "let me have that. Get back with the others!"

"It's all right," Chemoise argued. "I can help."

"You've a child in you," Dearborn said. "You can risk hurting yourself all you like, for all that I care. But we have to take care of the babe."

Chemoise handed him the broom, and held his eye for a moment. She went back to the far corner of the wine cellar with the other women. When she turned to look back, Dearborn was still gazing at her.

For a long while, the rats chewed, filing away at the door.

As they did, something strange happened. The ferrin in their holes began to snuffle and whistle plaintively. They poked their heads out of their burrows and sniffed the air, whiskers twitching. Then, one by one, the pudgy creatures began to emerge, squinting in the lamplight.

Chemoise had seldom seen a ferrin in such good light. The ones who came stalking out of their lairs now were big males, the hunters. Each stood a little more than a foot tall. Each wore rags almost in mockery of human clothing. One might wear only a mouseskin belt, into which a weapon was slung, while another wore an old dishrag as if it were a cape. The ferrin ranged in color from brown to a sort of mottled gray, and were lighter on the belly than on the back. Each wielded a weapon of some kind—an eighteen-inch spear made from an old fisherman's arrow, an ax with a blade chiseled from broken glass, a dagger formed from a gold cloak pin.

Growling and snuffling they approached the door, and then stood whistling.

Rats were the ferrins' favorite prey—a delicacy as beloved by them as venison was by the men of Rofehavan. Dozens of ferrin crawled from their holes, and as their courage grew, more hunters followed, grizzled old ferrin with the hair on their snouts gone gray, young ferrin with sleek brown coats. Soon, two hundred ferrin warriors swelled into the room—more ferrin than Chemoise would ever have imagined could have been hiding in the old wine cellar.

Uncle Eber warned his men. "Step back. This is their battle. This is why the Earth King warned us to stay belowground."

And so the humans fell back and watched in awe as the battle began. For long minutes, rats gnawed the door. The thunder raged, the wind wailed and pounded at the entrance.

Suddenly, a huge black rat lunged under the door.

Instantly, half a dozen ferrin spears rushed to impale the beast.

Then one ferrin lord growled menacingly and raised the rat victoriously into the air. Its legs kicked in vain as it struggled to break free, and it wrenched its incisors around and bit at the spear. The rat was far dirtier and more bedraggled than Chemoise had imagined it could be. It looked half-starved, as if it had been running for days. Its eyes were glazed with a yellow, crusty film. Its matted hair was full of mud and filth.

The ferrin lord swung his spear, sent the wounded rat hurtling through the air, so that it landed in the center of the hall. The poor vermin lay on its side, wounded, and began snuffling and kicking, as if seeking escape.

Three female ferrin bolted from their holes. They grabbed the wounded rat, pulling it in all directions, ripping the small animal with their sharp little paws, so that the rat shrieked once in pain and then died.

The ferrin women dragged their kill toward their warrens, leaving only its turds to litter the floor.

No sooner was one rat gone than the warriors hurled another back to take its place—then a third and a fourth.

But what started as a slaughter soon became a grim struggle.

The rats continued to gnaw, widening their access, so that soon dozens could scurry beneath the door at a time. Ferrin warriors in the front ranks stabbed and hacked at the beasts, blocking the passage with the bodies of the dead. So the rats attacked. They began leaping through the opening, sinking sharp teeth into ferrin flesh, piercing bones and severing arteries. The ferrin grimly fought, whistling and growling curses at rats that surged into the room, attacking with the abandon and strength of madness.

Swarming past the ferrin, some rats managed to race through or leap over the beleaguered ferrin warriors.

Once through, they bolted across the room toward the villagers and charged in a rabid fashion.

The first time it happened, it was a shock. The ferrin warriors hurled a wounded rat into the back of the room from the front ranks, and through pain-clouded eyes it peered into the recesses. Recognition suddenly seemed to dawn in its glazed eyes, and the rat scrabbled and pawed toward the villagers like a wounded hound seeking a boar.

No common madness drove it, Chemoise knew. It moved with a will other than its own.

As it approached, a queer sound emanated from back in its throat, a sort of quavering growl. Chemoise had never heard such a sound from a rat.

But she had heard rumors about rats, how they spread disease. A rat bite could easily become infected and ooze pus for days. The wounds could fester, and bite victims sometimes died.

Chemoise feared that these sickly creatures, which raced beneath the door and attacked with grim abandon, carried some unthinkable plague.

The rat came slowly, and one of the Drinkwater boys, a child of nine, leapt on the beast with both feet, crushing it with a crunching sound.

Chemoise's stomach turned. Back home at Castle Sylvarresta, there had always been plenty of ferrin to keep the town free of rats.

Their behavior wasn't natural. The storm outside wasn't natural. Thunder boomed in a menacing, unending chorus.

We killed the Darkling Glory, she realized, so now it sends this curse upon Heredon.

"Form up ranks," Uncle Eber shouted. "Men in front, women behind. Don't let the rats get near!"

Soon more rats came rushing past the ferrin, and not all were wounded. They raced across the room as fast as terriers, jumping ten feet at a time. The young men from the village pretended to make a game of it, racing out and batting the rats with brooms, skewering them with long-handled meat forks from the dinner table, swatting them with their hands or stomping them into oblivion.

But it was no game to the rats. The nasty things, driven by some dark force, seemed impelled to strike with a suicidal zeal. They charged into the ranks of villagers, biting into the first person they reached.

Uncle Eber and some other men grabbed tables and threw them down, forming a protective barrier.

The nightmare began in earnest. Rats streamed under the door so fast that the ferrin could not fight them all. The small warriors stabbed and hacked. The only light in the room came from a pair of lanterns, so that Chemoise could not see the battle well. The ferrin became a writhing, snarling mass. Their whistles and growls, which Chemoise imagined to be battle cries, soon turned to squeals of terror and pain. She could see ferrin spears rising up, impaling rats as they leapt. Axes swinging, chopping the heads off rats.

Wounded and bloody rats crawled about the room in a daze. And still more rats came, soaking rats, black with mud. Rats with crusted yellow eyes, or eyes filmed green from the plague. Rats that oozed white saliva from their mouths, and vomited as they died.

The ferrin battled fiercely, slaughtering the vermin by the thousands. But killing a rat was no small task for a ferrin. A ferrin was only a foot tall, and a large rat nearly reached his waist. Thus, in size, a ferrin was to a rat what a man was to a boar. And even though they were small, the rats were remarkably strong and ferocious, driven by madness. A ferrin armed with a spear or a makeshift dagger could bring one of the monsters down, but it was not easy.

So the battle raged.

Chemoise took her place with the women, and any rats that made it past the ferrin and past the men, she dealt with as best she could, kicking and slapping.

The female ferrin got weapons of their own and stood guard at the openings of their dens, where they waded into the midst of the rats. Chemoise heard a plaintive cry from one of them, saw two rats latched onto the ferrin woman, dragging her down. Chemoise raced to her, grabbed the rats and squeezed until their jaws unlocked. The rats twisted in her hand and turned their rage on her.

The battle became a jumbled nightmare. Chemoise could never say exactly how long it lasted—an hour, two at the most. But it felt like endless days.

She fought with heart racing, mouth dry with fear. She killed hundreds of rats, and was bitten once on the wrist, once on the ankle. One little monster scampered up her dress and would have taken an eye, but Dearborn Hawks swatted it away.

The number of rats swelled, until finally they surged into the room in a dark tide. Chemoise could not imagine where so many rats had come from. Certainly they did not come from local fields.

Old Uncle Eber shouted, "Everyone, stay back!" He ran to a keg of lamp oil, and hoisted it under one arm. Then he grabbed a lantern from the floor, and hurried toward the front door, shouting at the ferrin, "Make way! Make way!"

Rats leapt on him, latching onto his legs, racing up his shoulder to sink their teeth into his throat. Soon, the rats clung to him by the dozens, so that it almost looked as if he wore some macabre cloak.

Aunt Constance cried out in dismay. Uncle Eber would never make it alive through such an attack. Chemoise lurched forward to rescue him, but too late.

The ferrin scampered from his path as best they could, and then Eber hurled the useless door open.

Outside, the thunder was a snarling fiend. Lightning arced through green skies, and Eber stood for a moment, defiant, limned in its light. The wind raged this way and that, like a maddened beast. But for all its fury, the storm brought no water. No rain fell on the fields. Only a dry wind beat the last of the summer's crops to the ground. The wine barrels that Dearborn had stacked so carefully now all lay in a jumble, cluttering the path ahead.

Eber slogged forward a few steps, wading now through rats that broke off their assault on the door and assailed an easier victim, uttering fierce growls of triumph. The rats scampered up his legs and onto his shoulders, weighing him down so that Chemoise could not see her uncle at all, only a surging, struggling mound covered with rats.

Eber dashed the oil barrel to the ground, smashing dozens of rats in the process. They growled in rage and squealed in pain. Oil spilled over everything. He threw the lantern.

Flames surged up before him, forming a wall. Hundreds of rats had latched firmly onto Eber now, and he spun about crazily for a moment trying to dislodge them.

But he must have known that he could not survive their noxious bites. He staggered into the midst of the flames, dragging the rats with him.

All around Chemoise, the children and women uttered cries of horror. Aunt Constance struggled to reach Eber, but the other women grabbed her arms and held her back. The flaming oil ignited a savage blaze. The old wine barrels were dry as kindling and fed the flames. The tall grasses and wild daisies became an inferno. A wall of fire raged eighty feet high now, just outside the winery door, fanned by the keening wind.

Still the rats came, racing into the fire.

A few burst through, roiling in flames. But few of them survived the wall of fire, and the ferrin easily dispatched the rest.

The wind hammered at the door so that it swung on its hinges, and then slammed closed. The lift bolt slid back into place.

Outside, the storm continued to rage and the fire blossomed. Oily smoke billowed under the door. Dearborn Hawks hurried up and shoved his coat under the cracks.

The rats stopped coming at all.

Chemoise felt numb. She slumped to the floor and sat, exhausted, fearing that more of the vermin would come rushing through, worried that the battle would renew at any moment, only hoping for a brief rest. Many women and children were crying.

Grandmother Kinnelly warned, "Everyone, tend to your wounds! Now is not the time to rest." She took a keg of wine and went around the room, pouring it on the rat bites and muttering supplications to the Powers.

Chemoise got up to help. The children searched among the rats, clubbing to death any that were found wounded.

The sheer number of bites on some men was astonishing. Long into the night Chemoise worked. When she finished ministering to her own kind, she went to work on the ferrin. The ferrin folk had taken the worst of it. A dozen had died in the battle, and many others had gored ears, swollen muzzles, torn legs, and the like. One old fellow had his tail gnawed off. It broke Chemoise's heart to see so much pain.

The ferrin, which were normally afraid of humans, suffered her touch now.

Never again will I think of taking a bounty on the ferrin folk, she promised herself. And I'll take a stick to any man or boy that I hear of who hurts one of them.

Thus she worked through the night, tending each ferrin in turn. When she finished, she found that many wounds on both man and ferrin alike had begun to fester, so that she was forced to minister to them again.

Chemoise worked until she was too feverish and weak to continue. She sat with her back against a rough stone wall to rest for a moment. Her eyes felt as if they were weighted with lead, and so she closed them, still unwilling to let down her guard.

She worried about others that she knew, friends from Castle Sylvarresta. Where was Iome? Where was Gaborn?

Gaborn had sent his warning all through Heredon. Chemoise realized that battles such as this were happening everywhere—in storage cellars and abandoned mines, in dungeons and dank caves. She imagined rats swarming through each village in black hordes, and men and ferrin fighting them bravely, side by side.

The wind howled and snarled outside, and thunder pounded, until its rhythm seemed to beat its way inside of her, become one with her.

Shaking with sobs, Chemoise fell asleep, dreaming of rats.

ಬ 23 ಆ

A LAND WITHOUT HORIZONS

Those who surrender to despair forge the bars of their own private prison.

—King Jas Laren Sylvarresta

A dispute erupted only a few hours after the Consort of Shadows threw Averan in with the other prisoners.

There were only sixteen people here, sixteen left out of hundreds who had been brought down over the years. They were of all ages, taken from villages miles apart.

"We have light," one man said. "We have light for the first time . . . since we've been here. That's a weapon. It's the one thing that has kept us from making a run for it before. You yourself, Obar, you've said a hundred times that if you had a light, you would make a run for it, whether you lived or died."

"But what good is light?" Obar asked in a thick Indhopalese accent. "We are miles below surface, and tunnels go everywhere. We never find way out!"

"So what choice do you have?" asked Barris, the man Averan had taken to be their leader. "Now that you have a light, you'll sit here and huddle around it until flowers grow out your arse?"

"We're not all Runelords," an Indhopalese woman, Inura, pleaded. "We can't all fight."

"Barris is right," Averan said. "We need to escape. But we don't have to fight alone. Help is coming."

"Help?" Barris asked. "Down here?"

"Yes," Averan said. "Gaborn Val Orden, the King of Mystarria, is coming."

"Praise be to the Powers!" Inura cried.

"Why?" Barris asked as if he thought Averan had gone mad. "Why would a king come down here?"

"He's coming to find the Lair of Bones, to fight the fell mage that guides the reavers," Averan said. "I was trying to show him the way when the reavers caught me. Gaborn will have no choice but to follow. He should be able to track me. He has taken endowments of scent from twenty dogs.

Barris demanded, "And why would a child like you be leading a king?"

"Because I'm an Earth Warden," Averan said truthfully, "or at least an apprentice."

"If you're wizardborn," Barris suggested, "then maybe there are other things you can do to help us."

"Like what?" Averan asked.

"Could you summon animals to fight for us?"

"I don't have my staff," Averan apologized. "Besides, I don't think there is anything bigger than blind-crabs for miles."

"Please," Inura said. "Try anything."

These people were desperate. Averan looked in their grimy, hopeless faces, and could think of no way to help. But anger still burned in her at the thought of her father, and she, too, wanted revenge.

She squinted, wondering. "I'll try," Averan said. Silently the prisoners crept near, peering at her in the darkness. She slowed her breath and let her thoughts stretch far away.

Her mind lit first on Gaborn. She imagined his face. When she pictured it clearly, she tried to match the pace of his frantic breathing. He was running. She could sense that much at least.

She tried to envision what he saw as he ran, tried to feel the hard stone earth pounding beneath his feet. But it was useless. She couldn't gain entry to his troubled mind.

She needed an easier target, someone more accessible. Binnesman had had her summon a stag back in the hills above the Mangan's Rock because it was a stupid animal.

What kind of animal do I know that's stupid? Averan wondered. A world worm, she thought. That's what Gaborn summoned.

But the idea of some vast worm tunneling through the warrens was too frightening. She dared not try to call such a monster.

She cleared her mind, and an image came slowly: the green woman, Binnesman's wylde.

Averan stretched out with her thoughts.

She envisioned the green woman, and tried to touch the wylde's mind. But the creature was so far away. After long minutes, she began to see through the wylde's eyes, hear as it heard, smell as it smelled. Averan felt astonished at the keenness of every sense. The green woman had a nose sharper than a hound's and eyes keener than an owl's. Every nerve was alive. She felt the slightest currents on her skin, and could taste the lively air with a flick of her tongue. Binnesman had wrought his wylde well indeed. Never had Averan imagined that any creature could feel so vital, so in tune with its surroundings.

The green woman reached a great abyss where a canyon cut across her path. Below, stone trees grew along a riverbank and canyon walls like twisted, leafless caricatures of oaks, and wormgrass flourished beside riverbanks where elephant snails huddled in packs like rounded boulders.

Reavers and humans alike would have had to spend long hours negotiating the dangerous climb past the canyon. But the wylde merely stepped off the precipice, falling hundreds of feet before she grasped a rock on the far wall.

Averan could almost feel the stone shift, as if to mold itself to fit the green woman's hand, and then she scampered up the cliff as quickly as a spider.

Averan marveled at the wylde's endurance. The creature drew its strength from the Earth, and now Earth was all around it, enclosing it, suffusing it with energy. Averan could feel endless vigor in the creature's taut muscles.

"Spring," Averan called. "Help me."

Those three words cost her. Averan felt spent merely to think them, and her head suddenly reeled.

The green woman leapt like a cat, spinning in the air.

"Averan?" she asked.

"Help us," Averan begged. "We've been caught by reavers, deep in the warrens, near the Lair of Bones." Averan poured herself into the wylde's mind. Averan enticed her, "The enemies of the Earth are here."

Averan fell down in a swoon. She could hardly hold contact.

The green woman's head snapped up. Her nostrils flared. The wylde howled like a hollow wolf and began racing down the tunnel. Averan caught the scent of a reaver's marker as she met a sudden crossroad. Averan frowned in concentration, recognized the spot.

The wylde had been following the reavers' horde up to the surface. The creature was hundreds of miles away.

"Help," Averan cried. "Turn around."

Bitterly, choking back her own sobs, Averan withdrew from the creature's mind, unable to maintain contact, and fell into a black place, void of desire.

❧ 24 ☙

SARKA KAUL

For centuries the Days have claimed to be politically neutral. Their sole desire, they say, is to "observe" the lives of the lords and ladies of the Earth. But what lord, I wonder, can remain unchanged in the face of such scrutiny? What king among us does not seek to seem wiser, gentler, and more admirable than our base nature craves? We are forever reminded that our lives are short, measured in single heartbeats, gathered into a seeming handful of days. Thus, I believe that in observing the lords of the Earth, the Days unavoidably alter the course of history.

Given this, I can only conclude that it is not the mere recording of history that they desire: it is the alteration of affairs. Their hand is subtle but sure, and I suspect that in time of great need, they will reveal themselves.

—King Jas Laren Sylvarresta to the Emir of Tuulistan

Myrrima's captor hustled her down a long tunnel, shoving her forward. Verazeth was not a gentle man. It was too dark for a northerner like her to see, but he forced her to rush forward blindly. She could hear the sounds of the sea—the dull crash of slow-moving waves breaking over sullen rocks, the distant cry of a gull. The scent of salt water hung thick in the air.

Something stirred inside of her. She had never heard sea waves before, and had not really been able to imagine them. She had thought that they might sound like waves in a lake, lapping on a shore. She had been to a lake before.

But the sound she heard now was nothing like a lake. She could hear waves crashing upon shores that stretched far beyond what the eye could ever convey. The waves beat against the rocks at the base of Palace Iselferion, sloshing around them, making the very foundations of the palace tremble. She didn't just hear the ocean, or smell it. She could feel it quivering through her bones.

She had never felt such power in Water before. It seemed to call to her.

Myrrima's captor pushed her from the tunnel, and suddenly there was starlight overhead. Myrrima saw the sea, vast and limitless, stretching beyond the horizon. It was almost morning. A soft light hovered in the east. At her back, Verazeth, as pale as if he were dead and bloodless, gave her a shove, backing her over a stone parapet that leaned out over the ocean.

The water lapped the rocks below her, only a hundred yards or so. With a small push, Myrrima would fall into the deep.

Prince Verazeth pushed her backward, his black robe open, revealing his pale chest. He was a handsome man, with a sharp nose, a strong chin, and well-defined muscles in his chest and abdomen. His long silver hair had been braided in cornrows and knotted together, so that it hung over his right shoulder.

"What are you doing?" Myrrima asked.

Verazeth stroked her face just once. She saw undisguised lust in his expression. "It would please," he said at last, "if you give endowment . . . metabolism."

She knew what he desired. Once she gave metabolism, she would go into an enchanted slumber until the lord that received her endowment died, and her own metabolism returned to her. In such a state, she would not be able to protect herself from his lust. She would not even know when he violated her. And when she woke, she would be pregnant with his child.

"I'll give you nothing," Myrrima growled.

"Husband love you very much. He give will to save you. Make us promise to let you live. But if we let go, you make trouble for us. No can let you go. So, you must give endowment."

"I'll kill you first," Myrrima said.

He grunted as if annoyed at an idle threat. "You not understand. Give endowment, you live. Not give, I push you over." He grabbed her roughly and held her over the ledge.

Myrrima threw her arms around his neck. If he tried to push her over, he would come too, and Myrrima had no doubt that she would fare better in the water than he. She spat in his face.

Verazeth's eyes glittered cruelly, and his nostrils flared. He clenched his fists impotently.

"I give you day to think. Sun very hot." He let her have a moment to ponder this. Inkarrans, with their white skin, had no protection against the sun. They burned easily and deeply. "While sun come, you think. Maybe not so bad give endowment. Maybe both you and husband give endowment to king. That way, when he die, you both get endowment back, you and husband. Is not better to live in hope than die in despair?"

He grabbed the chain that bound her, and wrestled her arms down. Then he pulled off her traveling cloak, leaving her with naught but tunic and breeches. He grabbed Myrrima's chains once again and pushed her against a wall, even as he lifted her arms.

The next moment, Myrrima found herself hanging from her fetters, unable to touch the ground with her feet.

Verazeth said, "Many crab on rocks. Hungry crab. They climb cliff, look for food. Maybe help you think better."

The prince turned and entered the tunnel, bolting the iron door behind him.

Myrrima glanced down to see a pair of small green kelp crabs scuttling for shelter under the rocks. She pulled at her restraints. The heavy fetters cut into her wrists. They fit so tightly, it was almost as if they'd been made for her. With her endowments of brawn, Myrrima knew that she could pull her hands out. But she'd break every bone in her wrist doing it, and would cut away much of the flesh at the same time.

What good would escape be if it left her crippled?

So she hung for a long hour as the morning sun crept over the waves. The water reflected the deep blue of the sky, and deep swelling waves were wrinkles upon the sea's ageless face. The water stretched everywhere, limitless. Myrrima had never been in the presence of anything that made her feel so small, so humble.

She could feel it calling to her. With every wave that surged against the rocks at the base of the cliff, with the distant hiss of breakers like the clamor of spectators at a joust, she could feel the tug of the ocean, pulling her toward it, pulling her under.

Down below the cliff, seals swam about, their heads bobbing in the waves. Myrrima longed to swim with them. Cormorants and gulls and other shorebirds flew past in flocks. A little green crab scaled the rock and regarded Myrrima with its eyestalks, drops of water oozing from its mouth.

"Come, little friend," Myrrima told it. "Come gnaw at my metal bindings." But Myrrima was no summoner. The little crab scurried off.

The early morning wore away, and Myrrima was still hanging quietly when she heard the soft pad of footsteps.

She craned her head just as an old Inkarran woman opened the iron door. She was as white as clamshell, and hunched with age. She crept furtively, as if afraid that someone might hear.

She whispered in Rofehavanish that was surprisingly free of accent. "You came here looking for Daylan Hammer?"

"Yes," Myrrima managed to answer through parched lips.

"Long have I wondered what has become of him," the old woman said. "He was my tutor once, when I was a girl. My father hired him to teach us about the distant past, faraway lands, and the tongues of nations. I loved him greatly, but I could never tell him. I was a princess, you see."

Myrrima understood. It would have been considered scandalous for a woman of the Inkarran court to love a man of Rofehavan, even a hero like Daylan Hammer.

"But as much as I loved him, my sister loved him more. Often she tried to be with him alone, and at night she would tell me how she dreamed of him. As often as she sought him, he rejected her.

"Her marriage had been arranged before her birth, you see. She was to marry Sandakra Criomethes, Prince of Inturria. As the date of her marriage drew near, she grew sick in the heart, and at last thought of a way to revenge herself against our teacher. On the night before her wedding, she cut out her own womb, and died."

Myrrima stood for a moment, unsure what she was hearing. "Why?"

"It is the Inkarran way," the old woman said. "When a woman has dirtied herself with a man, this is how she confesses and makes it right."

So, Myrrima realized, to spite Daylan Hammer, the princess implicated him in her death.

"My father gave me to the prince in my sister's place, and so I have heard over the years some of what happened next. My lord Criomethes was outraged, and demanded revenge upon your Daylan Hammer. The immortal one fled north, and many men went to hunt him. There was a great battle in Ferecia. Many of our men never returned."

"Did they kill him?"

"I do not know," the old woman answered. "I know only this. I did nothing to save him, a man that I admired and loved far more than I could ever care for my lord Criomethes. So, I ask that you forgive me."

The old woman opened her clenched fist, and held out a key. Swiftly she climbed up on the lip of the parapet and unlocked Myrrima's fetters. Myrrima slid to the ground.

"Go now," the old woman said. "Almost everyone is asleep in the palace. Now is your chance to escape!"

"Not without my husband," Myrrima said.

"It is too late for him," the old woman said. "He has already given an endowment of will. He is one of the living dead."

"Then I'll take the endowment back," Myrrima said dangerously. She stripped the chains from her, and only then did the old woman seem to recognize her mistake.

She let out a yelp, as if she would scream, but Myrrima grabbed her by the throat. The old woman pawed and kicked, but Myrrima had many endowments, and she choked the old woman until she lost consciousness, and then chained her, and hung her from the peg.

"I'm sorry," Myrrima whispered as she locked the old woman into place. "I'm sorry."

Myrrima turned the woman, so that she wouldn't be burned by the sun, and crept back into the dark tunnel.

Sir Borenson lay upon his wooden bed, breathing in, breathing out. A cozy fire burned in the hearth, and Borenson could see the room clearly for the first time in more than an hour. He was in the main chamber of King Criomethes's apartments. The Inkarran facilitator hunched over Borenson's bare foot. He painstakingly dipped a long needle into an inkpot, and then inserted it into Borenson's foot. He was constructing a tattoo to cover the whole of Borenson's leg.

I could look down, Borenson told himself. I could see the shape of the rune of Will.

But he had no desire to do it. For ages the men of Rofehavan had sought to learn the secret of its making. But Borenson did not bother to look. There was a fat black spider on the stone ceiling, meandering along. Borenson watched it, unblinking. His eyes felt dry and itchy, and each time that the pain grew too great, he would try to summon the energy to blink them. This he did only because his tormentor forced him to do so.

His tormentor was a woman. She had stood over him with a bamboo rod since he first bestowed his endowment, and had given him orders. "Breathe for me, or I shall hit you," she warned. And whenever he stopped breathing, she would rap his shins with the rod, causing excruciating pain. And so he breathed in for her, and he breathed out. Thus she taught him to breathe.

Left to his own devices, he would have merely stopped and suffocated. He no longer cared if he breathed or not.

"Blink for me when eyes get dry," the woman told him after he had lain staring at the spider on the ceiling for an hour. She rapped him across the hands to show how much pain she could cause. And thus he learned to blink, though he did not care if his eyes went dry in their sockets.

Now she stood over him, lecturing. "I not feed you. I not your slave. When you get hungry, must out of bed and eat. Understand? If you not eat until full, I will beat you. Understand?"

Borenson understood, but he made no sign of it. To speak was a waste of energy, to nod a worthless gesture. He merely lay, staring at the ceiling.

The woman rapped him across the face with the rod. "You have tongue. You answer me. You understand?"

"Yes," Borenson said. He was angry and frustrated. The thought came to him that he could run away. He was not chained any longer. The facilitator had removed the chains so that he could create his tattoo. Yet the desire to flee was not strong enough to move Borenson's feet.

If I ran, how would I live? he wondered. And the answer was that it would be impossible. He would have to find his horse, a deed that could take hours. He would have to evade or fight the guards, a task that seemed too monumental. Then he would have to travel for days. For what? Everything he needed was here. Food, shelter, water. All he had to do was lie down, and others would bring it to him.

He felt the need to urinate, and announced it by letting his water flow. The urine soaked his pants and pooled beneath him, warming him.

The facilitator cleared his throat in disgust and issued an order to the tormenter. She had been busy across the room with something. She raced back to him.

"No!" she shrieked at Borenson. "You not animal. You not pee on floor or bed. You get up to pee like person. Understand?" She slammed her bamboo rod down. Borenson lamely put a hand over his groin to protect himself.

He heard a deep voice say something in Inkarran. From out of the shadows came King Criomethes himself.

"You well, I hope?" the king asked.

Borenson had no desire to frame an answer.

"Life without will is hard," the king said. "There no hope, only senseless desire. No real dreams, only longing for goals that one cannot attain. Life become burden, worthless to you. But we teach to live again. We teach to breathe, to eat, to pee. You will live like we tell you to. You will live because it easier than dying."

"Say 'Thank you,'" the old woman ordered.

Borenson made no answer, until she rapped him across the chin. "Thank you."

King Criomethes smiled and was about to leave when Borenson heard the scuff of a shoe across the room. Criomethes whirled to see the cause of the noise. A shadow came out of the darkness. There was a whistle of a swinging blade, and then the thunk of metal cleaving bone.

Blood spattered across Borenson's face as King Criomethes went down, a fine Inkarran sword blade cleaving down through his neck, into his rib cage.

The facilitator staggered back, and the old woman with her bamboo cane cried out and tried to duck, but the shadow whirled, yanking the blade free from Criomethes's dead body. The shining blade sliced off the old woman's head and hit the facilitator in the throat, slashing his windpipe. He fell back against the wall, blood pumping wildly.

Suddenly, in a rush, the will returned to Borenson. He pushed himself from bed, sitting up.

Myrrima stood before him, wrapped in her robes, her hood thrown up to make her one with the darkness.

"Come on," she said. "We're getting out of here!"

A moment ago, Borenson had felt empty, almost complacent. Now it seemed that some emotion had to fill that void, and the thing that he felt was rage.

Criomethes lay on the floor, struggling to pull himself up by grasping a chair with one hand. Borenson knew that the man was dead, that his body now only moved by impulse. Yet Borenson struggled against the urge to vent his rage. He watched the dying king as if through a red haze.

He grabbed Criomethes by the hair and lifted him up, raised a fist and would have struck him between the eyes hard enough to crush the man's skull.

But Myrrima touched Borenson's raised arm with one finger, and whispered, "Peace be with you."

It was more than a greeting, it was a powerful spell. Peace washed over him as if it were a flood, and all of the anger subsided.

He had only felt something similar once—at the pool south of Bannisferre, where an undine had kissed him and washed the guilt from his tortured mind.

He dropped the old king, embarrassed by his fury, by his lack of self-control.

A million questions came rushing at once. Where are my boots? Where is my warhammer? How did you escape?

Yet he held them all in, and for a moment just stared down at his leg. The skin burned from the tattoo. The old facilitator had begun at the sole of his foot and worked upward, creating an image of roots on a tree. It was as if Borenson wore a purple sock now, one that covered his foot up to his ankle. But there on his calf lay a rune that he had never seen before, the symbol for will. To Borenson it looked something like the head of a bull, all wrapped within a circle. There were squiggly lines above it that almost seemed to form a word or a thought in his mind. Runes often affected one that way.

Borenson peered about nervously, worried that Inkarran warriors would come storming into the chamber at any moment. Myrrima rushed across the room, stared down some dark corridor.

"Where's Prince Verazeth?" she whispered.

"I don't know," Borenson said. "I haven't seen him in hours."

She growled angrily and stalked back to Borenson. "We've got to get out of here!" Myrrima said. "If the Inkarrans find out what we've learned the shape of the Rune of Will, we're dead."

"Do you even know the way out?" Borenson asked, "This place is a maze."

Myrrima froze. She had no idea how to get out of the city, much less the country.

In the darkness, Borenson heard a grunt as someone cleared his throat. Then a voice spoke up in mild Inkarran accent. "Perhaps I can help."

Borenson whirled, ready to fight. In the darkness, against the wall, sat a man in dark robes. He had been so still that neither of them had seen him in the dark. He pulled back a deep hood to reveal skin as pale as milk and eyes that glowed red in the darkness from lack of pigment.

Borenson was about to launch himself at the man when he realized that he was a Days.

No, not just *a* Days, King Criomethes's Days, he realized.

"And why would you help us?" Borenson asked. For the Days had been politically neutral from time immemorial. They took no side in any dispute.

"Because the fate of the world sits upon a precipice," the Days answered. "For two days now, my people have argued whether to intervene. I have made up my mind, and the Council has made up theirs. They will not intervene." As if to announce his decision, he stood up and pulled off his brown scholar's robes. He was a tall man, with broad, powerful shoulders. Beneath his robes he wore a plain white tunic, and an Inkarran breastplate. A long Inkarran dirk rode in a sheath on his thigh. "It's time for any man who hopes to call himself a man to go to fight at Carris."

"Carris?" Myrrima asked.

"The Earth King has asked every man who can bear a weapon to ride to Carris to fight the reavers," the Days said. "If we're to make it, we must do so by sundown. I can get you out of Inkarra, but my kind are forbidden to enter Mystarria. Once we cross the border, my life will be in your hands."

"Fight the reavers?" Myrrima asked. "Last I saw, Gaborn had the horde on the run."

"No," the Inkarran said, "not that horde—a new one. The reavers are marching toward Carris in a black tide, larger than the first."

Borenson shuddered at the thought.

"Will Gaborn be fighting there?" he asked, for he hoped to tell Gaborn of his discoveries in Inkarra.

"He was last seen entering the Underworld two days ago, to fight a legend—the fell mage who leads the reavers, the One True Master," the Inkarran said. He rushed over to the fire, reached under some bags that were hidden there. He pulled out a kingly head plate as protection, took a long straight Inkarran sword from over the fireplace and strapped it on.

He finished buckling on the sheath, looked Borenson in the eye. "I should warn you that the chances for those who fight in Carris are slim. A host of enemies are arrayed against you, and not all of them are reavers."

"Who?"

"Raj Ahten has become a flameweaver, and even now he plots how to destroy Mystarria. As he does, his facilitators vector endowments to him as fast as they are able. They have resorted to bribing street urchins and blackmailing criminals. But he is not alone. Lowicker's daughter guards the roads north of Carris, preventing any help from reaching the city from that direction.

"Beyond that, King Anders is riding from Crowthen, claiming that the Earth has called him to be its new king, now that Gaborn has lost the power to warn his Chosen of danger."

Borenson snorted in derision, but the Inkarran said, "Do not laugh. For years he has studied the arts of sorcery, and already he has convinced many of the veracity of his words. But King Anders is full of treachery. He sent a plague of rats to destroy Heredon, and no Earth King would dare do something so vile. Gaborn managed to frustrate his plot, but Anders has others."

"Name them," Borenson said.

The Inkarran said, "At his bidding, the warlords of Internook have overrun the Courts of Tide. Olmarg himself led the attack, holding the Orb of Internook aloft. Three thousand gray longboats sailed into the city at dawn. Though Chancellor Westhaven surrendered, Olmarg gutted him. Then the barbarians of Internook hurled fire into the shanties along the docks, and have spent the morning raping and pillaging. Olmarg has seized the throne of Mystarria, and is even now looting its treasury of gold and forcibles. The Duchess Galent went before him an hour ago, begging him to restrain his men, for they slew her husband and deflowered her daughters before her eyes. In answer, Olmarg threw her on the floor and raped her, before slitting her throat. That is the kind of man that serves Anders." By now the Inkarran had taken a purse full of coins from the dead king's body and had grabbed some rice buns and fruit from a basket near the fire. He went to a peg on the wall and took down an Inkarran day cloak—a black cloak with a deep hood that would protect his eyes from the light—and wrapped it over his shoulders.

Borenson felt stunned at the news. He had spent his life in service to Gaborn's father, protecting Mystarria. Never in his darkest dreams had he imagined that his nation would fall.

The Inkarran studied Borenson for a moment. "I'll take you to the guards now. Act as if nothing is amiss. They'll return your weapons. Your horses should have been delivered to the king's stables. If not, we can steal mounts there."

"And what of Prince Verazeth?" Myrrima asked. "Where is he?"

"He is drinking honeysuckle wine and playing dice with his friends," the Inkarran answered. "With any luck, he won't return to these rooms until nightfall."

The Inkarran turned toward a door.

"One last thing," Borenson asked. "Do you have a name?"

The Inkarran glanced back, his face a white mask beneath his hood. Just enough firelight caught his eyes so that they reflected the red embers. "Sarka. Sarka Kaul."

ᙒ 25 ᙅ

A LOVE SO PURE

Since an endowment cannot be received unless it is freely given, it must be reasoned that it is emotion—rather than a facilitator's skill—that forms the glue that binds a Dedicate to his lord.

Fear binds a Dedicate to an evil lord, but such a bond is weak, for the Dedicate will often choose death rather than continue to serve one whom he despises. Greed is stronger, for those who sell attributes for gold usually crave life. But by far the strongest bonds are those created by love, for those who love their lords dearly are not dissuaded when they feel the bite of the forcible.

—*from* The Art of the Perfect Match, *by Ansa Per and Dylan Fendemere, Master Facilitators*

When Chemoise woke from her dreams of rats, daylight was streaming through the open door of the old winery. Chills wracked her, and she could not stop shaking. Aunt Constance helped her to her feet, and someone from town—Chemoises's eyes were too bleary to see who—guided her downhill to the house.

The ground outside the winery was burned bare. The hoops from the barrels lay in blackened rings. The pear trees were smoldering stakes. Fire had razed the hills to the west.

A wagon waited just outside the door, and Chemoise saw three people laid out on it with blankets draped over their faces.

"Who died?" Chemoise asked bitterly, for she had worked so hard to save everyone. To her knowledge, only her dear uncle Eber should have died. "Who is in the wagon?"

"Everyone is fine," Aunt Constance said, her voice choked with suppressed grief. "Everyone is well." She steered Chemoise to the house, and Chemoise felt too weak to argue. She'd discover who had died in time. She felt surprised to find the manor still standing, but the wind had blown the fire west of the old winery, across the fields, where it still burned in the hills nearby. Thus the house and town were saved.

Inside the manor, Constance poured cold water over Chemoise's wounds, and put poultices on them. She lay in a fever all morning. By and by she woke and heard a knock on the outside door, followed by women talking.

"The Fancher boy just died," someone from town said. "We tried everything, but he took too many bites."

"That makes nine," Constance said, her voice hollow from loss.

"It could have been worse," someone added. "If not for the king, we'd all be dead."

Chemoise lay in a daze, wondering who else might have died.

Not Dearborn Hawks, she found herself hoping. Not him.

It was an odd sentiment, one she felt guilty for even thinking, for in wishing him to be alive, she was wishing death on someone else.

But she had tended to his bites after the battle—twenty-four of them— and she could not help remembering the shy way that he smiled at her, and the way her heart skipped in return.

"Terrible, terrible," one old woman said. "My heart breaks for every one of them. Thank the Powers that the Earth King warned us in time. I only wish that I could repay him."

"We won't be seeing the likes of him for a while," Aunt Constance said. "Eber told me yesterday afternoon that there's terrible goings-on. There's to be a big battle down in Mystarria tonight—reavers. Reavers by the thousands. Everyone who can fight has been called to battle at Carris. And those who can't fight are giving endowments to the Earth King."

"Endowments?" the old woman asked. "Where?"

"At Castle Sylvarresta. Folks are gathering from all around. The king took endowments down at Castle Groverman last week, and the facilitators have brought Dedicates to Castle Sylvarresta to act as vectors."

"Really?" the old woman asked. "Have things gotten so bad?"

Aunt Constance was silent for a moment, and Chemoise imagined that she could hear her shaking her head. "I heard Eber whispering to some of the men. He told them to get weapons ready. The Earth King says that if we don't win at Carris . . ."

Chemoise crawled out of bed and steadied herself for a moment. Castle Sylvarresta wasn't far, less than thirty miles. Uncle Eber hadn't had a force horse, but he did have a boat, and the River Wye ran down through the forests right up to the castle. She knew that in the years past, Eber used to send his wine barrels downstream, so the water was deep enough to carry the boat all the way.

With luck, I can get there in a few hours, she told herself.

She threw on her riding cloak, and silently slipped out the window. She crept along the back of the house and was crossing the dirt lane when the door opened. Aunt Constance and her old friend Nan Fields stood there.

"I didn't know that you were up," Constance called. "Where are you going?"

Chemoise turned and looked her in the eye. "To Castle Sylvarresta, to give my endowment."

Immediately Constance limped across the street, her right foot swollen by rat bites. Her expression was grim. "You can't do that. You're already sick. Think of your child!"

Chemoise stopped, torn. Iome had always been her best friend, and Chemoise dearly wanted to give whatever aid she could.

"There are endowments I can give that wouldn't endanger the babe," she argued.

Dearborn Hawks must have heard them talking. Perhaps he had been waiting all day to see Chemoise. He came from the barn, his brow furrowed in concern.

"Dearborn, stop her!" Constance begged.

The Hawks boy looked at Constance, and then at Chemoise, and nodded thoughtfully. "There's not much water in the river at this time of year," he said at last. "You'll need help rowing if you're to make it by nightfall."

With that, he led her downhill to the boat.

ಜ 26 ಛ

THE CURTAINS OF HEAVEN

Many a warrior is wise in the ways of war, but only fools ignore mastering the fine art of retreat.

—from The Fine Art of Retreat, *by Colm Bryant, Diligent in the Room of Arms*

Borenson and Myrrima fled Iselferion with the Inkarran Days, Sarka Kaul, as their guide. The guards handed them their weapons at the door, and Sarka led them to some underground stables where Borenson found his horses already delivered. Many an Inkarran lord was visiting the city, and Sarka had no difficulty stealing a suitable mount for himself.

Thus the three rode from Iselferion into the morning light with the city still asleep, the Inkarrans unaware that a Rune of Will gleamed darkly upon Borenson's leg. He knew that the journey would not stay easy for long.

He suspected that once the Inkarrans learned what had happened, they'd send a legion of pale warriors to hunt them down. They'd kill him and anyone he spoke to.

Yet as Sarka guided them along lonely roads, there was no pursuit by daylight, no sign of Inkarrans at all. Empty fields lay all about the trails, cultivated and pruned, looking strangely bereft, for there were no workmen tilling them, no cottages or barns. The only sign of habitation came as the morning sun shone upon the stele that marked each city.

Borenson could not have hoped for a better escape. Sarka Kaul led them over desolate trails until they reached the shadowed forests, where winged lizards fluttered about, hunting for moths and gnats in the canopy.

Only once did anyone try to stop them. As they neared the foot of the

Alcair Mountains, a dark figure raced up behind the trio. The clatter of a charger's hooves announced that it was a force horse with great endowments, and Borenson looked back down a mountain trail, where he glimpsed the rider galloping through the trees.

"I'll get him," Myrrima said fiercely as they neared a meadow. She had kept her bow strung all morning, and she slowed her mount, leapt off, and slapped its rump. Her horse raced after Sarka and Sir Borenson, following them through a meadow full of white flowers so delicate that the sunlight shining through made them glow like ice.

Sarka Kaul led the way and reached a line of trees just as their pursuer exited the woods. Borenson glanced back. An Inkarran prince raced under the shadows, his blood red robes flapping behind him like wings. He rode a horse as black as night itself. The mount galloped into the meadow a few paces, and suddenly Myrrima stepped out from behind a gnarled sycamore and loosed an arrow.

The fellow cried and leaned forward, putting his heels to horseflesh. Borenson clearly saw the white plumes of goose feather from the arrow lodged in his back.

The black horse came to a halt in the meadow and spun about. Its rider was cursing, lamely struggling to get it to flee, while he struggled to keep from falling off.

Borenson raced to the wounded rider. The fellow's long silver braids announced that it was Prince Verazeth. He lay slumped in the saddle, clinging to his horse's neck, the arrow sticking up from his ribs. Myrrima had struck him near the heart. His horse danced around, frightened by the scent of hot blood.

Sarka Kaul rode up behind Borenson.

"*Cour as! Cour as!*" Help me, the prince muttered.

"Gladly," Sarka said, urging his mount forward.

He grabbed the prince by the hair and plunged his sword into the man's back. He flung the body to the ground and took the horse's reins in one smooth motion.

In a moment Myrrima came running up through the field.

"He's dead?" she asked unnecessarily. She stood over the prince, bow in hand, arrow ready to fire.

"He's dead," Sarka said.

"But . . . you watched him grow up from a child," she objected.

"And many a time I wished to put an end to his miserable life," the Inkarran whispered. "Here, take his horse. It might come in handy. It has many endowments of sight to let it run in the darkness."

"This is it?" Borenson asked. "This is the only man they sent to hunt for us?"

Sarka Kaul grunted. "Probably so. Inkarran politics are very complex. King Criomethes has secretly been in league with the Storm King's enemies for decades, so Verazeth couldn't dare risk revealing what his father has done. Their crime against you must remain a secret from the king. Nor could Verazeth tell his own cronies what has happened, for it will make him look foolish to be bested by Daylighters, people that he condemns as inferiors. He really only had one choice. He had to hunt you down himself. Only then could he pretend to avenge his family, and thus gain honor. So he came for you swiftly, foolish enough to hunt by daylight, and took his secret to the grave."

Myrrima seemed unsure. "Let's get out of here anyway."

She dragged the prince's body from the road, hid it under the trees two hundred yards into the woods. Then she leapt up on his black stallion and fought the beast for a moment, and led the way.

The trip over the Alcairs went quickly. The snow-laden arms of the mountains glowed as white as bone in the daylight, and the horses were eager to run in the cool air.

They raced up the jagged peaks, over roads that were almost never used, until at last they neared the Inkarran fortress. An icy gale was blowing spindrift from the peaks, so that by the time that they drew close, they did so in a dismal fog.

The road zigzagged down the steep mountain. Sarka Kaul bypassed the fortress by riding up the slopes until he met the road above. Even force horses had a tough job of it, lunging through the foggy ice.

When they neared the mountain peak, with its fearsome wall, Myrrima and Sarka both closed their eyes tightly, and Borenson led the horses. He only shivered once as he passed beneath the shadow of the gate, and noon found them all racing down snowy slopes.

In such fierce light, Sarka was almost blind. Borenson kept a keen eye out for Inkarrans. Sarka warned that the Storm King Zandaros and his men might be camped on the road, hidden in some dark fen. But the snow showed no sign that any large party had ridden past in the night, and Sarka decided at last that Zandaros must have kept on Inkarran roads, heading farther west, before taking their path northward. That way, the Storm King would avoid any well-traveled highways in Mystarria, taking most of his journey through the wilderness.

"He cares little for the fate of Rofehavan," Sarka Kaul warned Borenson, "but if the reavers manage to destroy your land, he knows that his own people will have to fight a war."

The sun seemed to be a great and brittle pearl floating in a distant sea, somehow vaster than any sun that Borenson had ever seen. Below him to the north, clouds covered the green fields of Mystarria like a cloak.

So they rode, racing the horses as fast as they would go down through Batenne and up the roads through the swamps at Fenraven. Verazeth's mount was as swift and tireless as any that Borenson had ever seen, and it carried Myrrima without complaint. His own warhorse and the white mare both tired more quickly, but Borenson kept from wearing them out by switching mounts each time one got winded. Sarka Kaul too had stolen a kingly mount, one whose coat was a peculiarly bright color of red. "They are called blood mounts in the south of Inkarra," Sarka told them, "and are highly valued for their ability to see in the darkness."

His mount followed along behind the others, apparently baffled to be running in the daylight. Sarka Kaul kept his head low as he rode through the towns and villages, his deep hood concealing his face, a pair of black riding gloves to hide his hands, and if any man of Mystarria noted that an Inkarran was riding abroad in the daylight, no one gave chase.

By early afternoon they left the swamps at Fenraven and rode west, where they began to draw near the reavers' trail.

A fire burned all across the horizon, and in the muggy air, the smoke billowed uncommonly black. It rose heavenward in thick columns, fulminating upward for miles. To Borenson, the columns looked like black vines espaliered against a stone cliff. At their crown, a breeze blew the smoke east in a thin haze, like tendrils of vine hanging over a garden wall.

Along the road, they began to spot refugees fleeing the coming war. Borenson saw a young woman driving an oxcart. Four children slept on a pile of hay in the back. Food and clothes were wrapped into a few meager bundles.

Then he began to see more exiles, old women with staves hobbling along the road, young women with babes in arms. But there were no men—no old men, no young men over the age of eleven or twelve. Not even the crippled or maimed were fleeing Carris.

The smoke's reach was tremendous. For twenty miles it hung overhead like a ceiling, and Borenson, Myrrima, and Sarka rode closer and closer to the dark columns. Powdery ash began to drift from the sky.

Borenson stopped at a stream near an abandoned farm to let the horses drink, and found a crowd of women who looked too exhausted to march any farther.

"When did the fire start?" Myrrima asked, nodding toward the clouds looming in the west.

"The Knights Equitable lit it yesterday before dawn," an old woman answered. "They're riding ahead of the reavers, setting fire to everything, hoping to slow the horde."

If Borenson knew the Knights Equitable, they would do more than just light fires. It was easier to take reavers in the open field than to fight them from behind castle walls. High Marshal Chondler would send sorties against the reavers.

"Have you seen the horde?" Borenson asked. "Do we have any estimates on how big it is?" The last horde sent against Carris had been nearly seventy thousand strong. Sarka claimed that this one might be over a million, but it was hard to credit such wild numbers.

The old woman spoke up. "You can't count them all. The reavers' lines stretches for a hundred miles, like a dark river, and the horde is so wide you can hardly see to the far shore."

"By the Powers!" Borenson swore. "There is no way that we can fight something like that. There aren't enough men and lances in all of Mystarria!"

But Sarka Kaul gazed off to the north and the west, and whispered, "Perhaps there *are* enough men to fight, if only they muster the will to do it."

They took off riding, moving ever deeper beneath the smoky shadow. For several leagues they met women and children fleeing in droves, until at last their numbers began to dwindle.

As the clouds of smoke thickened with each mile, soon it seemed as if night closed overhead. They passed a deserted village, and all the cocks were crowing as if to greet the dawn.

Deep under the shadow, they rode up to a peasant girl trying to carry her two weary sisters, even as a pair of toddlers trailed behind, crying of weariness. Borenson asked, "Where are your mother and father?"

"They went to Carris, to fight," the girl said.

"Don't you have any food?" Myrrima asked.

"We had some, yesterday, but I couldn't carry the children *and* the food. So we left it. There are farms along the way. I was hoping to find something to eat."

There was a moment of silence as Borenson considered the girl's predicament. The land was full of rocks, and there wasn't a village for forty miles. Half a dozen farms spread out along the road, but other refugees were picking the last apples from the trees as they marched. This girl and her brothers and sisters would never make it.

Borenson would never have abandoned his own offspring like this.

"Give her the spare horse," Myrrima urged.

Borenson felt torn. He looked to the west. He could see evidence of flames now—an angry red welt on the horizon. If these children didn't seek shelter soon, the fire would get them before the reavers did. "Nay," he decided. "We may need the horse for battle. But give them some food."

"We *may* need the horse," Myrrima said, "but they *do* need it."

Borenson hung his head. He understood some of the pain that Gaborn must be sensing. If he gave a warhorse to these children, he might save their lives. But he needed the horses for battle, a battle where he could save more than just five small children.

He looked back to Sarka Kaul for advice, but the Inkarran merely shrugged.

It was a bitter choice. He gave the girl some plums and a loaf of bread he'd bought fresh in Battenne, counseled them to head east toward the River Donnestgree, and then rode on.

As he moved toward the shadow, a strange thought took him: this is the road my father traveled to his own death.

It would have been only a week ago now that his father had ridden to Carris. The skies would have been blue and clear, and certainly his father hadn't known what awaited him, but it was the same road, the same farm-houses and trees, the same dull pond in the distance reflecting the sky.

Still the shadows lengthened, and darkness deepened. The air grew still, motionless. Almost the inferno did not seem to be belching smoke at all. Borenson could imagine that invisible hands had reached into the earth, and were pulling out its entrails, just as a huntsman guts a stag.

At last he rounded a bend and could see a line of red beneath the smoke, the sputtering of flames. The road led through the fire.

They raced the horses then, past scorching flames that rose up on both sides of the road, and found themselves completely beneath the shadow. Ash and smoke filled the air so thickly that they all wrapped scarves over their faces.

The sky was black above, as black as dusk, and the ground was charred and black beneath the hooves of the horses. The only light came from brush-fires that raged everywhere in a ragged line, like a fiery snake that stretched across the horizon.

The thundering of the reavers' feet could now be heard, rumbling beneath the sputter and hiss of flames. Howlers trumpeted mournful cries. Borenson, Myrrima, and Sarka Kaul raced toward the horde. Soon, gree began to whip overhead on wriggling wings, squeaking as if in agony.

Deep in the blackness, the reavers charged. They thundered along beside the charred highway, running hundreds abreast, and the line extended each direction for as far as the eye could see. Firelight reflected crimson from their carapaces. The ground shuddered beneath their feet, and the hissing of their breath sounded like a gasp.

Blade-bearers made up the vast bulk of the army, along with large numbers of pale spidery howlers whose eerie calls frequently were borne through the shadows. Among the mass of dark bodies, Borenson saw few scarlet sorceresses.

"What's that?" Myrrima shouted to be heard over the commotion. She pointed to a trio of enormous reavers that loped along about a quarter of a mile off. To Borenson's eye, they looked like any other reaver he had ever seen except that each of them had dozens of large, bulbous black growths all over their backs.

Myrrima raced her horse toward the monsters, and Borenson followed more warily. Sarka Kaul hung back, afraid of the reavers, for he was but a Days, a commoner without benefit of endowments.

As Borenson drew near, the mystery was solved: the huge reavers looked to be nurses, reavers charged with rearing the warren's hatchlings. Each nurse was oversized, nearly forty feet in length, and the humps on their backs were young reavers, each no more than five or six feet tall, and eight feet in length. Ten or fifteen young clung to the backs of some nurses.

"Why would they bring their young?" Myrrima shouted, nocking an arrow.

Borenson had an inkling. He imagined the young reavers charging through the rooms of a keep, breaking into cellars to hunt for women and children. He could envision them climbing turret stairs—going any of the places where people might hide when fleeing reavers. How vicious such young creatures might be, he could not guess.

At that moment, an enormous blade-bearer must have smelled them. It came rushing out of the column at tremendous speed, the philia along its head waving wildly. Instantly Borenson saw that the horses wouldn't be able to outrun it.

He had never seen a reaver move so fast.

"Shoot it!" Borenson warned as he pulled his warhammer from its sheath.

The monster charged Myrrima. It stood over twenty feet tall, and its mouth was wide enough to swallow a horse. Fiery runes glowed on its battle arms, as pale blue as a will-o'-the-wisp in the swamps at Fenraven. The reaver hissed.

Myrrima reined in her black stallion, drawing her bow as the blade-bearer charged. But her horse threw back its ears, and its eyes grew wide. It began to dance backward.

Borenson veered his own mount toward the beast, shouted a war cry, and charged.

He was nearly on the monster when a dark shaft sizzled overhead and disappeared into the reavers' sweet triangle. The monster's right legs buckled, and it skidded in the ash for a moment, then floundered as it tried to regain its feet. The arrow had struck its brain, but had not killed it instantly.

"Flee!" Borenson shouted, wheeling to see where Myrrima might be. She had already grabbed her reins and was urging her horse away from the reaver's lines—not a moment too soon.

The wounded reaver struggled unsuccessfully to regain its feet, even as two of its kin raced out of the horde.

Borenson put heels to horseflesh and set his charger galloping over the blackened fields. Myrrima raced ahead. Before them, Sarka Kaul's mount galloped like the wind. Borenson looked over his back. The wounded reaver was spinning about in circles while its comrades charged after him.

They were gaining on him.

Borenson had his little white mare on a tether, and was trying to lead her out. But she wasn't as fast as his old warhorse. He considered cutting her loose. If nothing else, she might serve as a decoy for the reavers.

He glanced up toward Myrrima. She was drawing another arrow from her quiver, trying to nock it as she rode.

The reavers were gaining. He could hear their hissing breath closing in on him; their feet pounded the earth. Borenson had taken but one endowment of metabolism at Carris. Over the past few days, his facilitator had vectored him more. But he still moved more slowly than these reavers. He dared not face them with only a warhammer.

He peered ahead.

Myrrima was racing away from him, over the dun fields. Sarka Kaul still held the lead. The great smoke clouds above threw a broad shadow, so that it looked as if they fled beneath a storm. Her mount's hooves threw up turfs, then leapt over the blackened limb of a fallen oak. Yet even as Myrrima fled, she held her reins in her teeth and nocked another arrow.

Borenson put heels to horseflesh and struggled to hold on. He clung to his long-handled warhammer. With so few endowments, he would not be able to use it effectively, but it was all that he had.

He could hear the reavers gaining, lurching forward, their massive bodies thudding with each step, weightier than elephants. Their hissing came loud.

Once, in his youth, Borenson had been to the shipyards on the north coast of Thwynn where King Orden's warships were built. There a huge iron battering ram was being fashioned for the prow of a ship. It was longer than a mainmast. The shipwrights had said that much of the ram would be hidden within the hull of a small, fast vessel, built solely to ram and thus disable the big, heavily armored "floating castles" of Toom. Borenson had seen the new-forged ram lifted from its cast and levered into a ditch filled with oily water. When it touched the liquid, it hissed with the tongue of a thousand serpents and sent plumes of gray steam writhing into the air.

As the reavers advanced, their hissing reminded him of that now.

Ah, he thought, what I would not give for a good lance!

Suddenly he heard Myrrima cry out, and he looked ahead. She spun her horse about and was racing toward him.

"Watch out!" she warned.

Borenson let go the reins of his white mare, and she split to the left. In order to avoid colliding with Myrrima, he spurred his stallion to the right.

Myrrima raced between them, head down, charging the reavers, who were startled by her sudden attack.

The foremost skidded, trying to stop, its philia waving in alarm. Clouds of dust rose from its feet, and it raised a knight gig as if to gaff her horse. The light of distant fires flashed red on the long black pole. The reaver just behind it bungled on, striking it in the rear legs, so that the foremost reaver tripped.

Myrrima was nearly upon the tangled pair when she loosed an arrow. It blurred toward the foremost reaver and struck its sweet triangle with a *thwack*.

The monster pushed off with its back legs and leapt nearly straight in the air, its four back legs kicking as if it sought to run. Then it flipped forward and crashed headfirst into the ground.

The felled reaver did not get up. It lay facedown in the black ash, its rear legs kicking in vain.

Now there was only one reaver. Borenson wheeled his mount to face it.

The last reaver had drawn to a halt. Myrrima raced away behind it, and the huge blade-bearer spun to confront her. Yet Borenson was now charging at its back, and the reaver swiveled its head, trying to gauge the threat. Sarka Kaul found some courage and brought his own mount galloping toward the fray.

The monster leaned back on its rear legs and raised its claws, as if it were cowed. Two of its companions were dead, and it couldn't tell whether Borenson, Myrrima, or Sarka Kaul represented the greater threat.

"Two hundred yards!" Myrrima shouted across the expanse.

She had now raced her horse about that distance from the last remaining reaver, and she wheeled her mount and drew an arrow from her quiver. Borenson suddenly understood what she meant to do.

Averan had said that a reaver's limit of vision was two hundred yards. The reaver here could certainly smell them, but he couldn't see them clearly at such a distance. Borenson, too, now retreated outside the reaver's limit of vision while Sarka Kaul raced near, distracting the beast.

Myrrima took her great steel bow and drew back an arrow even with her ear. At such a distance, she had little hope of hitting the monster in its sweet triangle. Borenson wasn't sure that her bolt would even pierce the reaver's skin, no matter how sharp her bodkins.

She let her arrow fly. It arced up into the air and struck squarely in the reaver's haunch, burying its head in the monster's buttock.

The reaver snarled and leapt in the air, then wheeled and snapped, biting off the offending arrow. But it was no use. He could not pry out the head of the shaft from beneath his skin without doing greater damage.

Now he hissed in vain and spun about, looking for sign of his attacker. For all the world he reminded Borenson of a wounded bear snapping at the encircling hounds. The reaver looked forlorn and confused.

And why not? he asked himself. In all our battles, the reavers have faced men with lances and warhammers and javelins. Never have they had to contend against men armed with Sylvarresta's bows of spring steel. Never have they faced men who could strike from horseback beyond their limit of vision.

Now the reaver spun about, snarling, clawing at the air, and blindly waving his philia, seeking to catch sight or scent of its enemy.

"Go!" Myrrima called. "I'll come around and meet you."

She hadn't hoped to kill the last reaver at all, only slow it enough so that they could escape. Sarka Kaul turned and headed back toward the highway. Borenson raced north to retrieve his white mare, while Myrrima circled downwind of the reaver, coincidentally putting the body of its fallen comrade between her and the monster.

She already had another arrow nocked.

Borenson went to his white mare, whispered soothing words, and took her reins. The little mare peered at him with frightened eyes, ears drawn back, and danced away at his approach.

"It's all right," he said. "I won't leave you to the reavers again."

He patted her, and heard the reaver roar wildly. He glanced back.

Myrrima was charging the wounded beast. She had the corpse of its fallen companion between them, and she was racing from downwind. She was less than a hundred yards away now.

She swung north, rounded the dead reaver, and suddenly its companion became aware of her. The monster leapt forward a pace, holding its giant blade in the air. It rose up on hind legs and gaped its maw wide in a fierce display.

Myrrima fired an arrow into its mouth, sent the shaft blurring up into its soft palate. Then she gouged the flanks of her horse and veered away, fleeing toward Borenson.

The great blade-bearer hissed in anger and lunged toward her, giving chase. It hissed cruelly as it ran, and Borenson realized to his dismay that Myrrima hadn't been able to fell the creature. Her arrow had missed its mark.

She was nocking another arrow even as she fled.

The huge monster bore down on her, ignoring the shaft buried in its leg. It muscled forward, strengthened by rage, intent on rending Myrrima to pieces.

"Ho-ooo!" Borenson cried.

He spurred his own mount, went charging straight toward Myrrima. She was two hundred yards from him, then a hundred. He could see the whites of her eyes, broad and frightened. Her dark hair flew behind her.

Then she brushed past him, and Borenson faced the reaver. It lurched to a halt, skidding, and then bobbed its head up protectively, believing that it faced a lancer. But Borenson had no weapon to fight it effectively. He merely veered his horse to the left and raced away.

For a second the brute stood, trying to decide whether to give chase. Then another arrow blurred from Myrrima's bow, striking it in the sweet triangle, and burying itself in the reaver's brain. The monster tensed for a moment as if to spring. Then it stepped forward and gingerly lay down in the grass, as if it merely sought a place to sleep.

It moved no more.

Myrrima wheeled her horse, and it came prancing back to meet Borenson.

There was a look of worry on her face. "Three arrows," she said. "I spent three arrows on one reaver."

Borenson knew what she meant. She had precious few in her quiver, and an army of hundreds of thousands of reavers marched in the distance, rumbling over the prairie.

"I'd say that three arrows to kill a reaver were well spent. Besides, you killed three reavers with five arrows, not one with three."

Myrrima bit her lip. He could plainly see that she was cursing herself for her poor bowmanship instead of rejoicing to be alive. How many men had ever killed a reaver with a bow? Few that he knew of. And here she had just slain three!

Sarka Kaul rode back to the meet them.

"How many steel bows like that do you think there are in Heredon?" he asked.

Myrrima shook her head. "I've not seen many. I'd guess that maybe there are three hundred in all the land."

"I would that you had a hundred thousand of them, and that someone had the good sense to bring them all to Carris," Sarka Kaul said, "along with all of your ballistas."

But Borenson could see that his heart was not in his words, for he knew that Carris would boast no such weapons. Sarka Kaul turned his blood mount and they galloped on beneath clouds of smoke-curtained light from the heavens.

ಬ 27 ಆ

THE WINDING STAIR

Until you embrace your own mortality, you cannot truly be free.

—*Omar Owatt, Emir of Tuulistan*

Iome had urged Gaborn to forge ahead to the Lair of Bones, but she never intended to lag far behind. So she ran, straining to keep up.

True to his word, Gaborn had marked a path for her through tunnels and caves, down canyons and watercourses, past wonders that Iome suspected no man had ever seen. She passed once through a long tunnel carved in crystal, its walls as transparent as ice. She beheld forests of stone trees, twisted and surreal in their beauty, climbing in whorls along the wall. She'd raced through migrations of blind-crabs and climbed down endless chasms. She'd passed under waterfalls, where the roar of an Underworld flood deafened the ear.

And all along the way, one thought rang in her memory, "And while you are saving the world," she'd asked Gaborn, "who will be saving you?"

It wasn't an idle question. It had been a promise, one that she hoped to keep. She wanted to stand beside him, but she had no weapon, and she had no way to catch up with him.

It was not until she reached another old Inkarran outpost that she had a hope of gaining a weapon.

A hole near the floor of the reaver tunnel marked the sanctuary.

Iome quickly crawled inside, hoping to find something that might be of help. Pocket crabs had gnawed countless burrows in the walls. The pale creatures looked much like small reavers, with heavy fore-claws and thick shells. They scurried about on the tunnel floor down here by the millions, rushing for their burrows as soon as they sensed movement. Some were no larger than roaches, while others were more the size of a rat.

As Iome crawled through the narrow opening, the pocket crab dens dug into the wall made the outpost look so worn that she thought that it must have been abandoned, but just inside the room a stone jar held a store of hazelnuts and buckwheat with dried melon, apples, and cherries. Iome scooped up a handful of it, and found that it tasted salty but edible. By the taste, she suspected that it had been sitting for more than a year. A second clay jug held some sweet winter-melon wine.

In the far corner, four Inkarran reaver darts stood propped against a wall. One was bent, another so old that it had rusted through, and the other two had each lost the diamond from one tip. None was ideal. But any weapon was better than nothing.

As Iome picked through the darts, wondering if she could repair them, she glanced over her back, at a faint charcoal drawing upon the wall. It showed squiggling lines, marked with Inkarran symbols. It looked like a map.

If indeed it was a map, she suspected that it would do her little good. The pocket crabs had dug so many holes in the walls that one could hardly follow the lines, and the pigment itself seemed to have faded. The map had to be hundreds, if not thousands, of years old.

"I must be here," Iome said, seeing an icon that looked like a shield with Inkarran numbers on it. "And that is the path ahead." She traced her finger along a sloping line that shot off in a far direction, then circled back below her, then intersected a corkscrew that went down and down. The path ahead led to the unbounded warren, she suspected. But the map seemed to indicate a shortcut, a small trail written as arrow points.

"A shortcut?" Iome wondered. Her heart pounded. With all of his endowments of metabolism, Gaborn was certainly far ahead of her. At her current pace, Iome would never reach him in time to be of help. But if she had indeed found a shortcut . . .

At the top of the shortcut was an icon, like the head of a crevasse crawler.

It's an old crevasse crawler tube, she realized excitedly. It could save me . . . a hundred miles, maybe two hundred. That is, if Gaborn keeps following the main tunnel.

I couldn't be so lucky, Iome thought. Even if there had been a shortcut once, what was the chance that it still existed? With all of the pocket crabs around, the walls of the tube would be pitted and scarred at least, and might even have caved in.

Iome studied the drawing. Dare I take the risk? she wondered.

She took her newfound weapon and raced down the tunnel, where she soon found a wall brimming with burrows dug by a large crevasse crawler.

Each passageway was three or four feet in diameter. An Inkarran icon had been chiseled above the entrance to one burrow. Iome peered in, the light from her opal crown dancing off the pale stone.

The crawlway wormed this way and that, as if dug by a madman. As Iome had guessed, the walls were pitted with burrows from pocket crabs, but the tunnel seemed passable. Dark lichenous plants felt almost rubbery beneath her palm, and dozens of mushworms—green sluglike creatures that squished into a syrup under the slightest pressure—fed upon the plants. Iome wriggled in, clutching her reaver dart. Only a hundred yards in, the tunnel shot down nearly straight, just as the map had shown.

Iome's heart pounded. The only way to go forward was to let herself drop and hope that the slope at the bottom would be gentle.

But she imagined what might be down there—a cave-in that choked the passage with rock so that when she hit, the impact would shatter every bone in her body—or a chasm carved by water that would send her falling into some void.

Iome turned around, so that she could go feet-first. She hesitated, suspecting that once she dropped blindly down the tunnel, her life would come to a swift end.

She pushed herself over the edge.

Deep shadows peeled away with each foot that she dropped. She slid over mushworms that formed a thin oil, slicking the way. Now and then, some blind-crab would be clinging to a wall, and these she kicked free, so that they tumbled all around her.

The tube plummeted down and down, but she took no serious harm. Suddenly it veered right, then left, then right again, and Iome found herself spinning, thrown down face-first as she slid ever onward.

Darkness flowed in behind her to reclaim its territory.

❧ 28 ❧

THE LIGHT OF HEAVEN

Alliances should be like flowers in the desert: quick to blossom, quick to fade.

—Feykaald Kalizar, Chancellor to Raj Ahten

In the hills twelve miles west of Carris, Raj Ahten's army gathered before dawn, a hundred thousand strong. His flameweavers raised a cloud of oily smoke that clung to the ground like a morning mist, hiding them from view, and the morning sun was so obscure, that it looked like a blood red pearl hanging in the air above.

His troops cut trees for scaling ladders, sharpened their weapons, ranged their catapults, and otherwise prepared for war. Raj Ahten spent most of the early hours listening to reports from scouts and far-seers he had sent abroad during the night.

The news disturbed him. To the south the reavers marched in a horde that blackened the lands, heading toward Carris as a host of Knights Equitable vainly fought to forestall their attack.

To the east, the far-seers spotted only ragged bands of women and children, fleeing the coming battle along the highways, or floating in boats and makeshift rafts down the River Donnestgree.

But to the north, his spies found things to be a bit more interesting. Lowicker's daughter, Queen Rialla of Beldinook, had marshaled a powerful army, some 180,000 strong. Most of these were archers, armed with the yew tallbows common in Beldinook. They rode in war carts drawn by heavy force horses, and thus could be conveyed quickly to the battlefront. The army also boasted many powerful Runelords, cavalrymen mounted on heavily armored chargers that were both swift and powerful.

But Lowicker's daughter, it seemed, was unsure what to do. The scout said, "We saw her march some troops within a stone's throw of the gates of Carris last night. Then she retreated twenty miles back north, to a place where the reavers' curses have not blasted the grass. There she has set camp on the road, where there is plenty of forage for the beasts. Even now her troops squat, holding the road against any allies that might seek to lend aid to Carris."

"Is there help from the north?" Raj Ahten asked another pair of scouts that had ranged farther afield.

"Indeed there is, O Light of Heaven," his spies answered. "Several thousand lords have ridden from Orwynne, along with warriors of Fleeds and Heredon."

"What of Crowthen?" Raj Ahten asked.

"We could see no troops from Crowthen," the spies said.

Raj Ahten smiled. He could see Rialla's plan. She had ridden south to lay siege to Carris, only to discover the reavers coming. So she had ridden back north, to get out of their way. She would let the reavers do her dirty work.

Carris didn't stand a chance. Raj Ahten had already gutted Mystarria, throwing down the northern fortresses, killing the Dedicates at the Blue Tower. The warriors that held the city were weak, lacking endowments.

And once Carris fell, nothing could stop Lowicker's daughter from overrunning Mystarria—except Raj Ahten.

Her army worried him, though. Her archers and heavy cavalry could easily defeat his common troops, though with his wizards and Runelords he could probably even the score. But if the two giants wasted their strength fighting each other, who then would win Mystarria?

A plan began to form in Raj Ahten's mind.

"Gather together a thousand lords to act as an honor guard," Raj Ahten said. "I think I shall pay Lowicker's daughter a visit."

As Raj Ahten's most powerful lords and wizards prepared to ride, he sat in his crimson tent. He could feel himself growing from moment to moment as his facilitators in Deyazz vectored endowments of stamina to him.

He had never felt so hale, so robust. He sweated profusely, though he had done no labor to warrant it. It was as if his body recognized that the time had come to cleanse away all impurities, make him something more than human.

He felt as if life and virility were combining in him so powerfully that it bled from every pore.

This is it, he told himself. This is the moment I have been waiting for. I shall be the Sum of All Men.

෨

"Food for the poor!" a small girl called in the markets of Ghusa in Deyazz.
"Food for the poor!" The market streets were still gloomy as the morning sun
rose like a ruddy coal beyond the sand hills.

Turaush Kasill, a large man grown fat from years of convenience,
rounded a stall stacked with tall clay urns to discover the source of the call.

He overshadowed the waif that he found. She was small, no more than
eight or nine, with huge eyes like almonds. Her brown skin was paler than
the black hue of the folk of Deyazz. She gripped the hand of a small boy, perhaps five years of age.

"Please," the girl said holding out an empty wicker basket. "We need
food."

Turaush smiled pleasantly. "I could give you food. How much do you
want? A basketful? I could give you that." The girl's eyes went wide, and her
lips parted hungrily. "What would you like to eat? Peaches? Melons? Rice?
Duck? Sesame cakes with honey drizzled over them? If you could have anything to eat, what would you like?"

"Sesame cakes!" the little boy cried.

The girl squeezed his hand and nudged him, begging the boy to be quiet,
as if fearing that he asked too much.

"Anything," the girl pleaded. "Anything you offer."

"Ah," Turaush said. "You are that hungry?"

"I have two sisters to feed, and a big brother who is hurt," the girl said.
"My father was killed by bandits, and my mother went to her sister's, and we
have heard nothing since. We would be grateful for anything."

"And what if I offer you a trade?" Turaush asked. "What if I offer to feed
you all the food you want, every day, for as long as you live, and give you a
beautiful home to live in?"

The girl hesitated. She must have been warned about sinister men. She
studied him warily, but at last put a hand over her empty stomach, as if by
pressing it she could assuage the pain. "What house?"

"The finest in all Ghusa," Turaush said, waving toward the Dedicate's
Keep. "Good food, as much as you can eat, every day for as long as you live."

Turaush was one of Raj Ahten's most persuasive facilitators. With five
endowments of glamour, he could use his smoldering eyes to lure young
women. With three endowments of voice, he could mesmerize the simple-
minded. He bent his whole will upon the child now.

"Think of it," he said. "Fresh fruit—tangerines and melons and dates
for breakfast. Fine lamb ribs basted with honey and cumin, cooked over
applewood coals; red bass fresh from the sea; peacocks stuffed with rice and
mushrooms."

"I want some," the little boy at her side said, tears coming to his eyes. She squeezed his hand, warning him to be quiet.

"And what if I did it?" the girl asked. "Would you feed my brothers and sisters."

She was only a child, and perhaps knew that by custom, if a man or woman gave an endowment, their children would be well cared for, for life. Turaush shook his head sadly. "If you were a grown woman, we might make such a deal. But you are only a child half-grown, and so your endowment is not worth much to us. Being so small, you don't have as much stamina as an adult," he lied. After all, he had a quota to fill. "So, if your little brother here wants food also, he will have to give up his endowment."

He smiled kindly at the boy. Turaush had rarely resorted to taking endowments from children so young. But these two looked healthy enough.

"I hear that it hurts," the girl objected.

"Only a little, and only for a moment," Turaush said. His tone promised a lifetime of joy afterward, though to be sure, it would not be a long life. Raj Ahten needed stamina, and a starveling like this was not likely to live through the winter plague season.

"But what of my sisters?" the girl asked. "Who will take care of them?"

"How old are they?"

"One is three, and the other barely a year."

Turaush frowned. Such children were too young to surrender endowments. A Dedicate had to want to give his endowment with his whole soul, and small children, not understanding the consequences of their decision, could not muster the proper resolve.

Still, Turaush thought, we could raise them for a couple of years, until they are old enough.

"I will make you a deal. If you and your brother give your endowments, perhaps I could arrange that your sisters get fed, too. In fact, I know a nice woman who has long wished for a daughter of her own. She would count herself fortunate indeed to be blessed with two."

"And my big brother?"

"Tell me about your brother."

"His name is Balimar. He's big enough to work. But he was gored by a water buffalo last summer, and is only now beginning to walk."

"So Balimar is mending?"

"Yes," the girl answered. "He is very strong."

Turaush considered. Balimar might not be able to give stamina now, but he might give his brawn. He would of course feel accountable for the younger children, and if they were suddenly spirited away to the Dedicate's Keep in the palace, he would be easily persuaded to follow. "I'm sure that an arrangement can be made. Come now, let us go take your endowments and get some food in you. Then I will talk to Balimar."

Turaush took the girl's tiny hand. In the distance, borne on the dawn winds, he could hear the keen piping of a facilitator as he coaxed the stamina from someone, followed by a howl of pain as the attribute was wrenched away. To him, the sound seemed sweeter than the coo of the wood doves as he led the children to the palace.

ℬ 29 ℭ

A BEND IN THE RIVER

There is nothing more noble than to give of oneself out of love. There is nothing more humiliating than feeling compelled to take that gift.

—*King Jas Laren Sylvarresta*

Dearborn rowed the boat steadily in the late afternoon, his eyes dull from fatigue. Beads of perspiration trickled down his cheek and off his nose, and sweat liberally stained the armpits of his work shirt.

"Almost there," he said. "We should see the castle as we round this next bend."

For hours he had rowed, seeming never to tire, never stopping to rest. He watched the currents, keeping the boat in the center of the **V** each time he rounded a bend, in order to borrow more speed from the fast water.

A chill shook Chemoise. She tried to ignore it. Instead, she watched the flat green water and rejoiced in the warm sunlight on her skin. It made her feel clean, as if its heat could burn the infection from her.

"Have you decided what to give?" Dearborn asked.

"Metabolism," she said at last.

It was the least dangerous endowment to grant. It wouldn't hurt Chemoise's child, and would hardly inconvenience her. She could give it easily. If Gaborn won, and killed the reavers, then she would wake in some distant day when the war was over, only a bad dream, fading into insignificance.

"Hmmm . . ." Dearborn muttered. He was obviously displeased. By giving metabolism, she would leave him in a way. She'd sleep as he grew old. But she wasn't about to let some minor attachment deter her.

Her journey downstream had been almost like a pleasure outing. The banks of the River Wye were overgrown with cattails along the route, and trout could be seen slapping the water in their quest for midges. Mallards paddled near shore, ever vigilant as their ducklings followed behind. Once, Chemoise saw a huge stag leap up from its bed beneath an apple tree.

All of the sudden, they rounded the bend, and Chemoise spotted Castle Sylvarresta ahead, a walled city built upon a long hill; the tall watchtowers looked like gray arrows taking aim at the sky. From here, you could hardly see the damage wreaked by the Darkling Glory. The Graak's Aerie hid most of the wreckage of the King's Tower and the Dedicate's Keep, and the burnt front gates remained concealed by the castle walls. Only blackened grass on nearby hills reminded one that a battle had been fought here.

Chemoise felt surprised to see crowds surrounding the castle. Tens of thousands of bright tents and pavilions were pitched upon the nearer hills. The smoke of cooking fires hung above the fields like gray cobwebs. Horses were tethered along the riverbank ahead.

Chemoise had lived in the city before the Darkling Glory came. Four hundred thousand people or more had camped in the fields round about, eager to meet the Earth King. They'd fled at Gaborn's warning, fading into the forest to hide from the Darkling Glory. Now it looked as if nearly everyone had returned.

"Look at them all," Chemoise said in wonder. "It's like Hostenfest."

Dearborn craned his head as he rowed, glanced over his shoulder, and grunted in dull surprise. Soon, they passed along shores where hundreds of women and children were washing clothes or fetching pails of water.

Chemoise shouted to one washwoman, "Why is everyone at Castle Sylvarresta?"

"The Earth King needs endowments," she replied.

"That can't be it," Chemoise whispered to Dearborn. "That many people wouldn't give endowments. There must be another reason. Maybe they came to hide from the rats."

"Did the rats come last night?" Dearborn asked the washwoman.

"They came," she answered. "Drowned trying to swim the moat. The ferrin took those what made it over the city walls." She seemed little concerned, and Chemoise envied her. In Ableton the rats had given them a bitter struggle.

So it was that Dearborn beached the rowboat, and Chemoise climbed the banks of the River Wye, up through oat stubble, looking for signs of a great struggle like the one fought back home. The city looked peaceful.

"The rats didn't kill your horses?" Chemoise asked the old woman. "They didn't ruin your tents?"

"We were all in the castle," she answered. "Hiding. We filled every tomb and every cellar."

"There was room for everyone?" Chemoise asked, unsure if she believed it.

"Och, no," the old woman said. "Some folks went up to the old iron mines in the Dunnwood, and stayed as cozy as peas in a pod. The rats never even made it to their door. The ferrin folk had them all, I suppose."

Chemoise stared in disbelief. There was no sign of a struggle. The sun shone golden over the fields. The cottages by the river sat undisturbed. The farms spread out along the road in a patchwork quilt of colors—white of oat stubble, the forest green of a field of mint, the yellow of mustard flowers, the ruddy gold of winter wheat.

It wasn't until they had walked a hundred yards toward the castle that Dearborn discovered sign of the attack. With his boot he pointed out a dead rat curled up under a clump of grass beside the road, a ferrin's broken spear still in its gut.

A chill shook Chemoise, and she noticed a bit of sadness in Dearborn's eyes and a thoughtful look on his face.

"What is it?" Chemoise asked.

"We're the lucky ones," he said. "It's only little rats we're fighting. Imagine if this thing was as big as a farmer's cottage, lumbering about. That's what our folks will be facing at Carris."

It was worse than that, Chemoise knew. Rats didn't have hide as tough as armor. Rats didn't have mages that cast foul spells. Rats weren't as cunning as men.

She peered into Dearborn's face in wonder. "Our folks," he had called the people of Carris. But they were strangers, hundreds of miles beyond the city's borders.

It's the war, she realized. A common foe had made brothers of them all.

She hurried her stride, reached the city gates. There were boys beside the moat, using rakes to pull drowned rats from the water, then throwing the nasty things into wicker baskets.

One boy had waded into the depths up to his chest, and used a spear to try to fish some rats out of the lilies that grew in the shadow of the castle wall.

The vermin would have been able to crawl over the moat on the backs of their dead, Chemoise imagined.

She glanced behind. Shadows were growing long. The sun loomed on the horizon, splendorous among some golden clouds. Soon it would be night. Chemoise hoped that she still had time. She raced up Merchant Street, where vendors hawked food, filling the evening air with scents of fresh bread and meats that made her mouth water.

It wasn't until she passed the King's Gate, out of the merchant's quarter, that she saw how strange the world had become.

She heard the distant birdlike singing of facilitators as they took endowments, and found that just inside the King's Gate, a crowd had formed.

A thousand people stood waiting to give endowments, jostling one another in an effort to be first. One woman called, "Tell the facilitators to hurry. We haven't got all night!"

The King's Tower and Dedicates' Keep were naught but ruins after last week's battle with the Darkling Glory, and little had been done to clean up the pile of broken stone. But the old barracks and attendant Great Hall still stood, and these had been turned into a makeshift Dedicates' Keep.

Pavilions in a riot of color covered the green, and everywhere Chemoise saw hundreds of people lying in their shade, as if in a faint.

Dully she realized that the barracks was full, and the tents were full, and there was nowhere else to put the Dedicates except to lay them on the grass until something better could be arranged. Those without brawn lay as slack as newborn babes while attendants clustered around them. Dozens of blind men and women sat beside a cooking fire, strumming lutes and singing an old ballad, which had served as a call over the ages:

> "Come give yourself, come give yourself,
> Before it is too late.
> Together we stand when darkness falls.
> The need is growing great.

> "Come give yourself, come give yourself,
> We know the cost is dear.
> Together we'll stand when our lord calls.
> Let's have a rousing cheer."

"Are all of these people Dedicates for the Earth King?" Chemoise asked in wonder.

"Aye," a young man called out. In the crowd, Chemoise hadn't spotted him. But at a nearby table sat a facilitator's apprentice with a quill and inkpot, writing on a long scroll. He was a young man, no more than thirteen.

"How many endowments does he need?" Chemoise asked.

"We'll give him every forcible we've got, and hope that its enough," the apprentice answered. "With any luck, we'll make him the Sum of All Men." Chemoise gazed out over the field in wonder. There weren't just hundreds who had given endowments. Instead, thousands of people lay on the green. And as she glanced back downhill, she could see carts and horses coming from afar—from Bannisferre to the south, and Hobtown to the east, and a hundred villages to the west—people bringing all that they had with them to Castle Sylvarresta. Tens of thousands would offer themselves as Dedicates. And those who didn't win the honor of going under the forcible would gladly hold the walls against any enemy that might try to take them, making them-

THE LAIR OF BONES 257

selves human shields between the enemies of the Earth King and the source of his Power.

It was grand and glorious to see so many people coming together to create the stuff of legend: the Sum of All Men. For a moment, Chemoise was swept away. The young facilitator cleared his throat, and asked, "Are you here to give an endowment?"

Chemoise's stomach fluttered nervously. "Aye."

"What can you offer?"

"Metabolism," she volunteered. "Metabolism won't hurt my unborn child."

"We're full up on that," the facilitator said. "He's got more than a hundred now. We really need stamina, grace, and brawn." He listed the greater endowments. Chemoise thought he sounded like a merchant in the market who demands more for his wares than one can easily pay. Giving any one of those endowments could kill a person. Chemoise was already sick from rat bites. She didn't dare offer stamina, lest her current illness take her. And those who gave brawn sometimes found that their hearts stopped, or their lungs quit working, simply because they hadn't the strength to go on. Chemoise didn't think she could face the terror of that, to lie helpless, unable to breathe, knowing that death was moments away.

"Grace," Chemoise said, struggling to sound more eager than she felt. Perhaps by giving Gaborn my grace, Chemoise thought, I can atone for my father's transgression.

Her father had once given grace to Raj Ahten, Gaborn's most feared enemy, who had also sought to become the Sum of All Men.

The scribe made a mark in his book, adding her endowment of grace to the Earth King's tally. She was but one of thousands. He didn't ask Chemoise her name or thank her profusely or make the normal promises of care and compensation for the rest of her life.

Her endowment was a gift, and the giving of it was its own reward.

"And you, sir?" the scribe asked, peering behind Chemoise to Dearborn.

"Oh," Chemoise explained, "he's my friend. He just brought me—"

Dearborn put a hand on her shoulder, gently pushed her aside. "Brawn," he said with a deadly resolve in his voice. "I'll give him my strength. And may the Powers grant that he deal a blow . . ." He made a fist and shook it, as if he'd strike with his own hand if he could.

Chemoise looked into Dearborn's face and saw a hardness she'd never imagined. She'd thought him a moon-sick pup. But now she recalled how he had rowed the boat all day without rest. Something in him had changed.

The plague of rats was sent to break us here in Heredon, Chemoise realized, but instead we have only fixed our resolve.

ᛞ 30 ᛒ

THE GLORY

*The Glories speak not as men speak but whisper words that can only be heard
in the heart of one who yearns for understanding.*

—Erden Geboren

Gaborn raced down a seemingly endless winding stair that a commoner
would have spent days trying to negotiate. Hot winds from the Underworld
swirled up it, blasting his face. There was no water here, no refreshment.

In Heredon the battle was over, and those that would die had died.

Now Carris was braced for the slaughter.

Gaborn could sense Averan, still alive, far below.

Over the past few days—as Gaborn sensed time—the Consort of Shadows had led him through doors that no commoner could open, climbed down
chimneys and up stairways that no human was meant to follow.

More than just reavers burrowed in the Underworld, and the Consort of
Shadows was as likely to take some route formed by the passage of a great-
worm as follow the reaver tunnels. Gaborn had run past huge waterfalls and
through drowned caverns. Twice he had lost his way and managed to find it
again.

As he ran, days seemed to pass, and he pondered what he would do when
he met the One True Master.

She would be prepared. She was strong in the ways of sorcery, strong
enough to challenge the very Powers. More than that, she harbored a locus
that had existed from the beginning of time.

Had Erden Geboren planned to fight her with his spear? Gaborn hefted
the ancient reaver dart, studied its diamond tip. Runes were carved into it—

runes of Earth Strengthening to keep the shaft from breaking. Beyond that, the weapon was nothing special. It was only a spear carved from bone.

Not with a spear, he thought. You can't kill a locus like that. It is evil, the very essence of evil.

Gaborn's stomach was knotted, but he craved an answer to his dilemma more than he hungered for food.

A chasm crossed his path, some hundred feet across. He ran and leapt effortlessly, but snapped an ankle when he landed on the far side. He straightened the ankle and sat for a moment, letting his endowments of stamina take over. Shortly, the bone healed and he was on his way again.

He tried to dredge up everything that he'd ever heard about the Glories and the Bright Ones, about Erden Geboren, about the great enemy, the one that his own lore called the Raven. As he pondered, something that Iome had read came to mind. Erden Geboren had described the Bright Ones on his first meeting, and said of them, "Virtue was their armor, and truth was their sword."

He had imagined then that Erden Geboren was trying somehow to express the goodness that he saw in these people, these true men of the netherworld.

Yet it struck Gaborn that these words weren't written upon first meeting the Bright Ones, but decades later. What if, Gaborn asked himself, Erden Geboren meant this literally?

What if . . . a man is like a vessel, Gaborn thought. And what if that vessel can be filled with light, or it can be filled with darkness?

If I fill myself with light, how can the darkness find place within me?

What darkness is there to purge within me? Gaborn wondered. He remembered the book that the Emir of Tuulistan had sent to King Sylvarresta, and the drawing within it. The drawing displayed the Domains of Man, the things that he owned. These included his Visible Domains, the properties that he owned that could be seen—his home, his body, and his wealth. His Communal Domains included all of his relationship to his community—his family, his town, his country, and his good name. His Invisible Domains encompassed all of those things that a man owns that cannot be seen—his time, his freedom to act, his body space.

According to the emir, whenever a man invades one of these domains, we call him evil. If he seeks to ruin our reputation, or steal our gold, or control our actions, we feel violated.

But if a man enlarges our domains, if he gives of his wealth or offers us praise, we call him good.

By this definition the One True Master was pure evil. It was seeking to devour Gaborn's world, strip him and his people of everything, including life itself.

The Three Domains of Man

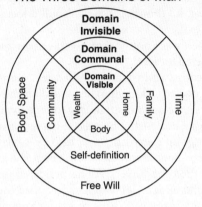

But how could he fight it? How could he destroy it?

Gaborn was so deep in thought that he was running almost blindly. He rounded a corner, and heard a moan. It sounded like a man in pain.

He halted there in the ribbed tunnel, gasping for breath. He tried to hold silent, to still his breathing and the pounding of his heart.

"Help me!" someone called from up the tunnel. It was a man in pain, choking out his words. He sobbed, and the sound of it echoed through the tunnel so that Gaborn half feared that he had passed someone in the dark.

"Hello?" Gaborn cried.

He moved forward carefully. The pale green light of his ring was fading, and didn't penetrate very far. The sobbing stopped.

Gaborn neared a corner, saw something on the ground—a human leg, drained of blood and as pale as snow. Its toes had gone black, and all of the muscles in it clenched painfully.

The sobbing began again. Just up the tunnel, around the corner.

Gaborn's nerves came alive. His Earth Senses warned of danger ahead.

It's a trap, he realized. The reavers must have left someone here as bait. And when I round the bend, they will spring on me.

His heart hammered in his throat, and a cold sweat condensed on his brow. Gaborn gripped his reaver dart, began to inch around the corner, his back to the wall.

Just a few feet ahead lay a pair of arms, blackened fingers curled up like claws.

By the Powers, Gaborn swore, what have they done?

He imagined someone alone and helpless, arms and legs ripped from him, lying in a pool of blood. Only a powerful Runelord with dozens of endowments of stamina could cling to life for long under such circumstances.

"Help!" the cry came again, nearer now, but weaker.

Gaborn suddenly realized how weary he'd become. He had been running for days now, almost in a trance, and even with his endowments, it had taken a toll on him. The walls of the cave seemed dreamy, insubstantial, and he felt disconnected from his body.

"Hello?" Gaborn called. "Are any reavers near you? Is this a trap"

He heard a choking sound, as if the man rejoiced to hear a fellow human's voice. "No, no reavers," he answered weakly. "It was no reaver that did this to me." The voice sounded almost familiar, and Gaborn rounded the corner, surprised to see a shadow on the floor so near.

He peered on the ground. Blind-crabs had burrowed holes in the wall of the tunnel, and there near them lay a stump of a man—armless, legless. Peppered gray hair and beard. His face was turned toward the darkness. The crabs were atop him, eating him. Yet he still managed to cling to life, for Gaborn could see the rise and fall of his chest.

"It was no reaver that did this," the fellow whispered, his voice a bit stronger. "Unless *you* are a reaver."

He turned to look at Gaborn, but peered at him with only bloody sockets. The crabs had torn out his eyes. It was King Lowicker, whom Gaborn had left for dead in Beldinook not a week past.

"No!" Gaborn cried, fearing that what he saw was Lowicker's spirit.

Lowicker began to laugh painfully. "Gaborn," he said, and the name echoed in the tunnel. Gaborn distinctly heard it whispered in his left ear, and almost immediately it came again behind him.

I'm dreaming, Gaborn told himself. There was no way that the foul King Lowicker could still be alive, down here. Runelords with great endowments of stamina seldom needed sleep, but when they did, the need was often announced thus, in a waking nightmare.

Lowicker laughed, as if amused at Gaborn's predicament.

"So," he said. "You come to meet me. Or do you hope to slay my master?"

Gaborn did not answer, for his mind was a whirl. A dream, he wondered, or a sending?

"You cannot kill her," Lowicker said, "without killing yourself. For she lives inside of you. You are her sanctuary, and her breeding ground."

"No," Gaborn said. "I want no part of her. I hate her."

"As you hated me?" Lowicker asked.

"You were a murderer. You killed your own wife, and would have killed me. You got what you deserve."

Lowicker stared at Gaborn with empty, accusing sockets. Blood had crusted on the stumps of his arms and legs, and now the crabs tore into him with relish.

"And you will get what you deserve," Lowicker said.

At that moment, Gaborn felt as if a cold wave washed over him, and darkness gathered about him. The world seemed to spin.

He felt as if he were in the center of a maelstrom. Invisible winds swirled about him, winds of darkness, and he wanted to cry for help, but his tongue felt like wood in his mouth, and even if he screamed, only the blind-crabs would hear.

He fell to the ground and knew that he was not alone in the cave. Some unseen power swirled about him, intent on his destruction.

His heart pounded. He found it almost impossible to breathe. The Raven circled. He could sense the One True Master, her ageless maleficent intent. She whispered in his ear, "How can you fight an enemy who has no form, who controls your very thoughts?"

Gaborn curled into a ball. He wanted to flee, but there was nowhere to run, and in his current state, he could not tell what was real from what was imagined.

He saw as if in a vision a young boy of four or five. The skies were clear and blue, and the day seemed warm and bright. But thunder could be heard, and the child was rushing from his house with deadly intent, a stick in hand.

There is a fox among the hens, the boy thought.

But as he rounded the back of the house, Gaborn suddenly realized the source of the thunder. Reavers were charging in a vast horde. They thundered over a nearby hill in a black line. The young boy saw them, and his knees went weak and his mouth fell open. He held up his pitiful little stick, as if hoping to drive them back the way he would a fox, but the horde raced forward, unstoppable.

The first reaver to reach the child swallowed him whole, and the vision faded.

The Master whispered in Gaborn's ear. "You are the child, we are the horde. Against us, you cannot prevail."

Gaborn felt with sick certainty that the vision was accurate. The Master had showed him something that had happened as the reaver horde charged toward Carris.

The darkness thickened. For long moments Gaborn thought that his spirit would be torn from his body, wailing, to be carried off and used as a plaything by the Raven.

But at long last he had a realization. She didn't have that kind of power. If she had, she'd have swept all of mankind from the face of the Earth long ago.

With that thought, the swirling darkness began to abate, and after a time, it departed altogether.

As if it had swept all evidence from the ground, Lowicker and his severed limbs had disappeared. Only the cavern floor, polished clean by the tramping of reavers, lay before him.

Gaborn's heart pounded.

The Master had attacked him. Why?

Gaborn could think of only two possibilities. The first was that she did it for mere sport, tormenting him for her own delight. But the second was that she did it because she was afraid.

Why would she fear me? Gaborn wondered. What threat do I pose to her?

He thought back to when the vision started. Gaborn had been wondering how he could defeat a creature of pure evil, one that lived not in the body but in the spirit.

He crawled to his knees, realized what had happened. She had tried to distract him from his line of reasoning. Indeed, Gaborn suspected that if he returned to his line of reasoning, he would invite another attack.

Let her come, then, Gaborn told himself. I want an end to her. I hate her. He got up.

"Then she will use that hate against you," a voice whispered in the back of his mind. "She will invite you to hate those who serve her, and in the end, she will overcome you. When you expand the bounds of virtue, the evil ones wail and mourn."

The swirling winds of darkness were gone now, and peace filled Gaborn's heart, even though he could hear, as if far off, the wailing voice of the locus.

"Learn to love all men equally," Erden Geboren had written, and the words seemed now to ring in Gaborn's ears, as if Erden Geboren stood beside him. "The cruel as well as the kind."

The cruel as well as the kind, Gaborn repeated. Doubt assailed him. He thought of King Lowicker the wife-killer.

What should I have done with him?

He recalled the hundreds of cruel men that he had refused to Choose. He recalled how he'd hated Raj Ahten.

"*Learn to love all men equally. The cruel as well as the kind.*"

When Choosing those who would live and those who would die, Gaborn had tried to set some sort of standard. He had refused to Choose only the strong, letting the weak die. He had refused to Choose only the wise, letting the foolish die. He had Chosen old and young, male and female, Rofehavanish and Indhopalese.

He'd set only one standard. He had rejected the wicked. In that, he had felt justified. For men may be born stupid and weak and ugly, Gaborn had told himself, and fortune may abandon even the most frugal, but a man must be held accountable for his own character. Otherwise, we invite anarchy.

"Hold them accountable for their weakness, then," the voice whispered.

But punish them for their own transgressions in the measure they deserve, and not to gratify your wrath."

Gaborn held that thought.

He felt foolish. He had grieved the Earth Spirit and lost his ability to warn his Chosen warriors of danger. Because of Gaborn's weakness, women and children would die in Carris tonight.

Who will punish me for my weakness? Gaborn wondered.

He knew the answer. People would die, and he would live, and that would be his punishment.

But was there something more that he could have done?

Erden Geboren had said that he was to love the cruel and the cunning, to seek their benefit, even when they were too blinded by greed and hatred to recognize their own best interests.

Something didn't fit. Gaborn wondered about Iome's ability to translate. In his book, Erden Geboren had often found it difficult to select a word, had crossed out a word to insert another, only to cross it out again. It was as if his own tongue were too imprecise to fit with that of the Bright Ones.

What did he mean, to "love" the cruel? How could he love a cruel person without also loving cruelty? Unless "love" were not an emotion but a determination. Perhaps to love another perfectly meant to seek to expand his horizons, to help him become better, even if he had no desire to do so himself.

Gaborn ran blindly down the tunnel, almost by instinct. Blind-crabs and other vermin seemed frozen in fear. Gaping holes in the floor showed where chervil, tiny insects, had eaten away the rock. Stonewood trees hung from the roof above, whorls of branches crazily twisting.

From the corner of his eye he noticed a brightness near the roof of the tunnel.

He glanced up, and the brightness departed.

An illusion, Gaborn thought, thrown by my cape pin.

He remembered something that his grandfather had once told him. "Goodness is like a stone, tossed into a still pond. Its effect causes ripples everywhere, touches everything around it, and in time its effect will return to its source. You say hello to a man, praise his work, and you brighten his day. He in turn brightens those around him, and soon the whole town is smiling, and people you don't even know seem glad to meet you. Goodness works this way. Evil does, too."

Erden Geboren had called the locus a shadow, a blackness that spread forth vapors to touch those around it.

Can there be a good locus? Gaborn wondered. Can there be creatures of light that do the same?

Something came to him strongly then, a knowledge that pierced him. It came powerfully, as if it were a shouted word, or memory long forgotten. Yet it came as if in words spoken outside himself.

"Yes, there are Glories," the voice came to him again.

Again he saw that furtive light hovering above. It was shaped like a vast bird, like a gull with graceful wings, gliding silently in slow circles overhead.

I am not alone, Gaborn whispered in his heart. Am I?

"No," the voice answered. "I am near you."

A sure knowledge filled Gaborn. He understood now why the Master had attacked. She had also sensed the presence of a Glory.

"Can you help me?" Gaborn asked. He did not know why he asked. He felt unworthy to ask it. He had promised his people protection, and through his own weaknesses had made that promise a lie. He had taken Dedicates only to see them destroyed. He had killed men rather than work to redeem them.

"Perhaps, if you crave it enough," the voice whispered.

"I do," Gaborn said.

Suddenly the brightness above him flared, becoming white hot. The light was blinding, and Gaborn threw his hands up to protect his eyes, yet he felt little heat. Instead, there was only wisdom and power, vast reservoirs that until that moment had been unimaginable to him.

The light dazzled him. Every bone in his body quivered as if to an invisible rhythm. And still the light grew fiercer.

The shadows in the cave fled, and Gaborn pulled his hands from his eyes, hoping for only a glimpse of the Glory. But if the creature had a body, Gaborn could not see. It was only an indescribable brightness, more dazzling than a noonday sun, and Gaborn felt that at any moment he would melt in its presence, or be blasted into pieces.

And then the light pierced him.

It was like a flaming lance in the heart, a lance that struck him and burned through him, consuming the evil hidden within, until every hair of his body felt energized, and every pore of his body bled illumination.

Things that he had never understood suddenly made perfect sense—the relationship between good and evil, between men and loci and Glories.

The light bursting within him was unbearable.

"I'm dying!" Gaborn called out in fear.

As silently as the light had filled the chamber, it began to fade. The shadows grew and lengthened. The tunnel darkened as the winged bird of light fled before the shadows.

Gaborn sat, panting, alone.

He stopped and looked at his hands. He could feel the radiance within, and brightness seemed to illumine his mind. But he could see no physical mark upon him.

Did I really see a Glory? he wondered. Or was it a waking dream? If others were here, would they have seen it?

He knew. He could not deny his senses. It was no dream.

So he got up and ran, down, down, deeper into the Underworld, carrying the brightness in his heart.

❧ 31 ❧

GEMS OF THE DESERT

There is nothing wrong with greed. It is the attribute that allowed your ancestors to amass the wealth that we have today. If you would honor them, revel in greed, and make yourself strong enough to grasp all that you desire.

—*Lowicker's counsel to his daughter, Rialla, at age four*

Glittering like gems against a backdrop of black ash, Raj Ahten and his retinue of lords from Indhopal rode to the camp of Rialla Lowicker.

His lords wore bright silken armor that flashed in the sunlight, whites so bright that they hurt the eyes, golds so bright that they looked as if they were freshly minted coins, rubies far redder than blood. The horses and camels were all caparisoned as brightly as the lords.

They rode down out of the hills through lands the reavers had blasted with curses a week before. The dead pine trees along the road all smelled of premature rot, though gray pine needles still clung to their black branches. Every blade of grass had turned to gray straw, and now lay desiccated upon the ground. Every vine and bush had withered.

No rain had fallen here in over a week, and all of the dead grass and bracken and pine forests now were as dry as tinder. A spark thrown up as a horse's hoof struck a rock caused a small fire along the way. One of the captains warned the men to beware the danger.

Raj Ahten only smiled. It was only sixty miles to Queen Lowicker's camp, and on swift force horses, it took less than an hour of the morning.

As Raj Ahten's criers announced that he had come for a parley, Raj Ahten sat straight and proud upon his gray imperial warhorse, resplendent in white silk.

He rode warily into camp. He did not trust these northerners, for oft Lowicker's men had sought his life in the past, but he did not let his wariness show. He came under a green flag of truce and let his glamour waft over the soldiers. Though he asked no man for allegiance, many a stout warrior looked upon him for a moment and then dropped to one knee, bowing his head.

Rialla herself came out of her great blue pavilion and took one look at him. She was big of bone and homely, but she had a masculine toughness to her demeanor that he had always admired in women. He knew at once what kind of woman she was: knowing that she could never compete with the dainty ladies of court, she had chosen instead to challenge the lords and war-riors around her.

Yet when she looked upon Raj Ahten, her mouth opened in awe, she trembled visibly, and then ducked back into her tent.

A moment later, her chamberlain came out of the quarters and announced, "Her Royal Highness, Rialla Val Lowicker, will parley with you in the privacy of her tent."

Raj Ahten leapt lightly from his mount and strode into the pavilion as the chamberlain pulled back the flap.

Rialla Lowicker stood alone in the center of the tent. On the floor was spread a huge map of Mystarria, painted upon four steer skins, all sewn into one piece. She stood just above Carris. The map showed Lake Donnestgree to the east, the mountains to the south, and the reavers marching toward them, as signified by a little black wooden carving of a reaver. To the west were the Alcairs, where Raj Ahten's troops were signified by another wooden carving of a warrior in a white turban. To the north, her maps showed King Anders riding through Beldinook, while young King Orwynne streamed south through Fleeds. But to the east was something of a surprise.

At the Courts of Tide, the King of Mystarria had been toppled, and in his place stood a barbarian in gray, with the Orb of Internook upon his round shield.

"Your intelligence is better than mine," Raj Ahten said, looking at the map. "Who is the warlord at the Court of Tide?"

"Olmarg," Rialla answered. She was breathing hard. Raj Ahten glanced at her. When she had first stepped outside, her long-sleeved dress had been buttoned severely up the collar to the top of her throat. Now she had unloosed the top five buttons, to reveal a hint of cleavage.

Raj Ahten smiled. He had thousands of endowments of glamour and Voice, and few women could resist him for long. Beyond that, he was now a flameweaver. As such, the Power of his master was upon him. His very pres-ence in a room inflamed certain passions in commoners—lust, greed, the desire for combat.

Raj Ahten took one look at the young queen and knew that she could not resist him. The combined effect of his magics overwhelmed her.

He toyed with her, stepping near. He took her right hand, stooped, and kissed it. As he did, he made sure to keep eye contact throughout, except for one calculated instant, when he glanced at her cleavage.

Her response gratified him no end. Rialla Lowicker began to pant as soon as he touched her. Her nostrils flared and her eyes rolled back as he kissed her hand. And when he glanced at her cleavage, her whole body trembled in ecstasy.

He knew that she was his to claim.

"How long ago did Olmarg attack the Courts of Tide?" he asked.

"He was to have sailed in at dawn," Rialla answered, "under the orders of King Anders of Crowthen."

"But the Courts of Tide are heavily defended. Are you sure that Olmarg can take them?"

Rialla breathed heavily as Raj Ahten's magics wreathed about her. "He was . . . my spies tell me that Gaborn Val Orden has fled to do battle with reavers in the Underworld, and commanded all of his warriors to come here. The coasts were left defenseless."

"So what do you plan?" Raj Ahten asked. "Your map shows lords from the north riding to the aid Carris. Will you fight them?"

He held her hand, and Rialla Lowicker clutched his in return, not willing to let him go.

"Until I know what you and Anders are up to, I can't decide."

"King Anders?" Raj Ahten asked.

"He's a slippery one—plots within plots within plots."

"And . . . you don't like him?" Raj Ahten asked.

"I was afraid to stand against Gaborn after what he did to my father. I wrote to King Anders and told him that any deals my father made died with him. In response, he sent messengers south, claiming to be the new Earth King. He says that Gaborn has lost his powers, and the Earth has called him in Gaborn's stead."

Raj Ahten laughed aloud. "First Anders claimed that Gaborn was no Earth King, and now he claims that Gaborn was an Earth King, but Anders is a better man still?"

"In my experience," Rialla said, "when a man cannot choose between the lies he loves, it is because there is no truth in him. Mark my word, there is no more dangerous man in Rofehavan than King Anders."

"I'm in Rofehavan," Raj Ahten said, still holding her hand.

"And do you claim to be more dangerous than he?" she teased.

Passion filled her eyes now, and laughter, and lust. Raj Ahten decided that he liked this woman. Her boldness was tempered with caution, and he sensed a streak of cunning and cruelty in her.

Raj Ahten reached up with his right hand and smoothed back her drab brown hair. Rialla closed her eyes and grasped his hand, held it to her cheek.

There was nothing lovely about her, but at the moment, Raj Ahten felt an excess of wholeness. So many endowments of stamina had been vectored to him that he felt as if light and life were oozing from every pore. If he did not plant his seed in a woman soon, the desire to do so would become pure torture.

"Let the lords of the north ride into Carris," Raj Ahten suggested. "The city is indefensible, and they will die together, leaving all of the north and west of Rofehavan vulnerable to attack. Orwynne, Fleeds, and even South Crowthen could be ours along with Mystarria and Heredon. Meanwhile, I suggest that you hold your army here and I will keep mine in the hills to the west, until after the reavers finish Carris. Thus, we will have them boxed in against the lake. Only then will we muster our armies and drive the reavers back to the Underworld."

Raj Ahten held her eyes, and Rialla moved in closer.

"You think we could do it," she asked, "with only three hundred thousand men between us?"

"Reavers," Raj Ahten said, "frighten easily when their leaders are stripped from them. They become confused. And I have brought with me from Maygassa a few surprises that even the reavers have never seen before. Once I slaughter their fell mages, our men will strike fear into them."

"What do you want out of the bargain?" she asked.

"Reaver curses have blackened the land through all of the southern kingdoms of Indhopal. My people need food to last out the winter."

"The stores at Carris won't be enough to do much good," Rialla argued.

"It will be enough to ensure that the strong and the cunning survive," Raj Ahten said. "The rest can starve.

"Beyond this," he continued, "I'll need Dedicates to grant me endowments. Any lords that I capture in Rofehavan will become mine, spoils of war."

"And what do you offer in return, if I grant your request?" Rialla asked.

"In a year's time I will rule as king of all Rofehavan, and you shall rule beside me as my queen."

Rialla was breathing hard. Now she stepped back, and though her lust had nearly overpowered her, her face took on a calculating look. Indeed, Raj Ahten realized that she had been playing him as much as he played her. He had just revealed his heart to her. Now she revealed her heart to him. "You have many wives in your harem. If I'm to rule at your side, there must be only one."

Raj Ahten liked her pluck. "They are not wives, merely baubles, toys. I had but one wife, and Gaborn took her from me as surely as he took your father from you."

"If your wives mean nothing to you," Rialla said, "kill them for me."

Fire whispered within him, "Yes, let her have them. Thus will I make her mine."

"Better than that," Raj Ahten said, "I will give you a knife, and let you kill them yourself."

He waited to see if she would flinch or back away from the deed. Instead, Rialla Lowicker, the future Queen of Rofehavan grabbed by him the throat and pushed him to the floor as she struggled to tear off his clothes.

Shortly after dawn, a bloody sun rose over Deyazz. The roosters crowed loudly in the streets of Ghusa, as if they were seeing the sun for the very first time.

Raj Ahten's facilitator Turaush Kasill trudged down the streets of the city, until he found an old ramshackle hut behind the brickyard. The hut was a lean-to made of sticks angled against an ancient stone wall. Hides atop the sticks served as a roof to keep out the rain and the noonday sun.

The smoldering ashes of a campfire still burned before the hut. The smell of human waste was everywhere. Turaush wrinkled his nose in disgust, and clapped his hands twice.

"Balimar?" he called. "Balimar Mahaddim?"

A young man quickly thrust his head out from behind a hide flap of the lean-to. His eyes were red, as if he had been weeping or had lain awake sleepless the whole night.

Surely he had been searching for his little sister and brother, the beggars from the market. Now, worn from a lack of sleep, his wits would be dull. At least, Turaush hoped that they would.

"Yes?" the boy asked. "You called"—he glanced at Turaush's fine robes and lowered his eyes in respect—"O Great Kaif?"

"I called," Turaush said. "Your little sister and brother were found begging for food in the markets last night."

"You know where they are?" Balimar asked with a tone of relief.

"I do," Turaush answered. "Would you like to see them?"

The boy Balimar pushed himself out from under the flaps of his lean-to, and grabbed onto the wall for support. Turaush could see the white weal of a scar on his hip, and the boy's leg was still bandaged, but he looked to be mostly healed. He had a brawny build, with a thick neck and strong biceps, but his eyes showed no intelligence. He was a facilitator's dream—brawn, stamina, perhaps even grace. Such a young man had a wealth of possibilities.

"Where are they?" the boy asked suspiciously.

"They sold themselves for food," Turaush said.

"As slaves?" the boy asked, his voice thick with disbelief.

"As Dedicates," Turaush said. "They now serve our lord Raj Ahten." Turaush put all the power of his voice into this last, hinting by his tone that theirs was a noble service, something to be desired.

"I . . ." the boy's voice faltered. Words failed him. "I've never met the man," he apologized.

"He is a great lord," Turaush said, "the greatest who ever lived. Not two days ago, they say he slew a great reaver in Kartish, the Lord of the Underworld. And even now he rides to defend our realm from the evil kings of Rofehavan. You should be proud of your brother and sister. They render a great service to our lord."

Balimar looked about in confusion. He was a bit darker of skin than his brother and sister, almost as if he were a bastard, fathered by a stranger. His eyes were darker than almond. He had his hair cropped short, in the style of young men who like to wrestle in the streets on feast days, hoping that by their skill they may win entry into the Raj's army. "My mother will be sad to hear this, when she gets back."

"Where is your mother?" Turaush asked.

"She went to see her sister, who lives in Jezereel. She was hoping that her sister's husband would take us all in. But that was last spring, and she hasn't returned."

"The village of Jezereel is less than a week's walk from here," Turaush said after a moment's thought. He was an inspired liar, and often amazed even himself with the way he managed to twist the truth. "But the trail through the hills is rife with robbers and thieves. I suspect that your mother will not return. I fear that she fell to them." Turaush let a note of false grief accompany his tone, as if to confirm the woman's death, rather than just raise the possibility. "How will you ever take care of your brothers and sisters?"

Balimar looked down hopelessly. "My leg is healing well. I'll be able to work again in a month or two."

"Without nourishing food," Turaush whispered, "you will only languish. And when you die, the little ones will surely follow."

Balimar looked about hopelessly, his eyes watering with grief at the thought. "What can I do?" At his back, a pair of toddlers now appeared. Two small children with big eyes, staring plaintively at Turaush. Their hunger was plain on their faces.

"Come follow me," Turaush said. "Give yourself to our lord, and we shall feed you well—you and the little ones. You can tend them there in the palace. They will not be left comfortless."

Balimar looked about helplessly. "What can I give that would let me care for the children. My hearing?"

"You would not hear the cries of the young ones in the night then,"

Turaush argued gently. "Give stamina, I think. You will be able to care for them."

"And what of my leg?" Balimar asked. "It will never heal."

Turaush merely smiled, letting his glamour argue for him. *You fool*, his smile said, *to be so full of concern*. He added after a moment, "The finest physics in all of Indhopal grace the Palace at Ghusa. For a thousand years, the lords of the land have come to take the air in its lofty towers, to bathe in the healing springs at its base. We shall find herbs and balms for your wound. In a week or two, the muscles will mend, and the pain will be gone."

Balimar's lower lip was quivering, and he stood belligerently, the way an ox will stop at the butcher's stall when it smells the blood of its fellows.

This one is not as stupid as he looks, Turaush thought. The leg will never heal once he grants his stamina, and the boy knows that.

He reached out his hand, and grasped Balimar's. "Come," Turaush urged. "The time is short. Your brother and sister call for you, and breakfast awaits. . . ."

∞ 32 ∞

THE GIVING

Each of the greater endowments—brawn, wit, stamina, and grace—can be transferred only at great risk to the giver. Often the death is instantaneous. For example, if a man gives too much brawn, his heart may stop for lack of strength, or a man who gives wit may simply forget how to breathe. But with both stamina and grace, the death is more often lingering. . . .

—*excerpt of a letter sent to Raj Ahten by his chief facilitator, Beru Shan*

Chemoise tried her best to wait patiently to give her endowment. She discovered as she stood in line that all the facilitators in Heredon, along with all of their apprentices, had gathered at the castle. Sixteen of them worked near the hilltop. They'd been slaving for nearly two days in an effort to complete their great work, taking no time to eat, no time to rest.

Their voices were weary and coarse.

"Are you sure that you dare do this?" Dearborn asked at her back in a whisper. "Won't giving grace put your child at risk?"

"It's a small risk," Chemoise said. "Yet don't we ensure our destruction if we refuse to stand against our enemies?"

"Let someone else stand in your place," Dearborn said.

"I can't," Chemoise whispered. "Iome was my best friend at court, and in the short time that I've known Gaborn, I've learned to admire him as much as any man I've ever known. The facilitators need your love and devotion to transfer an endowment. How many others here really know the Earth King?"

"I've never met the man," Dearborn admitted, "but I know what he's up against, and I'm willing to give whatever I can."

"So, you offer an endowment because of your love for a principle, while I offer mine for love of the man. Do you think our love is equal?"

"It could be," Dearborn said, "if one loves one's principles enough."

There was a cry up the hill from an attendant. Chemoise glanced up, knowing before she looked what she would see. One of those who had granted brawn lay on the lawn, and several healers quickly threw a black sheet over his body, then hustled him away, lest the death of one Dedicate poison the resolve of others who had come to grant endowments.

Chemoise took that moment to push her way to the front of the crowd, past others who offered themselves as Dedicates. Darkness was falling, and soon full night would be upon them. Gaborn had warned that the attack would commence by sunset.

She only hoped that she could give her endowment in time.

"Let me through," she said, elbowing past a fat man to the front of the crowd.

Almost immediately, a blunt-faced facilitator came downhill. "Next?"

Chemoise didn't recognize him. If he had been King Sylvarresta's old chief facilitator or one of his apprentices, she'd have stayed in the crowd. For the facilitator would have known of her pregnancy and refused to take her endowment.

"Here," Chemoise called.

She burst from the crowd just as the facilitator reached the front. "An eager one!" he rasped. "What's your pleasure?"

"Grace," Chemoise said. "I offer my grace."

He took her elbow. "Thank you," he said. "Few there be who will give up grace. I'd walk in your footsteps, if I could."

"You have your job to do," Chemoise said, "and I have mine."

He led her up to a tent, past Dedicates who lay all around the entrance in piles, like the wounded on some macabre battlefield. People were moaning, like the sound of wind through rocks, and nearby crickets had begun their nightly carols. The scent of stewing meats wafted over the fields.

"Tell me," the facilitator asked. "By any chance, do you know the Earth King?"

He threw back the flap to a red pavilion.

"I know him and love him," Chemoise said. She knew what he wanted to hear.

"Good," the facilitator rasped. "Good. Think of your love for him during the endowment. Think only of that. Can you manage that?"

She entered the pavilion. Inside, a single candle burned in the center of the small room, shining like a star. On a cushion, curled in a fetal position, lay a young woman. Every muscle in her body was clenched, unable to move.

Her fingers were balled into a fist, and she grimaced as if in pain. Even her eyelids were clamped tight, unable to relax. She wheezed as she breathed shallowly, unable to draw much air.

The facilitator stopped, let Chemoise see the woman for a moment.

"This is Brielle. She was a dancer at an inn at Castle Groverman until she granted her grace to our king. She will serve as his vector. By giving grace to her, you will be transferring it to your king."

"I understand," Chemoise said.

"This is what you will look like in a few minutes, if you proceed," he apologized. "Do you dare to go on?"

Having her muscles corded into knots was not the worst of it, Chemoise knew. Giving an endowment of grace affected the gut. The first few weeks would be hard. From now on, she would only be able to eat broth and thin soups.

"I'll bear it gladly," Chemoise said.

"Good," the facilitator said. "Good girl."

He went to a small pile of forcibles and picked one up, held it near the candle for a moment, studying the rune on its head. It looked like a tiny branding iron. He must have found some imperfection, for he pulled out a small blunt instrument and began pressing one edge of the rune outward.

"Forgive the wait," he apologized. "The blood metal bends easily, and is often damaged during travel."

"I understand," Chemoise said.

Chemoise watched Brielle. Aside from her shallow breathing, Brielle showed little sign of life. Chemoise saw a tear seeping from one eye.

It's painful to be so clenched, she realized. Giving an endowment of grace is torture.

When the facilitator finished, he glanced at Chemoise. "Now," he said. "I want you to look at the candle." Chemoise glanced at the candle, then turned her attention back to Brielle. Each time that she had seen the endowment ceremony before, the potential Dedicate had stared at the lord who would receive his gift.

"No, don't look at her," the facilitator warned. "Keep your eye on the candle. Look to the light."

Of course, Chemoise realized. We look at our lords because they are handsome, with their endowments of glamour, and it makes it easier for us to give ourselves. But staring at a wretched vector would only unnerve a potential Dedicate.

Chemoise looked at the candle as the facilitator began to half chant, half sing, in a rich voice. She couldn't understand the words. As far as she knew they were only sounds. But they were sounds that comforted her, and made her want to give of herself. She could feel that yearning grow, like a potent fire.

The candle flame flickered and sputtered as the facilitator whirled around the room several times, and then placed the forcible on Chemoise's arm.

The touch of it sent a thrill of shock through her. Often she'd heard of the "kiss of the forcible." She imagined from this that the touch of the metal must somehow be soft and sensual at first. But it wasn't a kiss. Instead, she almost felt as if the forcible were a leech that hooked its round mouth to her skin, and began sucking something vital from her.

As soon as the forcible touched her, the head of it began to heat, and the elasticity in her muscles drained away. Her right biceps cramped inordinately, so that she caught her breath.

She gave herself, willed herself to think about Gaborn in his hour of need. The candle flame flickered like the tongue of a snake, and she watched it, ignoring the urgent sound of the facilitator's chant. Outside in the city, she heard cocks crowing, serenading the sunset.

The pain in her arm spread down to her elbow and up to the socket of her right arm. Beads of perspiration broke on her brow, and one trickled down the ridge of her nose. The forcible seemed to become a flame itself. It burned her arm, and she smelled singed hair and cooking flesh.

She glanced down at the tip of the forcible in surprise. She'd been listening for hours as people gave endowments, and in turn nearly all of them had cried out in pain. Some said that the pain of a forcible was unspeakable, unbearable, but as Chemoise's arm burned, she felt determined to bear it.

So she closed her eyes, focused upon her king, and upon the people that she loved. The pain flared so that suddenly she felt as if her whole arm was on fire. She gritted her teeth.

This I can bear, she told herself. This I can bear.

And suddenly the pain blossomed a hundred-fold. Every muscle in her body seemed to cramp at once, so that she bent over in pain far more exquisite than anything she had ever imagined. Though she wanted to scream, to give voice to that pain, all that issued from her lips was a grunt.

Chemoise's world went black.

ಐ 33 ೞ

IN HIS FATHER'S FOOTSTEPS

It is the duty of every man to conduct his affairs in a manner that will make it both an honor and a challenge for his offspring to follow in his father's footsteps.

—Sir Blain Oakworthy, counselor to the Kings of Mystarria

Borenson, Myrrima, and Sarka Kaul rode away from the reaver lines, putting a mile or more between them and the marching horde that spanned from horizon to horizon.

Sarka Kaul stared ahead, his eyes unfocused. "There is good news and bad. Raj Ahten and Queen Lowicker have formed an alliance. They will allow troops to enter Carris from the north, in hopes that all of them die, leaving half of Rofehavan open to conquest. But even they do not guess what aid the night might bring."

"Hah!" Borenson laughed in sheer delight to have a Days as his counselor. "Tell me, friend, what will this 'Council' of yours do when they discover that you've betrayed their secrets?"

"There is only one punishment for such as me—death," Sarka Kaul answered. "They will torture my twin first, a slow, laborious process. When minds are twinned, you share more than common memories. I will see what she sees, feel what she feels, hear what she hears, until the very last moment. When she dies, I will most likely die with her, for one cannot hope to live after being torn from a bond so intimate as the one that we share."

Borenson fell silent, ashamed that he had laughed. "I'm sorry," he said at last.

"It's not your doing," Sarka Kaul said. "I made that bargain long ago. Right now, my twin lies to the Council, saying that you threw me into the ocean and that I am adrift at sea, clinging to a bit of wood. My only hope is that I live to help guide you until nightfall."

"And my hope for you," Myrrima said, "is that the Council never learns what has happened, and that your twin can escape."

They had not gone far when they met a lone rider, galloping south along the prairie. He was a Knight Equitable by the look of him, wearing some outdated beetle breastplate from northern Mystarria, along with a black horned helmet with ring mail that flowed like hair down his back, a style seen only among the Khdun warriors of Old Indhopal. He bore an ornate lance of black basswood, a rather princely weapon.

He came riding toward them on a gray horse, grinning broadly. Borenson recognized him as Sir Pitts, a castle guard from the Courts of Tide.

"What do you plan to do?" Borenson called out, nodding toward the line of marching reavers, "terrify them with your fashion sense?"

"Got in a tangle with a scarlet sorceress this morning," Pitts said, grinning broadly. "She ripped off me chainmail and chewed up me helm! Luckily, I skinnied out of 'em, or she'd have had me for breakfast, too."

Pitts rode near. Obviously, he'd scavenged his armor from dead warriors, and was forced to wear anything that seemed a close fit. Across the brow of his saddle were half a dozen philia taken from the bunghole of a reaver. They dangled from the saddle like dead eels, smelling of moldy garlic. Averan said that that smell was the death cry of a reaver. Borenson could see the dried blood now that blackened the man's brow. It was dark and copious, and if Pitts managed to live through the coming battle, he would surely carry some enviable scars. After all, how many men could say that they'd escaped from a reaver's mouth?

Borenson laughed aloud. "Someday you'll have to tell me the tale in full, and I'll pay a couple of pints of ale for the honor. But for now, how goes the battle?"

Pitts nodded toward the north. "The Earth King warned us to guard Carris, and that's what we'll do. But High Marshal Chondler isn't waiting for the reavers to attack. He's sending lancers against them, near the head of their column. It's a bloody row up there."

"How far to the front?" Borenson asked.

"Thirty, maybe forty miles," Pitts replied.

The news chilled Borenson. Forty miles to the front? And their line extended south for as far as the eye could see.

"How far to the back of their lines?" Myrrima asked.

"Hard to say," Pitts replied. "Some make it a hundred miles, others a hundred and twenty." Borenson was still trying to guess how huge the horde might be, but Pitts was well ahead of him. "There may be a million of them," Pitts said grimly. "We don't have enough lances to take them all, not even a twentieth. The Earth King used them all last week. So we're concentrating on their leaders. Their fell mage is well protected, near the front of the lines. It has been a bloody row." His voice sounded shaken as he said this. "We've lost lots of men already. Sir Langley of Orwynne has fallen."

"By the Powers!" Borenson swore.

"How are we to fight them," Myrrima asked, "without lances?"

"We'll fight them on the ground, at the gates of Carris," Pitts said. "We'll use warhammers and reaver darts, and resort to fingernails if we have to. But we'll fight." His sentiments were as foolish as they were brave.

"Chondler knows more tricks than a trained bear," Pitts said. "Go to Carris, and see for yourself!"

"It will take more than a trained bear to win Carris," Sarka Kaul said. Borenson glanced back. Sarka Kaul looked ominous upon his red horse, his face draped with a black hood. His voice seemed almost disembodied. "But be of good cheer. Young King Orwynne is riding into the city gates even now with three thousand men at his back. He has found his courage at last."

Pitts peered hard at the figure all draped in black robes. He asked Borenson. "Who's your friend?"

"Sarka Kaul," Borenson said, "meet Sir Pitts."

"An Inkarran?" Pitts asked in wonder, clenching his lance. "What's he doing here?"

"I go to fight in Carris, friend," Sarka Kaul answered.

Pitts barked in laughter. "Well then, I hope to meet you there!"

"Come before the darkness falls," Sarka Kaul said.

Borenson and Myrrima spurred their horses on. Ahead the land grew dark. Columns of smoke roiled upward, creating a vast curtain that leached all light from the plains. The marching of reavers caused the earth to tremble, as if the ground would shatter beneath them.

Borenson, Myrrima, and Sarka Kaul were nearly to Mangan's Rock before they reached the head of the reaver horde. There, knights on tired mounts raced across the reavers' path, setting torch to every blade of grass, every copse of scrub and bracken, every tree.

The flames roared to heaven and smoke blackened the skies. The light grew faint indeed, for by now the sun slanted low to the west, and here the dense forests of the Hest Mountains were wet so that the smoke that roiled up from that furnace was inky black and laden with soot.

Still there was no sign of any cavalry. The group passed beyond the vale of fire into the mountains, racing their horses. They stopped on a southern slope for a while, in the cool shadow of a rowan, and glimpsed the sun for the first time in hours. Even here, beyond the line of smoke, the sun glimmered like a hot coal in a torrid sky. High up, the smoke acted as a lens that colored the world in shades of ash.

So they hurried over the mountains, down through lesser towns, into the dead lands blasted by reaver curses, where at last they saw Carris gleaming upon the banks of Lake Donnestgree.

Here, the green fields had all gone gray a week ago. Vines and trees lay in twisted ruin. Every blade of grass had withered. Nothing lived. Even the crows and vultures had fled. Only the corpses of rotting reavers, monoliths, their mouths frozen wide in a rictus smile that brimmed with teeth, offered mute testimony to what had happened here.

For a moment as Borenson rode into the blasted lands, he had an odd sensation. He felt as if instead of riding from Fenraven to Carris, he was riding from the past into the future. Behind him lay the sweet green fields of the world he had known. Ahead lay rot and oblivion.

Sarka Kaul sniffed the fields. Borenson could smell old reaver curses on the dead ground. "See no more." "Be thou dry as dust." The ground seemed to whisper the curses. "Rot, O thou child of men!"

"Those who saw the battle tried to describe it," Sarka Kaul whispered, as he stared out across the killing fields, "but words failed them. I could not envision this. I couldn't imagine how wide the destruction went, or how perfectly it had been carried out."

Borenson spat onto grass that was as gray as ash. "No rain here in a week. A stinking inferno this shall all make."

As the three approached Carris, the sun slowly descended beyond the rim of the world, hidden behind towers of billowing smoke. The wind was ominously still, and the heat that rose from the soil leached the stink from the blasted lands and left it hovering in a fetid haze. To the west the foothills were all gray with decay, and to the east Lake Donnestgree lay flat and dull. Not a single wave rippled across its surface. Gone were the seagulls that had winged above its shore a week past.

Ahead, Carris was a city of ruins. The plaster had all cracked from the castle walls, so that only a few bright strips still gleamed above the gray stone. The walls had buckled and bulged. Gone were the doves and pigeons that had wheeled above Castle Carris like confetti.

It was a far fairer sight that greeted my father's eyes, Borenson thought.

Why Carris? Borenson wondered. Why would the reavers attack it again? There is nothing here worth winning, nothing worth defending. Yet we keep on fighting, like a pair of crabs squabbling over a worthless rock.

Unless there is something here that the reavers value? he wondered.

But what it might be, he could not guess. The land was a broken waste.

Still the armies had gathered. A million reavers were marching from the south, while men and women paced along the cracked castle walls, armor gleaming dully like the backs of beetles in the dying light.

Borenson caught wind of a noxious odor, and noted that to his right were the trenches that the reavers had made to channel water from the lake. The reavers had thrown in some huge yellow stones.

At the time no one had comprehended what the reavers were doing. It wasn't until Averan explained that reavers could only drink water rich in sulfur that anyone had understood: the monsters were creating drinking water.

But now the ditches were filled with lumps of white lye soap, brown human turds, and an oily scum that colored the water's surface. Chondler's men had poisoned it so badly that even a whiff of the putrid mix made Borenson's eyes burn.

"Even if the reavers manage to win Carris," Myrrima said, "I don't think that they'll be enjoying their stay."

The sun dipped behind the peaks, and suddenly the black plains plunged into near darkness. Borenson heard a cry rise up from the city, and he glanced back to the south.

A rim of fire could be seen on the mountaintops, twenty miles behind, and columns of smoke rose straight up like the black boles of vast trees. High in the atmosphere, the smoke spread like a mushroom cap, or like the limbs of an oak. Already, clouds of smoke arched overhead.

But it was not the encroaching darkness that caused the cries of alarm. There, in the distance, behind the rim of fire, reavers marched in a broad band, and raced down the mountainside like a black cataract. The distant hissing of their breathing and the pounding of their feet made it sound as if a dam had broken, and trees and boulders tumbled in the glut of the flood.

The city of Carris squatted on an isle out in Lake Donnestgree. The city was more than two miles long from north to south, and a little over a mile wide at its widest point. One could only reach it by boat or by walking up a narrow road that led over a long causeway.

Here on the causeway a week ago, towers and gates had guarded the city. But the reavers had pushed the towers over and thrown down the city gates, and Marshal Chondler, despite all his good intentions, had not had time to replace them.

Instead, at the head of the causeway, his people had dragged wooden rubble from all around—thatch from cottage roofs, timbers, fence posts, broken wagons and chairs, a girl's straw doll—and heaped them all into piles beside the road. This would become a firewall to protect the city from the reaver's advance, but even a firewall would not hold for more than an hour or two.

Amid this heap of trash, the heads of several huge reavers lay in the rubble, their mouths thrown wide. Borenson recognized the enormous fell mage that had led the first attack on the city, along with the heads of other monsters. Their mouths were filled with philia cut from the bungholes of dead reavers, so that the scent of moldy garlic wafted over the fields.

Straw lay strewn over the fields at the mouth of the causeway, a sure sign that Chondler's men had lain down *caltrops*—wicked bits of sharp metal bolted together in order to puncture the hooves of charging horses.

But would a caltrop harm a reaver? Borenson wondered. He peered hard until he saw a twisted piece of metal rising up through some straw, a blade at least five times larger than a normal caltrop.

Where would he have gotten so much metal? Borenson wondered, and then recalled the tens of thousands of knight gigs and blades that the reavers had lost here a week ago.

Borenson rode toward the city. A few dull rays of dying sun still managed to penetrate the smoke. All along the city wall, people gazed out at the newcomers—men in bright helms; old women with jaws set in determination, their faces framed by graying hair; young boys pale with fear—so many wan faces like scattered leaves cast upon a field of soot.

The castle gates were still down, along with some of the towers, but the rubble had been shifted, forming barricades of stone that bristled with reaver blades all along the causeway. Such barricades were not meant to stop reavers, only to slow them so that archers and artillerymen could have time to take aim.

Wooden platforms had been set along the wallwalks, and rafts floated in the lake, and on these and on the towers sat an array of ballistas and catapults that perhaps had not been matched in all of Rofehavan's history. In the lee of each artillery piece crouched a pair of archers from Heredon with bows of spring steel. Farther back, those who had not steel bows were armed with Indhopal's horn bows. And archers with longbows perched along the castle walls.

"Look at that!" Myrrima said. "Chondler must have gathered artillery from every castle within a hundred miles."

"Two hundred," Sarka Kaul said, "though little good it will do him."

Borenson's heart was full of foreboding.

Why did Gaborn tell his people to gather here? Borenson wondered. The city had not fared well in the first attack. Only a miracle had saved it. Only the Earth King, summoning a world worm in its defense, had managed to free the city. The mound of dirt around the worm's hole still rose up like a crater, several hundred yards to the north.

Perhaps, Borenson wondered, Gaborn hopes for another miracle.

He reached the city "gate," an open space between two tiers of rubble, and found Marshal Chondler there, atop one pile, gazing off toward the south. At his feet lay a pile of stinking philia, and Borenson could see more loathsome pieces of flesh hanging like talismans of doom from the castle walls.

"Hail, Sir Borenson, Lady Myrrima, and . . . your friend?" Chondler said mirthlessly. "Any news from the south?" His voice was oddly high, and he moved swiftly. Borenson could tell that he had taken several endowments of metabolism, and that he could only slow his speech with great concentration.

"The reavers are coming," Borenson said. "But that you can see for yourself."

"No sight of the Earth King?" Chondler's voice was husky, as if he sought to mask his fear.

"None," Borenson said, "or of any other comfort."

"You have your endowments intact," Chondler said. He eyed Borenson in particular. "I had your facilitator vector more to you yesterday, hoping that you would return."

"I got them," Borenson said, "and none too soon. Are you telling me that my Dedicates are still here, in Carris?" The news unsettled him. A million reavers were marching on the city, and his Dedicates would be helpless before them.

"Aye," Chondler said. "We'd hoped to get them out, but we'd sent our boats downstream to ferry out the sick, the women, and the children. There have been none to spare for Dedicates. So we will guard Carris, as is the duty of Runelords, and if the reavers take our Dedicates, they will have to do so over our dead bodies."

"This place is a death trap, you know," Borenson said.

Chondler challenged, "Name a better castle to defend in all of Mystarria."

Borenson couldn't. "Do you have any lances? Perhaps we could make one last charge on the open field."

"I wish we had a few. But our lances are gone. We'll rely now upon arrows and warhammers and whatever other weapons we have at hand."

"I found Sir Pitts riding south," Borenson said. "He told me that you were full of more tricks than a trained bear. I do hope you have more than a firewall and ballistas to show for your trouble."

"We have ten thousand ballista bolts, besides balls for the catapults," Chondler said. "We can shoot the reavers from behind the safety of the firewall. Once those fail, we'll rely upon our archers. They'll fire into the reavers from the castle walls as our men engage them at the gate. We have three million arrows and five hundred good force archers who can hit what they're aiming at."

"Three million arrows may not be nearly enough," Borenson said. "Those horn bows might pierce reaver hide, but I've never heard of a longbow that could do it."

"Nevertheless, we will try," Chondler said. "I've ordered the men to refrain from shooting until the enemy engages at ten yards."

Borenson bit his lip, wondering if it could work.

"I've had the facilitators here working night and day," Chondler said. "They reforged all of the forcibles that we could lay hands on. I've got three dozen men to act as champions, each with twenty endowments of metabolism. Working together, they should be able to hold the gate for a good long time. As it so happens, we still need another champion. How about it?" Chondler asked with a wicked smile. "Want to die young?"

Borenson glanced sidelong at Myrrima. Had someone asked him the same question a week ago, he would not have hesitated. But now he was not living just for himself. Taking such endowments meant that even if he lived through the battle, he would never be a real husband to Myrrima. He would die a solitary creature, isolated from all mankind by his speed.

Myrrima seemed to read his mind. She glanced back at the approaching horde, spilling down from the mountains. The darkness had deepened, and all that Borenson could see was a line of fire raging up there. But suddenly the flames took a whole pine, lighting it up like a vast torch, and in its light he saw the dreaded foe, red light reflecting from their dull backs. At the rate that they ran, they'd be here within the hour.

"It will take more than a few champions to save you," Sarka Kaul said, speaking up at last.

"We have hopes of reinforcements, sir," Chondler said. "Lowicker's daughter is leading a good army south, and at last word was less than a dozen miles away."

"And Raj Ahten has an army hidden in the hills to the east," Sarka Kaul said. "But neither of them wish you well. They come like crows, hoping only to take the spoils once you have fallen. They will enter the fray only when you are dead."

"And how could you possibly know this?" Chondler asked with worry on his brow.

Sarka Kaul drew back his black hood, revealing skin whiter than bone. "Because I have been privy to their councils," he said. "Grant me your twenty endowments of metabolism so that I can fight, and I think I can show you how to win this battle."

Chondler eyed the Inkarran suspiciously, glanced toward Sir Borenson.

Borenson gave him the nod.

"Very well," Chondler said. "We could use a man who knows how to fight in the dark."

As Borenson, Myrrima, and Sarka Kaul entered Carris, riding along the causeway, the evening sun dipped below the teeth of the world and plunged the city into blackest night.

❧ 34 ☙

A BRIDGE IN TIME

Signs and wonders follow those of whom the Powers approve.

—*from* A Child's Book of Wizardry

Erin Connal rode south over the muddy fields of Beldinook that morning, heading to war in the retinue of King Anders. On swift force horses followed nearly six thousand knights.

They held their black lances in the air so that they bristled like a gloaming wood. The ground rumbled from the pounding of hooves. Horses snorted and neighed, and the knights raised their voices in grim song.

The strange storm had passed, and the morning dawned bright and clear. Erin felt betrayed by the weather. The storm had paced her all day yesterday, and though clear weather was good for riding, it was not good enough. The ground was as muddy through the morning as if the rain were still falling, so the sun gave them little benefit. She'd rather have had the storm. There would be reavers at Carris, tens of thousands of them, and reavers feared lightning. The creatures could only see the force electric, so a bolt of lightning blinded the monsters, as if they were staring into the white-hot sun.

But the skies dawned clear over Beldinook.

Anders's troops rode south over the Fields of the Moon, where the ancients had carved a huge basalt boulder into the shape of the moon and set it upon the peak of a volcanic cone. One could see mountains and craters carved into the moon, but the features had long since worn away. The plain all around was relatively flat and featureless, with sparse clumps of grass. Volcanic gravel had rained down upon it in ages past, killing all plant life. All across the fields for hundreds of miles, half-sunken in the gravel, lay large strange stones carved in such a way as to represent stars, with rays bursting from them. Ancient paths led from one star to another, forming a map of the heavens.

"But a map to where?" one rider in the king's retinue asked.

"To the First Star, and thence to the netherworld," Anders told him with a smirk. "The ancients longed to return there after death, and so they would practice walking a path through the stars, to learn the way."

After a while, Erin fell back behind the king's retinue.

The Nut Woman reined in her own mount to ride beside Myrrima. She was short and broad, dressed in drab rags. She held a sleeping squirrel curled in the palm of her left hand, and petted it softly as she rode.

"Is there something you want?" Erin asked.

"I've been thinking about you," the Nut Woman said. "I've been thinking about you and King Anders. You've made no secret of the fact that you distrust him." Erin did not deny it. "But I've been thinking. You know, a squirrel can always tell a bad acorn from a good, just by the smell. Did you know that?"

Erin shook her head no.

"They can," the Nut Woman said, her eyes shining. "They can smell worm, and they can smell rot. They only bother to crack open the good nuts."

"What does that have to do with King Anders?"

"Don't you understand?" the Nut Woman asked. "The squirrels would know if he had rot inside. But you see how they love him, don't you? They jump on his saddle; they climb in his pocket. They're not like that with bad folk."

Erin peered ahead. A squirrel was riding on Anders's shoulder even now.

Erin studied the Nut Woman's eyes. They were filled with adoration for the king. But Erin saw something else. The woman didn't focus on anything. It was as if she peered beyond Erin, into some private vision.

"Yes," Erin said. "I see your point."

The Nut Woman smiled. "Good! Good. Most people don't understand. Most can never understand."

Erin forced a smile. Celinor had suspected that his father was mad; and King Anders accused Erin of being crazed. At the moment, Erin felt certain of only one thing: the Nut Woman was madder than them all.

As the day wore on, they passed far south of the Great Rift and through tortured lands into the sweet fields of Beldinook where the grass grew tall and green, even in autumn. Nestled among valleys and low hills, castles and cities sprang up everywhere. Beldinook was the second largest kingdom in all Rofehavan, with nearly twelve million souls.

Erin clenched the reins of her mount as she rode through. She was a

horse-sister of Fleeds, after all, and the folk of Beldinook were ancient enemies. Each time they neared a castle, she expected a mob of cavalry to issue
from the gates and put up a fight.

But King Anders rode through without hindrance. Indeed, he had been
expected, and several times through the morning, dukes and barons issued
out of the castle gates only to swell his ranks.

Gaborn's call for aid had gone through every kingdom, and had been
heard even here in Beldinook, and as each lord joined with King Anders, they
would laugh and bark out some variation of, "So, Your Highness, what think
you? Do we ride to save Carris, or to watch the reavers feed on our enemies?"

And each time the question was put, King Anders would frown at the
men, and with the patience of a father with an errant child ask, "How could
you think to laugh at the plight of another? We go to save Carris, and in so
doing, save ourselves."

Often then, he would raise his left hand and Choose the lord to aid him
in his fight, and ever again Erin was forced to wonder: is Anders truly an
Earth King, or does the Darkling Glory's locus sway him?

The travel went more slowly than Erin would have liked through the
middle of Mystarria. Villages and cities clustered along the fertile banks of
the River Rowan. The farms were the lushest that Erin had ever seen, and
people choked the roads. With winter coming on, the villeins were herding
pigs and cattle and sheep into town to be butchered. Indeed, Slaterfest was
celebrated on the fifteenth of Leaves in these parts, only a ten-day from now,
and at the fest the folk would celebrate the slaughter by eating huge amounts
of sausages and hams, lamb ribs and sweetened meats, along with turnips and
licorice root fried to a crisp in butter, and tarts and puddings and cakes, all
washed down with dark Beldinook beer so rich that you could smell it in the
sweat of your armpits for a week after you drank.

Erin rode close to King Anders and his son all morning. Anders spoke of
little. His mind was on the road ahead, and often he would peer south with a
worried brow and mutter beneath his breath, "We must hurry."

Celinor tried to cheer him, and often he would lead the troops in song,
as if in hopes of raising their spirits.

When they reached the River Langorn with its broad banks, the road
ahead jogged far out of their way. To travel by road would have wasted hours,
and some of King Anders men swore that it would be faster to swim the
horses across. But to do so would force the knights to abandon their own
armor along with that of the horses.

King Anders settled the argument by shouting, "Behold the Power of the
Earth!"

He raised his sword as if it were a staff and pointed it to the heavens. He
raised a cry and began to chant, but a great wind arose, circling the troops,

screaming with a voice like dying eagles, swirling down from the sun. Whatever words he spoke were carried off by the wind.

Then he pointed his sword at a nearby knoll and the wind struck, blasting it into dust. Dirt and stone flew up like a sheet, hundreds of feet into the air, raising a plume of soot in the sky. It was as if a great hand had taken hold of the hill and begun to stretch it, pulling it from its place. Lightning flew out of the ground and split the heavens, and the fields rattled beneath the impact of the wind. The horses snorted and shied away in a panic, and for a long minute Erin only fought with her mount, trying to keep it from fleeing.

Then the dirt and stones rained down into the River Langorn, making a broad road, like a crude peninsula.

"Hurry now to Carris!" King Anders shouted. "There is no time to waste!"

He spurred his horse down to the river and galloped across. His army followed after. The earthen dam was a crude thing, and as Erin's horse raced over it, its hooves sank in the loose clay and gravel. The soil rose only a few feet above the waterline. The dam would not hold for long. The river was slow moving and languid in the fall, but the water would soon back up. As pressure built, it would wash over the dam and send it downstream.

Still, King Anders's troops made it across on dry land, and his men began to cheer wildly, "All hail the Earth King! All hail Anders!"

The rest of the day, Erin rode as if in a dream. Whether it was from shock at what she'd seen or from a lack of sleep, she wasn't sure.

When the army halted for a short meal, Celinor rode up to meet her. "What do you think now?" he asked with the glazed eyes of a fanatic. "What do you think of my father now?"

"I do not doubt that he holds some great Power," she admitted. "But what is its source? Did the Earth indeed grant him his gift, or does it come from elsewhere?"

"What do you mean?" Celinor asked. "Of course it comes from the Earth."

"I did not see the Earth moving so much as I saw the wind blowing," Erin told him.

"You'll never believe," Celinor countered. "Will you? No matter that you see with your own eyes, or hear with your own ears, you'll never believe."

He sounded like a little boy convinced that he has the greatest father in the world, when along comes a doubter.

"I believe that you love him," Erin said.

He walked off angrily.

Erin tried to find sleep as she rode, hoping to speak with the owl again in her dreams. But the road remained slick and treacherous, and she could not rest easy. Like the wind and the lightning, sleep abandoned her, left her feeling betrayed.

All too soon she found herself south of Beldinook, riding into Mystarria as darkness fell. The stars overhead burned brightly as they passed through the hills and meadows. The locusts serenaded the troops, buzzing in the scrub oak, while the crickets sang in harmony.

The ride seemed surreal. Erin felt as if she were riding home from a relaxing hunt rather than riding to face the end of the world.

Only the empty cottages and villages along the highway revealed that anything was amiss.

When she reached the road that led to Twynhaven, she wondered if the green flames still licked the ground, and if she rode into them, would she find herself in the netherworld? She glanced toward Celinor, and found her husband watching her as if he feared that she would make a run for it.

She held a steady course. Shortly, distant fires could be seen in the mountains beyond Carris. Tall pillars of fire-lit smoke roared into the sky. As King Anders's troops entered the blasted lands, the odor of rot replaced the perfume of summer fields.

Scouts forged ahead and returned bringing word: "Reavers are already swarming the fields west of Carris, and Queen Lowicker of Beldinook has drawn her troops up within three miles of their lines, just beyond the Barren's Wall."

King Anders blew his trumpets and his men raised a cheer. All day long they had held their lances to the sky, making a black forest of their polished shafts. Now Celinor began a battle song and the lancers drew into lines, riding three abreast down the road. They prepared to drop their lances into a couched position, in preparation for a charge.

All too soon the sound of reavers racing across the fields came to Erin's ears above the thud of horses' hooves and the jangle of chain mail. Their hissing roared like distant surf, and the earth trembled beneath their feet.

Erin came up over a hill and saw Carris to the south—ten thousand torches glimmering upon the gray castle walls. The torches reflected in the still waters of Lake Donnestgree, and smoke clung to the water in a haze.

Before Castle Carris a turbulent, roaring sea of reavers blackened the land.

ॐ 35 ॐ

IN THE DEDICATES' KEEP

He who supports my enemy is my enemy.

—*Raj Ahten, upon slaying the Dedicates of Raj Bahreb,*
Lord of Old Indhopal

Gaborn sprinted through the ribbed tunnels of the Underworld, down, down, as if toiling through bones of an endless worm, and beheld a strange sight: a bright light shone ahead in a place where no light should be.

For a moment he suspected that a Glory filled the tunnel before him, but he didn't feel the overwhelming power that had surged through him before.

Instead, as he rounded the corner, he saw only Iome in the hall, her back toward him as she raced deeper into the Underworld. She moved relatively slowly, now that he had so many endowments.

He nearly stumbled in surprise.

He raced up to her back, drew ahead, and saw Iome's face contort with shock. "How did you get here so fast?" he asked slowly, so that she would understand.

"I found a shortcut," Iome replied.

"Follow me," Gaborn said.

Iome looked into his eyes, and must have seen the pain there. "It's time, isn't it? The battle has begun at Carris?" Her words came slowly, each syllable drawn out and deepened by the variance that came by reason of Gaborn's vast endowments of metabolism.

Gaborn nodded. His three days were drawing to a close. A struggle was about to flare up in Carris, one such as had not been seen since Erden Geboren led the nine kings in their charge against the reaver hordes at Vizengower.

Gaborn could sense his army of Chosen warriors above him, dozens and dozens of miles, and this caused him to wonder. His Earth Senses let him place them precisely. In traversing the caves, he had ridden by horse nearly two hundred miles south, and from there the caves had wound south and west toward Indhopal. But in time the trail looped back north and east, so that now he was directly below Carris again.

He suspected that this was vitally important. The reavers were trying to secure the ground above them—or perhaps above the Great Seals that they had fashioned. But why?

He could only guess at the answer.

"Follow me," Gaborn said slowly.

"Where?" Iome asked.

And he wondered in his heart what he should do. He had come to slay the One True Master, but his Earth Senses warned against it. He could not prevail against the monster—yet. Even now, though he felt as if he radiated vigor from every pore, he was not her match. Nor would the Earth permit him to seek out the Great Seals and destroy them. The Earth allowed only one task. "We must find Averan! Follow as best you can."

Comprehension dawned slowly on Iome's face.

She nodded.

Gaborn ran.

Three days have passed, he thought in despair, though with his endowments of metabolism it felt as if he'd run for thirty days through this endless night.

Death was about to rain down upon his people. He imagined reavers scaling castle walls, hurling dire spells.

He veered through tunnels. He was near the very bottom of the unbounded warren. The ground grew as hot as the chimney stones on a hearth, and the endless tramping of reavers' feet had polished the floor like marble. Little grew in these tunnels, just a bit of wormgrass on the walls. Few blind-crabs scurried along the floor. He was not in the wilds any longer.

Every few strides carried him past some side tunnel or cavity. He met several reaver workers that bore no weapons. He paused only long enough to stab them through their sweet triangle, and then hurried on, leaving a trail of dead in his wake. They did not even register his presence until he fell upon them.

He ran up a tunnel, following Averan's scent. He could feel her nearby. A mile, a half a mile, a quarter of a mile, and he was at her door.

A cavelike recess opened to the corridor, with guardrooms dug into either side. As Gaborn approached, two huge reavers sprang out to do battle.

The first raised a blade overhead, and hissed in fear. Gaborn smelled a spray of words fill the air, probably shouts of surprise or warning. It threw its head back and gaped its maw wide, crystalline teeth bristling like daggers.

He leapt up into its mouth, landing on its dark tongue, and plunged his reaver dart through the soft spot in the creature's upper palate, into its brain. The weapon slammed into the top of the monster's skull.

Gaborn gave the dart a twist, scrambling the reaver's brain.

Purple blood and bits of gray brain rained down from the wound.

Gaborn leapt from its mouth as the huge blade-bearer crashed to the ground. The second reaver reared high on her back legs. She was a mage, bearing a crystalline staff. A perfume of words wheezed from her anus as she tried to cast a spell. Gaborn would have none of it.

He dove between her forelegs and plunged his reaver dart into her breast, through her tough carapace, into an organ that the knights of Rofehavan called a kidney. The reaver's perfumed words transformed into the garlicky reek of a death cry.

Gaborn raced into the cave.

Averan stood there, turning to peer at him with frightened eyes, lit by the opal that gleamed from her silver ring. Around her squatted a crowd of starved, half-naked people. The reek of their prison was astounding—the stench of unwashed bodies, of urine and feces, and of the rotting carcasses of both fish and the unburied dead.

"Averan," Gaborn cried before she had time to react to his presence. He took her staff of black poisonwood, which he had been carrying in his free hand, and threw it to her.

With ten endowments of metabolism, Averan responded before the others even registered Gaborn's presence. She caught the staff, moving with a liquid slowness.

Gaborn cried, "The battle in Carris is about to begin! But I'm not ready to face the One True Master. How do I defeat her?"

Averan seemed to leap in slow motion to grab the staff as she peered at him. Her voice sounded unnaturally deep and tediously slow as she asked, "What?"

Gaborn forced himself to speak slower, to modulate his voice, as he repeated his request.

Worry dawned in Averan's face, and she leapt over the squatting prisoners. Her movements seemed painfully deliberate. She ran two paces, and stopped. "Wait!" she shouted.

She struggled to pull off her ring, twisting it on her finger, and then turned and threw it to the prisoners. She could not leave them comfortless.

As she worked, two of Gaborn's Chosen died on the walls of Carris—a proud knight and a young girl. With their deaths, he felt as if a hole gaped in his heart, as if he were rich soil and his Chosen were tender plants, cruelly plucked away. It pained him no end.

Averan raced to Gaborn, sprang past him. "This way!"

She ran with all her might, straining every muscle, intensity plain on her face. Then the green glow of Gaborn's opal bathed her back, and threw her dancing shadow on the tunnel floor.

Gaborn followed, disheartened at how sluggishly she seemed to move, even with ten endowments of metabolism.

He ambled beside her. A hundred endowments? Gaborn wondered. Perhaps the facilitators have given me more. They'll kill me, he realized.

He followed at Averan's heel. She sprinted with all her might, her every movement smooth and graceful. Tears streamed from her eyes, tears of frustration, Gaborn imagined, that came from yearning for greater speed.

He walked ahead of her, slaughtering any reaver that barred their path.

And ever closer, he felt the approach of danger.

"There!" Averan called. "Up the corridor, three more passageways. The Dedicates' Keep."

Of course! Gaborn realized. Averan had warned that the One True Master was experimenting with giving endowments, though he could not guess how much success she might have. That was why he could not hope to face her.

Gaborn left Averan behind, sprinted round the corner.

"Leap!" his Earth Senses warned, and Gaborn sprang fifteen feet into the air.

A reaver stood before him at the mouth of the Dedicates' Keep, a great black blade-bearer. Its blade whistled beneath his feet, then sang through the air as it whipped behind its back.

The monster did not open its mouth. Instead it leaned back, moving with a speed that nearly matched Gaborn's. The philia on its head and along its jaw raised into the air and waved like snakes as all its senses came alert.

This is no common reaver, Gaborn knew. Dull blue runes glimmered along its forearms.

As Gaborn reached the apex of his leap, he hurled his reaver gig with all his might, aiming for the soft spot in the monster's sweet triangle. He threw so hard that he felt the ball joint in his shoulder rip from its socket.

The reaver gig struck home, plunged into the monster's flesh, piercing its brain, and then stood quivering like an arrow in a tree.

But the great blade-bearer still lived. Its blade whirled round, sang through the air before Gaborn even touched ground.

Gaborn twisted, catlike, as the blade whistled toward him. It struck his chest a glancing blow that shattered the rings in Gaborn's chain mail and jogged him to the side.

He darted away as another blow clove the ground at his feet. He threw himself backward as the reaver charged.

He had no weapon to fight with. His reaver gig stood transfixed in the monster's brain.

Averan came rushing up the tunnel, and the reaver whirled its massive head to gaze at her, all of its philia quivering.

In that instant, Gaborn struck. He leapt twenty feet in the air and grabbed his reaver gig on the way up. He did not pull it free but instead wrenched it violently as he reached the apex of his leap, then jerked it down with greater force as he fell, slashing the monster's brain.

It shuddered and crumpled to its knees. Ahead, in the hallway, two more guards barred Gaborn's way, but neither moved as quickly as the monster that Gaborn had just fought. He dispatched them, and rushed into the Dedicates' Keep.

In all his dreams, in all of his nightmares, Gaborn have never imagined a place such as this. The light glowing green from his opal could not pierce the murk. Shadows fled as he entered the vast chamber, but the ceiling was so high that even with all of his endowments of sight, Gaborn could not view a roof overhead, only the steadily curving braces and supports constructed by the glue mums. These were not like the beams that men would use to brace the ceiling of a Great Hall. Instead, they looked more like cobwebs dancing along trusses, spanning over chasms. Not even the fabled Songhouse of Sandomir could have rivaled the complexity or grandeur of the workmanship. The supports, gray with age, rose up like lacework along the ceilings. Gaborn imagined that spiders might build such webs if they could only hope or dream. The designs were as alien as they were beautiful.

And beneath this glorious webwork, reaver Dedicates milled in an endless reeking herd.

The smell of them astonished Gaborn no less than the sight of them. A cloud of alien scents smote him—the odor of reaver dung and rotting carrion, suffused with the scents of reaver endowments as brittle as ice and as dank as mold.

There were hundreds of Dedicates, down in a bowl-shaped enclave. The room was black with them, but the dull light of fiery runes burned among them, so that a glimmering haze shone all about.

A huge, spidery creature the size of an elephant lay on its back about two hundred yards off, with its legs curled in the air. Reavers tore at the beast with their forepaws and teeth, rending its flesh.

Beyond that, a fetid stream ran, sending up vapors of sulfur water. Some Dedicates knelt in its shallows, dipping their heads and then craning them back like birds as they drank. Overhead sprawled a pair of massive stonewood trees, like vast leafless oaks, their limbs twisted in ineffable torment.

And all through the air, flocks of gree wheeled about on squeaking wings, like nervous bats.

Gaborn could not see the far reaches of the Keep. Nor could he guess how many hundreds of Dedicates it might hold.

Upon spotting Gaborn, many Dedicates rose up and began to lurch away, hissing and spraying a scent of warning in the air.

Gaborn raced in, leapt, and plunged his reaver dart deep into the sweet triangle of the nearest Dedicate. The creature hissed and sprayed moldy garlic scent, then swatted feebly at his dart until its legs went out from under it. The reavers lurched to attack, creating a fearsome wall of flesh, of flashing teeth and raking claws, as Gaborn raced into the room. They scrabbled over one another's backs in an effort to reach him.

Gaborn attacked the nearest reaver, leaping and spinning. He plunged his weapon into its sweet triangle, dodged a blow, and lunged after another.

In moments purple blood and gray brains made his weapon slippery. Gore clung to his hands and elbows, spattered his face. He wiped it from his eyes, and moved on.

Each Dedicate had a rune upon its head that glowed a soft silver. Gaborn suspected that it marked the endowment that it had given, but somehow the glowing runes were not shaped anything like those that men took. Since the reavers wrote in scents, the runes drawn upon them were meant to be judged by their musky aroma.

Gaborn smelled a particularly rank stench, with an odor like rotten cabbage, just beyond a wall of reavers.

As Gaborn tasted the scent, he felt the Earth's sudden warning: "Strike!"

He leapt upon a reaver, raced up its head, and peered behind it. Some sixty feet off, a reaver was retreating through the horde. It had a single silver rune gleaming on its forehead, but dozens of fiery blue runes ran the length of its legs. A vector, Gaborn realized.

"Strike!" the Earth warned again.

Gaborn leapt twenty feet in the air, somersaulted over three reavers, and landed with his reaver dart plunging through the monster's sweet triangle.

By now all of the reavers around him hissed, and warning scents filled the cavern.

"Gaborn!" Averan called desperately.

He looked back at her, only three dozen yards away. She stood close to the mouth of chamber, her black staff of poisonwood in hand. "I can't help you! I can't kill helpless Dedicates. What shall I do?"

Gaborn felt in his heart, sensing for danger to the girl. "Do you know where the Great Seals are?"

Averan nodded.

"Go destroy them," Gaborn said.

Indeed, the Earth now warned him that she must go. Danger was coming, and if Averan stayed, she would die.

Gaborn took off his green opal cape pin and tossed it to her. The glowing runes on the reaver Dedicates was the only light he would have to fight by.

Wordlessly, Averan whirled and sped off as fast as she could.

Gaborn redoubled his pace, plunging among the reavers. The monsters hissed and lashed at him, ripping with talons and gnashing with teeth.

Gaborn charged into them, dodging blows, lunging with his reaver dart, tasting the air for the scent of vectors.

Time and again his weapon stabbed.

He saw the Earth's plan now. Danger was swelling all about him. The One True Master had sensed his presence, and would come for him, as would any Runelord who sought to protect his precious Dedicates.

He was glad that he had given up his light, for now he could see the reavers' glowing runes even better.

He could sense a rising wave of danger.

She was coming. Gaborn darted into the reavers, raced beneath the legs of one monster, vaulted up onto the back of another and struck down a vector.

She was at the door.

He had killed perhaps fifty Dedicates, including three vectors. He whirled toward the chamber entrance.

A blackness swirled at the door, a shadow that blotted out the night. It wasn't just Gaborn's imagination. Dark vapors flowed into the chamber like a fog. Whatever was coming, it was more than a reaver.

And suddenly, Gaborn saw it.

A monstrosity appeared among the shadows, a reaver larger and more bloated than any fell mage he had ever encountered. Her feet clacked and her swollen belly groaned as she slid across the floor. A loud hissing followed as she scrabbled forward, air streaming from her vast anus.

The reek was magnificent. Gaborn could smell musty endowments, like putrid fat and rotten cabbages and moldy hair, so thick in the air that it choked him.

Darkness spread out from her, and as she advanced, shadows groped about Gaborn's knees.

He suddenly felt dazed. The creature twisted in his vision, and his eyes could not focus on it. In his mind's eye, the reaver seemed to expand suddenly, to grow taller and loom over him, as if to fill the whole chamber, as if to fill the universe.

෨ 36 ଓଃ

ALL DARKNESS FALLING

Let me be remembered not for how I lived but for how I died!

—last words attributed to Sir Marten Braiden,
who died heroically in the Battle of the Boars

Night fell swiftly over Carris. The sun slanted east beyond the mountains while the haze of distant smoke curtained off the light. Twenty miles to the north, reavers rushed in a horde down the mountainside, their feet making a dull rumble that shook a man's very bones. Borenson could not see them well, for a cloud of gree blackened the sky above. Howlers emitted their strange cries, like unearthly trumpets, and all of the reavers hissed. But there was another sound that bothered Borenson, a dull concussive *boom, boom, boom* that preceded the reavers like distant thunder.

The horde was less than an hour away. On the castle wall, men took up battle song to cheer their hearts.

In the failing light, Chondler led Borenson to his post as commoners began pulling up planks from the old drawbridge and tossing them into the lake.

"Rider coming!" someone shouted from the rooftop.

Borenson turned to see a lone rider racing from the south in the dusk, his swift gray imperial warhorse thundering over the road. The rider bent low, his robes flapping wildly in the wind of his passage.

He raced along the road and rounded the bend. The bridge was more than halfway destroyed, but his powerful steed leapt the gulf and skidded to a halt not more than a dozen yards behind Borenson.

"Hail, Sir? . . ." Marshal Chondler said.

The rider came to a halt, and sat on his horse, peering critically at the defenses. He was an old man in gray robes, with gray hair and ruddy cheeks. A strange light was in his eyes, and Borenson felt unreasonably that he knew the man from somewhere.

As he tried to imagine where he'd met the fellow, his mind returned to his childhood. Near his home there had been a peach orchard where he'd liked to go. He'd spent many an afternoon beneath a crooked old peach tree, its boughs so heavy with fruit that they swept the ground, and he'd imagined that he was in a deep forest filled with wolves and lions. He'd always felt a great sense of peace there, and now he felt that peace again.

"Binnesman!" Myrrima cried. "What are you doing here?"

The old fellow looked down on Myrrima, and Borenson finally recognized the old wizard. He had aged forty years in the past two days. "I've come to protect my charges," he said. "Perhaps for the last time."

He said no more for a moment, just peered up at the defenses, studying the stonework for signs of weakness that only a wizard could see. Just ahead, blocking the causeway where the barbican had been, piles of stone bristled with sharpened reaver blades, forming odd little humped barriers. Borenson had seen drawings of them in a book. They were called hedgehogs. They had been laid out in a staggered pattern to slow any reaver charge enough so that archers and artillerymen atop the towers could use the causeway as a killing field.

Beyond that, two new guard towers rose north and south above the city gate.

"The mortar is far from dry in those towers," Binnesman muttered under his breath. "The reavers could knock them down with a thought." He frowned with concern and began muttering a spell, sparing no thought for Borenson, High Marshal Chondler, or any other man.

Chondler asked the wizard, "How did you come here? Why did you leave the Earth King's side?"

Binnesman peered down at the High Marshal. "Foolishness. I came here by my own foolishness," the wizard said at last. "I was wounded in the Underworld, and Gaborn buried me for my own protection. For long I lay beneath the Earth, healing, and pondered. As I did, the reaver horde thundered over my head. By the time I woke, Gaborn was far gone, beyond my power to reach him.

"I suspected then that the Earth suffered me to get wounded for a purpose. I led Gaborn into the Underworld because I felt that he needed me. But you are all under my protection, and I knew that I was needed here, also.

"So when I had healed enough, I took care of some urgent matters to the east, then came as fast as I could."

"I thank you," Marshal Chondler said. "A wizard of your stature will be welcome indeed."

Binnesman peered at the castle walls. Worry etched his brow, and he shook his head. "I fear that there is little that I can do. But I will try."

He dismounted and looked as if he would march into the castle. But he stopped and peered hard at Myrrima, then put a hand on her shoulder.

"Your time is at hand, woman. The enemies of the Earth are gathering, and perhaps only you can resist them. Help us." He squeezed her shoulder, as if to comfort her, and then strode away.

Myrrima stood for a moment, then went to the moat. She reached down and dipped an arrow into the water, sat there for a long moment drawing runes upon the water's surface, dipping each arrow from her quiver in turn.

Borenson watched her for a long moment. He did not understand the significance of the runes that she sketched, but he dared not disturb a wizardess at her work.

He headed toward the castle, just behind High Marshal Chondler, Sarka Kaul, and the Wizard Binnesman. As Borenson walked the length of the causeway a garlicky scent wafted up, a scent so powerful it nearly brought tears to his eyes.

"What's this?" Binnesman asked, peering down.

"Onions and garlic, boiled with reaver philia," High Marshal Chondler said. "I'm hoping that this reek bothers them more than it does us."

A dangerous smile worked on the wizard's lips. "Yes, this may be more help than all of your walls and all of your arrows."

Just before the curtain wall of the castle stood one last low wall, a bulwark of substantial proportions. Here, once again, the reavers' own weapons would work against them. The wall bristled with bent reaver blades, so that they looked like a crown of wicked thorns set atop the stone. Logs and oil-soaked rags were worked into the mix.

Three sally ports just wide enough to let a horse pass through were placed beneath the bulwark.

Chondler led the party into the town square, where similar bulwarks ringed the square. Streets led west, north, and south beneath the bulwarks. Sally ports let men pass under. Binnesman studied the bulwarks with a critical eye, as if what he saw worried him. He suddenly raised his staff overhead and began sketching runes of strength upon the wall.

The men on the castle walls cheered to have a wizard of Binnesman's stature blessing their fortifications.

Marshal Chondler halted. Binnesman turned and uttered a spell over the garlic-strewn causeway. As he worked, Marshal Chondler bent in his saddle, and said, "That will be your station, Sir Borenson." He nodded toward the sally port beneath the ramparts on the left. "You'll be fighting in a team. In our last battle, the reavers took the walls in minutes. The only thing that gave them pause was men of sound heart, banded together. When confronted by such a force, the reavers grew confused. They didn't know which adversary might strike next, or which might pose the greatest danger.

"When the reavers charge, you'll set the bulwark here afire. It should give you ample light to see by and provide extra protection from the reavers."

"The dead reavers will pile up quickly," Borenson said, "leaving us no room to fight."

"I've taken that into account," Chondler agreed. "We expect that you will need to retreat, if only to give you room to fight. As you fall back, you'll defend Garlands Street. There are three more bulwarks like this up the lane. We have archers stationed atop the roofs and in the windows of every market. You must hold the reavers as the commoners fall back."

Garlands Street ran the length of the whole island, a distance of some two miles. Ramshackle merchant shops lined the street for the first half mile, shops that stood three or four stories tall. The buildings leaned so close together that the pitched roofs from every shop nearly joined. After that, dilapidated warehouses and smaller hovels squatted along the street's margins.

"As a last resort," Chondler said, "we have boats in the marina, enough to carry out a few hundred people. You'll hold the reavers there, if you can."

"Fair enough," Borenson said. He'd never been down to the old underground marina, and didn't even know the way, but he wasn't worried. He could simply follow the fleeing warriors. Besides, he doubted that he'd live long enough to make it to the boats.

"Good luck," Chondler said. He eyed the south tower just above Borenson's head, not a dozen yards away. Myrrima had just come from washing her arrows. "Lady Myrrima," he continued. "Take your steel bow up to the third story, and relieve the archer there. I suspect that you will want to guard your husband's back."

"Thank you," Myrrima said.

Binnesman finished his spell, and Sarka Kaul peered up at the wizard and Chondler. "Now," the Days said, "let us take counsel together and see if we can figure out how to save this city."

As Chondler, Sarka Kaul, and Binnesman hurried up toward the duke's old Keep on the hill, Borenson watched the wizard.

Despite the fact that an innumerable horde of reavers marched on the city, Borenson felt a flicker of hope.

Myrrima stood with him for a long moment, her hand wrapped about her bow. She bit her lower lip nervously and tapped her foot for a moment, but said nothing. Borenson realized that she felt shy about making public displays of affection, though she made up for it in private. Atop the walls, commoners began to sing a war song.

"Beyond the battle lie better days,
So let my blood be honored here.
Raise your mug and sing my praise
Like some sweet lark in coming years."

Myrrima leaned forward, wrapped one arm around his shoulders, and just held him for a long moment. She didn't say anything, and finally Borenson whispered, "I love you. I think I was destined to love you."

"I'll tell you what," Myrrima said. "After this battle, you can show me how much you love me, instead of jawing about it."

Borenson said nothing. He was standing inside the castle where his father had died, and the ground trembled from the tread of advancing reavers.

"This is a good place to fight," Myrrima said. "Water is all around us. Can you feel its power?"

"No," Borenson answered. "I can hear the small waves lapping on the rocks, and I can smell the lake in the air. But I don't feel anything."

"It whispers comfort to me," Myrrima said. "Don't resist the reavers too much. Don't stand against them like a wall. They'll break you if you do. You have to yield like waves of water. Rush forward to meet their fury, and rise when you must. Flow back when you have to. Learn to dance away like perch before the pike, and then leap in again for the strike." She had a peculiar light in her eye.

"I'll do the best I can," Borenson said, somewhat bemused by her advice.

He kissed her then for a long moment. A far-seer on the wall shouted, "Reavers are charging in advance of the army! Hundreds of them!"

"Come," Borenson said. "Let's have a look."

He quickly ducked beneath the sally port on Garlands Street and climbed a wooden ladder to the castle wall. Archers and footmen guarded the wall-walk, one every three feet or so. But there were no commoners up here, no gawkers to get in the way of the fighting men, as Borenson would have expected. Chondler had wisely forbidden them.

The air up here smelled of fresh rye bread and roast beef. The guards on the wall were eating one last hasty meal. They'd need the nourishment for the battle ahead.

Borenson squinted to the south, but could see little in the failing light. The reavers marched down the mountainsides in a black tide, their main front hidden among the hills. Nor did he see much in the way of advance forces, only a few shadowy reavers out in the fields—black monolithic bodies racing among the corpses of dead cohorts.

"Any sign of Lowicker's troops?" Borenson asked a stout warrior.

"Nothing to the north yet," he said, gripping his war hammer nervously.

Just then a flight of fire arrows arced from the castle wall and struck piles of bracken along the road at the end of the causeway. The oil-soaked piles quickly took fire.

By their light, Borenson could see a bit better. Reavers were indeed coming, racing across the fields like madness. They zigzagged this way and that, weaving like ants or bees, trying to catch a scent.

Some of them raced up to the lip of the vast pit where the world worm had breached, and crawled precariously about the rim.

They're trying to learn what they can of the previous battle, Borenson realized. They smell the words written on the ground.

A couple of reavers raced toward the castle, to the end of the peninsula. One stepped on a caltrop hidden under the straw. It hissed in pain and raised its tail high, spraying a warning, as it pulled the caltrop from its foot.

Its companion suddenly darted about on the straw-covered fields, plucking up the hidden caltrops and hurling them into the lake.

"They're smarter than we give them credit for," someone grumbled at Borenson's back.

Neither of the scouts dared step onto the causeway. Instead, they approached the head of the fell mage, whose mouth was stuffed with garlicky philia.

They drew near, quivering in fear at the scent, and then both scouts darted south, toward their front lines.

Borenson doubted that they would have to go far. The castle trembled beneath his feet and the earth grumbled loudly, like approaching thunder. To his surprise, he could make out a mass, a greater darkness blurring aboveground not ten miles south. The reavers were closer than he'd imagined.

"It won't be long now," Myrrima said.

Several dozen reavers had gathered just a few hundred yards south of the castle, over on the shore. During the previous battle, reavers had begun to build some sort of a strange tower there, with blue spires made of mucilage that twisted up like narwhale horns. These had all come down when the world worm surfaced.

Now the reavers began lifting the spires, tilting them upward, so that they rose hundreds of feet in the air.

In moments they somehow secured the base of these towers, and reavers began to climb up.

A far-seer nearby shouted, "There's something new here, up on them towers, a kind of reaver we ain't seen before."

Borenson squinted, but could barely make out the dark shapes. Only three towers were up, and each of them leaned precariously, like broken narwhale horns. Half a dozen reavers clung to the tops of these towers. Borenson could discern that the reavers were somehow misshapen.

"Describe them," Borenson called to the far-seer.

"They look like blade-bearers," the fellow answered, "but thinner and longer of body. And their capes are at least twice as long as a common reaver's, with more philia."

A reaver's "cape" referred to the bony head plates that extended from the sweet triangle to the crown of the head.

"They're looking at us," the far-seer called, "studying our defenses."

"Impossible," Borenson grunted. The reavers had to be six or seven hundred yards away, and Averan had said that they couldn't see more than two hundred. Yet as he squinted south, he could clearly see that these odd scouts had topped their towers, and hung like mantises clinging to twigs. Furthermore, they seemed to peer toward the castle, all of their philia waving madly.

He spotted movement not far away, perhaps five miles, and realized that a huge contingent of reavers was racing toward them in a dark tide.

He had imagined that the main front of the horde was an hour away. But reaver scouts charged ahead of the common ranks. He didn't have an hour. He didn't even have fifteen minutes.

"You'd better take your post," he told Myrrima, as dozens of powerful Runelords issued to the castle gate, making their stand beneath the rampart.

Borenson squeezed Myrrima's hand, and she reached into a pocket of her tunic, pulled out a red silk scarf. It was the same one that Borenson had tied to his lance when he'd fought High Marshal Skalbairn in the tournament a week ago, at Castle Sylvarresta.

"Here," she said, tying it about his neck. "Keep this safe for me."

Then she turned and raced into the tower, disappearing beneath a dark arch.

Borenson slid down the ladder and went to his own post. He watched the castle tower, until he saw movement in the window on the third story. Myrrima reached out a pale hand and waved, but he couldn't see her face.

Borenson had been so preoccupied with watching the reaver scouts, he had failed to notice that several men had taken their posts beneath the rampart on Garlands Street. A pair of torches were stuck in the dirt by the sally port, and by their light he spotted someone he knew, Captain Tempest of Longmot. Like Borenson, he was a stout warrior but did not have a wealth of endowments. A third man was a Knight Equitable, Sir Greenswar of Toom, who had taken enough endowments of metabolism to ensure an early grave. Two more champions beside him wore the golden surcoats of Indhopal. They introduced themselves with thick accents. One was a swarthy fellow named Hamil Owatt, ninth son of the Emir to Tuulistan. The second was a tall black man from Deyazz, a warrior from the fierce Tintu tribe named Nguya Kinsagga.

Nguya looked Borenson over, and blinked once in a sign of respect, but took the lead of the small band. "I fought reavers at this gate a week ago," Nguya said. "They do not fear a man who backs away from them or one who stands his ground. But when you advance against them, it stops their hearts." He studied each man, as if by staring he could bore the information into him. He raised his spear and shook it mightily.

"Don't wear yourselves out," Borenson suggested to those who had great endowments. "There are five of us here. If any of you start to tire, fall back and let someone else strike the killing blow."

Nguya nodded appreciatively, and the men took their posts.

From the barbican, Borenson could see nothing. The ground began to rumble in earnest as the reaver horde approached. The rumble grew steadily louder, and soon gree began to whip above the courtyard, a sign that reavers were here.

Borenson found his heart pounding, and he measured the seconds by its beat. He wished that he could go back up on the wall and take a look.

Excited shouts rose from far-seers, and he listened to their reports. "They're almost to the city gates, but they're hanging back."

The *thwonk, thwonk, thwonk* of artillery fire rose from the rafts out on the lake as the marksmen shot at reavers near the shore. "Milord," one far-seer cried after a few minutes. "I see Lowicker's troops cresting the hills beyond the Barren's Wall," and seconds later, "Milord, a spy balloon is taking off to the east!"

Only Raj Ahten's flameweavers used spy balloons, he knew. He could feel no wind down here in the town square. The castle walls rose up all about him. He peered up, and saw stars twinkling in the heavens, but smoke from the south was covering them like a gauze, and little light reached the streets below. But outside the wind had been blowing lightly to the east. The balloon would soar above the city, above the battle, and from there Raj Ahten's flameweavers would be able to watch in comfort. In an hour's time, perhaps, the balloon would drop to the east, among his troops.

Borenson glanced south and thought he spotted a man on the castle wall, beneath the dark arch of a tower.

The man had red hair and a familiar stance, and for a moment Borenson's heart leapt in his chest, for he thought it was his father.

But he looked again and no one was there.

He gulped. It was his father's wraith, he felt sure. He had been smiling, as if in welcome.

Am I to die here? Borenson wondered.

He looked about, and began to feel panicked for the first time in his life. Always before, he had met battle with grim determination, laughing in the face of death.

Now he wondered where his father lay. He had found the man's body a week ago, up on the green beneath Duke Paldane's palace. Carris was built on some low hills that rose out of the water. To the east, the hills were riddled with ancient caves and tunnels—tombs for the dead, warehouses meant to store food and troops in time of siege. Most likely, Dorenson's father was down in the tombs by now.

"The reavers are massing," a watchman shouted. "I see their fell mage! By the Seven Stones, she's big! Get ready!"

But for long minutes there was no movement from the reavers. Someone in the streets begged, "What's going on?"

"They came near the causeway, but after one sniff, they backed off. Now they're out near the worm hill," the far-seer shouted. "There's a bunch of sorceresses. It looks as if they want to rebuild that rune they had out there, the Seal of Desolation."

Borenson peered about. Fires were springing up all along the castle walls. Young men, torchbearers, were racing along the wall-walk, bringing light to anyone who wanted it. He could hear people shouting messages all up and down the length of Carris, but the hiss of reavers, the pounding of reaver feet, drowned out their cries. Where he stood everyone waited in anticipation of the battle, but he had a sense of the city as a hive, a vast hive filled with men and women who bustled about in preparation for war.

The Wizard Binnesman came down into the courtyard, then went rushing up Garlands Street toward the marinas.

Moments later, Marshal Chondler came running into the town square, a torch in one hand, a reaver dart in the other. "All Runelords," he called, "hold your positions. All lords to the east and south of me," he called, "on my command will begin an orderly retreat to the tombs. All commoners, head for the marina immediately."

"What?" one lord shouted down from the wall-walk. "You would have us retreat before the battle begins?"

In answer, Chondler ordered, "Any man who wants to live will do as I say—now!"

Hundreds of commoners, archers and healers alike, began to race down from the towers and hurry up Garlands Street, following Binnesman.

Borenson saw immediately what Chondler intended. Sarka Kaul had warned that Rialla Lowicker and Raj Ahten would not send their troops into battle until Carris was defeated. So Chondler hoped to feign defeat in order to lure them into coming to his aid. By sending lords to guard the tombs, and commoners to the hidden halls that led to the marinas, Chondler would be hiding most of his men underground.

Gree whipped overhead, squeaking as if in pain, and reavers hissed like a sea.

Chondler climbed atop the wall, looked down for several long minutes.

In that time, Borenson saw the spy balloon hovering in the air like a giant graak. The wind was blowing it right over the city. It peeked over the castle walls. Flameweavers glowed within its gondola, as if the fire would burst from them at any moment.

Chondler shouted to his men, "Don't let the reavers build that rune. Loose the catapults."

His marksman shouted, "Sir, at this range we can't hit it with anything larger than grape shot!"

"Then use grape shot!" Chondler insisted.

Moments later the artillerymen atop the tower cut loose, sending a hail of iron balls from the walls.

The reavers hissed in outrage.

The far-seers began to cry, "They're coming!"

The *thwonk* of ballistas filled the air and the *twang* of a thousand bows arose as missiles rained down, clattering on the causeway.

"By the Powers, they're fast!" someone swore.

It won't be long, Borenson thought, even as screams of terror rose along the walls. He grabbed a torch and threw it onto the rampart overhead. The torch landed among the spikes and oil-soaked rags. The rampart blazed, filling the courtyard with light.

Suddenly a reaver landed in the town square, snarling, a huge mage with a crystalline staff. A pair of ballista bolts protruded from her flank.

Borenson froze in astonishment.

She whirled and let fly a spell as arrows rained down on her. A red cloud boiled from her staff, and poisonous vapors filled the courtyard, even as arrows pierced her sweet triangle and she shuddered to the ground.

"Where did she come from?" Borenson wondered, and realized that she had leapt from above. He glanced up and saw three more reavers scurry over the castle wall, sending stones flying as they crashed into merlons.

A reaver atop the wall lurched forward and swung his long blade, hitting three men at once. The force of the blow sent a spray flying toward Borenson. A pile of guts landed sloppily at his feet, while blood showered from the sky.

"They're over the walls!" someone cried. A reaver suddenly bounded from the castle wall to the top of a merchant's shop across the street. Sixteen tons of monster hit the roof, which collapsed under the weight. Timbers shattered and rock from the walls tumbled away. Floor after floor buckled, while the men and women inside cried out in pain and horror.

Archers fell back from the castle wall firing toward the monsters in terror.

The mage's spell hit in a cloud, and Borenson heard words ring in his ears, "Crawl, thou son of man." Immediately, dismay coursed through him, and his legs went so weak that he could hardly stand. His bowels felt loose, and his heart pounded as if it would burst.

Along the walls, men dropped in panic. Bows fell from the hands of archers. Stout warriors collapsed in terror.

A huge blade-bearer plunged from the castle wall, into the street behind Borenson, landing with a crash as its massive body thudded to the cobblestones, shattering the street.

Borenson screamed a battle cry and charged.

ℬ 37 ℭ

IN THE LAIR OF BONES

Erden Geboren spent seven years searching for the fabled Throne of the Underworld. The fact that he never found it suggests that it may not exist.

—*excerpt from* A Comparison of Reports on Reavers, Hearthmaster *by Dungiles*

Averan peered down the tunnel that led to the Lair of Bones. A huge blade-bearer was rushing toward her, all the philia along its head waving in alarm at the scent of blood. It skidded to a halt as it became aware of her.

Averan cleared her mind and sent a thought to the monster. "I'm not real. You are worm dreaming."

The reaver froze for an instant, confused, its huge blade in hand. Averan used that moment to strike. She leapt, waving her staff in the air as she did, forming the rune that she had seen Binnesman's wylde use so often.

She whacked the blade-bearer on the head, striking the bony plates above its muzzle. The monster's skull imploded, sending shards of bone lancing into its brain. The creature collapsed.

Averan scrambled past the dead reaver, toward the Lair of Bones. She imagined that no one had ever felt as lonely as she did, rushing through the ribbed tunnels. Averan was heading into the heart of the boundless warren, deeper than any human had ever been.

Sweat streamed down her face, and the silence seemed like a leaden weight. The only sound was the echo of her footfalls, the gasp of her breath.

If I get hurt or die down here, Averan thought, no one will ever find me.

The tunnel wound through the warren, joining others at frequent junctures, becoming a twisted maze. Crawlways led in all directions—one to her left ran a dozen miles to underground lakes where reavers raised enormous blindfish. Another to her left dropped to an old hatching ground where young sorceresses studied the making of fire runes. Another tunnel plummeted down to reaver foundries where brutish workers forged tools of steel.

Another to her right plummeted down into a tunnel whose walls were pure blood metal, a vein of metal so rich that Raj Ahten himself could not have imagined it in his grandest dreams.

Averan sniffed as she went, making sure that her recollections were correct. She had spent hours communing with the Waymaker, plumbing the depths of its memory. He had known the path well, and Averan now negotiated the twisted warrens with ease.

But she had miles to go.

She raced to a pair of howlers, huge yellow spidery creatures that were lugging stone buckets of ore down to the mines. The monsters discarded their buckets and trumpeted an eerie warning as Averan raced past.

Even the big howlers were more afraid of Averan than she was of them.

A dozen miles she ran, meeting no reavers. In Waymaker's memory, these tunnels had always been bustling. For the first time Averan began to understand how many reavers the One True Master must have sent to attack Carris.

She had emptied the Underworld.

Averan was panting from thirst when she reached a side tunnel that sloped down a hundred yards and then leveled out again as it emptied into the Lair of Bones.

Here, the ground burned hot. Even with endowments of stamina, no human could survive long.

Averan sprinted into the chamber. The Lair of Bones was vast, part of a cavern that had existed for millennia. Dripstone hung from the roof, covered with feathery grasses and roots that slowly stirred the air. Reaver bones littered the floor—ancient skulls with gaping crystalline jaws, serrated teeth as long as Averan's arm, and huge leg bones as thick as logs. Dried claws groped the air like scythes, while everywhere lay piles of horny carapace plates so exotic that humans and other surface creatures had nothing to compare them to. The bones were as clear as crystal. Some were so old that they were as dull red as amber, others were the citrine hues of the newly dead.

The bones climbed upon the ground to a depth of four dozen yards in places, forming small hills, and the reavers had cleared a path between them. Averan trod through a valley of bones.

These were the vanquished foes of the One True Master, left as trophies so that other reavers might be properly humbled as they sought audience before her.

Until Averan saw the aged skeletons, she had not truly understood how old the One True Master might be, how hoary her malevolence.

She knew that the monster had subjugated all of the other reaver hives. But she hadn't guessed how many queens had been destroyed in the process.

The dead numbered in the thousands.

Averan slowed as she wound through the vale.

There should be more reavers here, she thought, at least some of the queen's Shadow Guard.

But the vast chamber lay silent.

That means they must have gone to the surface, Averan thought. They'll be leading her troops.

Still, Averan's gut warned that she wouldn't be able to reach the Chamber of the Seals without passing some guards.

She wouldn't smell them. The reavers could hide their scents, make themselves smell like rocks and plants. Nor would she see them if they chose to hide.

She cleared her mind, reached out with her senses, and felt *him* there, the Consort of Shadows.

He was up the trail, waiting patiently. He'd suspected that someone might try to make it here.

"It's me," Averan whispered to the creature's mind. She timidly ambled forward. "I had to come. I have to destroy the Seals."

Faintly, almost as if against its will, she heard the Consort of Shadows answer. "I smelled you. I knew you were coming."

"Let me pass," Averan said.

Ahead lay a great hill of bones that rose seventy feet into the air, so that they almost scraped against the ceiling. At the very top lay the skulls of giant reavers, noses pointed outward like the petals surrounding a daisy, their open mouths gaping in every direction.

They formed a nest. The staves of mighty sorceresses were thrust between the skulls, sticking up like a crown. This was the great throne of the One True Master, the seat of power from which she peered down upon her servants. Above the nest, enormous stalactites hung like teeth.

"The scent of command is upon me," the Consort of Shadows replied. "I must guard this place."

Some bones beneath the throne suddenly shifted, and the Consort of Shadows scrambled up, looming above Averan. In one clawed hand he held a great blade, a weapon unlike any that Averan had ever seen. The metal was cold and black, and the blade rippled in waves. She could smell runes written

in scents by powerful reaver mages along the length of it. In the other claw
he held a black net woven of reaver hide.

He was huge, and Averan now recognized the scent of hundreds of runes
upon him, and could see their pale blue light flickering like a low flame along
the lengths of his arms and on the bony ridge of his enormous head.

He moved with tremendous speed and grace, and Averan dared not
fight him.

"Your ancestor ate the brains of an Earth Warden," Averan reminded
him. "You know what he knew. I don't come to destroy your people but to
help them."

The monster lunged.

Averan raised her staff and imagined a rune on the ceiling above, a rune
of stone breaking. Instantly the stone bubbled and the rune took shape.

The roof of the chamber began to collapse. Massive stalactites sheared
away under their own weight.

The Consort of Shadows darted to the side to avoid the first of them.
Averan sprang back, running as fast as she could.

Stalactites lanced down while slabs of rock flaked from the roof. Above
her the Lair of Bone was collapsing.

Averan ran for her life, racing through the valley of bones. She dodged
just as a boulder crashed in her path.

Raining stone pummeled ancient piles of reaver bone. It thundered, and
the floor shook beneath her.

Averan sprinted toward the mouth of the chamber, fearing that the Consort of Shadows would leap on her at any moment. Rubble pounded the floor.
A choking cloud of dust as black as night roiled out from the mess, filling the
cave, so that the light of her opal pin was almost worthless. Averan could see
no more.

She threw herself beneath a reaver skull. Stone roared down around her
and chunks of rock bounced from the path and slapped her ankles. Blinding
dust rushed over her as Averan threw her hands in front of her eyes for protection. Thick dust worked its way into her ears, settled down the back of her
throat, clogged her nose. There was nothing to do for it. She waited a long
moment for the cave-in to finish.

She opened her senses, reached out with her mind, and sought the Consort of the Shadows.

The huge reaver lord was in pain. Rocks by the ton weighed down upon
his back, slowly crushing the air from him. His right arm was pinned, and with
his left he tried to dig his way out. But even with his incredible strength he did
not seem to have a hope of escape. He was not a hundred yards behind her.

I'm sorry, Averan sent the thought to him. I didn't want to hurt you. I
don't want to hurt anyone.

The sound of falling stone tapered away. Only a few rocks clanked down from the ceiling and bounced as they settled among the debris.

Averan climbed up from under the overhanging skull and tried to peer around. The dust was so thick that it blinded her, and it would hang in the air for long hours, hours that she dared not waste.

She sprang up and picked a path over broken stones, hurrying toward the Chamber of the Seals. Tons of stone and rubble covered the Lair of Bones. Large rocks shifted each time she stepped on them, and she had to wend her way around massive boulders. Averan peered up to the great throne, but the reaver skulls were crushed beneath the tonnage. Averan squinted painfully as she fought through the dust.

She climbed to the stones where the Consort of Shadows lay buried, worried that at any instant his massive paw might reach up and crush her.

She peered into his mind, felt rage and frustration. He struggled to free himself, unaware of how close she might be. Gingerly, she climbed onto a large stone, fearing that the monster might sense her added weight.

Suddenly a stone shifted beneath her, along with dozens of other rocks nearby that sank a foot as if they had dropped into a sinkhole.

He's coming! she realized.

She leapt thirty feet, landed on a large stone, and leapt again. Froglike, she bounded past her buried foe.

She reached the far side of the Lair of Bones. A tunnel gaped before her, and the rubble suddenly came to an end.

The Chamber of the Seals was just down the corridor, only three miles. Averan could run it in minutes.

She raced into the tunnel, bypassing crawlways that led to the One True Master's personal quarters, to her egg chambers. Averan wiped her eyes, fighting back tears.

The face of Gaborn burned in her memory, and for a moment she worried about how he fared. She was so shaken that she didn't notice the tremors at first.

An earthquake began to build. The riblike supports on the walls swayed with the motion, and the floor beneath her began to rise and fall as if in waves. Chips of rock and dust peeled from the roof and cracked to the ground.

The Earth is in pain, Averan thought. She could feel it, the dull sustained ache that cut through the very bones of the world, adding to her own distress.

She rounded a corner, and a reaver blocked her way, a big lumbering matron. It became aware of Averan charging headlong, and wheeled to flee into the egg chambers. Averan could smell its distress call.

In the pocket of her wizard robes she carried a sprig of parsley that Binnesman had given her days ago. He had told her to tie it in seven knots and throw it on her trail if anything gave chase. She had tied it in knots, but hadn't needed it until now. Suddenly, the sprig blossomed in her memory.

She grasped its dried leaves between her fingers, dropped it to the floor, and gave a little chant.

> "Round the circle, round the bend,
> Round the corner and back again
> Seek my scent, and when it's found,
> Twelve times twelve, follow it around."

Averan raced along the tunnel. The floor trembled wildly as another tremor hit, and suddenly ahead it buckled. Slabs of rock tilted up. Averan leapt over them, racing like a hare.

It wasn't far now—up one tunnel, round a bend, over a bridge where burning white mud pots splattered against a wall, round a corner.

And Averan was there—a chamber much smaller than the Dedicates' Keep had been. It was only a couple of hundred yards from one end to the other. As in the keep, sluggish water flowed through a small pond, bubbling up from a hot spring. A few stonewood trees grew from the ceiling.

The whole room was eerily lit.

Upon the floor lay a vast rune, fully a hundred yards across: the Rune of Desolation. It was evil to behold, and seemed all the more depraved for being carved in stone. It was no simple shape. To Averan's eye, it looked almost like two snakes seeking to devour each other within a vast circle. But other protuberances jutted up among the scene to monstrous effect. A noxious haze circled above it, obscuring the symbol.

The rune itself was made of earth. Knobs and ridges of carved stone rose from the ground in varying heights, forming a bas-relief.

Actinic flashes of red and blue shot from the rune, eerily lighting the vast chamber, as if the flames of a hearth flickered upon the walls. Averan could discern no source for the fire. The ground seemed to fulminate, for she could see glowing embers, yet earth remained unconsumed.

Averan peered about, searching. Gaborn had told her to destroy the seals. But she saw only one seal before her, a Seal of Desolation.

Where are the others?

She tried to imagine what nearby rooms they might be hidden in. But the Waymaker's memory only confirmed that the runes stood before her.

Then she gasped: there, among the flickering lights she discerned a shape. If she squinted hard, she could see it, a rune carved not in earth but formed in the sourceless fire. The Seal of the Inferno.

And there, above the earth and fire floated a noxious gray haze, swirling in lazy circles. No wind made the smoke swirl so. The third rune was also here, the Seal of Heaven, written in currents of air.

The seals were stacked atop one another.

Her first instinct was to break the Seal of Desolation.

I can collapse the roof on it, Averan thought.

She stretched out her staff, and prepared a spell to weaken the stone.

ಜ 38 ೮

BENEATH THE SHADOW

To give your life in the service of a higher cause, one must first renounce all self-indulgence.

—*The Wizard Binnesman*

Gaborn danced away as the One True Master advanced. With every step backward, the Earth warned him, "Flee," and then again, "Strike!"

Thus he knew that it was not his task to face the monster yet. She was beyond his strength to battle. He raced away from her, slaughtering her Dedicates as he did.

In Carris the battle was in full swing. Dozens of his Chosen were torn from him in an instant, and Gaborn cried out in pain.

Dark tendrils of vapor wrapped around his leg, and ice seemed to freeze his heart. The voice of the One True Master whispered in his mind. "You have failed. Because of your weakness, your Chosen will die."

Gaborn saw as if in a vision from the hills west of Carris, reavers roaring across the causeway in a black tide, leaping onto the castle walls. The city seemed to be aflame, the only light in a blackened world. Outside the castle, a fell mage and her sorceresses sought to complete a new Seal of Desolation. Actinic blue lights rose from the ground where it took form.

Above the castle, a balloon shaped like a graak wafted through the smoke.

Gaborn's army was crumbling. Men raced from the gates, fleeing in terror atop the castle wall. From this distance, Gaborn saw a reaver reach up to pull a young boy from a tower window. Gaborn knew that what he witnessed was true, for the boy was one of his Chosen, and Gaborn felt the boy's life ripped from him.

And then the view changed and Gaborn saw, as if from above, Raj Ahten to the west of Carris, high on a hill, with his troops behind him. His face was a mask of ruin, with his ear burned off, the skin seared from his jaw, and his eye puckering white and blind.

He exulted at the slaughter in the distance, watched the reavers bursting through walls to get at the people that hid in their homes and cellars.

"This is your doing," the One True Master whispered. "You made him your enemy, and sought his life."

The Master sought to crush Gaborn with guilt, like a massive stone, but he would have none of it.

"Liar!" he shouted. "He made himself my enemy—at your bidding!"

The One True Master is only seeking to delay me, he realized. Gaborn raced to another Dedicate, and plunged his reaver dart into its kidney.

"Duck," the Earth whispered, and Gaborn threw himself flat to the ground, dodging beneath the knees of a reaver.

As he did, the One True Master snapped her vile whip, slicing the air above his head.

"Dodge," the Earth commanded, and Gaborn leapt aside as the monster hissed a curse.

"*Gasht,*" the words sounded, and a black funnel of wind issued from her staff, racing near the spot where Gaborn had stood. The ground boiled where it touched, and flakes of rock splintered from the floor. Three reaver Dedicates, seemingly frozen in time, fell beneath the blast. Their blood and bones spattered through the chamber.

The floor bucked beneath Gaborn's feet as a strong earthquake rocked the chamber. Stones and dust fell from the ceiling.

"Strike!" the earth commanded, and Gaborn leapt over a reaver and plunged his dart into another vector. He craned his neck and felt gratified to see one of the ghostly blue runes on the monster fade to gray.

The tendrils of darkness swept over him, and Gaborn found himself wishing to curl up on the floor and die. The monster fought him, sought to take control of his limbs.

As if uttering a curse he shouted, "The Glories deliver me!"

In that moment, Gaborn wished for nothing more than to become pure light himself, to fight the corruption he beheld.

The monster wheezed as if stricken, and the shadow withdrew.

The way his very desire seemed to engender pain in the creature gave Gaborn sudden insight.

I can do it, he thought. I can call upon the Glories, and she knows it!

"No," the monster whispered. "You're not worthy." Images flashed before his eyes: a pair of reavers tearing a man in two as they fought to eat him; a woman rushing from a reaver as its blade whipped down, cutting her in half. "This is your legacy," the beast whispered.

But Gaborn did not believe it. By making him view the world's corruption, the beast hoped to dishearten him.

"I am worthy," Gaborn said. "The Glories have made me so."

The One True Master wheezed and lunged.

Gaborn found that he had backed beneath a twisted stonewood tree, and the bole of it bored into his ribs.

The monster sprang forward in an astonishing leap.

"Jump," the Earth warned. Gaborn leapt thirty feet in the air, rising between two branches of the tree. "Dodge." He felt the warning, and Gaborn twisted as he leapt. "Dodge," the earth warned again, and he twisted once more as he dropped toward the ground.

The One True Master raked the air with her crystalline staff, swatting at him with incredible speed. Once, twice, three times she sought to strike him as he fell, and each time he only barely managed to twist away from the blow.

As he dropped, Gaborn saw a light at the mouth of the chamber, and huge dancing shadows. Iome had come to help.

Gaborn landed on hard rock. The ground began to buck from the force of the earthquake, and stones showered from the ceiling.

For miles Iome had run, following Gaborn, until at last she rounded a bend and saw a light ahead. She could make out man-shapes, dozens of them, and her voice caught in her throat, for she imagined that Gaborn had found an Inkarran war party.

But when she neared she saw only a tattered band of skeletal beings, the shadows of people dressed in rags, and she recalled Averan's tale of prisoners in the dark places of the world.

She rushed up to them.

"Where is Gaborn?" Iome begged.

No one answered at first, for she had many endowments and spoke too quickly, but one finally pointed down the tunnel. "That way! Hurry!"

Iome raced down the trail, over a floor polished as smooth as marble by millions of reavers that had trundled over it during the centuries. Her heart hammered with every stride. She knew that Gaborn's need was upon him, for he had left no marks at side tunnels.

She glanced down each crawlway that crossed her path, afraid that she might lose the way. She saw great rooms carved in stone, and longed to search them, to learn what she could of the secret ways of reavers.

Over the weary days of travel she had lost her ability to track time. Her race seemed unending, measured only by the sense of urgency that drove her.

She rounded a bend, saw a trio of dead reavers, and the mouth of a tunnel. As if from a great distance, Gaborn shouted, "Iome, stay back!"

The ground bucked and swayed beneath her feet. Iome threw herself against a wall for support, and warily peered up, afraid that the roof would collapse, but the walls and roof were reinforced with mucilage from glue mums.

She raced into the mouth of a huge chamber. Stones tumbled from the ceiling. Dead reavers lay in humps all about. But in the distance, wading through a swarm of companions, Iome saw a reaver far more enormous and hideous than any that she'd ever imagined.

Its abdomen was so swollen with eggs that she looked bloated to the bursting point. Yet she danced over the battlefield with a speed and grace that left Iome breathless.

Then Iome spotted Gaborn, a second shadow lit only by the big reaver's glowing runes. He was in something of a clearing, created as reavers rushed to escape his presence.

Gaborn and his adversary moved as if in dance, seeming to read each other's minds. Gaborn recoiled backward some eighty feet, spinning in the air as he dodged the monster's whip.

Never had Iome imagined such grace and speed in a man. It was like watching lightning arc across the heavens. To her, it seemed that Gaborn had become a force of nature, the Sum of All Men.

But the One True Master lunged toward him with equal speed, and if Gaborn was the Sum of All Men, then she seemed at this moment, with her power and deadly intent, to be the Sum of All Reavers.

Together, Gaborn and his attacker raced between a pair of grotesque stonewood trees.

"Iome," Gaborn called. "Kill the vectors."

All throughout the cave were countless reavers, each marked by softly glowing runes. Comprehension dawned in Iome. She peered about, searching for targets. To her left, her keen eyes detected a bright glow. Half a dozen reavers clustered around it, as if to shield it from view.

Iome raced down the hill, straight toward the light. Several young guards lunged toward her. As she neared them, she leapt toward one's face. It lurched backward, and Iome dove under its legs, then sprang up behind it.

She saw a reaver lying there, with dozens of pale blue runes along its shoulders and head. She plunged her dart into the vector's sweet triangle. Blood and brains gushed from the wound.

Two hundred yards away, the One True Master hissed in anger.

A stone plummeted to the floor nearby, shattering and sending its shards into the reavers all around. Several of them hissed in pain.

Iome peered about, seeking another victim.

In the city of Carris, Borenson raced to meet a reaver, heart pounding in terror.

"For Heredon!" Captain Tempest cried, rushing forward at Borenson's side. The reaver whirled to meet them, rising up in a defensive posture. It's huge blade arced overhead, and came swinging.

Borenson rolled to the side as Tempest lunged with a reaver dart, striking the beast in the thorax. The reaver lurched backward ripping the dart from Tempest's hands, and began to roll about, kicking.

Another reaver came leaping over the castle walls and landed nearly atop it. It was one of the juveniles that Gaborn had seen from a distance, riding the back of a matron. The monster was small for a reaver, just smaller than an elephant, but it seemed to be all legs, and it moved swifter than any adult. The thing raced a few paces, grabbed some fleeing warrior from behind and bit him in half.

An arrow from the tower behind Borenson whizzed into its sweet triangle. The monster curled in on itself, like a wasp, and vainly began trying to pull out the arrow.

Vaguely, Borenson realized that great shadows were leaping over the castle wall—other juveniles—a hail of the swift creatures.

Borenson could see no sign of the heroes assigned to guard the gate. They were still inside the courtyard.

Flames roared to the south of Borenson. The oil and the wood on the burning ramparts sent a wall of flame searing forty feet high. The heat was so intense that Borenson didn't dare try to run beneath the sally port. He was cut off from the others.

Borenson glanced up at the castle walls. The sound of artillery had all but gone silent. Reavers, both adult and juvenile, had already taken the top of the north tower, and a dozen monsters had scaled the castle wall above. Some men were rushing to face them, but the reavers would soon be swarming over the walls.

"Gasht!" came the sound of a spell. Borenson ducked by instinct.

He dodged toward the north tower, shouting "Myrrima, get out!"

A reaver raced along the wall-walk, and having seen the damage that its weight alone could cause, it bounded atop the tower. Rocks and debris rained down. The first three stories crumbled.

Borenson leapt to avoid a hail of falling stones. One burst near his foot, sending shards everywhere, and he heard Captain Tempest cry out in pain.

He glanced back. The warrior of Heredon was staring down in shock. A shard of stone, as sharp as a dagger, had lodged in his shin.

"Get to the healers!" Borenson shouted, even as the reaver above surged through the tower wall and leapt into the street.

To the north, at the far end of the island, various trumpeters began blowing distress calls and retreat, as if hoping that Queen Lowicker would send her troops into battle.

Borenson charged the reaver, a huge mage. He bounded a dozen feet in the air and brought his warhammer down with all his might, piercing the monster's sweet triangle.

The long spikes on the head of the hammer hit with a *chunk* sound and bit through the mage's flesh. But the sorceress was so large, he couldn't penetrate deep into her brain.

The reaver shook her head, and her bony cape slammed into Borenson, hurled him thirty feet, where he crashed into the wall of a merchant's shop. His mail and padding absorbed the impact against the mud-and-wattle facade, but the blow drove the breath from his lungs.

Borenson hit the ground and lay gasping for half a minute. The reaver mage whirled and peered at him, fanning the bony plates of its head wide, all of its philia waving wildly in alarm.

He could see dark blood pouring down its face. He had sorely wounded the creature. It must have decided that he was dead, for it whirled and was about to lope down the street, giving chase to commoners and lesser men who had begun fleeing in a crowd.

It's leaving, Borenson thought. I should let it go.

But he couldn't.

He scrambled to his feet and raced down the street a hundred yards, chasing the wounded reaver. It pounced on some retreating guardsman and halted a second as it made sure of the man.

Borenson sprang at the reaver from behind and swung his hammer, striking deep into its haunch.

The reaver hissed, and a stench exploded from its hind end. Too late, Borenson realized that it was a spell.

"Be as dry as dust, thou child of man."

Immediately sweat gushed from Borenson's every pore, and came streaming down his face. His bladder contracted, and warm urine rolled down his leg.

The mage whirled to face him, its jaws opening just the slightest.

"Damn you!" Borenson screamed as he dove into its mouth. The monster's serrated teeth scraped his forehead, and he landed on a tongue as rough as stone.

The reaver snapped its mouth closed, but too late. Borenson was inside. He lunged to his feet, reversed his warhammer, and stabbed upward with the handle, trying to drive it through the beast's soft palate. But in an instant Borenson was thrown off-balance and his weapon struck only bone.

He went flying sideways as the reaver shook its head, trying to dislodge him. He crashed against its sharp teeth, and grabbed onto one.

For only an instant the reaver shook, then stopped to feel if there was still movement. In that instant, Borenson lunged with his warhammer, and hit the creature in the soft palate again. Hot blood washed down on him in a gratifying burst.

The reaver stumbled forward, and then it dropped. Borenson was thrown from his feet, and scraped his face on the monster's gravelly tongue.

He lay for a moment in pain, bleeding from a dozen small wounds, struggling to catch his breath. Sweat poured from him, and his own tongue began to swell from thirst.

He crawled to his knees. Reaver blood pumped hot from the gaping hole above, gushing out in a steaming shower.

Borenson laughed and crawled forward. The reaver's mouth was closed. He couldn't even see beyond its lips. A large reaver can top twelve tons, and much of that massive weight is in the bony plates of its head. Even a Runelord with all of his endowments of brawn can rarely lift more than a few hundred pounds.

Borenson set his feet in the reaver's gums and leaned his back against its upper palate. He lifted with all of his might, but could not get the head to budge.

Outside, he could hear warhorns blaring, calling a retreat from the front gate. Folk were screaming in terror. By now dozens of reavers had breached the walls.

What do I do? he wondered.

He rolled onto his back, tried pushing up with his legs. But it was no use. The reaver's jaws were locked.

He pondered his predicament.

After the battle at Carris, he'd seen the reavers in the fields, jaws gaping wide as their muscles tightened. Before rigor mortis began to set in, the beast's mouth would open of itself—in a few hours.

The safest thing would be to stay here until the battle was over. But he couldn't just sit while others fought and died. Besides, Myrrima was in the north tower, where the battle raged hottest. If she was still alive, the reavers would soon block her escape.

"I've got to get out!" Borenson muttered.

He could think of only one thing to do: cut his way out. The only place he might do it was in the monster's throat, just below the neck. He grabbed his warhammer in his right hand, drew his dagger in the left, and raced to the reaver's throat. He was trying to wiggle his way down when the dead reaver suddenly seemed to gag. Its mouth choked open, while bile rose from its stomach.

A flood of bile sent Borenson washing into the street.

He got to his knees, and peered about, to make sure he was safe. As he did, he sheathed his dagger and then wiped bile and blood from the handle of his warhammer. Reavers were stampeding over the walls, unimpeded. The north tower had completely collapsed. Only the bottom floor seemed to be standing, and there was no movement in its darkened doorway.

He looked about frantically. "Myrrima?" he shouted, but his heart went out of him.

If Myrrima was still in the tower, she'd be crushed under the rubble.

A few arrows still rose from the roofs of markets across the street from the castle wall, and a guardsman was crawling along the street toward him. Borenson saw no other sign of people, though all through Carris he could hear their cries.

A reaver pitched from the wall and crushed a shop that had served as a station for archers. Borenson whirled and looked up the street to the north, to see if Myrrima might be fleeing.

Dozens of reavers rushed ahead of him, already racing toward the marina, clearing the streets.

He was behind enemy lines!

He heard a hiss nearby and whirled. A reaver charged him.

Borenson held still, as if too frightened to move, until the reaver was upon him. Then he sprang a dozen feet in the air and struck with his warhammer, biting deep into the monster's brain.

The reaver went down, skidding beneath him, and Borenson landed on its back.

He had been told to guard the street, to hold back the reavers as best he could while the commoners tried to reach the marina.

But he feared that Myrrima was still in the north tower, and he imagined her crushed and bleeding beneath the rubble.

He could not leave her.

He raced south, toward the tower. A reaver vaulted from the castle wall, seeking to crush him. Borenson rolled away from the attack, then jumped up and slew the reaver. A mage on the castle wall cast a horrific spell, and Borenson waded through a red cloud, holding his breath while his eyes burned so badly he thought they would boil from their sockets.

Two more young reavers dropped from the castle wall, while a third climbed over the rampart, ignoring the flames.

There is a difference between bravery and foolishness, Borenson knew. He was cut off from Myrrima. He dove through the window of the nearest merchant's shop and raced through a back room while a reaver gave chase. The reaver bulled into the shop's wall, and the building collapsed as Borenson exited out back, into a narrow alley called Bleak Street.

The street was too narrow for an adult reaver to negotiate easily, but a juvenile came rushing toward him.

He ran to the nearest door, found it bolted. Borenson lowered his shoulder and hit the door. It shattered, and he tumbled in.

He stood for an instant, wondering what to do. The reavers would come after him any second. He bounded across the room, heading for a back door.

He felt a wrenching in his gut, as if something vital had torn away, and realized that one of his Dedicates had died.

It could mean only one thing: Reavers hunted uphill where his Dedicates hid in the tombs beneath Paldane's Palace.

Deep in the Underworld, Iome stabbed with her javelin, and another reaver died, her fifth kill.

Across the black chamber, Gaborn yelped.

She looked up.

"*Gasht!*" A curse boiled from the One True Master's staff. Gaborn flung himself away, a shadow in the darkness, moving so fast that for a moment he seemed to vanish.

The One True Master became mindful of her. The reaver lord lurched back from Gaborn and scrambled to cut off Iome's advance. Tendrils of darkness, like a wispy fog, flowed out from the monster's feet, surging toward Iome.

Gaborn howled like an animal, leaping to attack. He raced to the One True Master, moving so fast that Iome could not track him as he stabbed her in the thorax.

The creature whirled to face him, cracking her whip. For a moment she blurred, and the surging fog halted in its progress.

Iome kept racing toward a knot of reavers, where a strong light burned, bounding over Dedicates both living and dead.

"*Gasht!*" a spell hurtled from the monster's staff, a dark cloud of destruction.

"Jump!" Gaborn shouted.

Iome sprang thirty feet in the air, somersaulting as she did. A funnel of destruction, glittering like ash, touched the ground where she had stood, blasting several reavers to oblivion, smiting the floor so that flakes of stone and dust flew up beneath her.

The wind was a tumult as she fell.

Iome came down into the mess. Her left ankle twisted violently, and she cried out in pain. She crawled to her knees and used her reaver dart as a staff to hobble into the midst of the reavers. One struck out at her, and she dodged its blow.

Their bodies formed an almost solid wall. They moved so slowly that they almost seemed to be monoliths. Iome passed beneath their shadows as if into a dark wooded dell. For a moment she was reminded of the glade amidst the Seven Standing Stones of Heredon, where Binnesman had raised his wylde.

But amid these monoliths, there was no vast reservoir of Earth Power, nothing so grand and glorious.

Sir Borenson gripped his warhammer in bloody hands and stood panting in some poor merchant's hovel. Outside, reavers raged through Carris, knocking down buildings, digging through rubble. The death screams rose, a continu-. ous wail of fear and pain all across the island.

Smoke filled the air as the whole district went up in flames.

And he could do nothing to stop it. In the past few moments, his Dedicates had all been slain, stripped from him.

Without his endowments of brawn, his armor weighed like an anvil about his shoulders, and his long-handled hammer proved so unwieldy that he could hardly swing it.

Without stamina, he felt sick near to death. The exertions of the past few days had taken their toll—his ride to Inkarra and back, the torture he had endured at the hand of King Criomethes. His legs felt so worn that they threatened to collapse beneath him.

He wanted to work up some strength, to go across the street and hunt for Myrrima, the reavers be damned. If she was alive still, perhaps he could help her. And if she had died, then he had no reason to live out the day.

Strength is an illusion, he thought in his torment.

Twice now in his life, Dedicates had been torn from him, dozens of good men and women killed in an effort to prove him weak.

Screaming a war cry, he grabbed his weapon and burst out into the night.

Flames licked the sky in every direction, and smoke reflected the light in such a way that it seemed that the heavens had taken fire. It was brighter than dawn.

Almost directly overhead, Borenson saw a great balloon hundreds of feet above, nearly lost in smoke, a balloon shaped like a graak in flight. It floated in eerie silence.

At the far north of the island, trumpets blared wildly, calling once again for the folk of Carris to retreat.

A sudden roar shook the earth, like rising thunder. The earth began to quiver beneath his feet. Buildings trembled as if a giant jarred their foundations.

A reaver barreled down the street at the end of the alley, a juvenile blade-bearer, with grotesquely long legs and a small head.

It skidded to a halt and whirled, its philia writhing as it spotted Borenson. It opened its maw and charged.

"Death!" Borenson roared as he raised his hammer and rushed to meet it.

Raj Ahten looked down on Carris from a far hill.

The city was an inferno. Reavers thundered everywhere, slamming into homes like battering rams, raking through the rubble to pull out anyone who might still be alive. On the north end of the island, horns desperately blew a call for retreat while people climbed the castle walls and flung themselves into Lake Donnestgree.

But they couldn't climb the ladders and tower steps fast enough to escape, and so they crowded the walls in a seething mass, trampling one another in their terror. Some tried to fight back as the reavers advanced, shooting with their puny bows or raising their weapons, but the reavers waded into them. As well might hens try to fight when the hollow wolf is in the pens.

The speed at which the reavers overwhelmed Carris astonished him. Powerful lords had protected the gates, but the young reavers merely sprang over them or slammed into them, grinding them to ruin.

Men were no match for such monsters.

Above the city, Raj Ahten's spy balloon wafted on hot thermals. He could hear the whispering thoughts of his flameweavers, exulting. Sweet-smelling smoke roiled upward in great clouds, enticing them to battle. Their gondolas were loaded with arcane powders made of sulfur, potash, and herbs, brought from the south of Indhopal just for this night. "Give us the signal," their thoughts whispered, "and we will drop our load."

"Patience," he whispered in return. The balloon had been drifting toward the reavers' fell mage as she squatted in the midst of a great rune, her Seal of Desolation.

As the wind carried the balloon toward the seal, he whispered, letting the Power of Fire carry his words to his flameweavers. "Now let the heavens blaze!"

The flameweavers rejoiced, crying in tongues of flame, "Long live Scathain, Lord of Ash!"

Three miles north of Carris stood the Barren's Wall, a rampart that rose chest high and spanned from Lake Donnestgree in the east to the Alcair Mountains some dozen miles to the west.

King Anders's troops came up behind it, riding hard in the darkness, only to find Queen Rialla Lowicker's army, more than a hundred thousand strong, huddled in its lee. Ballistas by the hundreds were ranged higher on the hill, to help hold back any charge by the reavers, while archers and footmen manned the wall. Lowicker's intent seemed obvious: she would hold the wall if the reavers sought to range north.

Beyond the wall, Carris flamed. Horns blared on the castle walls as the folk of Carris called for help, yet the screams of the dying overwhelmed the horns.

Reavers by the hundreds could be seen racing north along the wall-walks, dispatching any guardsman who dared try to withstand them.

At the foot of the city a vast reaver horde blackened the land. Howlers trumpeted in their midst, and the earth seemed to groan beneath their feet while clouds of gree whirled above the throng.

Near the great worm mound, a fell mage squatted, covered with glowing runes. She wielded a staff that gleamed as white as lightning. A rune was taking shape beneath her, a malevolent thing that gathered mists and sent them swirling about like a tornado.

"By the Powers!" King Anders swore when he saw the mess.

There was nothing to save at Carris, it seemed.

Even if we charge the city now, Erin thought, the reavers will wipe out its people before we get there.

Erin's horse stamped nervously, and she leaned forward. Many a brave knight clutched his lance, as if to race into battle at any moment.

The lords at the front of the column stared hard at Anders, to see what he would do. He claimed to be an Earth King. Would he call a world worm, as Gaborn had done?

Erin shouted, "Your Highness, sound the charge!"

But Anders raised his right hand in warning, and said in a bereaved tone, "I cannot. The Earth warns against it. Those in the city are Gaborn's Chosen, and they must die for his sins."

"What?" Celinor shouted in horror.

Anders shook his head sadly. "I am to be the new Earth King. He is the old. But I cannot be crowned until the old is swept away." He peered forward as if he could see through the walls of Carris.

What kind of man is he? Erin wondered. Gaborn could never have sat idle while folk were in danger.

Erin's head spun. She was dazed with fatigue. More than that, she reeled from the shock.

She felt as if she were in a dream, or at least half in a dream. She wanted to call out to the owl of the netherworld for help, to touch his mind with a sending.

A thought struck her.

The owl had warned that Asgaroth could bend his will and read the minds of others. Could she reach Asgaroth with a sending?

Even as the thought struck, Erin silently screamed the name, "Asgaroth!"

King Anders sat on his horse just ahead of Erin, slouched wearily in his saddle, his long gray hair flowing out behind a kingly war helm.

In answer to her silent call, he whirled as if she had slapped him. His mouth parted in surprise, and he glared at her.

The mask of kindliness fell from his face.

The One True Master raced toward Iome, its feet a blur.

"Noooooo!" Gaborn screamed, veering to block the monster's path.

He raced forward, weapon in hand.

For an instant, Iome watched them both, frozen in pain. Gaborn bounded toward a creature part light, part shadow. The One True Master blurred, her whip snapping like fire. Gaborn cried out, stumbled, and ducked beneath the lash.

Iome charged toward a Dedicate, a huge reaver that lay as if asleep. She cocked her arm back, preparing to stab with all her might.

The iron javelin ripped from her hand as a reaver swatted at her, missing by inches.

Gaborn shouted, "Iome, flee!"

The room shuddered. The ground rolled beneath Iome's feet, and stones rained down from the roof as another temblor struck.

"Gasht!" a spell hissed from the monster's onyx staff. Gaborn took two steps forward and sprang high in the air as a dark green cloud flowed forward. He hurled his javelin.

The monster twisted to her side. The javelin glanced off her skull. Gaborn was still flying toward the beast, and hit it with a sickly thud, then fell away like a broken doll.

"No!" Iome cried.

The One True Master regarded Gaborn for a second, dismissed him, and turned toward Iome.

In her mind, Iome heard Gaborn's last words, as if he shouted them anew. "Iome, flee!"

The reavers circled Iome all around, their features twisted and cruel. She frantically peered toward the far corners of the room. Even with a dozen endowments of sight, she couldn't see how to escape.

There was no pain where Gaborn went. He'd smacked into the bony head-plates of the monster. Then nothing.

He woke in a realm as light as day. All about him were fields, brown from the farmer's plow, the rich soil spilling from the ground. Hills rose in gentle humps in the distance, with oak trees sprawling on their sides. There was no wind, no sun, only a sourceless light that shone above. Ravens cawed and wheeled overhead, their raucous cries full of malice.

Tender shoots shot from the ground all about him, as if the soil could not hold the abundance of life.

The ravens dove and tore at them, drawing the seeds from the soil, ripping the pale roots.

A dozen yards away, a man-shaped creature slumped upon a large stone, his back toward Gaborn. He wore a shapeless robe of gray, and gray hair spilled down his back. But where he should have had skin, Gaborn saw only sand and pebbles.

The Earth Spirit sat before him. "I am but fruit to the crows of fortune," he muttered. "They hover on jeering wings. My stones cannot fell them. . . ."

Gaborn went to the creature, rested a hand upon its shoulder. It turned to face him.

The Earth Spirit wore the face of Raj Ahten, but no eyes peered from its head, only empty sockets.

The Earth looked at Gaborn helplessly, threw up its hands. "The ravens. The ravens feed. . . ."

Gaborn saw the Earth's torment.

"Why do you wear the face of an enemy still?" Gaborn asked. "We should be friends."

The Earth took on a pained expression. "You turned from me."

"No," Gaborn said, "only once, in a moment of weakness. But never again will I turn from you. All that I am or ever hope to be, I give to you."

The pebbly face of the Earth Spirit began to shift. It took on a new form. Gaborn's father appeared for a moment, and then his face became young. Gaborn thought that the Earth might be showing him his own face, or the face of his father as a child, but then realized that it had revealed the face of Gaborn's son. The pebbles and grains of sand flowed once more, and Iome was smiling up at him.

Gaborn felt something within him ease, and saw that he was bleeding from a wound to his chest, but instead of blood, light flowed out. He let it flow. All around him, the crows began to caw and flap into the air, wings exploding into the sky.

ଊ 39 ଓ

A TREE BENEATH THE SHADOWS

No tree or plant can grow in daylight alone. Given only light, a seed will not germinate, roots will not take hold. It takes a balance of sunlight and shadow. Men, too, grow their deepest roots in the darkness.

—Erden Geboren

Gaborn woke and scrambled to his feet, heart hammering. His ribs felt like broken twigs. The great reaver was chasing Iome, scrabbling on powerful legs as it scrambled over a knot of its precious Dedicates, crushing them.

The effect of its curses putrefied flesh and set wounds to festering. Now dozens of reavers nearby rasped loudly as they sought to breathe. But with the apparent slowing of time, the sound came as an ominous drone.

Iome ran from the monster. Its ghostly runes still glowed, but darkness seemed to flow beneath its feet, obscuring the view. Gaborn wiped tears from his burning eyes.

Iome ducked between two reavers that seemed to move at a crawl, seeking to use them as cover. But Gaborn knew that she couldn't hide for long. The reaver queen raced toward Iome at blinding speed.

Gaborn could feel death approaching her.

Gaborn reached down, picked up Erden Geboren's ancient reaver dart.

The One True Master waded over its own Dedicates, grinding a pair of them beneath her.

"Strike!" the Earth warned.

Gaborn shouted a battle cry and lunged forward, bounding twenty yards to a stride. The reavers around him were dark monoliths, almost motionless.

He darted between the legs of a large Dedicate and plunged his spear into the One True Master's hind knee.

The leg buckled. She whirled toward Gaborn, and he jumped backward, throwing himself high in the air and somersaulting as her whip snapped beneath him.

Runes simmered on the face of the One True Master. The triad of bony plates on her head was nearly covered with ghostly blue fire. Despite all of the Dedicates that Gaborn had killed, few dark splotches appeared at all.

Gaborn landed on a Dedicate, then sprang backward again and again, drawing the One True Master away from Iome.

The monster approached, rasping. Wisps of darkness curled about Gaborn's ankles. His thoughts became confused. He struggled to remain standing.

"Cut the child from your lover's womb," a voice whispered cruelly in his mind, "for it is tainted with evil."

A vision passed before Gaborn's eyes, in which he held the child from Iome's womb, a vile monstrosity. He clutched its scrawny neck, peering at it, wondering how it could be so hideous, and the thing twisted in his hands. He saw now that it had four legs and two arms, that it was eyeless, and where its face should have been, bony head plates appeared while philia dangled like pink worms from its jaw.

Gaborn hurled the thing to the ground.

It peered up at him and made a mewling sound.

"Something wicked grows within her," the One True Master whispered. "Cut it out. Save your people."

Gaborn felt a horrible compulsion. He had a knife in his boot. It would be easy to reach down, slip the knife from its sheath, plunge the blade into Iome's womb.

"You could rid the world of evil," the voice whispered. "Isn't that what you want?"

No! he told himself. It's a child, not an evil. But a greater will seemed to seize him, and he heard a voice in his head whisper, "Yea, master, I do thy bidding."

The One True Master lunged toward him, and Gaborn fell to his knees. He was lost in vision, sinking into a maelstrom of darkness that swirled all about.

"Master!" he called. And simultaneously, the One True Master and the Earth spoke at once, "Yes, my servant."

"No," Gaborn said to the One True Master. "I am not your servant."

A strange light suddenly blazed in his mind. The horrid vision fled, and Gaborn found himself shaken, standing in the reavers' Dedicates' Keep. In his right hand he clutched his gore-covered reaver dart.

A light glowed at the far end of the cavern.

A strange animal cry came from the throat of the tunnel, and the One True Master whirled away from Gaborn.

Binnesman's wylde stood there.

"Now," the Earth whispered, "summon the Glories."

The green woman raised her left hand in the air, forming runes swiftly. She spoke as if in a trance, her eyes vacant of thought, void of emotion. "The time has come, Old One, to leave your body behind. The lords of the nether-world demand it."

The One True Master hissed in alarm, retreated from Gaborn. Her massive head swiveled left and right, as she sought to track both Gaborn and the wylde. Her philia waved frantically as she scented for danger.

The green woman howled and leapt a dozen feet at a stride, her face contorted in fury. Above her, white lights appeared, small at first, and dim, as if seen from a great distance. But they grew in brightness and size swiftly as they neared. Suddenly, the Glories were there, dozens of them, white ghostly shapes with wings of light.

The green woman raised her hand, and balls of lightning issued from it, went scattering through the air like flower petals tossed into the wind. The light snaked through the air, sizzling and crackling, and the whole room suddenly smelled as if a storm began to rage.

The reaver Dedicates hissed in despair and lurched backward, seeking to escape. Many threw their paws over their heads and dropped to the ground.

Gaborn watched calmly.

The green woman has come to kill the One True Master, Gaborn realized, and he thought, But I won't give her the honor!

In that instant, the reaver queen swung her muzzle toward him, exposing her sweet triangle. On a monster this huge, the soft spot above her brain was a good eighteen inches across. She stood less than forty yards away.

Gaborn rushed from between two reavers and hurled his dart with all his might. Pain wracked his shoulder from strained tendons. The iron pole became a black blur. There was a *thwack* as it struck reaver flesh, and Gaborn stood for half a second, gazing in triumph.

The reaver dart struck, and then went ricocheting off the monster's bony head plate. Purple blood pumped from the grazed wound. Yet the One True Master's head still swiveled about.

The monster held her black staff and lunged as if to strike Gaborn, then glanced back, as if deciding that the wylde presented a greater danger.

The green woman raced forward as the monster pounced. For half a second, Gaborn was not sure if the green woman would strike before the monster crushed her.

But the wylde raised up both hands, as if to embrace the falling beast. Her arms and fingers lengthened, as though they were branches and twigs, growing thick over the years.

The two met, as if in an embrace, and the wylde howled one last time, a howl of triumph and release. In that instant, Gaborn saw her as she had been at the Seven Standing Stones when Binnesman had summoned her—a collection of twigs and stones and roots and dust.

And then she caught the One True Master.

There was a rumbling, and a violent rending, and roots broke into the rock and a thick trunk formed and began to spiral upward. The One True Master fell onto the wylde and let out a cruel hiss. She struggled violently, like a tarantula caught in the grasp of a scorpion, her huge legs scrabbling and tearing.

But a tree grew beneath her now, a tree with a trunk thicker than oak, and branches that pierced her and grew up through her body. The sinuous limbs shot through armored breastplates, sent tendrils and twigs growing through her skull and shoulders.

In an instant, a vast tree took form, its green branches as alive as snakes. It held the monster and crushed her and pierced her all at once.

The One True Master gaped and hissed. She craned her head back, as if suffering indescribable agony. Purple gore coursed from her wounds.

The monster swung its head left and right, trying to dislodge itself.

But the wylde held it, made it one with the Earth.

Within seconds the ghostly runes that simmered across the One True Master's body winked out, like candles extinguished by a breeze.

Gaborn dropped to the ground, panting. You cannot kill a locus, he suspected. Its evil would only pass on to another.

Help me, he cried in his heart, seeking aid from the Glories.

There had been a darkness about the creature, a shadow that followed as it walked. Gaborn saw that specter now. It surged upward, like a sooty cloud, or a winged shadow. It hovered above the dead reaver, above the living tree.

And the Glories came. Distant lights seemed to break through the rock above, swirling down from the netherworld. They were faint at first, as if seen miles and miles away. But in a matter of seconds they were revealed.

They swooped like swallows upon wings of light, creatures at once beautiful and impossibly cruel. Larger than men they were, and though they had arms and legs, Gaborn thought they looked nothing like men. Their heads hinted at the ravenous faces of jackals, with sharp fangs and large eyes. Whether they were covered in hair or feathers, Gaborn could not tell. For to look at them was to invite death.

Gaborn threw up his hands, squinting.

The Glories circled the mist of darkness, like starlings mobbing a crow, driving it around and around and upward, spiraling through the air.

As Gaborn gazed up, it seemed that a conduit opened between worlds, and for just an instant he saw the skies of the Netherworld—stars so fierce that they made his heart jump, in a heaven so vast that it seemed forbidding.

The Glories pursued their prey upward through those heavens, lights as bright as the stars chasing a strange, amorphous shadow, spiraling up as if all of them were caught in a cyclone.

And then the earth closed above them, and the Glories and the locus all were gone, and Gaborn stood among the dead reaver Dedicates with Iome.

Averan faced the Great Seals that the One True Master had formed, and peered through the shadows toward the roof. She pointed her staff and imagined the runes of stone-breaking that would cause the ceiling to collapse.

The ground buckled and swayed beneath her. Pebbles and soot dribbled down.

And as if in her ear, she heard Binnesman's voice. "The Earth is in pain. Heal it. End the Earth's suffering."

An image came to mind from her dreams. Runes appeared, two vast wheels to join with those that lay before her.

Averan gazed at three great runes, each patterned after the Seals of Creation that had governed the One True World. The runes themselves were not evil. They were tools. And Averan, if she dared, could bend them to her purpose. She could heal the Earth, remake it in the image of the One True World that had been mankind's first home.

Do I dare? she wondered, trembling.

The ground heaved as another quake shook, causing the room to sway.

Averan stretched forth her staff and stared into the rocky floor, tried to recall from her dreams the great Rune of Life.

She began to shape the stone.

There was a ridge like a hook, where eagles had soared. As she imagined it, the ridge slowly rose from the ground. There were three knobby hills where rabbits had run, and the hills buckled up from the rock. Here was a valley where she had seen elephants sprout from the soil, waving their trunks to the sky, and a rift appeared.

Averan raised and lowered the stone in each place, using her gifts to conform it to her will.

Erin Connal sat upon her horse, frozen in astonishment. King Anders glared at her maliciously. But in an instant his expression changed to one of alarm.

"No!" he cried, whirling to peer at the battlefield.

A pale light shone above it, as if the moon suddenly peeked out from a cloud.

An unreasonable hope suddenly filled Erin.

She took no time to wonder what caused Anders such dismay, or to wonder at the light. She spurred her horse forward, throwing down her lance, for she was too close to use it in battle. She pulled out her half sword, and fell upon Anders before he had time to react.

She plunged the blade into his side, angled it up into his chest. She watched his skeletal face.

"Mother," he cried, peering toward the battlefield. Then he turned slowly to look at Erin.

What she saw in his eyes terrified her, for there was no dismay, no fear—only cunning.

King Anders gripped the hilt of her sword with his right hand, so that she could cut no deeper, and then grabbed her shoulder with his left hand.

He fell forward, so that for half a minute he leaned into her, his mouth to her ear.

She thought he would speak, and then he would die, but instead he only uttered a strangled laugh.

Cries of dismay rose all around as men witnessed Erin's attack. Celinor shouted, "Grab her! Hold her!"

Lords instantly surrounded her. Erin spurred her horse, tried to bolt away, but she was boxed in.

Celinor flung himself from his horse, crying, "Father! Father!" while Anders slumped in Erin's arms and fell to the ground, clutching the blade that still lodged in his gut.

Rough hands seized Erin, dragging her to the ground beside him. Three stout warriors threw themselves atop her. A fat man with a red beard began shouting, "A rope! A rope! Let's hang the bitch!"

Weakly, King Anders raised a hand to Celinor's face. "No!" he cried. "Save the poor mad creature. She carries your child, a—a queen who will rule the world. Cage her. Promise. . . . to cage her—until the child comes."

Anders's head dropped to the side a little, and he peered at Erin in pain. A physic rushed into the knot and began pushing Celinor aside, preparing to bandage the wound.

Celinor whirled and glared at Erin, a snarl of rage marring his face. "Tie her!"

The earth was shaking. Erin felt it beneath her, shuddering as if it would break.

A far-seer cried. "Ships! Ships on the lake! The warlords of Internook are bringing longboats upriver."

The men that held Erin finished tying her arms behind her back. They climbed off her, and stood on the hill peering down at the city. One man jerked the rope, pulling Erin to her feet, while the physic applied a healing balm to the king's wound.

Erin pulled against her knots, trying to break free, but her captors had tied her in some cunning manner so that the more she struggled, the more tightly her bonds cut into her wrists.

To the east, roaring arose in the wilderness, the battle cries of frowth giants. It was their feet that caused the ground to rumble.

"Giants, thousands of them!" someone shouted. "They're coming out of the hills." Erin peered toward the source of the noise, but could see nothing for a moment. Then they rushed over the brow of a hill, huge staves in hand, fur glowing red as it reflected the light of distant fires. They trotted toward the reaver hordes, taking twenty feet to a stride.

Above Carris, Raj Ahten's spy balloon had been floating like a graak on silent wings. Suddenly, beneath the balloon, light flashed, and there was a tremendous explosion. A great mushroom cloud of fire and smoke blossomed above the battlefield, filling the scene with light.

The ball of fire rose directly above the Seal of Desolation, where the reavers' fell mage had been working. Some reavers seemed stunned, but Erin could see the monstrous fell mage along with dozens of other mages standing fast among the flames.

The reavers' far-seers hissed and looked skyward, and Erin could see the lines of communication race through the crowd as each reaver in turn recognized the threat from above, and then raised its hind end and hissed warning scents to its neighbors.

The fell mage whirled and aimed her staff skyward, sending a dark bolt to blast into the air. It ripped through the fabric of the balloon, and the balloon plummeted into the reaver horde.

Reavers lunged to rip the wizards apart.

An instant later, the flameweavers died. Three creatures of fire rose up, man-shaped elementals of white-hot fury, each sixty feet tall.

They surged into the reavers, touching one and then another, so that they boiled and burst into flames.

One elemental raised its hand. With a thought, it sent its power quivering through Carris.

Torches suddenly flared, escaping their bounds. Fires already raging through merchant hovels exploded with new intensity. Fire raced like lightning along beams and up poles.

The city erupted into a blaze, and as it did, the cries of tens of thousands of city folk joined the roar of the inferno.

Pillars of smoke mushroomed upward, glowing as red as coals. Indeed, even the attacking reavers balked, and began backing from the elementals, which had now begun to dissolve, losing their human form as they became simple beasts of malevolent flame.

Erin stared in wonder. The fiery elementals waded through the horde like warlords among a pack of dogs. The flameweavers sent lines of fire racing into the midst of the reavers, and infernos sprang up in the hills.

To the south and west, warhorns suddenly blared, the deep-voiced ram's horns used by the lords of Indhopal.

Raj Ahten's men charged into the fray.

Lowicker's daughter shouted commands to her troops, downhill just below. Her own silver warhorns trumpeted a high note, as if to answer Raj Ahten's call. Her knights on their chargers leapt the Barren's Wall and raced toward the reavers like a gale. Lowicker's archers and footmen roared their battle cries and raced to catch up.

"Sound the charge!" Anders called weakly to his son. His trumpeter sounded the warhorn, and Anders's lords leapt on their horses.

Many would have urged their mounts into battle instantly, eager to obey what might well be their lord's dying wish. But Celinor knelt, holding his father up to witness the contest, while a pair of lords stood guard over him.

"Go, now!" King Anders told his son feebly. "This is our day, your hour of triumph. Let the Earth King's son make a name for himself in battle."

Celinor's troops were all mounted. Celinor leaned close, squeezing his father's right hand in an effort to comfort him. A physic leaned close and sniffed the king's wound.

"He'll be all right," the physic said. "The blade nicked his liver, I think, but missed the heart and lungs. With his endowments, he'll heal in a week."

"Very well," Celinor said. He rose to his feet and vaulted onto his horse. He glanced down at the guards that held Erin and warned, "Kill her if she tries to escape."

ଐ 40 ଓ

EARTH RISING

*History affirms that the wounds of a nation can never be healed by the sword.
Vengeance may be had in battle, justice may be won, freedom restored, but
with every stroke of the blade, we carve for ourselves bright new scars.*

*Therefore, bestow your greatest honors not upon those who make war
but upon those who heal.*

—attributed to Daylan of the Black Hammer

Averan finished roughing out the Seal of Creation, and began the second
rune she'd envisioned in her dreams.

In the pool in the far corner of the chamber, water bubbled and boiled.
She raised her staff and caused geometrical shapes to chase across its face—
circles and triangles, and bizarre arcs—as if great fish sped just beneath the
surface, dorsal fins cutting waves.

Sweat poured from Averan's brow, and her lips grew parched, but she paid
no mind. She was so deep in the act of creation that nothing else mattered.

Soon the Seal of the Deep began to glimmer in the pool. Waves stood
up, as if frozen in time or sculpted in ice.

Averan studied her work. To look upon the runes filled her with joy. It
was a great work, she knew, a slow magic, such as Binnesman had attempted
when he sought to heal the plagues at Carris. Her labor would not bear full
fruit for many centuries.

Yet she felt potency in the runes. Vigor would come to the Earth, life and
health and mending. The grass would grow greener and taller than anyone
had ever seen. Children born on this new day would be fairer and wiser than

men of old. Fresh colors would be added to the rainbow, and wildflowers would sprout in the desert.

It conformed well to her memory. It was not perfect yet, but she could feel rightness in it, and she would have years to tinker and bend it into shape.

Only one thing remained for Averan there in the heart of the Underworld, to draw a circle and encompass the five Master Seals, make them one.

Averan raised her staff, felt deep in the Earth. She could sense the fault lines and cracks in the stones, the seams and blockages. To shape the stone required almost nothing, a simple release of the energy.

She let it flow upward.

Soil began to rise, bursting up as if a crust of bread had cracked. Then it raced along, leaving a trail within its wake. The circle began to form.

Suddenly she sensed a presence at the mouth of the tunnel, smelled the death cry of a reaver, and whirled.

Gaborn strode toward her, the light of his opal pin blazing like a meteor. Over his shoulders, like a pair of huge eels, he'd slung a pair of reaver philia, taken from the One True Master.

It was her garlicky death cry that Averan had heard.

Gaborn looked on in awe as he peered at the seals, feeling their potency. He spoke slowly so that she would understand. "What are you doing?"

"I'm fixing it," Averan said. "I'm healing the Earth."

"I feel the change coming," Gaborn replied. "Yours is a great work, and I fear to hinder you. But I need your help. The battle goes ill at Carris, and only I can hope to change the tide of it."

"How can I help?" Averan asked.

"We're almost directly below the city. I need you to open a path for me."

"I'm not sure that I can," Averan said.

"You can," Gaborn told her with certainty.

Averan was growing accustomed to Gaborn's uncanny Earth sense. If he told her that she could help, then she believed that he was right.

Averan took a last glance at the seals. She felt exhausted, too tired to do more now. Though sweat soaked her clothes, she took a moment to draw strength from the ground so that she could secure the chamber. With her staff, she drew a rune upon the wall. As she did, the stone flowed together slowly, like boiling magma, until the opening closed.

"Here let the seals be hidden," Averan whispered, "unaltered and unmarred by the hand of the enemy."

"Come," Gaborn said. "I left Iome and the prisoners behind."

He fled the chamber, striding down the tunnel. She rushed to keep up for nearly a mile. As they neared the Lair of Bones she heard shouting in a side corridor.

"Milady, over here!" someone cried. "I've found their nesting grounds."

"Break the eggs," Sergeant Barris commanded. "Break them all."

Averan's heart hammered. Iome and the prisoners had found the hatching chamber. The clutch of eggs was precious.

Averan followed Gaborn round a bend in the tunnel, found Sergeant Barris, Iome, and the other men and women from the reavers' prison peering into the egg chamber. Iome stood using a reaver dart as a crutch, a bandage wrapped around her ankle. Iome held her opal crown aloft to reveal leathery gray eggs upon the steaming ground. They lay wrapped in nests of silk spun by cave spiders, each nest holding a cluster of twenty or thirty eggs.

"Stop!" Averan cried.

Barris turned first. Anger blazed in his eyes. "Why?"

"They're the last of the reaver eggs. The One True Master made war on other hives for years. Each time she took control of a hive, she destroyed the eggs of her enemies. These might be the only reaver eggs left in the world!"

"Good," Barris said. "Then we can kill every last one of the damned monsters."

There comes a moment in the life of every Earth Warden when she discovers the purpose of her existence. Binnesman had told Averan that when he realized that it was his lot to protect mankind, the knowledge had flowed into him with a purity and power that could not be denied.

Averan felt that now.

For this purpose I was born, she thought, and empowered by my master. For this reason I learned to commune with reavers and have been granted dominion over the deep places of the world.

"I forbid it!" she shouted. "I serve the Earth, and I will do my master's will."

Averan pointed her staff above the door to the egg chamber, and formed a rune there. She had no time to draw power from the Earth at her ease, and instead had to rely upon her own meager reserves.

The stone cracked instantly, and a circle appeared on its surface. Within the circle a rune burst forth. The whole wall warped and flowed together, barring entry.

Averan felt so spent from the hasty spell that she nearly swooned. She leaned precariously on her staff, peering at Barris, Iome, and Gaborn, wondering if they would hate her, or fight her.

These people had all suffered horribly at the reavers' hands. The monsters had stripped everything from them—homes, health, and families. If any had cause to hate the reavers, these did.

"The Earth loves all life equally," Averan whispered. "It loves the snake no less than the field mouse, the eagle no less than the dove, the reaver no less than you."

Barris growled angrily in his throat, as if he would spring. But Gaborn grabbed his arm, holding him back.

Iome merely peered at Averan, her lips parted in surprise. "You have grown, little one," she said. "You have grown great indeed." Tears glistened in Iome's eyes, as if she gazed upon someone who was now dead to her. It nearly broke Averan's heart.

"Oh, Iome," Averan said in a small voice. "It's only me. I'm still the same."

But Iome shook her head sadly. "No, you're not. You're an Earth Warden now. Look at your robe."

Averan looked down and saw a great change. Her wizard's robe had been growing for days. It was as if tiny seeds had taken sprout in her old coat, and the new roots had been growing among the fibers. But in the last moment or two, their color had turned a vibrant green.

All trace of her old robe was now hidden under the twined embrace of the rootlets.

I am an Earth Warden, she thought, called to serve the reavers. And she understood why Iome had shed a tear.

This is my home now. Perhaps in some far future, I might visit the surface of the world and gaze upon the fields of wild grass, or walk under the stars, but not soon. Not often.

Averan shook her head. "Get ready to go," she told Iome, Gaborn, and the prisoners. By habit, she thought of what she would do if she were preparing for a journey by graak. "Go pack your things."

Barris nodded toward his ragged people. "We have nothing to pack."

"We're ready," Gaborn said.

Averan raised her staff, considered what to do. Hers were the powers of the deep Earth, so she reached out with her mind, as if summoning an animal, and could sense the rocks and boulders all around her.

Gaborn was right. She felt a shaft overhead, not more than a few thousand feet. The world worm had cleared the way a week ago, when Gaborn had summoned it to Carris.

Averan reached out with her senses, felt the stresses in the rock all around her, the tiny cracks and fault lines. With all of the vast tonnage of stone above, it would take a great deal of energy to open a crack and floor beneath them.

It would take more Earth Power than Averan could ever hope to have. To even think about it pained her mind.

"I can't," Averan said plaintively.

"Hold up your staff," Gaborn told her.

She raised it slightly, felt the Earth Power within it. No. She was too tired even to try.

Gaborn suddenly reached out and grabbed the black staff of poisonwood.

At his touch, the wood seemed almost to burst into flame. Earth Power surged through it, as warm as the breath of a newborn babe, as sure as stone.

Averan looked into Gaborn's weary eyes with renewed awe. Nothing in his manner suggested that he had such reservoirs.

"Thank you," was all she managed to say.

She knelt and cast a spell, by drawing a rune on the ground, and the earth began to tremble.

Sir Borenson clutched his warhammer and dove for cover in a wrecked wine merchant's shop. Reavers had collapsed the roof, so that it stood even with the front windows. Flames sizzled along every beam. He dropped to the floor on his hands and knees, just below the sill, while reavers raced into the city unimpeded. Hundreds of them flashed past his hiding spot.

His heart hammered. Reaver gore covered his hands and face. Fierce heat battered him from fires on every side. Black ash and cinders swirled around like falling snow. Borenson spotted a bottle of wine lying unbroken on the floor, pulled its cork, and relieved his thirst.

In the fields north and west of Carris, he could hear Raj Ahten's and Lowicker's horns blowing the charge. Men screamed wildly.

The reavers were in for a bloody row by the sound of it. But here in Carris, the city was becoming ominously quiet.

How many have died? Borenson wondered.

He wanted to get a view of the battle. He only needed a little height to see over the city walls. A set of stairs in the shop led up to what had once been a second-floor apartment. Now the stairs conveniently opened to the sky, and only a few flames licked their base.

Borenson crawled through rubble—stones and splintered boards and broken wattle—making his way to the stairs. He gripped his battle-ax and climbed to the top. He heard the distant *thwonk, thwonk, thwonk* of ballistas.

Near the shores of Lake Donnestgree, longboats plied the waters, thousands of them. One could hardly see the lake for all of the masts. The warlords of Internook, in their horned helms, fired a hail of ballista bolts from longboats, lancing into reavers that waded along the shore.

To his north, Lowicker's knights surged into the reavers' lines, horses whinnying as riders drove lances home.

To the northwest, the frowth giants waded among the reavers, their huge iron-bound staves rising and crashing down. The reavers had no choice but to fight.

And fight they did. A wall of reavers surged north toward the Barren's Wall, and west toward Raj Ahten, even as their fell mage and her companions raised their staves and sent bolts of ice whirling into the elementals.

The reavers were boxed in, Borenson realized.

He looked for a sign of Myrrima. Below him, reavers thundered down the road unimpeded. The north tower, where Myrrima had been, lay in ruin. The reavers were climbing over it, cracking its beams, knocking down the ramparts. A tower that had stood sixty feet was now crushed down to thirty. Part of it had spilled outward into the lake.

He peered into the shadows at its base, hoping for some sign of Myrrima, but he could see nothing.

If she had been on the third floor when the reavers attacked, the chance that she still lived was slim.

"Myrrima?" he called hopefully, but heard no answer. There was no movement there at the base of the rubble, except for one young reaver that seemed to be digging, like some monstrous beagle, digging for rats in their burrow.

"Attack!" Raj Ahten bellowed above the sounds of battle. His voice, amplified by reason of thousands of endowments, seemed to come from everywhere and nowhere, and so compelling was it that against all reason, Borenson felt constrained to leap from the roof onto the nearest reaver.

Heart hammering, he ducked, trying to keep good stone between him and the reavers below, lest they see him.

"Into battle now," Raj Ahten shouted. "Let your rage light the way. Teach them to fear us for another thousand years."

The words were like a spell that ignited Borenson's rage. A nervous chuckle sprang unbidden from his throat, and against all reason he longed to throw himself into battle.

Raj Ahten's command seemed to compel every man within its range. To the west, Raj Ahten's men screamed like berserkers as they bore down on the reavers. The armies collided in a boiling mass. Horses screamed and died. Men disappeared in a spray of gore as reavers clubbed them with blades and hammers. Reavers reared up, lances buried in their faces.

Reavers and men hurled themselves into battle, dying by the score with no sign of any clear winner.

To the north, Rialla Lowicker urged her cavalry downhill beneath skies a brighter red than any dawn. The light of elemental flameweavers reflected from clouds of smoke. Her men drove into the ranks of the reavers, and great was the slaughter on both sides.

To the east, the warlords of Internook blew their horns and fired ballista bolts into the reavers with renewed fury. The reavers continued hurling a hail of boulders toward the ships, and to Borenson's horror, the warlords responded by steering toward shore, as if to do battle. They too were fully under the sway of Raj Ahten's voice.

To the northwest, frowth giants cried out in renewed fury, as if heartened by the efforts around them. The elementals of fire raged, while reaver sorceresses fought grimly.

But the reaver hordes seemed endless, and for each reaver that died, three more scrabbled forward to take its place. They washed down from the hills in a tide that did not end for a hundred miles.

Borenson glanced east, uphill toward Castle Carris, and his heart nearly stopped. Below in the streets, reavers raced through the dead city unimpeded, surging up Garlands Street in a black flood. At its end they were digging up the streets, trying to get at the men who hid in the maze of tunnels below.

How did so many get in here so fast? Borenson wondered. It can't have been twenty minutes since they first breached the castle wall!

Rialla's soldiers suddenly began shouting, and some blew retreat while others blew the charge. Borenson glanced east just as her banner faltered. Thousands of knights had formed a knights' circus, a huge circle with lances bristling along its outside. They raced in circles and whirled about within this construct, felling every reaver that entered. But Borenson saw how it all would end. The knights had hemmed themselves in. Each knight would use his lance, killing a reaver or two. But Rialla's knights had nowhere to retreat. The reavers formed a ragged wall, like a canyon, and living reavers were crawling over the dead to get at the warriors.

Rialla herself was dead, and her men had doomed themselves. Footmen and archers who had been charging at her back suddenly turned and fled.

The frowth giants cried out in horror as the reavers lunged into their lines.

Raj Ahten's men continued to advance, but their war cries had turned to wails of pain and despair. "Onward," he cried, forcing them into battle like beasts of burden. From here it looked as if every foot they purchased, they bought with barrels of blood.

A meteor blazed overhead, sputtering so brightly that it shone even through the haze of war.

Borenson dropped to a crouch, and leaned against the stone wall of the shop. His mind whirled. He clutched his warhammer.

It's the end of the world, Borenson thought.

೫ 41 ೫

THE HEAT OF BATTLE

Learn to love all men equally, the cruel as well as the kind.

—*Erden Geboren*

The path before Raj Ahten's troops was black with reavers. Their blades and staves reflected firelight from the elementals at their backs. The philia on their heads waved like cobras. The colored smoke of their spells drifted through the battlefield in toxic clouds.

Their dead formed lurid mounds. He had spent many men to create those hills, hills that his troops could not easily climb. So they fell back and let the reavers come to them, slowing as they climbed over their own dead. His archers fired with their finest horn bows, piercing the sweet triangles of many of the reavers. Those that made it alive over the wall would have to face the most powerful lords of Indhopal.

Raj Ahten merely sat ahorse and watched. Hot blood thrilled through his veins, making him eager for battle. His men were fighting well, but he could see that they would not hold out long. His men were spending their lives too fast.

Only one thing could save them: Raj Ahten himself.

He needed them to know that. He needed to confront them with their own weakness, crush their hopes for the future, leave them debased and adrift. He needed their despair.

For only when they were bereft of hope would they begin to venerate the horrible light that filled him.

His common foot soldiers on the left flank had begun to fall back, weak-

ened by spells and facing a particularly fierce counterassault by a dozen reaver
mages that hurled blasting spells from behind their dead.

"Onward, you curs," Raj Ahten shouted at his men. They jerked like
marionettes, driven forward by virtue of his endowments of glamour and
voice. "Climb over the dead, kill those mages." Gree whipped over their
heads like bats. His soldiers held their breath and charged to their deaths.

Raj Ahten surveyed the battle. Carris was destroyed. Reavers could be
seen racing the length of its walls. The inhabitants had thrown themselves
into the lake in a last-ditch effort to escape.

Queen Lowicker's army to the north was nearly destroyed. King Anders's
flag flew safely behind the Barren's Wall, while his men rushed in and threw
themselves on the reavers.

Even the frowth giants roared in pain, and had begun a slow retreat.

The *thwonk, thwonk, thwonk* of ballistas from the lakefront now grew
quiet, for the warlords of Internook had nearly spent their bolts, to little
effect.

At the front lines, one great lord turned from the battle and called, "O
Great One, save us! The battle is hopeless."

"Fight on," Raj Ahten insisted.

In the moments that followed, first one and then another lord took up
the cry. "Help us, O Great One!"

He could hear the rising panic in their voices, the despair.

My time has come, he realized at last.

Ahead, the elementals of his flameweavers towered above the reavers.
Clouds of fire-lit smoke billowed above them. They had lost all manly form,
becoming mere monsters, mindless with pain, ravaged by the need to consume.
They struck at the reavers blindly, hurling fireballs, lashing with whips of flame.
Soon they would lose form altogether, becoming aimless in their desires.

Lust is a powerful force when skillfully focused. But these creatures
wasted their strength.

Raj Ahten stretched out his hand, as if beckoning the elementals. With
that gesture, he drew the heat from them in crimson cords that swirled about,
whirling toward him like a tornado.

Thus he took their fire into himself.

It was too much for any man to hold. In an instant, heat blazed from
every pore, and wrapped itself around him like a brilliant robe. His body
armor melted like slag.

The huge gray imperial warhorse screamed beneath him and died. It fell
to the ground instantly, its boiled guts gushing out beneath it.

Raj Ahten stepped lightly to the ground. He felt as if he had no weight
at all. He was only brightness and flame now.

He stalked toward the reavers' lines, and his men whirled. He could see them everywhere, their dark faces frozen in astonishment, like pebbles on the ground.

"Fear not," he told them, "for I will vanquish all of your foes. My sword will fall upon the Earth, and night shall be no longer."

Raj Ahten's light was whiter than sunlight, and he strode easily now toward the battlefront, as if all of the stars in heaven had combined, and now a creature of starlight took shape.

A reaver broke through his lines, came crashing in among his men. Raj Ahten pointed his finger, sent a shaft of fire swirling through the air. It touched the reaver's forehead, hit its sweet triangle.

The monster thudded to the ground as a smoking crater opened, revealing the brains that fried in its head. Raj Ahten sent a shaft toward another reaver, and another.

To kill them all would be child's play.

But in a heartbeat, everything changed.

Suddenly, the world shook, and as soon as Raj Ahten became aware of it, the reavers began to hiss. He had never heard a sound like it. A million reavers wheezed at once, like the sound that a blade hot from the forge makes when it meets the water.

Every reaver hissed, expelling gas from its anus, and filling the world with a single, strange scent, a smell that reminded him of mold.

Every reaver turned from battle, throwing down its weapon. The monsters drew back from their human foes, each of them turning to face something in the thick of the battlefield, just before the gates of Carris.

Raj Ahten could not see what had transpired there. But as he peered, he saw a mound of earth rising up. A hillock appeared, gray earth and stone spilling up from the ground. Atop the knoll crouched a dozen wary figures, like tender sprouts.

Iome wore a crown that glowed like moonlight on water, and Gaborn wore a cape pin that shone like a lantern. Gaborn stood in the light, and held something speared to a reaver dart—a reaver's philia, like the carcasses of wolf eels, gray and slimy.

He raised them aloft, and the reavers hissed and backed away en masse. All of them lowered their tail ends, dragging them on the ground.

Only one reaver dared confront him—the great fell mage that had marshaled the horde. She left her hillock some two hundred yards to the west, thundering toward Gaborn.

She held her head high, philia waving madly atop her regal cape, a livid crystalline staff in her hand. She drew near tentatively, as if undecided on how to do battle.

Gaborn merely raised his left hand and pointed south.

The reaver gazed toward him a moment, raised its massive head as if scenting the air like a hound, and then peered south. She seemed to take his meaning: "Your master is dead. Go home. Return to the Underworld."

Thoughtfully, she hesitated, and then dropped her head, laid her staff on the gray soil, and lowered her tail as far as it would go. A spray hissed from her abdomen, and behind her, each reaver in turn caught the scent and sprayed. There was a seething sound like the pounding of surf that rose among the reavers, rolling like a wave, until it could be heard repeated dozens of miles away.

The reavers turned, and the ground began to tremble as they raced to the south.

At Raj Ahten's back, his troops suddenly began to cheer, shouting and hooting at the tops of their lungs. Raj Ahten looked to his side, saw tears of relief flowing from the eyes of many a soldier. To the northeast, frowth giants raised their staves in the air and bellowed, "Wahoot! Wahoot!" To the east, the men of Beldinook began throwing helms in the air and dancing jigs. "Hail the Earth King!" they cried. "Praise the Earth King." The warlords of Internook, in their longboats, blew their warhorns in celebration.

Raj Ahten seethed.

By the size of the philia that Gaborn carried, and by the reavers' reaction to them, Raj Ahten surmised what Gaborn had done.

He has stolen my glory, Raj Ahten thought. He has slain the lord of the Underworld, and stolen my triumph.

He was still clothed in flame, and the light that shone from him blazed in murderous intensity.

Raj Ahten strode across the battlefield, past the ruined carcasses of men and reaver alike. A week past, the reavers had unleashed dire spells upon the land, blasting every tree and vine, wilting every leaf and blade of grass. Every living thing had gone gray, and Raj Ahten stalked now through a land drained of all color, a realm of horror.

He was the brightest light in a dark world. Scathain, the Lord of Ash.

As he passed among the dead, he spotted a great imperial warhorse, one that he'd given to Rialla Lowicker as a gift. The dead queen lay pinned beneath it, her blank eyes staring up toward the sky, as if to question the heavens. Raj Ahten gave her no pity. He hardly spared her a glance.

Clothed in white flames that sputtered in the evening wind, he stalked toward the Earth King.

The reavers were leaving, thundering over the plain. The ground trembled and groaned beneath Gaborn, as if complaining of the load that it was called to bear.

Overhead, a pair of blazing meteors hurtled, their red traces barely visible through the clouds of smoke and dark gree that hovered above Carris.

Gaborn held his javelin aloft, the philia of the One True Master impaled upon its tip, and felt unaccountably weary.

The reavers were fleeing, racing over the causeway from Carris in a huge line, shoving and jarring one another in their strain to flee. The last of them, it seemed, would be gone in moments. The fell mage and her minions were already a mile away.

Yet Gaborn sensed danger still.

The object of his fear strode toward him from across the vacated battlefield, a beacon in the night, a creature clothed in flames as bright as a Glory, a creature that seemed far hotter than any earthly forge. As it neared, walking between fallen reavers, even at four hundred yards Gaborn could begin to sense the heat that boiled from it.

Gaborn dropped his javelin, and called to Raj Ahten. "That is close enough. I am the Earth King, and have sworn to save the seeds of mankind. I will honor my vows. I would save even you, Raj Ahten, if I could—though I fear that little of the man you once were abides now among the flames."

Warhorns echoed off the lake, and to the north and west, men were cheering. Whatever had transpired, Borenson knew that the battle was over.

He only wanted to find Myrrima.

The reavers had not all left when he sprinted across Garlands Street to the ruins of the north tower.

The stonework was heavy there, the walls thick enough to withstand artillery. Reavers had crawled atop the tower, collapsing the thick beams that supported the upper stories, but the first floor was still intact. A young man crouched on the floor, bleeding from the head. He peered at Borenson, witless with fear, his arms clasped about his knees in a fetal position.

"Myrrima?" Borenson shouted.

Borenson tried charging upstairs to see if he could make it to the second floor, hoping to reach the spot where he'd last seen Myrrima gazing from a window, but beams and broken stones blocked his path.

From the doorway behind him, Borenson heard a familiar voice. Sarka Kaul had suddenly appeared, and whispered, "Go on up!"

Borenson looked vainly for a way to the top of the tower, then rushed back downstairs, and out the door. Only a hundred feet up the street, a wooden ladder led to the walkway atop the castle wall.

He ran round the ruins of a merchant's shop, raced up the ladder. A severed human leg lay draped over a rung. At the top of the ladder sat a helm with the head still in it. Blood pooled hot upon the wall-walk.

Atop the wall-walk, there had been a massacre. Dead men lay everywhere. Some had merely been trampled, others chopped in half with reaver blades. The bottom of one man lay just in front of Borenson, guts splashed against the merlons of the wall. By the look of it, his head and torso had toppled into the water.

The scene was well lit. Fires raged throughout the city, and light reflected from boiling smoke.

Borenson hardly spared a glance out on the battlefield. The reavers were thundering south. He ran through the carnage until he reached what was left of the tower. The weight of the reavers had collapsed the roof, and then as the combined tonnage of reavers and wreckage hit the floors below, they collapsed as well. Part of the tower wall had fallen west, so that much of the wreckage had slid into the lake. Broken beams showed where supports had once stood.

As Borenson studied the ruined tower, pain wracked him. If he searched long enough, he feared that he would find Myrrima crushed in the wreckage below.

Borenson peered through a crack to the east. A brilliant flameweaver stalked over the battlefield. Borenson froze in surprise. Someone down below addressed the creature, speaking so quickly, having taken many endowments, that Borenson had difficulty understanding.

Borenson spotted the speaker, there on a small knoll among the dead reavers. It was Gaborn, speaking with many endowments of metabolism. At his side, a small knot of people stood. Averan held her staff up warily. Iome held a reaver dart at the ready, looking regal in a crown of light, while a crowd of ragged beggars crouched behind them.

Yet Gaborn intentionally slowed his speech, and spoke loudly enough so that a man on the castle wall could hear, almost as if addressing Borenson at his back. "I would save even you, Raj Ahten, if I could. . . ."

Borenson's nostrils flared with anger, and he peered toward the flameweaver. Raj Ahten?

Raj Ahten stopped and merely stood for a moment. Bright flames whipped about him, as if blown in a fierce wind, and he blazed all the brighter. Borenson heard a laughing sound, a hiss among the fire.

"You would save me?" Raj Ahten said, his voice high and almost unrecognizable from the great number of endowments he had taken. "I am not the one who needs to be saved. There is nothing that you have that cannot be mine, including your life. I will take it, as I took your father's, and your mother's, and your sister's and your brothers'."

Gaborn shook his head, as if saddened. "There is little in this world that I would not give you, but I will not willingly let you take another man's life, and I will not give you mine."

Borenson heard a noise below and looked down on the causeway, saw dozens of warriors racing out of fallen buildings, like creatures creeping from the edge of a forest at night. Sarka Kaul was there, and Captain Tempest of Longmot.

Borenson whistled to catch their attention, then spoke in finger talk. "Raj Ahten is outside the castle."

"If you would live," Gaborn said to Raj Ahten, "listen to me. I will do all that I can to save you."

The flameweaver peered at Gaborn, who now dropped his weapon and sat cross-legged on the ground. He bent his head, as if deep in thought.

Borenson peered down through a broken battlement to the scene directly below. Dead reavers lay piled before the city gates, blocking the street. The corpses were stacked two or three deep, attesting to the fact that the archers and champions at the gate had made the reavers pay a toll for crossing the bridge.

But it had not been much of a toll.

Sarka Kaul, Captain Tempest, and a dozen other fierce Runelords were already climbing over the bodies, sprinting to help Gaborn.

Borenson launched himself from the broken tower onto the back of a reaver, a drop of some twenty feet, and tried to ignore the pain that shot through both ankles on landing.

He raced to reach the other warriors. Several of them were already approaching Gaborn's back.

Borenson shouted to the men, "I want the first swing!"

The men fanned out quickly, stalking toward Raj Ahten. Dead reavers littered the battlefield here, so near the causeway. Most were impaled with ballista bolts.

Borenson headed toward the flameweaver, his heart hammering.

Raj Ahten, he told himself. It's Raj Ahten.

But looks belied the creature. It wasn't Raj Ahten. It was something more. Even at hundreds of yards, he could feel the heat rising from the monster, hotter than the blast of any forge.

Borenson rushed behind a dead reaver, using its shadow to keep cool as he sought to draw near. Around him, others did the same. Silently, warriors crept about in the shadows thrown by dead reavers, ringing Raj Ahten as dogs ring a bear. Some had nocked arrows in bows. Others held long spears or warhammers. Borenson noted that the men wore armor from several nations—Mystarria, Heredon, Orwynne, and Indhopal.

And more men were rushing over the causeway at Gaborn's back.

"Come ahead, little men," Raj Ahten shouted. He stood among a knot of dead reavers. "The first to attack will be the first to die."

One archer burst from cover and took aim at Raj Ahten's back.

"Raj Ahten, beware!" Gaborn shouted.

The archer loosed his arrow.

Raj Ahten whirled and stretched forth his hand. Coiling ropes of white fire flowed from it, incinerating the arrow in its flight. Then the fire traveled on.

At such a short distance, the archer had no time to escape. The coils whipped about him. His robes and hair flashed into incandescence, and his flesh burned an oily green. He stood like a living torch, crying out in agony.

Borenson had heard of such curses. Spells of flesh-burning were the stuff of legend.

Borenson peered toward Gaborn, who sat cross-legged on the ground, now a scant two hundred yards from Raj Ahten.

"I warn you one last time," Gaborn said to the flameweaver. "Turn back now."

At Raj Ahten's back, Sarka Kaul suddenly appeared from behind a huge reaver, whose legs rose up like the trunks of trees. The Inkarran Days, his face reflecting the fierce light of Raj Ahten, sprang a dozen yards and thrust with his long knife.

But the heat roiling off Raj Ahten was so intense, that Sarka Kaul succumbed a dozen feet from his target.

He dropped to one knee, weakened by the heat, and his clothes burst into flames.

Borenson ducked back under cover, behind a dead reaver's head, and grasped his battle-ax, thinking.

I'll have to throw my weapon, he decided. But he'd lost his endowments of brawn, and he knew that he could not hurl the weapon more than thirty or forty feet now.

Suddenly, from atop a nearby reaver, a commanding voice cried out. "Lord of Ash," the Wizard Binnesman intoned. "Leave here! I warn you one last time."

The flaming monster whirled and peered at the Earth Warden. The wizard stood with his staff in hand, held protectively high above. His robes billowed out, blowing in the evening breeze.

Raj Ahten laughed. "You cannot harm me with that old tree limb. I am beyond your power!"

"That may well be," Binnesman intoned. "But you are not beyond hers!"

Binnesman dropped his arms, and suddenly Borenson saw Myrrima hidden there behind his robe, her bow drawn to the full. Borenson's heart hammered wildly in relief to see her alive. She was bloody and wet, as if she had just come out of the lake, and Borenson realized that she must have dived to safety when the tower collapsed.

She let an arrow fly.

It blurred in its speed.

Gaborn shouted, "Raj Ahten, dodge!"

Raj Ahten saw the arrow blur toward him, and heard Gaborn's warning at the same moment. He heard, but refused to humor the little man.

He had no time to concentrate his energies, consume the arrow. Instead he reached up to catch it before it could bury itself in his eye.

He caught the shaft, and only then realized his mistake.

A force struck him, a Power irresistible.

He caught the arrow, and felt as if it shattered every bone in his arm. The flames that had encircled him, caressed him, suddenly guttered and died. The heat leached from him in an instant, and Raj Ahten stood naked but for the scars of thousands of runes matted over his body.

It was as if an impenetrable wall had formed between him and the source of his Power. Only then did he realize that the arrow had never been meant to pierce him. Far more disastrous were the runes that had been written on its shaft with water.

"No!" Raj Ahten bellowed. The sound of his voice, amplified by thousands of endowments, echoed over the low hills.

"Take him down," Myrrima shouted, "before my spell wears off!"

Suddenly men sprang out from the shadows at every turn. Arrows whizzed toward Raj Ahten, while men with spears and battle-axes charged to meet him.

I am no coward, Raj Ahten told himself, to be chased off by pups like these. I am a Runelord still!

He batted aside the first two arrows that neared him, pulled the spear from the hand of the first man to attack, and hit the fellow hard enough to crush his skull.

Whirling, he faced to meet his enemies.

In the palace at Ghusa, Balimar had been lying in the Dedicates' Keep. The ceiling rose high, some twenty feet, and soaring marble arches showed what had once been an open-air courtyard. But Raj Ahten had walled it in with cheap mud bricks, so that more Dedicates could be housed here.

Balimar's heart had pounded as he reached into the bandage on his hip, grasped the hilt of a long, narrow dagger that lay concealed there.

It had been easy to fake giving an endowment. As a warrior among the

Ah'Kellah, he had taken enough endowments himself. He had seen how the Dedicates sweated as the forcibles were pressed to their bare flesh, how they swayed and cried out as the endowment was taken, how their eyes rolled back and they fell senseless to the ground afterward. So he had feigned giving the endowment. The scars of the forcible were upon him, but in his heart, he had only hatred to give to Raj Ahten.

His face betrayed no emotion, though he grinned inwardly. Raj Ahten's endless appetite for endowments would be his own undoing. His facilitators were working so hard to strip attributes from the local villagers that they had not even bothered to question the street urchins whom Balimar had bribed to pretend that he was their brother.

He had let the facilitators carry him into the innermost sanctuary of the keep, among the Dedicates. They were an ailing lot. He could hear them coughing, see them limping about.

The facilitators had tossed Balimar to the ground like a rag, throwing him near the door, simply because the Keep was so full.

Now, outside, a ram's horn blew three long blasts—Wuqaz Faharaqin's call to battle. It was a mere feint. Wuqaz and thirty men would ride to the gate, shoot arrows at the guards, killing as many as they could.

Indeed, even as Balimar lay there, a death cry arose, and horses began to scream.

Two guards within the Keep rushed toward the door. Their leader shouted, "We're under attack! Bar the gate behind me." He rushed through.

The second guard was occupied for a moment, pulling the huge iron gates closed, placing the iron bar across it.

Balimar quietly sprang to his feet. For seeming days now he had sought to hold himself still so that his endowments of metabolism would not be revealed. Now he sprang with all speed toward the door.

The guard heard him, dropped the bar in place, and reached for the warhammer sheathed on his back. Balimar shoved him against the door and stabbed through the fellow's ring mail, angling the blade upward, so that the dagger sliced into his heart. He quickly drew the dagger out partway, then thrust it back in—once, twice, three times, and four.

The guard died with nothing more than a grunt escaping his lips.

Balimar made sure that the door was barred tight, and then turned to peer at the Dedicates in the Keep.

Silently, nine other men had risen up among them, all warriors of the Ah'kellah, each bearing a dagger to pierce a man's heart, or a cord to snap his neck. Already they had begun the slaughter. Balimar grabbed the warhammer from the hand of the dead guard even as the man dropped to the ground, then sprang among the Dedicates.

He bypassed the women and children who lay in heaps upon the stone floor, recalling Wuqaz's words: kill the vectors first.

"Raj Ahten," Gaborn shouted. "Flee!"

And Borenson wondered, What is Gaborn doing?

Raj Ahten seemed to have the battle well in hand. Dozens of men rushed to fight him, stabbing with lances, hurling axes, sending arrows to fly. Amid the swirling mass of bloodthirsty warriors, Raj Ahten danced naked, a dance that left many men dead.

An Invincible raced up to Raj Ahten's back and hurled a scorpion dagger. Its poisoned blade struck him full, buried to the haft between his shoulder blades.

Raj Ahten shook himself, sending the blade flying. He whirled and drove the point of his spear through the man's eye socket. He hardly slowed as the wound in his back closed and healed.

He swung his spear, almost as if it were a club, and took out a man's throat.

He's too fast, Borenson thought. He's too strong.

He dared not draw near.

And then suddenly Raj Ahten seemed to stumble. In the midst of his dance, he slowed dramatically. His eyes were full of light, as if a dozen stars reflected from them. Smoke issued from his nostrils. His face contorted in alarm.

Borenson had seen that look of dismay upon the faces of other men. He'd had it upon his own. His Dedicates are dying! Borenson realized. He's lost his metabolism!

The warriors around Raj Ahten raced for the kill. A fellow from Heredon drove a spear through Raj's knee. Another swung a warhammer and spiked him through the back of the head.

Borenson rushed forward and would have attacked, but in his mind he heard Gaborn's voice, the shout of the Earth King, warning, "Hold back."

He dodged back a pace, just as Raj Ahten thrust his spear toward him.

Then Borenson waded in and swung his warhammer, not with much strength, but with great accuracy. He struck Raj Ahten in the joint of the shoulder, taking off his right arm.

Blood gushed from the wound, and a Knight Equitable saw the game. He lunged with a great-ax and hacked off Raj Ahten's left arm.

Raj Ahten fell, screaming, and a dozen more warriors surged forward, eager to draw blood. They ringed him about and plunged in their spears, while the Knight Equitable lopped off both of the Wolf Lord's legs.

Raj Ahten wailed in horror, but such was the force of his endowments that he could not die.

"Stay your hands!" Myrrima shouted. "Don't kill him!"

Her fearful tone stopped the men cold.

"He's a flameweaver," she cautioned. "Kill him, and you'll loose the elemental within! Let the water have him."

Cedrick Tempest rushed forward, shouting, "I like that. Let him go for a swim. I'll even give him the loan of my armor!"

He grabbed Raj Ahten, who now was but a torso, with arms and legs removed. Though blood flowed everywhere, Borenson saw to his dismay that Raj Ahten had begun to heal. The flesh had closed over his stumps, so that they had regenerated in a matter of moments more than a normal man's would have in months. Indeed, the stumps were lengthening, budding new arms and legs.

Yet such healing came at a terrible price. Raj Ahten's body had to cannibalize fat and flesh and bones from his trunk in order to nourish the new limbs. He looked skeletal and sickly.

With the eager help of two other men, Tempest picked up Raj Ahten. As cinders rained down from above and a meteor blazed in the heavens, they bore him over the ash-covered field, through gore and mud, out to the ruins of the drawbridge. Gree still squeaked in the air, and the reavers charging in the distance made a distant rumble.

Raj Ahten's eyes glazed with pain, and he moaned in a daze. "My Dedicates!" Then his mind seemed to clear, and he cried plaintively to his enemies, "Serve me! Serve me. Let me go."

But he had not enough Glamour or Voice left in him to sway his enemies.

Borenson followed the men, a chuckle rising involuntarily to his throat, as they climbed over reaver corpses to the bridge. The fires on the castle wall cast a dim red glow, creating a surreal tableau.

They reached the water, and Borenson saw huge shapes moving in circles there in the blackness. Salmon, he thought at first, finning in the water.

But the shapes were too large. They were more the size of sturgeon, like the great fish he'd seen in the moat at Castle Sylvarresta.

Water wizards, he suddenly realized with awe. Dozens of them swam in circles, small waves lapping against their backs, creating runes upon the surface of the lake.

There on the bridge, the axman noted that Raj Ahten had nearly grown a new right hand. Indeed, a child-sized nub had regenerated. They took a moment to lop it off.

Captain Tempest stripped his coat of ring mail and began to wrap Raj Ahten in it clumsily. "You wanted to take Heredon for its steel," Tempest said. "But I'm afraid that this bit is all we're willing to give."

Borenson pulled off his own armor, and added it. Thus Raj Ahten was doubly weighted in mail.

With that, Tempest and another man grabbed the stump of Raj Ahten and hurled him into Lake Donnestgree.

He sank beneath the dark waves, his neck wrenching wildly as he struggled to scream. The water wizards circled him, as if excited, as he began to sink. The great fishes bumped him with their noses, like playful dolphins, pushing him up toward the surface, teasing him with the hope for air.

The water smelled so potent here, so omnipresent. The black waves lapped at the castle walls, and made soft sucking sounds.

Borenson stood on the causeway as if at the edge of ruin, unable to believe that Raj Ahten would die, unable to accept that anyone so powerful could be killed.

Light flashed underwater as a great red ball of flames erupted. The surface suddenly bubbled and foamed. Hot gases escaped, forming waves that rocked Lake Donnestgree. In the light, Borenson saw the monstrous elemental unleashed. A creature of flame took form, its hand seeking the surface, and it seemed to grow.

The stump of Raj Ahten's body fell away, burned so badly that ribs stuck out like ruined kindling, as it sank down into the waves.

The great fishes could suddenly be seen more clearly, darting about in excitement. The bright glow lasted only for a second, as the elemental faded, and then the water went dark again.

Still, the surface of the lake continued to boil for nearly a minute until the water grew calm and black and fell silent again.

Then there were only the dark waves lapping softly against the castle walls.

Borenson looked over his shoulder, saw Gaborn and Iome standing side by side atop some dead reavers, looking down. He could see no victory in either of their faces, no celebration. Gaborn looked grim, worn, while Iome seemed to be shocked and hurt by what they'd done.

Gaborn has lost, Borenson realized. The Earth King has lost one of his charges. Yet even then he noted a change in Gaborn.

Like the child Averan, or the Wizard Binnesman, his skin had taken on a green tone. No, it is darker, Borenson realized. More like the face of the green woman—or like the effigies we make for Hostenfest.

Only then did Borenson realize why Gaborn had sought to save Raj Ahten, the prize he had won through his forbearance. Gaborn had become the Earth King, at last.

ᴂ 42 ᴄ₆

THE EARTH AT PEACE

War is easy to come by. Lasting peace is rare, and to be treasured.

—*Gaborn Val Orden*

Gaborn strode into the streets of Carris and peered about. The few folk who saw him stared in amazement, and then drew back reverently. Someone muttered, "He has leaves on his face, oak leaves—the sign of the Earth King."

And inevitably those who looked at him dropped to their knees in reverence.

Gaborn could feel the change that had taken place in him. Until tonight, he had only glimpsed the power he would have as an Earth King. Now he felt it. He was sinking his roots into the Earth, sending up shoots. He was beginning to see ways to use his powers that he had never imagined.

In the city, fires sputtered everywhere, and the town was a pile of rubble. Buildings lay crumbled, with huge stones lying in heaps, or leaned to their sides with timbers thrust out like broken ribs. But he sensed life beneath the ground, life like tender seeds, waiting to spring forth.

He drew a rune on the ground, a Rune of Protection from fire, and in moments the flames that burned everywhere began to dwindle and extinguish.

He stalked down an alley, sensing for life, and found a door. Iome, Borenson, and dozens of others followed him in silent awe.

In the ground at the foot of the door, Gaborn's sharp eyes could detect runes in the starlight—runes to protect the hunted from the unwelcome attention of the hunter, Runes of Strength to bar the door.

There were hundreds of doors like this throughout Carris, Gaborn knew. The men of Carris had dug many tunnels and chambers over the ages—cellars to store goods, tombs for the wealthy, tunnels to connect hidden passages beneath the castle walls.

"You have done a great work, it seems," Gaborn told the Wizard Binnesman.

Silently he sent a message to his Chosen people hidden beneath the ground. "Come out. The danger is past, and the reavers are vanquished."

Long seconds later, someone threw open the door and a pair of frightened commoners, men with pale faces who gripped their spears tightly, peered out.

Then they began to exit. One after another, the folk of Carris ushered forth, an old woman here, a pair there, until soon they began to fill the streets. They peered up in awe, for higher overhead the smoke had begun to clear, and now the stars fell like a shower of diamonds, flashes of silver and gold raining down in a clear night sky.

Soon, folks took stock of the empty fields before Carris and began shouting in jubilation. The crowd swelled the streets, until it became apparent that though many had died in the battle for Carris, perhaps half had been saved alive. Borenson stared at the emerging crowds, his jaw dropped in wonder, and said over and over, "I feared them dead. I thought them all dead."

"Milord," Captain Cedrick Tempest called to Gaborn, "the warlords of Internook wish to parlay.

Gaborn climbed the nearest wall so that he could look down over the southern reaches of Lake Donnestgree. There, longboats drifted like leaves, and in every boat a few torches lit the night. They bobbed like censers on the water. Iome stood beside Gaborn, looking down, her regal crown glowing with a thousand gems, while Gaborn's green cape pin glimmered as if a star had fallen on his shoulder.

Near the base of the castle wall, great fish swam about in circles.

Old Olmarg, the warlord of Internook, drew near in his longboat, his oarsmen driving him forward in graceful strokes. He saw the water wizards ahead, and signaled for the oarsmen to stop. He gazed up at Gaborn and squinted with his one good eye, as if appraising him.

Gaborn looked out over the ships. He could feel a threat here, still. Olmarg was unsure whether to press the attack, or flee.

"The people of this realm are under my protection," Gaborn warned him. "Come against us, and we will destroy you."

Olmarg growled and said dangerously. "We came and fought a war for the plunder, and you'll give us nothing? My men spilled good blood here. A reward seems in order."

"Your name will go down in songs, as one who fought bravely," Gaborn said. "Your great-grandchildren will sing your praise."

Olmarg barked a laugh, and peered south. The pounding of reaver feet came like the roar of a distant ocean, and their backs were black in the starlight as they struggled over the hills.

"Damn," Olmarg said, "we came and fought for nothing but the joy of battle." He appraised Gaborn once again, and quickly decided that any man who could take on an army of reavers would not be cowed by the likes of him. He smiled broadly. "But it was worth it."

Olmarg raised high a bright sphere, an orb of purest white. Gaborn could see clouds and light swirling, as if storms raged within, and almost immediately a gale picked up, came speeding from the north.

"Hoist sails," Olmarg shouted. "We're going home."

Gaborn nodded thoughtfully. The sense of danger at Carris was gone.

As the warlords of Internook set sail, Averan turned and saw troops fleeing to the west. Many of Raj Ahten's troops raced over the hills, terrified that Gaborn would come and make an example of them. Rialla Lowicker's troops handled themselves in a courtlier manner. They banded together, and began blowing horns in long wailing notes. Her knights bore her body on a bier, with all of their flags flying about, and headed north in a sedate march as if to give her a heroine's funeral.

As if to echo their calls, the frowth giants climbed a hill to the west and called out, "Wahoot! Wahoot!" over and over. They beat upon hollow logs, and their leaders raised a dead reaver high overhead, as if to make an offering to Gaborn, and then laid it on the battlefield.

Only King Anders's men had refused to pack up and go skulking away in the darkness. In moments a knight came riding from his camp. The fellow looked fearful. He rode up to the castle wall and stood on the parapet, looking up. He called out to Gaborn, "Your Highness, my lord King Anders of South Crowthen sends his congratulations on a battle well won, and wishes you peace and a long life."

"Why does he not come and offer such words himself?" Gaborn asked suspiciously.

"I fear that moving him unnecessarily would not be wise. His surgeons tell me that he has taken a mortal wound, and wishes only to return and die within sight of his homeland. I fear that he will not make it. Still, we beg your indulgence, and ask that you grant us permission to leave the battlefield."

"What of Celinor?" Iome asked.

"The boy is with his father, trying to ease his way," the messenger said. "He also begs permission to leave the battlefield."

Gaborn peered across the battlefield, filled with misgivings. Anders had claimed to be the Earth King, and now he asked to leave the battlefield?

"I will come to bid him farewell," Gaborn said.

With that, he sped across the field faster than the messenger could have imagined, past dead reavers, up the hill to a small rise where Anders's startled guards barely had time to register his approach before he was at Anders's tent.

Erin Connal lay outside it, bound hand and foot. Inside the tent, Anders lay abed with Celinor at his side. His wound did not look mortal. Gaborn peered at the man with his Earth Sight, and saw within him something far more terrifying than any reaver. There was a shadow in him, a blackness deep and grotesque.

Celinor and the guards reacted slowly to Gaborn's presence. They shouted and began to fall back.

King Anders opened his eyes to slits, peered up at Gaborn, and merely smiled. "Will you kill me?"

"What would be the point?" Gaborn asked. "A locus cannot be slain."

Celinor had staggered back a step and was drawing his blade, as if to protect his father. Gaborn stopped him with a glance.

"You are wise, Earth King," Anders said.

Gaborn looked up to Celinor. "Your father harbors a locus, and is therefore your father no more. Bind him, and bear him to the deepest dungeon at Ravenscroft. There, you may tend him and feed him, but do him no harm."

Celinor peered at his father, horror showing in every line of his face.

At that, King Anders screamed in protest, his back arching up off of the ground. His eyes rolled back in his head, and when he slumped to the ground, he breathed no more. Gaborn saw a flash of darkness as the locus fled. A chill ran up Gaborn's spine. He rushed from the tent, and saw the shadow blurring away to the north.

"What happened?" Celinor called from within the tent. Gaborn peered back through the flap. The guards were looking about darkly.

"The locus feared imprisonment," Gaborn said with certainty. "So it tore your father's spirit from its body, and fled." Gaborn felt certain that it would make itself known in time.

Celinor went to Erin, and begging forgiveness, cut her free of her bonds.

Home, Averan thought, as Gaborn raced to Anders's tent. Everyone is going home. But where will I go? Her home was gone.

By her body's clock, thirty days and nights she had been in the Underworld, and in that time she had become accustomed to the smell of the deep earth, the overwhelming silence of the Underworld, the eternal shadows. The open sky above her seemed strange and foreboding, with all of its bright stars falling down from midnight blue skies in a steady stream, like bright coins of gold and silver tumbling through the darkness.

By dawn the folk of Carris had begun to bury the dead in two great mounds before the castle walls. In a cool gray mist Averan watched them as she rode south toward the Courts of Tide, the hills becoming smaller and smaller, fading into the distance. She imagined them as they would be some-day, with broad-leafed elms growing atop them, giving shade to the folk who would build cities here again. Rabbits would feed on the hillsides, and foxes would dig dens beneath the roots of the forest giants. Doves would call from the boughs in the evening while young men sat in the shade of the hillock and sang to the women they loved.

Soon, the Earth whispered to Averan. It will happen again soon.

On the road, the prisoners that Averan and Gaborn had rescued from the Underworld filed off toward their homes. Gaborn provided each of them with cloaks and horses and food and money for the road, and many a proud man wept in gratitude as he took his leave.

The ride to the Courts of Tide was not a hurried one. The Earth King traveled by day, and by night he ranged far from camp. With his many endowments he traveled quickly over hills and through the fields, seeking out the cottages of humble farmers and woodsmen, Choosing those that he fan-cied. He took to wearing a green travel robe, and carrying a staff of oak. Tiny rootlings took shape in the robe almost as soon as he put it on, and within two days they had so overrun the fabric that nothing could be seen of the original material. Instead, Gaborn wore a wizard's robe that seemed as brown as turned earth in some light, or as green as pine needles in others.

Within three days, they reached the soaring towers at the Courts of Tide, where the crystalline bridges spanned the ocean between the isles.

The warlords of Internook had already sailed away by the time they reached the city, but evidence of the damage they had wrought was every-where—scorched wood along the piers, walls of huge estates knocked over.

Still, the folk were delighted to see the Earth King, and came out in force. All of the warning bells in the city rang for joy, and the children and mothers cried.

Gaborn rode through the city slowly, for he was so pressed by those who wanted the Choosing that he could hardly move forward. So he sat atop his horse and held his left hand high, looking into the crowd at knots of people, calling, "I Choose you. I Choose you all for the Earth."

Averan wondered why he bothered. He had saved the seeds of the Earth, as was his duty. Why did he keep up the Choosing?

So she asked him one night a week after they had reached the city.

"I am the Earth King in times of peace, as well as in times of war," Gaborn said. "Indeed, now my Power will serve me best."

And he continued to Choose. Over the coming weeks, lords came from far lands—from the remote reaches of Indhopal, and the islands of the north, and from every realm in Rofehavan, all of them bowing their heads and offering up tribute from their realms. Wuqaz Faharaqin came from Indhopal, to make a peace offering from all of the kings of the desert, and brought with him a great store of blood metal as tribute.

Gaborn distributed the blood metal freely, but only to those who belonged to the Brotherhood of the Wolf. "The Earth King needs no standing army," he explained. "Our greatest enemy now is the evil that lurks among us, and the Brotherhood of the Wolf is hereby charged with excising that evil. Go into the hills and find the brigands and bandits there, and root them out. Go into the halls of your barons and dukes, and find the evil there, and cut them down." And though his orders sounded broad, the truth is that few men actually paid the ultimate price. The Brotherhood went out with great authority, executing judgment righteously, and all who dared to defy them were destroyed.

Only the men of Inkarra did not come be Chosen. Borenson told Gaborn that the Kings of Inkarra had gone riding to fight the reavers, but no sign of such a battle was ever seen, and whether they fought and died, or whether they discovered the reavers coming out of the Mouth of the World and decided to retreat, never became quite clear.

Averan waited at the Courts of Tide and took a room in the castle, a room fit for an honored lord. But though it was huge, and the chestnut paneling on the walls was inlaid in gold, and enough feathers had gone into the bolster of its huge bed to make cots for all of the farmers in a village, Averan did not feel at home. She found herself at night wandering from room to room, looking for a place to sleep.

Thus it was on the tenth night, just after sunset, that an old stargazer with a silver beard came to the castle, begging to see Gaborn.

The stars had quit falling every night by then, though the heavens seemed to be filled with light, as if new stars now shone above. Averan led the fellow to Gaborn, who was up on his tower, watching over his kingdom like a shepherd standing watch over his flock.

"Your Highness," Jennaise the stargazer said when he saw Gaborn. "In behalf of our guild, I thank you."

"For what?" Gaborn asked.

"For moving the Earth back near its normal course in the heavens."

Gaborn looked at Averan sidelong out of his eye. "I had no part in that," he said. "A wizard greater than I managed it."

At that, the stargazer gaped in surprise at Averan, and begged, "Then it is you that I must thank. However, things are not exactly as they were. . . ."

"In what way?" Averan asked.

"Our path through the heavens will take longer than before. Each year is extended by nearly a day, if our calculations are correct. Can you not repair the damage?"

"The damage is repaired," Averan said. "The new course will be better for us than the old."

"But," the stargazer gasped in exasperation, "the calendars—they will all have to be changed!"

"Then change them," Gaborn said. "Add a day to the calendar."

"But, what shall we call it?" the stargazer asked.

"Gaborn's Day," Averan answered. "In honor of our king."

"No," Gaborn said. "I don't want people celebrating me. Call it Brother-hood Day, so that men may celebrate their kinship with one another. Make it a day of feasting and games."

"Very well," the stargazer said, nearly sweeping the floor with his beard as he bowed and left.

ಐ 43 ೮

HOME

Home is anywhere that we find peace.

—a saying of Rofehavan

Iome stayed on at the Courts of Tide for the winter, though her husband soon left. She heard rumors of him ranging far and wide, stalking through the mountains of Ashoven and hills of Toom, racing through Orwynne. Many a traveler saw him on the road, a bent man with many endowments, hurrying toward some secret destination. On all of his journeys it as said that he Chose the common folk at large, selecting some, neglecting others, and executing men whose hearts had gone dark after committing bloody deeds.

Thus he was loved and admired by most, but feared by others, and it was rumored that evil men were gathering in the forests all through the kingdoms, lest Gaborn's bright eyes pierce them and discover their secrets.

Throughout the autumn Iome heard word of skirmishes here and there, where the Brotherhood of the Wolf rounded up villains and slaughtered them wholesale.

As for her babe, Iome had not even been showing when she made the trip to the Underworld, but her endowments of metabolism made the babe mature quickly within her womb.

It was on a cool winter night, not more than three weeks after the battle at Carris, that Iome gave birth to Gaborn's first son. She laid him in a cradle, and named him Fallion, after the hero of old.

To her surprise, Gaborn came home that very night and marched to her loft to look at the child. Iome had made sure that Gaborn received many endowments, and he moved swiftly now, and aged accordingly. Though he had only been gone a few weeks, his body bore the ravages of years.

He peered into the crib, and seemed to hesitate before he said at last, "This one is an old spirit, one that has been born many times. He does not come as others do, with a blank mind, empty of purpose. He comes on a quest."

"What is his purpose?" Iome asked.

Gaborn stared hard at the child, and whispered mysteriously, "To finish what I cannot."

Iome sensed sadness in Gaborn then, and she ached for what she had bought. She was losing him, losing him to his cause. Yet she was the one who had paid the coin, given him the endowments that he would not have taken himself. And though they had managed to save the world, they had paid a dear price. He would die of his endowments within a year. And her life too would be short.

Iome sent to Heredon for word of her dear friend Chemoise and learned that she had made herself Gaborn's Dedicate. Saddened, Iome had her brought to the Courts of Tide so that Iome could care for her until Gaborn's demise.

Gaborn remained near the castle for a few days more, and Iome healed from her labor and soon found herself with child again.

Almost immediately Gaborn headed back out on the road, for there came word that an army was gathering in Indhopal, an army that would challenge Gaborn. And so her husband slipped out in the night, and once again Iome heard little of him but rumors.

Then, at midwinter, when the first light snow had fallen over the green fields of Mystarria, Iome got word from Gaborn.

She dreamt of him, and in her dream, Gaborn walked beside her and told of his labors of the past few days, of Choosing the poor in Taif, those who were most ravaged from the famine that occurred in the south. He spoke in a language that used no words during the dream, so that she felt his thoughts and his desires, and thus in a way, the time she spent apart from him seemed more fulfilling than the time that they had spent together.

And when she woke, she spoke with her counselors and discovered that her sending was true, that Gaborn was in Taif. There he was using his Powers to warn men not of danger but to tell them who was in greatest need. Thus, those with plenty of food found themselves responding to the Earth King's warning, and were oft led to give a loaf of bread to a child beside the road, or an old woman holed up in her hovel.

Indeed, from time to time, she heard Gaborn's voice herself, as he told her what funds to send to the relief of various realms within his kingdom.

And he did not return. He passed into the southern realms of Indhopal at midwinter, and Iome heard rumor that he might have gone to Inkarra.

She ached to see Gaborn, for every day that she spent away from him, he grew another fifty days old. Iome herself had taken many endowments of metabolism, and thus had to bear her own burden. Her second son, Jaz, came a month by the calendar after her first. In their cribs the children looked almost like twins. And though the children hardly grew at all, Iome aged a decade over the course of the winter, while Gaborn grew past middle age.

As spring neared, Myrrima and Borenson took up residence in their estate at Drewverry March. The manor house there offered nothing in the way of defensible walls, and Myrrima preferred it that way. Borenson had hung up his shield and battle-ax, beneath the crystalline tooth of a reaver, and there she hoped the weapons would stay.

Myrrima invited Averan to live with her, and treated the girl as if she were her own daughter. But Averan had taken endowments of metabolism, too, and during the course of the summer, she blossomed into a young woman, the kind that Borenson would have admired only a few years before. The girl seemed restless, and wandered around the house like one who was lost, and often could be seen staring to the west with a faraway look in her eye. Whenever Myrrima saw her thus and asked what she was thinking about, Averan would only say, "Home." Then she would drop her eyes and look away in embarrassment.

It was obvious to Myrrima that Averan longed to be someplace else.

Over the summer, Borenson went to work beside his farmhands, and learned the fine art of growing string beans, and pulling weeds, and swinging a scythe.

Myrrima, in the meantime, spent much of the day up at a spring above the house. It opened into a clear pool, deep and wide, encircled by weeping willows. In the fall their leaves came on golden, and fluttered noisily in the wind in the evenings, and Myrrima liked to go there and cast rose petals upon the water. She gave birth to a daughter in the late summer, and gave the child no name for the first few weeks.

Borenson had not heard much of Gaborn in long weeks. The last that he'd heard, the Earth King was in South Crowthen. There were rumors that old King Anders had not died after the battle at Carris after all, and had been seen at night, standing upon the castle walls at Ravenscroft. Most of the other tales that Borenson heard, though, were good. The people of the world had nearly all received the Choosing, and among them there was a sense of deep and abiding peace that had never been known.

Often Borenson would find himself prompted to visit an old neighbor woman and help with her chores, and each time that he did, he knew that by doing so, he was saving the old woman's life. And a thousand times a thousand times a day, such deeds were repeated all across the world.

Borenson began to see now that though Gaborn had won the day at Carris, like Erden Geboren himself, it would someday be said of him, "He was great in war, but greater in peace."

That evening the Earth King came to them. It had been just more than a year since the battle at Carris, and with his many endowments of metabolism, Gaborn had grown old indeed. His hair had turned gray, and cracks lined his skin. The dark green blotches of earth blood upon his face stood out like tattoos of leaves, and the wrinkles on his cheeks became the veins in the leaves.

Gaborn came and stayed that night and talked to Borenson, Iome, and Averan of many things—of strange goings-on in the south, of rumors of Celinor's rising madness, and how his wife had gone into hiding. They sat in rough chairs in the kitchen, drinking warm ale, so yeasty that it built a new head of foam if left for a moment. Outside, the wind was growing cold, howling like a wolf cub.

"The children born this year see better than their fathers ever did," Gaborn told them. "They see new colors in the rainbow, and in flowers. And down in Inkarra, new animals have begun to appear, and many of those that we thought we knew are taking on new Powers. In Fleeds the grass grew long and lush this summer, and it smelled so sweet that I envied the horses that ate it. The colts that sprang forth run fast from birth, faster than their mothers."

"I've heard some stories, too," Borenson said. "My steward claims to have dreams, sendings from the netherworld. He does not say much about them, but I can tell that they frighten him. He spends too much time sharpening his sword."

"There's nothing to fear," Averan said. "The world is changing, and will continue to change."

"It's all your doing, then?" Gaborn asked Averan.

"The world is changing," Averan said, "taking on some of the shape of the One True World. There is nothing to fear in this."

So they stayed up late talking, and Borenson reveled in the company of his old master, until they heard a thump at the door late in the night, and Borenson opened the door to find the Wizard Binnesman there.

Borenson grunted in surprise, looked at the old gray wizard, and at Gaborn, and asked at last, "What's going on?"

"We came to say good-bye," Gaborn said. "To you, and to Averan. We four shall not meet again. I will not live out the winter, and when I pass, I will leave the world in your hands. And so I must ask a favor of you."

"Name it," Borenson said, and he saw that Averan and Binnesman were leaning near them, intent on Gaborn's every word.

"Protect my wife and my sons."

"What won't she be safe from?" Borenson asked. "Are the reavers returning?"

But Gaborn only shrugged. "I am not told, I only feel."

"Not the reavers," Averan said. "They will never bother us again, I think."

"There are darker things than reavers," Gaborn said with a shiver. "I have searched the world for them far and wide, but many yet remain hidden from me."

That morning at dawn, Averan, Gaborn, and Binnesman mounted up for one last ride. They told Myrrima that they would be back in three days, and they took force horses to the Courts of Tide.

There, Iome gave Averan a gift, and told her, "Let this be a light for you in dark places," Iome said. "You may only be a wizard, but you shall look the part of the queen of the Underworld." Iome gave Averan her crown of blazing opals.

Averan tucked it into her pack, hugged Iome, and said her good-byes.

A night later the three of them rode fast horses to the Mouth of the World. Averan bowed her head as they passed Keep Haberd, and would not look at the massive stones all thrown down, now covered with wild peas that had their blossoms open to the night.

It was a fine night, surprisingly mild. Starlight and a rising moon dressed the hills in silver. To Averan's senses, everything was a wonder. It was well past the first of the month of Leaves, and the trees had all begun to turn to their autumn colors. To the north, the hills rolled away, each hump riding the back of the last, until the fair fields of Mystarria glistened in the distance. Off to the east, the Alcair Mountains rose up as sharp as blades, with snow glistening at their peaks. Everywhere, crickets sang among the fields, and Averan peered up at the stars, which seemed to loom just out of reach up in the heavens. None of them were falling.

Averan felt as if a huge burden had lifted from her chest. She sat astride a gray mare, holding her black staff.

"Tell all the people," Averan said, "that the reavers will trouble them no more. The hosts of the Underworld shall never come against them again."

"Are you sure that you want to go back?" Borenson asked. "There will always be a place for you at the manor, if you wish."

Averan shook her head. "Don't worry for me. You're going to your home. I'm going to mine. There is much work to be done still, and I must remain vigilant."

Borenson nodded, unable to even guess what burdens the child would have to endure. The reavers needed an Earth Warden to protect them. Even he had to know what that meant. Dark times lay ahead.

"Still," Borenson said, "if ever you find yourself yearning for sunlight on your face, or a fair bed, or another person to talk to . . ."

"I'll know where to find you," Averan finished for him.

Averan climbed down from her horse, and gave Borenson a hug. He squeezed her tightly, and wished never to let her go. Averan still felt small in his embrace.

Averan hugged him close one last time, and Borenson saw tears glisten in the young woman's eyes.

At least there is still a small part of her that is human, Borenson thought, and he rejoiced in that.

Averan said good-bye to Gaborn and Binnesman, and of that tearful meeting, little can be said. She had found in Binnesman a father that she had never known, and now she would lose him again.

Then Averan stood in the mouth of the cave for a moment, just breathing the fresh air. A small breeze suddenly stirred the trees, and went hissing through the grasses, and Averan looked as if she took that as a sign to depart. Placing Iome's old crown upon her brow to light the way, she turned and strode back into the Underworld.

ᘒ GLOSSARY ᘓ

Blood metal: an extremely rare metal used for creating forcibles, the magical branding irons that are needed so that attributes can be transferred from one person to another. Blood metal is dull red in color, extremely soft, and melts at low temperatures.

Bright Ones: a race of beings in the netherworld, they are manlike, but better than men in every way—wiser, stronger, smarter, swifter. Those who have seen the Bright Ones describe them as "perfect" men. Wizards claim that mankind descended from them.

Darkling Glory: a creature of the netherworld, the Darkling Glory is a vile creature with vast wings, somewhat human in appearance, with dark skin and feathers. The Darkling Glory consumes light, and seems to have power over the wind.

Days: a Days is a historian who will typically follow a lord or lady about in an effort to chronicle the history of mankind. Each Days gives up his or her name upon joining the order, and simply is called Days for the rest of his life.

As a group, the Days claim to be in service of the Time Lords, a race of beings that most folk consider to be mythical. Though the Days have sworn never to interfere in the affairs of mankind, their influence is great, for every lord knows that upon his death, the Days will publish a history of his doings, and thus he will not want to be seen in an evil light. Furthermore, there are rumors that in the past, some Days have broken their vows and supplied information to their lords about goings-on abroad.

Upon joining the sect, each Days grants an endowment of wit to another, who then grants the same endowment in return. Thus, the Days become twins that share one mind. For most people, this arrangement would lead to madness. But the Days are so committed to their cause that they endure this arrangement gladly.

One of "twinned" Days thus spends his time observing what happens in the world, while the other chronicles what they have observed.

Since the chroniclers all live upon the same isle, it is possible for the Days collectively to keep track of all that is happening in the world and to share information almost instantly.

Dedicate: a person who has granted an attribute to his lord. A Dedicate who has granted brawn will be weak. One who has granted wit will be an imbecile. One who has granted stamina will be sickly. Thus, Dedicates are always handicapped in some way, but hold an exalted place in society. They are usually pampered and protected by their lord.

Dedicates' Keep: a special fortress or part of a fortress where a Runelord houses his most valuable assets, his Dedicates.

duskins: a race of small creatures, somewhat manlike, that long ago inhabited the Underworld. They were craftsmen of consummate skill and magicians of renown. The reavers killed the last of the duskins thousands of years before Gaborn Val Orden.

Earth King: a king who has been granted the greatest of all protective powers, the Power of Choosing, so that he may "save a seed of mankind" through the direst of calamities. With this power, the king may see into the hearts of men and Choose those that he wants to save. Once a person is Chosen, the Earth King not only recognizes when the person is in danger but will also be able to send a warning, which bursts into the Chosen's mind, telling them how to avoid danger. There have only been two Earth Kings in recorded history, Gaborn Val Orden and Erden Geboren, but legends say that long ago there were others whose names are now forgotten.

Earth Warden: a wizard who is committed to preserving the earth, usually a single species of plant or animal. The Earth Warden is granted protective and healing powers by the Earth in return for his or her service. Note that an Earth Warden may be either a human or an animal.

endowment: a gift of an attribute, usually given to a lord by his vassal.

An endowment remains in force only so long as both parties remain alive. Thus, if a lord dies, the attribute returns to the giver. If the vassal dies, the lord will lose the attribute. So it becomes incumbent upon the lord to keep his vassals safe and healthy.

Endowments can be transferred only between communal mammals. Thus, a magician can take an endowment from a dog and grant it to another dog, or to a man. This is sometimes done to create faster horses and camels for use in war, or to transfer unusually powerful endowments, such as scent, from an animal to a human.

Attributes that can be transferred include:

sight—the ability to see clearly and in low light.

hearing—the ability to hear soft sounds and broader frequencies.

smell—the ability to detect scents.

brawn—the ability of the muscles to constrict forcefully.

grace—the ability of the muscles to relax.

metabolism—increases the speed at which cellular processes take place

wit—allows the receiver to store memories in the brain of the giver.

stamina—increases the ability of the receiver to heal him- or herself and sustain trauma.

Voice—increases the ability to control the tone, pitch, and volume of one's speech. With training, a Runelord can use his gifts of Voice to become overwhelmingly persuasive.

glamour—reshapes the face and body of the receiver so that he or she becomes more beautiful and seductive. It also robs self-esteem from the giver and transfers it to the receiver.

will—transfers willpower to the receiver.

facilitator: a magician who specializes in transferring attributes from one person to another. He does this by use of magical branding irons called forcibles.

flameweaver: a wizard who serves the Power of Fire.

force horse, force elephant, force dog: an animal, usually used in war, that has had its natural abilities boosted by receiving endowments.

force soldier: a warrior who has been granted the right by his lord to receive endowments.

forcible: a branding iron, made of blood metal, which magically allows attributes to be transferred from one lord to another. The forcible is small, almost wandlike, and can have one of several runes at its tip. The shape of the rune determines which attribute that the forcible will transfer. The forcible is destroyed in the process of transferring endowments.

frowth giant: One of several types of giant in the known world, the frowth is the largest, standing nearly seventeen feet tall. The frowth is covered with long, silver hair. The frowth is omnivorous, but favors meat. Though unable to communicate with humans well, the frowth sometimes allow themselves to be hired as laborers or mercenaries.

Glories: a race of benevolent creatures from the netherworld that have sometimes made contact with men, and at least once aided them in times of trouble. Those who have beheld Glories describe them as creatures of light that communicate powerfully through thought. Beyond that, words fail.

Indhopal: a cluster of nations to the west of Rofehavan, most of which have either a desert, temperate, or tropical climate. The people of Indhopal typically have darker skin than those of Rofehavan, though there are many people of fair skin. Note that Indhopal is the most populace region of the world, containing an estimated half of all mankind.

Inkarra: a large realm south of Rofehavan that covers nearly half of the known world.

Inkarrans: a subspecies of human that are adapted to a nocturnal lifestyle. These pale men and women typically have white skin, silver or cinnabar-colored hair, and silver eyes. Though they do not look much different from normal humans, the offspring of a normal human and an Inkarran is like a mule, unable to breed.

Invincible: an elite warrior from Indhopal who has been granted a minimum of fifty endowments.

loci, locus: a race of creatures that seem to be pure evil. Undying and insubstantial, they will often take control of a man, like a parasite living within its host, in order to spread destruction. Wizards will tell you that they were created when the One True World was shattered, and that "just as our world is a shadow of the One True World, the loci are but a shadow of our great enemy, the Raven."

netherworld: sometimes called the One True World, the netherworld is another planet, most probably on another plane of existence. According to legend, the One True World was the first home of mankind, and was bound together in perfection by magic runes, until the Raven, a creature of pure evil and an enemy to mankind, sought to take control. The runes that bound the universe into one were shattered, and a thousand, thousand shadow worlds came into being. Gaborn's world is one of these shadow worlds, and the netherworld is all that is left of the One True World. It is unreachable by normal men, but powerful magicians can sometimes open doorways to the netherworld.

nomen: a race of fearsome, bipedal giants that came across the seas in times of old, riding in black ships. The nomen's appearance is somewhat like that of a jackal.

Powers, the: the four primal forces that grant gifts to mankind.
   Earth—grants primarily protective and restorative powers.
   Fire—grants primarily destructive powers and insight.
   Water—grants healing powers and stability.
   Air—grants chaotic powers.

Raj Ahten: one of the most powerful Wolf Lords of all time. *Raj* is Ind-hopalese for "Supreme Ruler"; *Ahten* is a Taifan surname that means "Lord of the Sun." Raj Ahten began his career as a rapacious young prince who never-theless gained the admiration of his people. By secretly raiding caravans that carried forcibles from one nation to another, he secretly amassed tremendous power and soon took over the nation of Kartish, gaining a near stranglehold on the blood-metal market. Using this position of power, in a matter of seven short years he was able to conquer half of the people in the world. In time he became a flameweaver of great power.

reaver: a type of subterranean carnivore that has long been an adversary to man. The reavers are large, often weighing as much as ten tons, and standing taller than a bull elephant. The reaver walks on four legs, but has a pair of long forearms. Their hides are so thick that they almost seem to be exoskele-tons. Reavers have no eyes, but instead use philia, eel-like sensory organs on their heads and jaws, to smell and to sense vibrations. Reavers seem to be as intelligent as men, and are capable both of making weapons and casting magic spells.

Rofehavan: a group of kingdoms in the northeast bound together by a com-mon heritage and language.

Runelord: any man or woman who has both been granted tracts of land to protect, and the endowments necessary to protect them.

runelore: the accumulated knowledge of the making of runes (magical sym-bols). Note that there many types of runes other than those that are molded onto the heads of forcibles. There are Runes of Protection, runes to strengthen metal and stone, runes that give magical properties to implement. Indeed, according to the mages, all runes are but one part of a huge master rune that once bound the universe together.

Sum of All Men: in myth, the Sum of All Men was Daylan Hammer, a lord who had taken so many endowments that he could not die. According to some, Daylan Hammer still lives.

Toth: a race of Underworld creatures with obvious similarity to reavers. The toth were hunted to extinction by the legendary King Fallion, whose world-ships crossed the sea so that he might hunt them in their lairs. The toth were smaller than reavers, and easier to kill. But they were also powerful magicians, and had domesticated reavers much as a man might domesticate a war dog.

Underworld: a vast region belowground that is inhabited by strange animals and plants—animals such as the great worms and the reavers. Caverns that connect the Underworld to the surface are rare, but those who dare enter find a world brimming with tunnels and warrens where strange creatures live.

vector: a person who channels endowments to a lord. This is a person who has received endowments from others, and then has granted an endowment of the same kind to his lord. Thus, for example, a man who has given brawn to a lord might be called upon to take endowments of brawn from others, so that the endowments can all be funneled together to his lord. This way, a lord who desires great strength, for example, might take a single endowment of brawn from a man and then ride out to war. As he rides, the facilitators can continue transferring endowments now to the Dedicate, so that the lord might receive hundreds or even thousands of endowments in this manner.

   The only problem with this methodology is that if the vector is killed, then the lord loses all of the endowments that the vector channeled at once. Thus, slaying a vector can significantly weaken a lord.

warrior of unfortunate proportion: a warrior who has taken endowments, but who is not well-balanced. For example, if a warrior takes several endowments of brawn, but none of grace, he will tend to become muscle-bound. If he does not take metabolism, then he will move slowly, and all of the strength in the world won't save him from a much faster opponent.

wight: the spirit of a dead man or creature.

wizardborn: a person who is born with magical powers.

Wolf Lord: originally a Wolf Lord was a person who took endowments from dogs, a practice that somewhat changed the nature of the lord, particularly if he ventured to take endowments of wit from a dog. The wolf lord tended to become more feral, more vicious, and more voracious than common men—a trait much prized in war, but shunned in times of peace. Thus, most Wolf Lords throughout history have not been noblemen but are instead highwaymen and bandits.

Note, however, that though the practice is shunned, many lords have posed strong moral arguments for the practice throughout time, and many a lord has secretly preferred taking endowments, such as stamina, from a dog, rather than risking the health and safety of a human.

Figuratively, a Wolf Lord is anyone who forces others to give endowments by blackmail.